The Best
AMERICAN
SHORT
STORIES
2018

The Best AMERICAN SHORT STORIES® 2018

Selected from
U.S. and Canadian Magazines
by ROXANE GAY
with HEIDI PITLOR

With an Introduction by Roxane Gay

HOUGHTON MIFFLIN HARCOURT
BOSTON • NEW YORK   2018

hmhco.com

ISSN 0067-6233 (print)
ISSN 2573-4784 (ebook)
ISBN 978-0-544-58288-0 (hardcover)
ISBN 978-0-544-58294-1 (pbk.)
ISBN 978-1-328-50667-2 (ebook)

Printed in the United States of America
DOC 10 9 8 7 6 5 4 3 2
4500742574

"Cougar" by Maria Anderson. First published in the *Iowa Review*, 46/3. Copyright © 2017 by Maria Anderson. Reprinted by permission of Maria Anderson.

"A Family" by Jamel Brinkley. First published in *Gulf Coast*, vol. 28, issue 2. From *A Lucky Man: Stories*. Copyright © 2018 by Jamel Brinkley. Reprinted with the permission of The Permissions Company, Inc., on behalf of Graywolf Press, Minneapolis, Minnesota, www.graywolfpress.org.

"The Art of Losing" by Yoon Choi. First published in *New England Review*, vol. 38, no. 2. Copyright © 2017 by Yoon Choi. Reprinted by permission of Yoon Choi.

"Los Angeles" by Emma Cline. First published in *Granta*, 139. Copyright © 2017 by Emma Cline. Reprinted by permission of *Granta*.

"Unearth" by Alicia Elliott. First published in *Grain*, vol. 44.3. Copyright © 2017 by Alicia Elliott. Reprinted by permission of Alicia Elliott.

"Boys Go to Jupiter" by Danielle Evans. First published in the *Sewanee Review*, vol. CXXV, no. 4. Copyright © 2017 by Danielle Evans. Reprinted by permission of Danielle Evans.

"A History of China" by Carolyn Ferrell. First published in *Ploughshares: Solos*

Contents

Foreword

I DO NOT think it hyperbole to say that in 2018, the rapidly changing condition of American democracy has become an absorbing narrative of its own, one that features larger-than-life characters, nonstop conflict, breakneck pacing, and incredibly high stakes. On the day that I write this, April 16, 2018, the former head of the FBI is on a book tour, railing against what he calls our "morally unfit" president, the man who fired him a little less than a year ago. Five days ago, and without the consent of Congress, the president authorized an air strike of Syria after its president used chemical weapons against civilians near Damascus. Six days ago, two black men were arrested and detained for eight hours at a Philadelphia Starbucks after simply asking to use the restroom. Eight days ago, the FBI raided the office of the president's longtime lawyer, seizing among many other things, evidence of hush money paid to a pornographic actress after an alleged affair with him. By the way, the FBI is also investigating Russian meddling in the 2016 election, the role of Russian hackers and Facebook in the election, and most likely a laundry list of related alarming occurrences. On Valentine's Day, a nineteen-year-old opened fire at Marjory Stoneman Douglas High School in Parkland, Florida, killing seventeen people and injuring seventeen more.

Fiction writers are now faced with the significant challenge of producing work that will sustain a reader's attention amid this larger narrative. Roxane Gay is just the right guest editor for this moment. With her keen eye for tension, voice, and structure, as well as her deep understanding of the forces at work in our cul-

ture, she chose stories that reflect and refract our time, stories
that exhibit mastery of pacing, surprise, and rich characterization.
Here are stories that hold their own in this day and age, no small
feat, and they do so with devastating realism, honesty, humor,
and courage.

Many of these short stories communicate deep longing. Maria
Anderson describes the loneliness of a nineteen-year-old rural man
whose father has disappeared. Cristina Henríquez writes of a Mexican woman who, after a grueling journey, crosses into the United
States only to face a far darker journey: "Where has she gone and
what has she become?" In Rivers Solomon's story, "Whose Heart I
Long to Stop with the Click of a Revolver," a black woman meets
her birth daughter, resuscitating memories of the girl's white father, whose "words sound like truth to me, like something to be
afraid of." In Yoon Choi's story, "The Art of Losing," a husband
and wife struggle with his excruciating memory loss: "Sometimes
she felt that patience and kindness could be stretched so far in a
marriage as to become their opposites."

I first encountered this series when I was an undergraduate in
college, and one of my favorite elements was the contributors'
notes at the back of the book. After reading a stellar story, I turned
to the mini-essay that provided access to what seemed like secrets:
confessions about the difficulties of writing, self-deprecating comments about the author's obsessions; profound assessments of the
themes of the stories. I admit that I still treasure the contributors'
notes. One by one, they fill my email inbox. After having fallen in
love with a story, I savor these notes. Given the escalating conflicts
in our country, I was unsurprised to see that this year, many au-
thors described in their notes the nonfictional territory beneath
their stories. Underlying Ann Glaviano's hilarious story is the fact
that wife camp is a verifiable thing. Jacob Guajardo writes, "Young,
queer people of color become adept at hiding, but it's hard to
hide that you are in love." The bloody assault of a black college
student by local law enforcement prompted Jocelyn Nicole Johnson's "Control Negro." Describing the seed of his story, Matthew
Lyons explains, "I've always been fascinated with the phenomenon
of American male rage." Alicia Elliott describes the vast dangers
of Canadian colonialism to Indigenous people and culture. Canadian stories and writers have always been a part of this series; all

stories submitted to me and written in English and published in North America are considered.

The stories in this book offer readers passageway inside contemporary and age-old questions of what it means to live together in a society, as well as what it takes to define and sustain oneself in difficult times. To read great fiction well is to live and breathe inside of it. A couple of years ago came scientific proof that reading literary fiction stimulates "theory of mind," or emotional intelligence and empathy. Fiction offers truths and humane understanding not found elsewhere. When we ally with fictional characters, we enlarge our understanding of the world, something particularly crucial these days.

In last year's foreword, I wrote about my reaction to the 2016 presidential election. I received a few letters requesting that I keep my politics out of my job. I read as any critic does, as a human being with a particular set of experiences. I read as the best reader that I can be, as someone who seeks out engrossing and important stories; beautiful, evocative, funny, or striking language; a sense that I am transported and unable to return to my life at least until I've finished reading, no matter the author, no matter the setting, nor the time period, nor the cultural or gender or sexual preferences expressed by the characters. As George Orwell wrote in a 1946 essay, "The opinion that art should have nothing to do with politics is itself a political attitude."

I am grateful to share these twenty stories that engage, impress, and transport.

The stories chosen for this anthology were originally published between January 2017 and January 2018. The qualifications for selection are (1) original publication in nationally distributed American or Canadian periodicals; (2) publication in English by writers who have made the United States or Canada their home; (3) original publication as short stories (excerpts of novels are not considered). A list of magazines consulted for this volume appears at the back of the book. Editors who wish their short fiction to be considered for next year's edition should send their publications or hard copies of online publications to Heidi Pitlor, c/o The Best American Short Stories, 125 High Street, Boston, MA 02110 or files to thebestamericanshortstories@gmail.com as attachments.

HEIDI PITLOR

Introduction

WE ARE IN the midst of a significant cultural moment. Of course, there has rarely been a time when we haven't been in the midst of a significant cultural moment. Donald Trump is president, and he is implementing his agenda with relative ease. He is subverting what we once knew as the presidency for his own personal gain. In the late spring of 2018 his wife, Melania Trump, wasn't seen publicly for weeks, sparking all kinds of speculation about where she was and what had happened to her, because with a man like Trump it was plausible that harm had come to her or that she had simply left him. His adult children are feasting at a bountiful table funded by American taxpayers while his oldest daughter plays at diplomat and part-time First Lady. The cronies the president has installed in office are grifting the American people and they aren't bothering to hide it, because they know that the Republican Congress is so enamored with the power they wield that they see no need to check and balance. Tensions are high in this country. Tensions are high nearly everywhere in the world. The news offers a constant barrage of terrible, overwhelming truths about the way things are. On social media, people parse all this information and become instant experts on everything from global warming to immigration law. The world feels like it is coming apart. For many vulnerable people, the world *is* coming apart.

In times of great personal or public upheaval, I turn to reading. I turn to fiction and how writers imagine the world as it is, was, or could be. I am not avoiding reality when I read fiction; I am strengthening my ability to cope with reality. I am allowing myself a much-needed buffer, a place of stillness and quiet. I read fiction to step away from the cacophony of the news and social media and the opinions of others. The reprieve fiction provides is a necessary grace.

Being chosen to edit this year's volume of *The Best American Short Stories* couldn't have come at a better time. I craved the distraction, no matter how overwhelmed I was by the task of reading 120 stories and choosing only twenty upon which I could apply the imprimatur of excellence. First, though, I had to get over my surprise at being asked to edit this anthology. I've been reading the series for nearly twenty years, always wanting to see what the best short story writers in America have to offer. Sometimes I read the stories while filled with envy, coveting such literary recognition. Other times I read the stories in a given year and was more frustrated than anything else. After reading the 2010 volume edited by Richard Russo, one of my favorite writers, I wrote about how too many of the stories focused on rich white people. I described that year's offering as having a "profound sense of absence." Despite the indisputable excellence of all the stories in 2010, I yearned for the collection to offer more, to better reflect the world beyond gilded existences. And then, when my own story "North Country" was selected for *The Best American Short Stories 2012,* I was gleeful. At the time, I was certain I had reached the pinnacle of my career. Then I called my mom and told her my story had been selected, and she asked, "What is *Best American Short Stories?*" The pinnacle was promptly dismantled. I was appropriately humbled.

As I read this year's stories, I was thrilled by the opportunity. I was also thinking about this ongoing, unfathomable cultural moment and how, if at all, these stories might address it. Often, during significant cultural upheavals, critics wonder when and how fiction writers will respond. Such questions are often voiced immediately following the upheaval, with little regard for craft, as if writers were simply sitting around waiting for cultural crises to which they should respond. Soon after the initial thrust of the Iraq War, I remember reading several treatises that wondered where all the good war fiction was, implying that American letters was failing somehow because this fiction had not yet been published. Those treatises overlooked the fact that writing takes time. Writing often demands distance and space to process events before writers can interpret them creatively. I knew I would likely never write any war fiction and resented the implication that I was somehow falling short because my creative interests lay elsewhere. I also knew there were different ways for me to engage with the world's turmoil. There were different ways for me to write politically.

Writers are divided on whether or not it is their responsibility to address the contretemps in their work. Some writers stubbornly cling to the idea that writing should not be sullied by politics. They labor under the impression that they can write fiction that isn't political, or influenced in some way by politics, which is, whether they realize it or not, a political stance in and of itself. Other writers believe it is an inherent part of their craft to engage with the political. And then there are those writers, such as myself, who believe that the very act of writing from their subject position is political, regardless of what they write. I know, as a black, queer woman, that to write is a deeply political act, whether I am writing about the glory of the movie *Magic Mike XXL,* or a novel about a kidnapping in Haiti, or a short story about a woman eating expired yogurt while her husband suggests opening their marriage.

Nearly every major writer has something to say about whether they consider themselves or their writing political. I often return to Chinua Achebe's thoughts on this matter. In a *Paris Review* interview Achebe noted, "There is something about important stories that is not just the message, but also the way that message is conveyed, the arrangement of the words, the felicity of language. So it's really a balance between your commitment, whether it's political or economic or whatever, and your craft as an artist." He succinctly addresses what naysayers love to bring up when the political is introduced into conversations about art—that somehow it is impossible to both write politically and make good art, as if the former compromises the latter.

When I am reading fiction, I am not always looking for the political. First and foremost, I am looking for a good story. I am looking for beautifully crafted sentences. I am looking for a refreshing voice or perspective. I am looking for interesting, complex characters that I find myself thinking about even when I am done with the story. I am looking for the artful way any given story is conveyed, but I also love when a story has a powerful message, when a story teaches me something about the world, when a story shows me just how much I don't know and need to know about the lives of others.

One of the first novels I read and recognized as political was Alice Walker's *Possessing the Secret of Joy,* a flawed but beautiful, unforgettable story, a sequel of sorts to *The Color Purple,* that deals with the repercussions of female genital mutilation. It is a novel about grief and trauma, as Tashi, the protagonist, grapples with the mutilation of her body as a young girl and years later trying to live in the world as a woman and wife, trying to make herself whole again. One of the most startling aspects of the story is the graphic way in which Walker details what Tashi endures as a young girl, the sheer physicality and pain of her experience. Because of those narrative choices, I understood exactly where the author stood on the issues she was addressing. This was not just a work of fiction. It was an indictment. It was a condemnation. It was the work of a writer using her craft to take a stand. When I read that book, I wanted to develop the confidence and skill to take such stands in my own fiction.

In the spring of 2017, I taught a graduate workshop on writing the political novel. I did so because I was still reeling from the results of the 2016 election and couldn't fathom teaching a regular fiction workshop, pretending everything was just fine when such was not the case. The classroom felt like an ideal place to use my own craft to take a stand. It was a small act of defiance, if not resistance, but I needed to do something. I scrapped my original plan for the course and quickly developed a new syllabus. I was nervous about how students would respond to the course's theme, having two years earlier taught a fairly disastrous workshop on writing "difference" and encouraging writers to use fiction to create interesting characters beyond their subject position. During that workshop, the students resented what they saw as a restriction of their creativity, and so this time around, I construed the political as broadly as I could without rendering the concept meaningless.

Our first task was to try to answer the question "What is a political novel?" The truth is, nearly anything could be considered political writing, given the right framing. We did, over the course of the semester, manage to come up with some interesting answers to this question. We identified common themes in political writing—protest, social critique or commentary, engagement with the world as it is and how a writer wants it to be, bearing witness, social responsibility, and, of course, creating accountability for those in power. We read several political novels, including *The Handmaid's*

Tale by Margaret Atwood, *The Sympathizer* by Viet Thanh Nguyen, and *Disgrace* by J. M. Coetzee, all novels that are explicitly political and beautifully crafted. We talked about strategies for balancing political ambitions and finding what Achebe so aptly termed "the felicity of language." We also talked about the limits of the political novel and how to manage expectations about what literature might accomplish, thinking about the challenging but mindful arguments James Baldwin made in his essay "Everybody's Protest Novel," where he worried, understandably, about the idea that books could provide salvation simply by existing.

Alongside this reading, where we explored the political ambitions of each work and what it taught us about writing a political novel, the students wrote political novels of their own. They engaged with the Cuban diaspora, the natural world and its endangered status by way of global warming, how soldiers deal with post-traumatic stress when returning to their lives after war, technology and reproduction, the oppressive cultural norms women navigate, and homosexuality in China. The students produced astonishing work in such a short amount of time. They each wrote a story where something important was at stake for the characters and the world of their novel and the world into which they might someday publish that novel. They did so without compromising the level of craft demanded of a good novel. I couldn't have been happier with how the workshop progressed and the ways in which these writers were willing to take their own stands.

As I considered the 120 stories I read for *The Best American Short Stories 2018,* I thought about this cultural moment and what it means to both write politically and read politically. If writers have a responsibility for how they narrate the world, certainly readers have a responsibility for what they consume and from whom. I wanted to read through these stories with as open a mind as possible, but I also wanted to make sure I was as open to stories from smaller, lesser-known magazines as I was to the reliably excellent stories published in *The New Yorker* and *Granta* and *Tin House.* I wanted to make sure that the diversity of identity was represented in terms of the writers I selected and the stories they told and how those stories were told. Reading for this year's anthology was as much a political act, and a way of taking a stand, as my writing. I was comfortable reading this way because the excellence of these stories was the one known quantity.

The twenty stories I finally chose, after no small amount of tense deliberation, are all stories I still remember with distinct admiration, months after first reading them. They are stories that engage with the world and reflect the diversity of the world. They are stories that offer fascinating insights into the human condition and the terrible ways people can treat one another and how beautifully people can love. These writers accomplished great feats of imagination and wrote stories that surprised me in the most unexpected ways. These stories challenged me and reminded me of how vibrant the short story form can be.

In "Boys Go to Jupiter," Danielle Evans writes a sly, subtle story about friendship and grief, but also about race and youth and small transgressions that become unintended acts of damage and defiance. "Boys Go to Jupiter" is one of the finest short stories I've ever read, and it embodies the ways in which fiction can be political without being heavy-handed or unnecessarily didactic. Esmé Weijun Wang wrote the one story in this year's anthology that explicitly addressed the 2016 election: "What Terrible Thing It Was." The story is about far more than the election, but it captures so well the chaos and confusion of that November night when so many things changed, while also capturing the chaos and confusion of a woman dealing with mental illness.

I am always drawn to darkness in fiction, and "The Brothers Brujo," by Matthew Lyons, did not disappoint with a story about dark magic and two hardscrabble brothers trying to survive their abusive father. The prose is brutal and bold. The story itself made me uncomfortable. It made me cringe. It made me read it three times, four, as it got under my skin. In "The Art of Losing," by Yoon Choi, there is tenderness and poignancy as the author details a man losing his memory but trying hard to hold on to what he knows and who he is. "Control Negro," by Jocelyn Nicole Johnson, depicts a father using his son in a social experiment to challenge what he knows about race in America. The story is strange but funny in that way where you laugh rather than cry through painful truths. "Everything Is Far from Here," by Cristina Henríquez, takes on immigration detention centers, where people are housed until the government decides whether or not to treat them like people. Many people are willfully excluded from the American dream because they have brown skin, and this story serves as a necessary reminder. My expectations were brilliantly upended by Curtis Sittenfeld's "The Prairie Wife," and when I finished the story, I was forced to consider the assumptions I make when I am reading a story and think I know everything I need to know about a narrator.

In everything I read and ultimately selected for this year's *Best American Short Stories,* writers were engaging with the political, sometimes explicitly, sometimes implicitly, always brilliantly and creatively. These writers used their craft to take a stand, and how. They represent the best of what short fiction can be.

ROXANE GAY

The Best
AMERICAN
SHORT
STORIES
2018

Cougar

FROM *The Iowa Review*

OUR TRAILER SAT on cinder blocks in a half-acre lot a four-cigarette drive outside of town. There wasn't much else around except Jenny's trailer and forest that started at the end of the lot and went on for as far as you could see, dim and impenetrable. Dad kept pink healing quartz on the porch steps, rocks he'd found in the deepest parts of forests, back when there was still old-growth forest to be logged. He was a sad, quiet guy. Never argued with me or knocked me around like dads of guys I used to know. We played cards with his old logging friends when they came through town. Summers we shot coyotes in the Rattlesnakes. Slept outside without tents or bear spray. I never felt safer. We hunted elk and deer. I loved having my hands deep inside something just barely dead, seeing what organs and muscles and fat looked like from the inside. Better than any science class. We had a decent, quiet life in that trailer.

Dad's logging operation went under. He got even quieter. When he wasn't sleeping, he would drink Heinekens and sit in the living room, which was really just a wide hallway between the bedrooms and kitchen, and watch the forest through the window. Most dads I knew drank Bud, but mine liked Heineken and was okay with paying more for it. Koda would sit protectively next to him. She was a mute Pyrenees, who like my father was parted from her natural vocation—her ancestral duties were keeping livestock alive—and so cared for us instead, herding our trucks out of the driveway and guiding them back in whenever we returned, that kind of thing.

What was Dad thinking about when he sat like this? Just going over things in his head? All the trees he'd run chainsaws through with crews of guys from all over, the few women he'd slept with, wobbly nights driving back from Bonner bars with old logging buddies. Dad loved the woods, and, I think, for him, felling the oldest trees in the oldest forests didn't mean he loved them any less. Maybe he was thinking about my mother, who left when I was two. Maybe he was just watching the trees and not thinking about anything at all. Maybe he was hoping to spot the cougar I'd seen a few times now, the one folks were saying killed Shively's new colt and came back for the rest of her before they could get her buried.

Dad disappeared the day I got my senior pictures back. Late April. His wallet on the table with everything still in it, empty Heinekens in the sink. I checked the closet and was relieved to see the rifle and shotgun. His truck was still there, key in the ignition, old Copenhagen cans on the floor, orange juice bottles half-full of his spit, SunChip bags crammed into the seats. I touched the chewed passenger's-side seat belt where Koda had worked on it all the way home from the pound. I pulled out my senior pictures. I was eighteen, but in them I looked like a kid. A dumb, smiling kid, because when people asked me to smile, that's what I'd do. I spat on the shiny surface, rubbed the water around, and scratched off all my mouths.

Search and rescue never found a body. One member of the search committee, a homeless asshole there for the free lunch, pulled me aside and told me it was "them aliens" who took my father, the ones who doodled on all the trees. He pointed at a larch.

"That's Dutch elm," I said.

He nodded. Licked a yellow stain at the corner of his mouth and wiped the area dry with his sleeve. "Nope," he said. Before he took off, he pressed fifteen dollars and the Snickers bar from his sack lunch into my hands.

The rifle was a gentle-looking black .22 semiautomatic. Polymer plastic blend. I associated it with the peaceful feeling of completing a hunt, the comfort of fresh-cooked meat. I carried it into the living room and pointed it out the window, hoping the cougar would choose this moment to stroll through. I peeled off a sock and clicked off the safety and aimed at my big toe. I stood there for what felt like hours, wondering what kind of hurt could come from something small as a toe. I tried to think about all the places Dad could have gone and might still be. Tried not to think about how he might have offed himself, if that's what he'd done. I clicked on the safety, turned the gun around, and swung it from the barrel like a golf club into my ankle.

The pain felt like something else in the dark room, dim and sweet.

For weeks I searched the woods, ignoring my busted foot. Hoping to find what search and rescue couldn't. Koda followed, licking the scabby blood off my ankle whenever I stopped to rest. She started sleeping in my bed at night instead of Dad's, arranging herself in the center of the mattress at crotch-level, so I'd have to lie on one side around her or else sleep with legs spread. She'd close her eyes but was awake in a way and watching me. Any time I got up during the night, she'd snap open her eyes and follow me to the bathroom or kitchen, making sure I returned to bed. There her rib cage rose and fell slower than I thought possible. Watching her breathe reminded me of the one girl I'd slept with. I used to watch that girl's belly go up and down and press my hand into it. Her stomach went concave when she inhaled, and my hand was sucked into her by her breathing. It was strange, pressing my hand into Koda's long white fur and feeling the same thing. That girl now sold eight-dollar coffee in Williston to creepy oil field guys.

A hawk or something that sounded like one made a long, ugly noise in the distance.

In June I went full-time washing dishes at one of Bonner's worst restaurants, a Chinese place by the interstate. Bonner was an old logging town, population 1,600 and shrinking. Business was usually slow. Even when we were busy it felt slow. And the food was rough. Real rough. Greasy piles of chicken or beef probably slaughtered years ago, thawed and slopped with sauce that left orange residue on the plates. I'd turn down a free ticket to China if anybody ever offered me one. They'd go, "Here, Cal. Round-trip to Beijing. On me." Thanks, but no fucking thanks. The only places Dad ever traveled were logging camps in Washington and Oregon. Except one time he'd gone to California, where a kid tried to grab his wallet. Hit him in the face with a busted lightbulb when Dad wouldn't give it up. The bulb nicked the artery in his cheek.

Washing dishes wasn't bad. You could go the whole day without talking to anyone if you didn't feel like it. A lot of jobs weren't like that—you had to bullshit with customers or your coworkers whether you liked it or not. Here you just stuck in your headphones and everything disappeared. Some days, though, I was happy to have company. I'd smoke a cigarette with the old grandma whose son and daughter-in-law owned the place. She chain-lit stale Montanas she got cheap off the rez, squinching her eyes shut and breathing the smoke in deep.

Slow days the owners had me drive trash to the Clark Fork and throw it in. They didn't want to pay for a dumpster. This got me out of the restaurant, but I hated leaving garbage in such a beautiful place. The river was so blue and clear I didn't have words for it. Dry heat wagged the horizon. I'd smoke on the muddy bank and stare at the water. Once a moose and her calf were drinking from the far shore. I wanted to shoot them, thinking of the nice, oily meat. The calf walked underneath its mom to get to the other side of her, then looked up at her to see if she'd noticed, but the mom was watching me. Other times I'd see what I thought were probably their heart-shaped tracks on my side of the shore, the toes splayed in the mud. After seeing the moose, I threw the trash in the back of my truck to ditch on my way home from work. I'd toss it in one of the abandoned sawmills, where the flies and bees buzzed so loud in the heat that I could hear them before getting out of the truck.

The owners of the Chinese restaurant, who were actually Korean, kept a quiet shrine on the floor in the corner of the dining room. The shrine had a picture of a sad-looking man with a dented head, a bowl of bruised clementines, and a plastic cat that waved its paw at you. An up-and-down wave. Maybe that was how Korean people waved. The cat waved at you like it was waving away all the stuff you thought about. Like it was urging you not to think, not to worry about being able to buy food or pay rent or feel like you should try to make some friends or have sex again because that was what eighteen-year-olds did. I sometimes stole clementines from the shrine. At home I peeled them and gave half to Koda. She'd accept them and gravely spit out the pulpy mess.

After Dad disappeared, Jenny would come over to pick up the rent. He'd trip on the quartz in the dark and cuss his way up the porch steps. The old Indian had a fat, long, gray rattail that looked like it was feeding on his brain. He lived across the lot in a trailer that was out of earshot but close enough for me to see the shape of him moving around, trimming the bushes around his property, dragging long, limp branches inside for his stove, pounding some skinned animal into the side of his shed. I'd heard Jenny had some kind of cancer, or some other disease. Something eating him from the inside.

"Met these women on the internet," he told me once, a few months after Dad left. We were on my porch again. He tucked the rent into the pocket of a grimy, striped T-shirt. His armpit skin was tanned and saggy, but the skin on his face was pale and smooth. I didn't know about meeting women online. Seemed desperate. If I met a girl, I'd want it to be in person. But then again I wasn't meeting anyone at all.

From the restaurant parking lot, I'd sometimes see Jenny pull into the Super 8 across from the Chinese restaurant and sit at the lobby's guest computer. What kind of picture was he showing these ladies?

I'd hear music blasting. See the shapes of Jenny and a woman playing a game of naked tag outside like kids. The whitish glow of a woman's ass in the porch light. Some nights I wondered if they weren't playing at all, and the woman was trying to get away from him, or if play had tipped into something else. When the campers took off, Jenny would usually come over, tripping on the steps, red-cheeked and reeking of sex. He was usually drunk and happy and had a joint he wanted us to smoke. This happened a couple times a month.

"Cal, you got to try it. Young guy like you, you need to get your dick wet," he said one evening. Koda was lying in the dirt but kept getting up and going inside and coming out again, wanting to go to bed. If she could speak, she'd whine, but instead she hovered, moving from one side of us to the other, trying to herd us inside.

"My dick's just fine," I said.

"Cal, I'm serious," he said. "You got to get out of Bonner. You got to start figuring out what you want to do next."

I was quiet. Koda gave up and lay down next to me.

"You're not living in this trailer for good, are you?" said Jenny. "You can't wash dishes forever." He sat on the porch steps and stuck the unlit joint all the way inside his mouth, pulled it slowly out to coat it with spit, and passed the lighter back and forth as he rotated it, drying out the paper, before lighting it.

"Your dad was a weird duck — never knew what that guy was

thinking. But guys like him, they're so nice they sometimes can't say what it is they want. I think wherever he is, it hurt him bad to leave you. That's all you need to know."

I took a big drag of the joint and coughed. We passed it back and forth, pressing our lips to the same soggy end, and sat there awhile after we finished.

"Man, I'm flipped outta my rig," said Jenny. "Flipped outta my fucking rig!" He hauled himself up by the porch railing, taking a last coughing drag, and stumbled down the steps. He tripped on a piece of quartz on the last one, picked it up, cussed, and chucked it toward the forest. It bounced off something and came rolling back into view.

Over a year after Dad left, I was still living with Koda in that trailer, working at the Chinese restaurant. I'd been alive nineteen years and had no idea what to do with myself. I'd finally cleaned out Dad's old wallet and threw it away. After staring into his face for a long time, I threw out his driver's license and old ID cards too.

I saw my friend Blake outside the gas station, holding a cup of shit coffee in a fancy portable mug. It was summer. The asphalt was starting to radiate heat. Blake had heard about Dad, and he didn't like that I was still living in the trailer.

"It's not so bad," I said.

He told me about Williston, where he worked on an oil rig. He was here to see his folks. "Hard living, but a couple years of this and I'll be doing anything I want." I didn't understand exactly what it was he did. "Two weeks on, one off, bud. Hundred thou a year. Pretty good for a Bonner High School grad, huh bud."

"It's not bad here," I said.

"Cal, you want to end up like these people?" He looked around the empty parking lot. Across the street, guys piled into a truck loaded with construction supplies, and we heard one give a loud, girlish giggle. They seemed all right to me.

"Williston's the kind of place that can change your luck," said Blake. "Make enough money to do whatever you want. Hell, you could live in my basement. Bring Koda. Think about it. We could get beach houses in Florida, bud. Watch ladies in bikinis walk through our yard every day. Track caribou up in Canada. You could finally teach me how to hunt."

I'd heard about guys losing a finger or arm at those jobs, or getting hooked on pills or whatever else they had down there. But a beach house sounded nice.

In the fall Jenny and I hunted together. Mulies, mostly. Once in a while an elk. He didn't need my help and I didn't need his, but I think we both liked the company.

Jenny's legs had gotten so thin his pants hung off them. Whatever sickness he had seemed to be getting worse. His face wasn't smooth and puffy anymore. His cheekskin hung on two cheekbones. Oily skin under his eyes the color of chow mein. Looking at it made me hungry, even though I hated chow mein. The rattail was the only thing that looked healthy about him. It looked fatter than before. It reminded me somehow of the waving cat at the restaurant, this long piece of hair rooted into his skull, wagging at me as I followed it through the woods. Slowly sucking the fat out of him, but also saying, don't worry, don't worry. I wondered where his meat was going, since we split whatever we got. He was so skinny. I figured he gave some of it as presents when women visited.

We had to walk farther than usual to find game, and the animals we did find looked hungry. On our longest hike, I shot a porcupine. Jenny showed me how to skin it. We roasted it over a fire, and he explained you have to cook it a long time because of tapeworms. The meat was greasy and crisp and tasted like pine.

"You think my dad killed himself?" I asked. That's what I'd come to believe. It was easiest thinking he'd made a choice and acted on it. That he hadn't left me to go live somewhere else, or died by accident in some far-off ravine in the woods. Even if I didn't believe it, it seemed like the best way to stop wondering.

"I don't think he would," said Jenny. "But you never know."

We never saw the cougar that killed Shively's colt. The Korean grandma told me she'd seen it on one of her nighttime walks around town. "My son thinks mountain lions are the most beautiful animal in Montana," she said. Her son was tracking him. Wanted to stuff him, mount him on the restaurant wall like he was about to jump. "Like a display he saw in a museum in San Francisco," she said. "It would bring business in. People like to see." I pictured a cougar crammed with stuffing, bigger than he'd ever been alive. Stuck crouching sadly above diners. Eyes made in a factory in China by little girls. Wanting to maim these Chinese-food-eating cretins. The gross orange sauce and greasy chicken smells seeping into his corpse.

A postcard came from Blake. A well spit up black oil on the front. On the back, in smashed-together handwriting, like maybe his hands were tired, it said, *Basemnt still free. Talked to my boss abt a job for you. Come out, bud.* I stuck it on the fridge.

At the restaurant, I came to look forward to talking to the grandma. There was never anything to report on her son's cougar hunt, so she'd tell me about the sad-looking man in the shrine photo and how he and her dad had sampled LSD and eaten gas-station steak and eggs every morning for a month. He'd also smuggled a lemon the size of a football from California to Korea in the '70s. This all seemed unappealing to me, stuff I'd never want to do. The lemon, her dad said, was from a famous lemon farm and would bring his family luck. She said she came from a place called Soul.

I started smoking rez cigarettes too. Mostly quit buying beer. Drove slower to save gas, so that the trailer was now a six-cigarette drive from town. Stole more than usual from the Missoula Walmart, filling a trash can in the self-checkout line with Koda's food and other junk and just ringing up the heavy can, which I'd later return. I'd save as much cash as I could every month, rolling the twenties and sticking them in a cigarette carton.

After work I'd sit with my back to the living room window and the forest, watching shapes the light and trees made on the wall. I made a beer last a long time, closing my eyes and sipping and looking at the shapes the sun made through the skin of my eyelids.

Blake called to tell me he'd spoken to his boss about me, but I needed to pass a test first. Over the next weeks he helped me study over the phone. I drove to Missoula for the exam. Most questions I had to just guess. At least, that's what I thought. A few weeks later a letter came. I'd passed.

When Jenny smoked a cigarette I'd go out and smoke one too, so I could wave at him and see him wave back. I'd wave up and down, like the cat in the shrine. I'd go inside, sit on the couch, and think about how many moments like this a man could have in a day, a week, a year. A year felt like an unbearably long time.

When Jenny didn't want to hunt, Koda and I roamed even far-ther from the trailer, and I guided us back by leaving little landmarks from torn-up construction vests I'd stolen from work sites. The Clark was muddy from runoff and no longer as blue. I was still leaving trash at the huge pile in the sawmill, which was drawing more flies and bees.

One day I was sitting on the porch hoping Jenny would come over after he was finished with the woman whose camper was parked in his yard. I hoped he'd bring another joint.

I heard a strange, muffled wheeze, the kind Koda would make if she had to make a noise. At first I just saw her running. A ways behind her was the cougar. The air smelled sour. The cougar was moving fast but with a limp. In front of the cougar was Koda, running along the side of the ravine. She was heading for the brush where the forest started. I needed to run inside for the rifle, but I couldn't move. I wanted to throw up. She was going fast for an old dog, but not as fast as I knew she could run. As she neared the forest, she became a white blur.

He got her before she could reach the brush pile. I went inside for the rifle. When I got outside they were one big shape, like a cartoon of the Tasmanian Devil I'd watched as a kid, churning up dust. He had her by the neck. I got a bead on the shape and shot. I'd hit Koda in the leg. The cougar dropped her and loped away.

I carried her back to the trailer and tried to pry the bullet out with a knife while I hugged her body to keep her still. She panted but otherwise made no sound. She grinned in pain. All I could do was move the bullet around. Finally I carried her inside and laid her on my bed.

The next morning when I woke up, Koda was gone. I got the rifle and ran outside. I ran along the ravine, thinking she maybe went for water. There was one spot with a lot of blood that looked shiny in the sun. It might not have been hers.

I looked for her until it got too dark to see.

That night I sat outside until I couldn't feel my hands or face. I thought of how the cougar had returned to eat the rest of Shively's colt. For the next few days I kept looking for Koda, barely taking time to eat, ditching work. I saw what I thought was cougar shit, which looks like cat shit, only bigger. There was no sign of Koda.

At work the son told me to start collecting uneaten meat from peoples' plates for his dogs, though I was pretty sure he didn't have any dogs. I turned the water to the hottest setting and sprayed my hands until they turned red, until I couldn't stand it anymore. When the cook warned me a pan was hot, I'd pick it up anyway. Soon my hands were covered with burns. I couldn't stop looking for Koda. I couldn't sleep. I'd lie awake looking at the friendly burns on my hands. In the dark they looked like puffy leeches.

After a week, I found her. There were big cat prints around her body. Smaller prints that looked like little hands—raccoon, probably—had been patting the ground around her, as if trying to comfort the tail and the paws that still looked like paws and the matted and reeking outsides of her. None of this looked like it had ever been part of the dog that used to watch me while I slept. Her eyes were closed and her lips were pulled back into a snarl, or a grimace. Her front paws were bent, as if trying to protect her stomach; this part of her that I'd watched rise and fall was gone. The middle of her had been eaten, everything inside her rib cage and some of the bones too, and the ground where her stomach used to be was dark. The fur around her back paws was pink. I hugged her head, stroked her big smooth teeth. I buried her under the living room window, inside one of Dad's old sleeping bags.

I threw out her bowls and blanket. I wouldn't need them in Williston. After a few years, I'd go to California to see the lemon farms, if those still existed. I'd go to Florida and buy a house with a pool and pay someone to clean it.

I'd wake up and find Koda's white hair everywhere. The hair both depressed and comforted me. I tried to pick it off my clothes, but it kept reappearing on stuff I'd already washed. I missed sleeping with her in my bed, letting her eat fried rice out of my hand, dumping out her water bowl, shouting her name to call her back inside, an excuse to yell as loud as I could. Later I removed her water bowl from the trash, running a finger along the rough white calcified crust. At breakfast I'd read the calcification rings like a cereal box, looking for something I could use.

A postcard arrived from Blake with the same oil well. Maybe they sold only one kind of postcard in Williston. It said in that same smashed handwriting, *Florida. Beach. Caribou. Come out, brother. Boss has ben asking abt you.* I put it next to the other one on the fridge. I took out the cigarette carton and counted the cash I'd saved so far. Not much.

The grandma was unhappy I missed work. She cut my hours. I

tried not to worry. I quit putting twenties in the carton. Sometimes I needed to borrow a few, and I could never pay myself back.

One morning I walked to Jenny's. He'd installed a Cherokee Nation sticker on the mailbox: a man's face inside a red square. Above him, a star and some kind of branch. The man looked tired, stuck to that mailbox, like he was sick of seeing the mailman's hand crammed inside his little metal establishment every day, stuffing circulars and impersonal letters, never a fat check or a *Penthouse* or a wedding invitation.

Jenny emerged from his trailer. He was wearing clothes that struck me as not being his, though of course they could be no one else's. I asked him if he'd seen the cougar.

"The thing killed Koda," I said.

"Dammit. Dammit, Cal, I'm sure as hell sorry to hear that." Jenny scratched his knee through a hole in his jeans, moving the hole around to reach more skin. He coughed and wiped his chin. "Sometimes those big cats, they come down from the mountains when they can't get enough to eat."

"Jenny." I'd never asked him for any help since my dad went away, tried never to be late on rent. I asked if he'd help me find the cougar.

"Why? You thinking of killing him?" said Jenny.

I wasn't sure why. Maybe I did. I wanted to at least get a good look.

"I'm not sure an animal deserves getting shot for being hungry," said Jenny. "Nope, I'm not sure it does at all."

I resolved to go out on my own but lost my nerve.

The grandma fired me from the restaurant. Her son's son had aged out of his paper route. "My grandson tried to find a job everywhere else in town, you know. He did not want to work here. But no one would hire him. You're a good worker, but he's family, you know? You know we are the only Korean people in Bonner?" She lit her cigarette on the third try and tucked my lighter into my sweatshirt pocket.

"We had a Korean restaurant but no one came. People here only want shit Chinese food. No *kalguksu*, no *gimbap*, no *bibimbap*. Nothing crazy. Nothing they wouldn't like. But they didn't want it. They wanted shit. They wanted very cheap, big portion of shit."

She closed her eyes. "What I decide is, people want shit, you give them shit," she said.

I finished my shift even though she implied I wouldn't get paid for it. I wondered if my trailer was shit, if my way of living was shit. If Dad's life had been shit. As I was leaving—I later regretted this—I kicked the shrine. Clementines rolled across the floor, and the grandma's dad, the lemon smuggler, tipped face-first onto the ground. The cat fell on its side but kept waving.

"Bibimbap! Bibimbap! Bibimbap!" I said. I shot the place up with guns I made with my hands. I didn't shoot any people, just the walls. Even this felt wrong to me. But something had clenched inside me when I got fired, Williston and beach houses and chicks in bikinis all shriveling up, and so I shot. I looked back before running out, and the grandma was standing there, looking tired and old.

I'd already sold Dad's truck, and the money from that was gone. The two oil wells had slid lower and lower on my fridge as the magnet lost its stick. It was almost winter. I daydreamed about jumping into a Florida swimming pool, my body cold all over and weightless. I'd keep a waving cat in the window where I could see it from the pool, reminding me that the times I worried about money were over for good.

When Jenny didn't come by to pick up rent a few days later, I went to check on him. He answered the door with his rattail in his hand. Its fat body curled over his shoulder like a snake. The planter of cigarette butts had been tipped onto the ground next to the porch. Someone had tried to peel the Cherokee man off the mailbox and failed, or the weather was slowly undoing whatever made it stick.

"Jenny," I started. I was going to tell him they'd fired me.

"You call your mom? Bet she'd like to hear from you." He was slurring. He seemed to be having trouble walking and took my arm. With his free hand, he put his rattail in his mouth and chewed. He chewed and stared at me and opened his mouth, using his lip to flap the end of the braid. He removed the rattail and held it in his hand, and we both looked at it. Up close, the hairs were all squiggly, like he'd been electrified.

"I don't talk to my mom," I said. "Never have. You knew that."

He wanted me to come inside. He went into the back room

where it was dark. He kept sheets nailed over his windows to keep out the light. I heard him take a big huff of something, moving around. I found him in his bathroom, pants down, lying on the floor. I decided for his pride to leave him there.

The next day I went again to tell him about getting fired. I wouldn't be able to pay rent that month or maybe ever. I'd brought the last twenties I'd saved to give him, but before knocking I'd tucked two or three back in my pocket.

We were standing on his porch. That morning I'd found a white, worry-doll-shaped mummy of hair the size of my thumb. One of Koda's hairballs. No matter how much I cleaned, parts of her remained.

"You know, maybe your dad did kill himself. Maybe it's best to think that. Man, I think about going that way, taking a rifle and going out back into the forest here, maybe on the river. I've lived a good life, you know. I'm about ready to give up." Jenny spit into the planter. "I think Koda maybe went that way too."

"I don't believe you," I said. "She ran. She was trying to get away from the thing. I saw it." But I did believe him.

Jenny looked in his mailbox. There was nothing inside but a few crumpled papers. Someone miles away was burning trash.

He pulled his rattail over his shoulder and arranged it in the middle of his chest. "I've been feeding him," he said. "The cougar."

He told me he'd been setting out meat for him for a while now. "I know he killed Koda, and I'm sorry, but being hungry's no one's fault. Everyone's hungry, everyone's got to eat."

I could taste the burning garbage on my tongue.

"I'd like you to keep feeding him for me, when I'm not around," Jenny continued. "That's one thing I need you to do for me."

He got me a cold beer with a soggy label, which I took but did not drink.

Jenny told me I reminded him of a son he once dreamed he had. He squeezed my armpit. It was horrible, standing there, listening to him. I remembered an old man I'd seen in the restaurant trying to get the plastic wrapper off his straw. You could tell it was important to him to get the wrapper off, and he kept trying. Finally, he set the straw down, and the waitress came over and undid it for him.

Jenny pulled open his mailbox again, and still nothing was there but those crumpled papers.

A few nights later I saw the cougar again. He was walking about twenty feet from my living room toward Jenny's trailer. His eyes were the size of clementines—big, black clementines. He was moving slowly, swinging his head low to the ground, looking toward my trailer and away and back again. I didn't want the cougar to have killed Koda, to have given my dog a scary, painful death. But there it was. I couldn't believe the way this lone thing walked, placing each foot heavily down, shifting one shoulder bone, then the other. His fur was gray in the dark. His tail was as big around as a bull snake. I could make out a pink smear on his flank where a wound might have healed. He made his way to Jenny's trailer, paused outside, and continued on into the trees.

A Family

FROM *Gulf Coast*

CURTIS SMITH WATCHED from across the street as the boy argued with Lena Johnson in front of the movie theater. She had probably bought tickets for the wrong movie. Or maybe Andre didn't want to see any movie with his mother on a Friday night. Her expression went from pleading to irate. The boy said nothing more. With his head taking on weight, hung as though his neck couldn't hold it, he followed as she went inside.

It was a chilly evening in November, the sky threatened by rain. Curtis blew warm breath into his cupped hands. Obedience, he thought, he could talk to the boy about that. He'd been making a list of topics they could discuss. The question of obedience was right for a boy of fifteen, when the man he would become was beginning to erupt out of him like horns. Though sometimes it was important to *disobey*. Curtis had known this since he was younger than the boy was now. Twelve years in prison hadn't changed that, and so Curtis was here, doing what his mother had asked him that morning not to do anymore. He'd been seen watching Andre and Lena, and his mother's friends were gossiping about what they saw. Maybe Curtis still had a grudge against Lena, they said, or maybe he simply couldn't let go of the past. He didn't care what his mother or her friends said. A man decided his own way, and there came a time when a boy growing into his manhood had to as well. *Unless your balls haven't dropped yet*. Curtis could say that to the boy, teasing him the way he and the boy's father, Marvin Caldwell, used to tease each other when they were young. Marvin dreamed most vividly of everything he would do for his mother one day, but even he knew to disobey her.

Curtis took a last look at the names of the movies and tried to guess which one Andre might have wanted to see, which one Lena would have chosen instead. He counted his money. He'd only spent twelve of the forty dollars his mother had left for him, so he decided to get a bite to eat while he waited for the movie to end. At the Downtown Bar and Grill, an old favorite, he ordered a hamburger and soda. Refills were no longer free, so Curtis kept asking for glasses of water. From where he sat he could still see the brilliance of the marquee.

The rain began before Andre and Lena came out of the theater, but they took a walk anyway. Curtis followed them. Lena opened an umbrella that was large enough for two, but as they strolled along the promenade Andre kept drifting away from her, exposing his body to the cold drizzle. Lena stopped at a bench and used a piece of newspaper to wipe it dry. Andre maintained a distance from her when they sat. Curtis stalled for a few moments, and then settled near the middle of the next bench. A large trash can partially blocked his view of them, but he could hear their conversation.

"Your daddy liked to come out here," Lena was saying.

"You told me that before," Andre said. Curtis had been following them for weeks, but had rarely been this close. He'd never heard them talk about Marvin.

"Well, it's nice, isn't it? Look at that view."

Andre gestured at the rain. "I can't see nothing."

Curtis had been out on the promenade several times since he'd been released from prison. There was plenty to see, he thought. A great, unseen hand depressed the keys of the city, sounding notes held constant in the many windows, a thousand little squares of humming light. These seemed to float independently, since the tall buildings themselves, their outlines obscured, were indistinguishable from the black enamel seal of the sky. The night grew more thickly clouded by storm, but in the shifting bands of reflected light from the bridge and the city, Curtis could see the surface of the river alive and puckered like so many restless mouths. Given all the nights he'd spent here since getting out, it felt like a triumph that he no longer thought of feeding himself to the water.

"Why we out here, Ma?" Andre asked. "It's wet. I'm cold."

"It's not so bad under the umbrella."

"Can we go?"

"I just thought you'd like to stay out a while longer. Might as well enjoy it now. I need you to be at home tomorrow."

"For what?"

"You know how the girls from work go out to Temptations after our shift," Lena said. "Well, this time they finally invited me."

"Tomorrow's Saturday, Ma."

"I know what day it is. And I need you to be at home. For my peace of mind."

"While you out shaking your ass at the club."

"What'd you say, boy?"

"Nothing," Andre said. "I'm cold." He stood and started walking back the way they'd come.

Lena chased after him, sounding pathetic as she called his name.

Curtis didn't follow. After a while, he got up and strolled along the promenade in the direction of the Brooklyn Bridge. The only other person he saw was a man with an unsettling face. The man's bouts of muttering formed clouds that flowered like visible emblems of his secret language before being pulled apart by the wind. But it was the way this man's hands jumped within his dirty coat as he shuffled along that marked him as dangerous and insane. Curtis had been both of these things, in those months after Marvin died in the fire. Those months before Curtis went to prison. It was danger lurking in the man's left pocket, he suspected, and insanity leaping around in the right. He liked the feeling of their passing him by.

Curtis huffed the name of his long departed friend—*my dead friend,* he told himself soberly—so he could see the wind take it, imagining that it too, along with the words steaming from the man's mouth, drifted off and seeded the East River. The river was badly polluted, but he liked it anyway. It flowed in either direction, reaching both ways until it licked the sea. As the man prattled on, now some distance away, Curtis again said Marvin's name, which rose from his lips and hovered there for a moment, clean as an unstrung bone.

He might have also said the name of the dead woman, the one he had struck with his car, the one who intruded on his dreams.

But his life was for other things now, he'd been desperately telling himself, beautiful and wondrous things.

The rain began turning to sleet, the sound of it an exhalation steadily hushing the world. Curtis indulged his sense of feeling contained but not trapped. Under the capacious dome of sky he was free, but bounded, so his newly freed limbs wouldn't fly apart. As much as he wanted to stay there on the promenade—often he stayed until the spell of night began to break—the sleet was penetrating his slicker and the thin coat he wore underneath. His hands and feet were already numb. Curtis shivered. It wouldn't make any damn sense to get out of the clink just to turn around and catch his death of cold. He walked quickly to keep the chill from settling into his muscle and marrow.

The next night, Curtis walked along Atlantic Avenue, not far from the movie theater and the Downtown Bar and Grill. It was eleven o'clock and he was enjoying the bustle and breadth of the thoroughfare. He was still amazed at how much had changed: the number of fancy restaurants and wine stores now. Then again, many of the old bars remained. And the new nightclubs were just the old nightclubs with different names.

An empty bus made its way past, the driver lit against its dark frame like an insect stuck in amber. On the corner stood a white woman trying in vain to hail a medallion cab, and Curtis stood beside her, as though waiting to cross the street. She wasn't dressed for the weather, wearing only a trim jacket and a scarf over her short dress. Her uncovered head twitched, shaking her cropped hair from her lips; her legs were thin but shapely, the color of rich cream. She was what Marvin used to call a "slim goody." Curtis imagined how soft the inside of her thighs would be. He imagined her open mouth.

It had been a long time since he'd had sex with anyone but himself, with his own clutching hand. In those first years in prison, he kept an old black-and-white picture of the actress Marpessa Dawn taped to the wall. Following those first years of her smiling in the swimming pool came explicit pictures of women opening their shiny, hairless bodies to the camera. When he first got out of prison he bought a couple of magazines with centerfolds, but then he discovered how easily videos could be found on his mother's computer. He still liked that picture of the actress in the pool most of all.

The white woman's phone began ringing, and she greeted the caller, apparently her mother, the simple words strained by her tone of heavy familiarity. The second Curtis heard her speak, a feeling of exhaustion overcame him; she reminded him, for some reason, of the woman he had struck with his car. But if that woman had been white, Curtis knew, he would still be in prison, with many more years there ahead of him. To get away from the voice now whining into the phone, he jogged across the street.

In front of Temptations, three men were lined up behind a black velvet rope. The bouncer wore dark glasses and appeared to have no intention of letting the three in. Curtis took his place in line as the first man began to complain.

"Come on now, chief. We been waiting out here for a minute."

"Damn near a half hour," another said. "Say it straight."

"And the hawk is *out,* big man. Come on."

The bouncer said nothing. Another man got in line behind Curtis as a livery taxi pulled up. Three women got out and were followed by Lena Johnson, an afterthought. The bouncer wasted no time letting them in.

Waiting with the other men in line gave Curtis plenty of time to reconsider going in, even after Lena's arrival. In fact, he tried to change his mind, calling up reasons he should—images of the promenade, of the white woman on the corner—but it was Lena's nyloned legs emerging from the taxi that were lit up on the stage of his mind. Moving slowly in a sapphire dress, she trailed the other women. The shock of seeing her dolled up was slight, but after she vanished through the door, every scene that proceeded on the stage of his mind featured the nylons and the sapphire dress and ended in foolishness. He kept thinking about Andre imagining these scenes unfold or trying to decipher his mother's face tomorrow during the broadcasts of Sunday afternoon football. The boy needed to be spared his mother's small tragedies.

About fifteen minutes later, the bouncer announced to the men that it would be a ten-dollar cover to get in, speaking as if they had only just arrived. He examined Curtis's clothes doubtfully before admitting him. Curtis wore jeans, but they weren't that dirty; the real problem was that he had on work boots instead of what Marvin would have called "slippery earls." This outfit wouldn't have gotten him into the places they used to frequent, back in the days when they used fake IDs.

"Good luck, playboy," the bouncer said. He stepped aside to let Curtis through the curtains. "Your broke ass gonna need it."

The nightclub had two floors. Curtis didn't spot Lena on the ground level, so he went down to the basement. He took a seat at the bar that gave him a good view of the room and recognized certain features: the low ceiling with its copper tiles, the four pillars that marked the boundary of the dance floor. He and Marvin had been here before, when there was only a basement level. The place used to be called Nelson's.

Curtis had extra money from an odd job helping his mother's neighbor move some boxes, plus what was left of yesterday's forty dollars. It was easier than he thought it would be to order a bourbon. The words didn't get stuck; the bartender didn't stare. The taste of the drink closed his eyes and warmed him from his throat to his navel.

The music blasting in the club sounded like pure racket, but this wasn't new. While he liked some of the rap other boys listened to when they were growing up, Curtis was always drawn to older music, songs from the 1960s and '70s. *All right, old man.* Marvin had a great time teasing him about this. *Look at the old head tryna get his groove!* He'd mock Curtis by bending over and holding his lower back, two-stepping with an imaginary cane.

Lena and her friends were already out there shaking their bodies, each with a drink in hand. Some new dances must have caught on from the music videos. As he watched, Curtis felt he was a man true to better times. He returned to the problem of Andre, how he'd manage to talk to the boy and what his first words would be. After a while, a tall man in a suit came up behind Lena and began to whisper in her ear. She laughed. Soon she had backed herself into him and they were fused in body and time. She pursed her lips and slapped her thigh with her free hand as they danced. Although he and Lena were the same age, thirty-five, Curtis was upset to see her carrying on like this. Feeling sorry for the boy and, somehow, for Marvin, he wished he had just gone to the promenade. He ordered another bourbon.

Lena and the man in the suit talked for a while at a different side of the bar. He had bought her another drink, but the smile was gone from her eyes. She seemed much less engaged now that they weren't dancing. The man must have noticed this too. He tried to pull her back onto the dance floor, but she refused. The man tried a few more times and then his mouth turned cruel. He appeared to curse at Lena before he walked away.

She stood at the bar for a while, staring into her drink. Then she tossed it back, the entire pour, and drew from her purse a thin cigarette that looked cold in her brown fingers. She said something to one of the women she'd come in with and went past Curtis upstairs. For a moment it seemed that her gaze had fallen on him, but in places like this people's eyes darted everywhere. He followed her. From the entrance, he saw her smoking out near the curb. Her coat was still checked inside and with her purse pinned under her arm she held herself, trembling against the cold. She dropped her cigarette and watched it smolder and die on the ground. She could have been some kind of bird staring down from a high perch, wings pinched against her blue body, refusing to fly.

"Hey playboy," the bouncer said. "You leaving or what? It's in or out, my man."

As Lena took out another cigarette and began the drama of lighting it, Curtis walked back into the club. He stayed on the ground floor this time, where the music seemed not quite as loud. Sipping from his third bourbon, he thought about how easy it had been to go from his first to his third, and beyond, on the night the girl was struck by his car. Dismissing this, he wondered instead about what Andre was doing, if he too was taking advantage of his freedom or compounding the little tragedies of the night by sitting timidly at home. A boy his age should be in the world, seeing as much as he could claim or aspire to. He should be terrified by the new sensation of a girl's modest breasts in his hands, by the new sensation of her hands in his jeans, not by thoughts of his mother in a short dress playing at youth out here in the drunkenness of night. They were thirty-five, yes, but they were old. The boy was still young and he had his father's face. Curtis had gotten close enough to see that. His face was the same, but his fate wouldn't be.

Curtis smelled the tobacco on her breath before he felt her cold hand on his shoulder.

"You might as well come on," Lena said.

When he spun around on his barstool to look at her, she grabbed his drink and finished it in one swift motion. "Come on and dance with me," she said.

He allowed her to lead him to the dance floor, less crowded than the one downstairs. He bent his knees, searching for their bodies' fit—it turned out he hadn't forgotten this, how to accommodate the body of a woman. They danced to old lovers' rock. Her breasts were crushed against his ribs, his leg planted between hers. She held his shoulder and rode his hip. He touched a hand to her back and found skin there, exposed and sweaty.

She was clearly drunk, and he, with the bourbon at work in his blood, had the impression that he was anonymous to her. He wished he could vanish on the spot and leave her to her phantom, but something begged him to stay. It didn't seem sexual—his body had yet to respond in that way to hers—so, he told himself, it had to be his obligation to the boy. But it felt like something more bewildering than an obligation. The yearning didn't belong to him, and it didn't belong to her either. It was beyond either of them, he felt, so it claimed them both. It was as though a bright delicate object they couldn't see, some filament, were held between them, along the length of her sapphire dress stretched taut by his thigh, the spark of it hot where he carried her on his hip, moving her in the rhythm of his stationary stride, and they had no choice but to pull each other close, to preserve the object between them, otherwise it would drift free and fall and lose its light. The exhilaration of her breathing and her slim clutching thighs and her hand pulling on his shoulder were the forces she exerted on him, and he carried her with his hip and his knees bent and his back dimly aching, but all that mattered was the fragile wire pressed between them, lit by something they could neither face nor abandon.

This feeling of being stuck persisted, and Curtis was horrified by it. When the long set of lovers' rock ended and released them, he averted his eyes from the sapphire dress going loose again between Lena's thighs. He knew of nothing else to do but go back to the bar and order another drink, and when she followed him there he ordered one for her as well. It was what anyone in the role of her phantom would do. Her drink was cooled by a sculpted sphere of ice that had the look of perfection and permanence, a little moon displayed in glass. When Lena drank she did so deeply, and the moon slid, and it wet the tip of her nose. Curtis's drink had no ice. When he took it up he tilted it so the liquor fell just short of his lips and he could inhale its heat before drinking.

What did she see when she looked at him? Added weight had rounded his face, and a beard darkened it. His hair had receded above the temples so that a blunt arrow pointed down at his nose. What would Marvin look like now if he were alive?

Curtis avoided Lena's eyes, hoping the rest of their time together would pass like this—in silence. He tried to lose himself in the music that was playing, but it wouldn't permit him access; its borders were dense, its patterns impossible to predict.

"I know who you are," Lena said. "You."

Curtis was overcome with a feeling that by entering this place he had once known, he had also elected for so much more. He sat and was helpless. Everything around him—the music, the carnal laughter, the spinning stellar lights—all of it was a frenzy. He'd forgotten this basic truth, that freedom was a wilderness.

There was no place for them to go. He explained that he was living with his mother for a little while, listened as Lena said that her son was at home. Then she surprised Curtis by suggesting they get a room. Just for a couple of hours, she said. She was lonely. It wasn't all that late yet. The nightclub itself would be open until four, and her son knew not to expect her home until after that. He'd already be asleep anyway, and she'd still wake up before he did. "All that boy's worried about is having his breakfast ready in the morning," she said. She told him she made pancakes and bacon on Sundays.

Curtis hadn't expected the drinks to be so expensive, so only six dollars remained in his pocket. His dignity would have been one reason to tell Lena no. Andre was another, but he was a reason to say yes too. Getting mixed up in her night wasn't the best way to get closer to the boy, but it might be the only way. "I spent all the money I had on me," he said.

"Don't worry," Lena said. "I got it."

Their motel was called the Galaxy Inn. A strange smell hung in the air of their room, which was nearly as small as his cell had been. A coat of silver paint had been recently applied to the walls, but there was something else, an organic pungency. Little effort had been made to mask the presence of former occupants. There were useless dials on the walls, mysterious blinking lights. Curtis felt trapped in some television show from the 1960s, a science fiction program he watched in syndication as a child.

Lena lay next to Curtis with her back to him. She was abruptly calm, abruptly still. He couldn't even hear the sound of her breathing. He'd been surprised by her wildness, which exceeded his. The rough sheet covered her to the waist, displaying her long neck and the slick coins of her spine. Curtis felt the urge to yank the spine out of her, to scatter those coins all over the bed and catch a true glimpse of her inner workings under the room's dimmed bulbs of winey light.

"I should go soon," Lena said. "See about my son."

"Tell me about him."

She sat up. "Andre?"

"That boy's asleep. You got time."

She studied his face. "What's in that head of yours?"

Curtis shrugged and made himself hold her hand. "Come on, tell me a little something."

Lena began hesitantly, but her initial vague description of her son eventually turned into a long complaint about her challenges with him, how easily she seemed to make him upset. He was a good child, she said, but their relationship was worsening and it was difficult to manage things on her own. "It's not just that he's a teenager," she said. "It's more than that."

"He's probably just girl-crazy," he said.

"Uh-uh, I don't think so," she said, and went on, speaking with more kindness about him now.

When she was done, Curtis insisted on giving his view of things. The question of obedience was on his mind, but nothing he said was profound. Still, Lena listened to everything he said and seemed thoughtful when he fell silent again.

"You know," she told him, "if it was my boy you were interested in, there were easier ways than sniffing after my behind. You could've just walked up to him on the street and told him who you were."

Curtis straightened against the headboard. To him that sounded like the most difficult thing in the world. "I was just looking out for Marvin's people, that's all." He felt embarrassed, a little angry. "I know it's not the usual way," he added.

Lena shook her head. "Look at you," she said. "I know you been gone, but you not invisible. People talk. I got eyes."

"How long have you known?"

"Long enough to think plenty on whether to do anything about it."

Curtis gestured at the blinking walls of the room, a tired old version of the future. He gestured down at the bed. "This what you decided to do about it?"

"Well, you were there, sniffing as usual," Lena said. "I had my notions, and you just happened to be the one. I knew you were safe. And I figured you'd go along with it."

He yanked off the sheet and exposed the full nakedness of his body. He sprang from the bed and glared down at her.

"I'm all done with that," she told him, "so you can put it away now."

"I'm not somebody you know," Curtis said. "I never was."

She rubbed the edge of the sheet between her fingers. "Look, I'm gonna go. You can stay the rest of the night if you want, if you don't want to sleep at your mama's house." She rose from the bed and watched him for a few moments, frowning. "You don't know me either," she said, and began to dress.

Curtis left not long after Lena did. No need to stay and stare at a dead end. Night was starting to drain from the edges of the sky, but he didn't go directly to his mother's house. Walking restored him when he was upset, helped him regain his focus, even before he went to prison, and now he savored it much more, despite the times he was harassed by cops. As adolescents he and Marvin would often stay out late, sometimes until dawn, romping all over Brooklyn. Marvin preferred walking or taking the bus to the half-blind underground careening of the subway. He liked taking different routes, preferring the slightest deviations or even dangerous blocks or neighborhoods to what he would have called the "same old, same old." But he did like the promenade.

When the two boys went there together and gazed out at the protruding jaw of the city, they spoke most openly of their desires. Marvin spoke as if the days and years to come were nothing but a cycle of restoration. "I'm gonna get my mother a house," he'd always say. This was his favorite thing. Not only would he pay off her considerable debts, he would do this too. The house he imagined buying for her was like a place he'd already been in, stepping past furniture bought from her catalogs and out to the little vegetable garden she'd keep. Looking up with her past the white slats to the blue roof where the birds would be rebuilding their nest. "She wouldn't want the birds there," he said once. "But I do. They do all the things I like."

Marvin spoke of girls as if he weren't a virgin, as if he knew a thing about the frightening business of female nudity and of sex, which Curtis understood was animal and floral: the odd nosing around, the smells and the sap, the near-violence of fingernails and coarse hair, the peeling back of language to a hard core, like the spiked stones of peaches the boys used to throw at stray dogs.

Then, for reasons Curtis never understood, Marvin got stuck on the idea of Lena Johnson. He talked about her constantly, and soon the boys' wanderings through the borough began to circle her old neighborhood, not far from where Curtis was walking now. There was the basketball court—still there, Curtis knew—where Marvin kept insisting they go, despite the busted rims.

One spring day they saw her there. She came from across the street and began to stroll the sidewalk along the length of the court, lifting her hand to take languid pulls from a cigarette. Marvin raced over with an odd look on his face, his hands in loose fists. He was carrying little rocks swelled and blanched by the sun, as though he wanted to roll them at her like gifts through the openings in the chain-link fence. Curtis followed, smelling the opportunity for mischief. The boys caught up and then kept pace with Lena on their side, daylight flickering in their faces, blinking madly through the diamonds of the fence. The flashing light did not transfigure Lena's appearance. She was still just a skinny girl with pointy elbows and spooky eyes, whose shirts and sweaters were always linted-up, whose flat ass made a pair of jeans droop and frown.

When Marvin greeted her, she blew out the smoke that had been held in her lungs. She was inhaling from a joint, they realized, not one of her usual cigarettes. At school she was made fun of for having stale breath. Curtis laughed at these jokes, and Marvin used to laugh too.

"My mama told me not to talk to strange boys," she said without looking at either of them.

"What? It's me, Marvin Caldwell. From school."

"I know who you are. Don't mean you not strange."

"But you talking to me anyway."

"Do you always do what your mama says?"

And that was it. She kept going without another word and left Marvin standing with his long fingers clawed into the fence, exactly where Curtis was standing now. Marvin somehow turned what she'd said into a genuine mystery, one he considered, on that day and afterward, by wondering aloud about her life. Had anyone ever seen her mother at the school? Did they get along or did they argue all the time? Did they look alike? He let Curtis know how deeply he imagined her. As Lena became a real part of Marvin's life, he talked less often to Curtis about her. And when they became a couple, Marvin hardly talked to him at all.

Curtis got him to go on a walk, like they used to, one Sunday afternoon. When they were near Drummer's Grove in Prospect Park, he confronted him. "We supposed to be boys," he said.

"Then be happy for me," Marvin said.

"I can't even remember the last time we hung out."

The shaking of gourds decorated the sound of the drums. Marvin said, "You know how it is when people first get loved up."

"You don't even talk to me no more."

Marvin laughed. "It's not like that. You're my boy. Trust. We'll be good."

"So it's just a phase?"

"Oh, it's real. Be happy I'm happy."

"But what about me?" Curtis said. The drumming got more layered and complex.

"Okay, I see. You want it to be about you."

"I just can't believe you let a bitch get between us," Curtis said.

Marvin stopped walking. He narrowed his eyes in the direction of the music. The head of a dancing man bopped up and down. Sounds from a wind instrument wove between those of the drums. "Don't ever come out your mouth like that," he said. "I'm serious."

"That's what you did though."

Marvin closed his hands into fists and then opened them. Curtis watched them close and open, close and open. Marvin approached him, got so near their noses almost touched. Curtis breathed through his mouth.

"I'm out, man," Marvin said, and gripped him in a strong lengthy hug.

Curtis let his arms hang limp at his sides, hands loose. As time

passed, until the fire and the death, he kept his arms and hands
that way, until he used them again to drink.

When Curtis came in, his mother was asleep in the easy chair
again, the glow from the television in the living room bluing her
form, the canned laughter a kind of murmured grace. He didn't
switch off the old sitcom and he didn't wake her. Instead he listened to her dogged breathing. On the small table beside her were
peanut skins on a paper towel, orange peels, a cup with the dregs
of tea. When Curtis stayed out until seven or eight in the morning,
his mother would be awake when he got in, looking tired as she
sipped strong coffee and stretched her sore back at the kitchen
table. Otherwise she'd be where she was now, floating on the mer-
est shallows of sleep. When he told her not to wait up for him, she
said this was nothing; she'd been waiting for him to come home
for twelve years.

There was still a little time before sunrise. Curtis would often
read in such circumstances; he'd become an avid reader of Wal-
ter Mosley's novels in prison. But he liked the feeling of being
near his mother now—he liked her when she was asleep—so he
sat with a tall glass of water and forced his gaze onto the television
screen. The off-hour commercials for ridiculous products held his
attention better than the show itself. Despite his efforts, his body
slumped against an arm of the sofa and he fell asleep.

Curtis often slept during the day, even when he was in prison, so
his dreams were full of light. At least, this was how he made sense
of what happened. Each dream was a city of houses and water and
clear sparkling glass. Every inhabitant wore white, against which
their brown skin was beautiful. People smiled and held the hands
of their lovers, their children, and their friends. The strange thing
about these light-filled dreams was that Marvin never appeared,
not a piece of him in the fragments Curtis could gather upon waking. He told himself that the grandness of the dreams—the pristine landscapes and spacious houses, the variety and richness of
color—was a symbol of Marvin's presence, or that the diffuse light,
the kind you see in old paintings, was the gold of his friend's fantasies. But he knew his claims were suspect. He was stung by Marvin's
disregard for his dream-life.

It was not yet morning now, however, so his dream had a different character. Aside from the darkness of waking life seeping

into it, there was the dim, gray shadow of the woman he'd hit with his car all those years ago. The woman sprang into the dream the same way she'd sprung out onto the street, and as she'd been that night, she was faceless, voiceless, and pale, gesturing woodenly at the edge of his vision. As she had been in the last few moments of her life, she was barely a smudge, nothing more than a faint mote in the air before suddenly looming. That night she seemed to fall upon the car like a burden dropped from the sky, and in the dream she acted the same way, flying at him, shocking him out of sleep. He jerked awake, shaken and afraid, with a metallic taste on his tongue. The taste offended Curtis, reminding him of the pit his mouth had become after Marvin's death, in those months of heavy drinking.

In the kitchen Curtis's mother was spreading butter and cherry preserves on slices of toast. "Glad it's Sunday," she said. Her job at the hospital gave her Mondays and Tuesdays off, so she was on the cusp of her weekend. She pushed his breakfast plate across the table and got up to place more bread in the toaster and fork scrambled eggs from the pan on the stove. She was already dressed for work. A saltshaker pinned two folded twenty-dollar bills, the amount she'd leave for him a few times a week to eat lunch and get around as he searched for jobs. While waiting for the toast to pop up, his mother hummed old gospel songs, something she'd never done when Curtis was growing up. She must have learned them as a girl back in North Carolina, and now as she drew closer to her life's other edge, the songs must have come back to her again.

When she sat back down with her plate, she watched Curtis, nearly done with his eggs, toast, and sausage patties, before touching her own food.

"Want some more?" she said.

Curtis nodded and grunted yes.

His mother gave him one of her hot triangles of toast and began to scrape some of the eggs from her plate onto his. "Go on and eat it, Curtis," she said. "Shoot, I'm getting fat anyway. I need to start back with my exercises."

Remembering his private vow, that his life was now for wondrous things, he accepted what ended up being almost all of his mother's breakfast so he could see her lips closed and smiling and her eyebrows settle back down to a sensible height, so there would be the satisfaction of silence. It was true that she was getting round in the midsection, but he knew she would never return to her exercises, because she'd never started in the first place.

Curtis felt her watching him eat the second portion of food. She'd be late for work if she didn't leave right away. She was sixty and he wasn't surprised by how old she was starting to appear. The visits she'd made upstate to the prison each month revealed the rhythms of her decline, and in the intervals he guessed accurately where and when age would touch her next. Her brown skin was somehow darkening. She had a soft pouch under her chin, and at the cheeks and around the eyes the skull was beginning to show itself behind her face. She was nothing to write home about anymore, but a man her age wouldn't complain much. When she and Curtis's father decided their relationship just wasn't going to work, she was still a young woman, and quite pretty, but she made only halfhearted attempts at romance, as if she believed you got just one real try at it in life.

Those energies she used in doting on Curtis, fussing over him the way it seemed Lena fussed over Andre. As soon as Curtis set his fork down on his plate, his mother snatched them up, along with her own, then went to the sink and began washing them.

"I was telling Shirley what we talked about on Friday," she said. "She thought you were gonna give me lip, but I said *Oh no, my boy gets it.* Look, I know you loved Marvin. He was like kin to you. But following his people around ain't what's right for you. I know you know it. Can't look back. It's like the Bible says: *Let thine eyes look right on, and let thine eyelids look straight before thee. Ponder the path of thy feet, and let all thy ways be established. Turn not to the right hand nor the left—*"

"Ma, don't you gotta go?" Curtis said.

She waved him off with a gloved hand, flashing yellow, flicking suds and drops of water across the kitchen. "My baby is home," she said. "Ain't no thing to put some soap and water to a couple dishes."

That's right, he thought. Your baby. Can't get a job, can't get my own place, can't open a goddamn bank account. You wouldn't even care if I pissed the bed.

His mother snapped off her rubber gloves and glanced up at the clock. She blinked slowly, keeping her eyes closed a beat or two longer than necessary, opening them as she took in a great draft of breath. Curtis steadied himself for what was coming. This had the look of one of her speeches, the ones that began, *Baby, you know the Lord has forgiven you. Now you just need to forgive yourself . . .* Curtis wasn't sure God had forgiven him. He wasn't sure God agreed that the accident couldn't have been avoided. He wasn't sure about God. If God was true and had forgiven him, then why did He keep sending the woman into his dreams at night? Curtis had to do it the other way. If he forgave himself first, maybe then God would follow.

He steadied himself, thinking of beautiful things and filling his head with their music: The words of the man on the promenade, grabbed by the wind. "The Payback." Freedom on his tongue like the taste of curry chicken and macaroni pie from Culpepper's. "Someday We'll All Be Free." A pretty woman opening her legs and arms for him. *Devil in a Blue Dress.* "Ruby." Marpessa Dawn taped to the wall. "A Felicidade." Marvin, his friend. Andre, who looked so much like his father. "They Reminisce Over You." "Little Ghetto Boy."

Curtis followed Lena into a bank one afternoon that week. He tried to make their encounter seem like a coincidence, but could tell she knew better. They talked uncomfortably for a few minutes, both averting their gazes. Then he apologized for the other night and told her he wanted to see her. After some hesitation that seemed to him like a ceremony, Lena gave him her phone number.

When they got a room together on weekdays, Lena would tell Andre she was working an extra shift, but they usually got rooms on Saturday afternoons. Curtis brought her home once, while his mother was at work. Lena told him it was fine, but he felt humiliated being with her on such a small bed, in a room filled with his childish things. He was morose after they slept together. Even the scent of their sex couldn't distract him from the pervasive smell of his mother. When Lena tried to comfort him, he asked her to tell him about the night Marvin died.

She flinched. "Y'all were like brothers," she said. "You know all about it."

"I wasn't there."

"I wasn't there either," she said. "You had to know that much."

"But tell me about the last time you saw him."

She was quiet for a while before she spoke. "I was waitressing

back then too," she said finally, "the late night shift at a diner over
by Coney Island. I like waitressing. You get to know folks and they
get a kick out of you remembering them and they tip you good
—well, as best they can."

"What about Marvin?"

"Like I said, I was working the third shift, and that started at
midnight during the week. Marvin had already lost his construction job. Then he lost his side gig too. You know how hard things
were for him."

"I didn't know."

"Well, he couldn't handle it. Poor thing was always beat from
looking for jobs all day, every day, but he liked to stay up and watch
me get ready for work. Tried to keep himself awake with a book of
all things. Can you imagine? He *was* one to think reading in bed
would keep a tired man awake."

"What was he reading that night?"

"I don't remember," she said.

"Did he like Easy Rawlins and Mouse?"

"I don't know."

"And the fire?"

She looked at him for a long time and then studied her hands.
Her voice, when it came, was cold now: "You must've heard how it
happened, Curtis. It was just like that."

"Tell me."

"I told him not to smoke in the bed, especially when I wasn't
around. But the man was tired, always, and with every job telling
him no, he was a bundle of nerves. I kept telling him to ask for
help, but he had to do things all by himself. Too proud. He wanted
life to be different for us, and for his mama. All that debt . . ." She
shook her head. "He thought we deserved to be in a better place."

"I heard his spirits were low."

"Sometimes."

"You would know better than me." Curtis tried to say this with
some tenderness, but she flinched again. For the first time she
seemed genuinely pretty, even beautiful to him, like a woman griev-
ing calmly in a painting. He pressed on: "Do you think he . . . ?"

"What?"

Curtis looked at her.

"Took his own life? Is that what you mean?"

He nodded. He knew he was being cruel, but couldn't help himself. He wanted to hurt her.

"What, in his right mind he just lit a match and let it fall on the damn pillows? You asking me if he meant to destroy his own self? Why would you say such a thing? Why would you even think it?"

Curtis sometimes imagined that his friend would understand what it was like to feel that blue, but he knew Marvin had loved life too much to take his own. "Maybe you're right," he said. The faded Knicks poster on the far wall hung askew. "He wouldn't have done that with Andre on the way. He knew about the baby, right?"

Lena seemed baffled. "Whatever did or didn't happen, it wasn't because of what was growing inside of me."

Curtis nodded, but meant nothing by the gesture. "Tell me the last thing he said to you."

"I don't know," she said. "As far as we were concerned, it was just another day."

"Last time we saw each other, he gave me a hug."

Lena lay with her back pressed to him, her knees drawn up and touching the wall. "That's no surprise. I never heard him say a bad word about you," she said. "What in the world happened between you two?"

Curtis didn't reply. After that Sunday afternoon by Drummer's Cove, Marvin eventually reached out to reconcile, but Curtis ignored him. He met any attempt to talk or spend time together with silence. When they finally did talk, Marvin begged to borrow some money.

"I lost both my jobs, man," he said, "and nobody's trying to hire a brother. I can't catch a damn break."

On the phone, Curtis stayed quiet.

"I'm having a real hard time, man."

Before he hung up, Curtis said, "Well maybe that bitch you got can help you out."

He didn't tell Lena any of this, and it was obvious that she didn't know. He listened to her breathing now, the steady in and out, the deepening. He closed his eyes. In a while he was startled awake by his recurrent dream, and then startled again by a cold hand on his shoulder. Curtis saw it had taken a great effort for Lena to reach out to him, even though they had no space between them on his bed. Her reddened eyes, taut mouth, and fingers roughly scratch-

ing at the points of her elbows meant she knew she could never
be loved by him—he had told her as much as they talked before
falling asleep. Maybe she already knew she couldn't love him either. He held her, though, in the little bed, and then she held him
too. As they lay there, he decided he would never bring her to his
mother's house again.

Lena eventually got in the habit of inviting Curtis to the apartment, just for meals at first: dinners or late Sunday breakfasts
where he got to see Andre. On Sundays, the pancakes were dense.
Lena piled the bacon in the pan, so it always came out soggy. It was
greasy and almost sweet on the tongue. As it slid down his throat,
Curtis held his hand to his mouth and gave Andre a funny look,
but the boy seemed to like the food. He didn't seem pleased with
much else.

   In the beginning, Lena told Andre the simple truth that Curtis was his father's good friend. "He's like your uncle," she said,
but the boy rolled his eyes. When he called Curtis *uncle* he said
it with a hint of derision. The two of them got along well enough
though. By the end of the fifth month, Curtis was frequently at
their apartment; by the sixth, he and Lena stopped getting rooms.
They both danced around the question in such a way that either of
them could claim the other had asked about him moving in. When
Curtis told his mother it was happening, she cried the way she did
when he was sentenced to prison. He invited her to visit them, but
she said she would need some time.

   Curtis pretended Lena had never called him the boy's uncle,
but Andre went on calling him that anyway, still with a mocking
tone. He liked to say it in the mornings when Curtis emerged from
Lena's bedroom, or right before he went in at night. "Morning,
Unc," he'd say, or, "Have a good night, Uncle Curtis."

   When they were in bed Lena would signal Curtis by rubbing her
cold feet along his legs, and then there would be lovemaking. The
first few times they slept together, he was surprised at how much
pleasure her skinny body gave him. He wasn't gentle with her, and
the things she whispered to him made it clear she didn't want him
to be. But now he hated the little sounds she made, the words she
said, loud enough that the boy would be able to hear. Sometimes,
not quite meaning to, Curtis covered her mouth.

                              *

When summer arrived, Curtis took Andre to the basketball court in Lena's old neighborhood and watched him hang listlessly from the rims. They took long walks together, though Andre complained. "Why don't we just take the train?" he asked. They had macaroni pie at Culpepper's, but the boy said Lena's was better. Curtis told him about his time in prison. Andre seemed uninterested until Curtis began to exaggerate, and then the boy asked him if being locked up was the way they showed it in some movie Curtis had never even heard of. His reply was yes. Exactly like that.

One of Andre's favorite things to do, because it made him laugh so hard, was to ridicule his mother. It bothered Curtis afterward but he joined in anyway, making fun of his own mother too. He laughed with Andre at the promenade when the weather was nice, tears wetting his eyelashes. Curtis often fell silent and made a show of watching the young women walk by.

"What makes mothers the way they are?" Andre asked one day. It was the first time he posed a question like this to Curtis, that of a boy seeking the wisdom of a man.

"They lose themselves and get all kinds of ridiculous," Curtis said. "Ain't no mystery to it."

But Andre was quiet, and it was hard to tell if he was listening. Curtis fixed his gaze on a jogger in red shorts, and leaned forward to keep her in sight as long as he could. He pointed so that Andre would look too. Then the joke from the old song leaped into his mind. "Goddamn," he said. "Do fries go with that shake?"

Andre turned to look out at the harbor, his eyes a bit dulled. His taut lips shifted from side to side, as restless as the river.

Curtis kept up the banter about the jogger. "You like that, huh?"

"If you say so," Andre replied with a shrug.

"Well, she looks like a college girl to me anyway, young buck," Curtis said with a laugh. "Might be out of your league."

"Man, I'ma be so glad when I go off to college."

Curtis nodded and listened as Andre continued talking about his future, his life of success, of accumulation and bachelorhood. "There's one thing you gotta do, though," he told the boy. "A house. When you make it big like that, you gotta get your mother a house."

Andre seemed taken aback, and was quiet for a long time as he considered the idea. "Ain't you supposed to do that?" he said. "I mean, I can come visit and everything. But you gonna be with her, right? You can make that happen. She'd like that, wouldn't she?"

Curtis didn't say so, but he supposed she would.

"Hey," he said, "you never ask me anything about your daddy."

Andre shrugged again.

"I got a lot of good stories. Don't you want to hear them? You should get to know who he was."

"What for? He's still gonna be dead."

"Your father was a good man," Curtis said. "And—"

"I know, I know. You loved him like a brother."

"No," Curtis said. "That's what people keep on saying but it was more than that, a lot more." He was startled by the sound of his own voice, the force of it. He gazed down at his curled hands, unable to bear the gentle, curious way Andre was looking at him. He couldn't find the words to explain the affection he felt, still, for the boy's father, and in this moment he didn't want to be misunderstood. Another jogger went past but neither of them paid her any mind.

"What happened the night you killed that lady?" Andre said.

"I was drunk," Curtis said. "They said she had some drink in her too. She came out of nowhere and got in my way. That's all." He rubbed his palms against the knees of his pants. "I did something I shouldn't have done."

Since no one would hire Curtis for steady work, he was often free to spend time with Andre, when the boy allowed him to. Lena supported them, sometimes working extra shifts at the restaurant. She stood aside and let Curtis try to deepen his relationship with her son. She put a smile on her face when Curtis, and sometimes Andre too, made fun of her Sunday bacon, picking it up by one end and wriggling it in the air. She must have noticed the way they both looked at her when she reached for her cigarettes. Soon enough she stopped reaching for them, and then Curtis no longer saw them in the apartment at all. She didn't buy tickets for movies on Fridays, unless she was going to the theater by herself. When the woman Curtis had struck with his car kept entering his dreams, Lena didn't put her hands on his shoulder. If she ever cried at night, she refused to be comforted by him. She still signaled him with her cold feet, however. She still made her little demands for intimacy, and sometimes he did too.

Before they slept, she lay beside him in bed and listened as he talked about Andre, unable to stop himself. "He seems happier, doesn't he?" Curtis asked one evening, and she agreed, as though he truly understood her son. It was true, Lena told him, and she called them her men, her two men, which she was in the habit of doing, as if they were all she had ever wanted. "I think Marvin would be glad," he said, but wondered. Lena agreed again and appeared pleased at the thought of all her contented men. Curtis forced a smile onto his face too. He kissed her cheek, lightly, his lips barely making contact with her skin. He and Lena wouldn't love each other, but there was love they openly shared, and that would be enough, for now, to make a kind of family.

The Art of Losing

FROM *New England Review*

WATCH THE BOY, she had said.

Or had she? Some things he knew for sure. His name was Han Mo-Sae. His wife was Han Young-Ja. They had been married forty years, possibly fifty. The wife would know. They had two children: Timothy and Christina. They would always be his children but they were no longer kids. He had to keep remembering that.

Tunes. He was good with tunes. He could retrieve from memory music he hadn't heard in decades. "The Mountain Rabbit," "*Ich Liebe Dich*," Aretha Franklin's "Operation Heartbreak," which he had first heard in his twenties on the Armed Forces Network in Korea. He had a good singing voice. He had been Tenor 1 in the church choir; years before that, he had led off the morning exercise song in the schoolyard. These performances had given him an appetite for praise and notice, although no one, seeing the old man he had become, would know it.

His wife had no particular distinction—had *had* none, even in youth. How could she? Her childhood task had been survival. She was the oldest of three sisters who were orphaned as they fled south during the Korean War. In Busan, she had worked on the rubber processing line, removing trapped air from rolled products. She told him about it years later, in another country, sitting on a weedy patch of campus lawn. Once, she had snapped a dandelion stem, allowing the milk to run. Did he know that the sap of the dandelion was a form of natural rubber? Latex? It was one of the few things he learned from her and he never forgot it. It altered in a small and precise way his notice of trivial things: the soles of his shoes, the elastic in his waistband.

They had met in Philadelphia—when was this, the 1960s?—through the area's one Korean church. He was working toward a master's in mechanical engineering; she tailored and mended for a dry cleaner. At church, he was a star. His fine singing voice, the impressive school he attended. But at the university, he was struck dumb. Every morning, he would tear out a page from his English dictionary, memorize it, and eat it. Still, the language would not take. And things grew worse. He began to dread not only the classroom, but also the grocery store, the post office, the blank pages of his dissertation.

One night, he had gone to Young-Ja's rented room. As he removed his shoes, he noticed a hole in the toe of his sock, which he made no attempt to hide. He was too good for her—that much was assumed. She made no argument for herself. She had not made herself up or even changed after work. Her hair was short, like a man's. Her hands were rough. Her dark sweater showed snips of thread and lint from altering other people's clothes. In a glance, he could see the perimeters of her life: the toothbrush in a cup that she brought to the communal bathroom, the single hot plate, the twin mattress on the floor.

Yet she brought to the low table a fermented bean curd stew still bubbling in its clay pot. How had she come up with such a thing in Philadelphia? That smell. It was the bean paste. Soybeans, charcoal, and honey placed in an earthenware vessel, buried deep in the frozen ground and over the seasons grown elemental. It stank of home.

They helped themselves from the same pot, bringing the silken onion or softly crumbling potato onto their plates of rice. They dipped again and again into the pot with their spoons. And then, stinking softly of garlic, he took hold of her wrist, drawing her down as she rose to clear the table. She showed no surprise.

Afterward, she asked for his sock, to mend it. The meek look of her bent head, her fluency with the needle, his deflated sock in her hand, had caused a movement in his pride that he didn't know then—or perhaps ever—to call love. Still, he began to spend nights, which he had previously devoted to his studies, at Young-Ja's place. And when he received news through an aerogram that his mother had died, when she was no longer around to be disappointed that her only, late-born son would not live up to his educator father, his thoughts turned to marriage.

Yes. That was how it had transpired.

Now, in later life, he began to see her with new fascination. That wife of his. She was always busy—cooking, cleaning, nagging, blindly pulling out of parking spaces without a rearview glance. Even now, she was bustling about on some mission that didn't involve him. She emerged from the bathroom, having drawn on eyebrows and applied rouge. He noticed a new fullness to her hairdo that revealed itself, as she came into the natural light, as a hairpiece. He followed her into the kitchen, where she acquired keys, phone, and bag. It came to him, what she was doing. She was leaving.

This made him anxious. He realized that with her gone, he would be obligated to himself. To remember to eat. To remember that he had eaten. To turn things off after he had turned them on. To zip his fly. To occupy the present moment. Suddenly, he hated her. He watched her jam her feet into her shoes, then bend to recover the collapsed backs. He hated her right down to the wayfaring look of those shoes.

At the threshold, she turned back for a moment. A change came over her expression, and he wondered if she had intuited his anxiety. But no. Whatever she saw was behind him, further down the hall, and caused what was honest about her face to come into bloom. *Be good!* she cried to that vision. Then opened the door and walked through it.

Vanishment.

What to do next. He placed his hands in his pockets and took them out again. He straightened a neat stack of mail on the entryway table without a glancing interest at their contents. Looking down the hall, he noticed the boy. Of course, the boy. He took a closer look.

The child was small, definitely under five. There was something about him that didn't seem perfectly Korean: some touch of dusk to his complexion and gold to his curls. The shirt he wore was yellow and read HAPPY. But the boy himself looked neither happy nor unhappy. He looked how he looked. Small. Temporary. Everything about him would change in another five years. In five minutes.

"Well," said Mo-Sae, heartily.

Ignoring this, the boy turned toward the kitchen. Mo-Sae followed. "What you looking for?" he asked in English.

The boy braced to open the fridge and surveyed the contents. He didn't seem interested in the child-size packs of yogurt or bendy sticks of cheese or even the various Korean side dishes in little containers. Instead, he pointed to a can of Coca-Cola on an upper shelf.

"This?" Mo-Sae asked, even as he took it down.

"Open, please."

The can was so simple, so presumptuous, as was the child's belief that an adult could open it. Mo-Sae held the cold, weighted shape in his hand, considering it. He felt his judgment was being tested. Was it wrong to give soda to the child? What would Young-Ja say? But at the thought of his wife and her little criticisms, he grew bullish. After all, he had had his first bracing metallic taste of cola as a boy. It reminded him of the K-16 Air Base in Seoul. The grinning GIs. As a boy, Mo-Sae had served as a kind of mascot for them. They would strap a helmet on his head, ask for a song, teach him to swear. How easily the memories came to him: Hershey's Tropical Bars. "Good-Bye Maria, I'm Off to Korea." He remembered how one soldier, a wondrously black man, could pop the cap off a cola bottle using only his strong white teeth. He wished he too had some entertaining way to open the can for the boy, to bring him to delight.

"Watch this," he said, although he had no plan. He tried a twisting motion on the tab. Nothing. Perhaps, then, a countering motion. The tab began to loosen, then broke off. This filled him with a frustrated gall that automatically made him think of his wife. "*Yeobo?*" he shouted. "*Yeobo!*"

Where was she?

Was she somewhere laboring over her devotions? Wiping down the leaves of her showy house plants? *Shala-shala-shala* with church women on the phone?

Then it dawned on him. Had she left him alone with the boy?

He began to move through the apartment. There were signs of her. At least half-a-dozen pairs of reading glasses; some unfinished work beside a sewing basket; something simmering on the stove. But no wife.

He entered the living room, which was set like a stage for the occasional visitor. Matching armchairs angled as if in conversation. An ornately framed print of a peasant couple praying in a wheat field. A bowl of fancy dusty candies. Even the piano bench wore little crocheted socks. This was all Young-Ja. All this stuff. When had she turned so aspirational?

At that moment, what appeared was the boy—appearing also in Mo-Sae's cognition—as he struggled to drag a large toy bin down the hall. Mo-Sae moved to help but was dissuaded by the child's look of fierce refusal. When he reached the living room, he threw his weight into upending the bin. Toys dumped everywhere. Mo-Sae surveyed the mess. He should have been angry at this demonstration, which, he suspected, was aimed at him. Instead, he was transfixed. A stray block. A plastic soldier. A marble on the run, which he nabbed.

Now he was fully engrossed—sorting, retrieving. Puzzle pieces, dinosaurs, cars. He put them in files, rows, ranks, and columns stretching across the living room floor. As he worked, he swore under his breath to mask the pleasure of having something to do, to make that pleasure seem obligatory. TS. Tough Shit. Fuck it got my orders. Goddamn Jodie. Goddamn Gook. Fucking Biscuit Head, shit for the birds.

When he straightened up, he noticed that the sliding door was open. As he drew closer, he heard whoops and shrieking laughter: the sounds of some exclusionary fun. He saw a boy standing on a chair to look way down over the balcony railing. Below, other children played in the communal swimming pool. Waist-high, the boy was clear of the railing.

Mo-Sae was suddenly overwhelmed with love for the boy, that yearning posture pitched against the open air. He was so small and his frustration was so great.

Mo-Sae called to him. "Danger," he said.

The boy did not move.

"Down, Jonathan," he said. The name had come to him.

No response.

In a few steps, Mo-Sae crossed the balcony and seized the child around the middle. A naïve fight went up in the live body: sharp kicking feet, valiant muscles.

"*Yeobo!*" Mo-Sae yelled as he attempted to embrace the struggle.

The kid wrestled free and ran back into the house. Mo-Sae found him back in the living room, breathing hard and scheming. When he saw his grandfather, Jonathan deliberately plowed through the organized toys with his feet. As Mo-Sae approached, he shouted, "No, Grandpa, no!" and picked up a car as if to hurl it.

Young-Ja always rushed home, handbag gaping, outracing disaster. She felt her heart do just what her doctor had said it must not do as she thought of the pool, the gas stove, the three-lane intersection beside their apartment. Sometimes the anxiety kept her homebound, but little by little, she would start again, coming up with errands that were really excuses to leave. Stamps, prescription pick-ups. Sometimes she would drop by T.J. Maxx for the small pleasure of buying something she didn't need or, as it invariably turned out, even want.

She was never gone long.

This afternoon, she even left a length of pork belly simmering on the stove with some peppercorns and a spoonful of instant coffee. She told herself she would just run to the bank and deposit the monthly check her daughter gave her for childcare. On her way out, she glanced at the mirror. She felt a complicated sense of recognition at her reflection, not unlike the feeling she had toward the look of her full name, Young-Ja Han, written out in her daughter's hand. *Payable to.*

As she waited for the elevator, she heard the door of a nearby unit opening. She realized that she had been listening for it.

"Damn chain latch."

It was Mr. Sorenson. He had trouble with small physical tasks, like opening jars or unhooking a latch from its runners. Sometimes she wondered if he kept his eye to the peephole and watched the elevator all day, so canny were their afternoon meetings.

"Young-Ja!" he called. "*An-yeong-ha-sae-yo?*" He knew a little Korean because he had been stationed near Seoul during the war.

It always caught her off guard, how handsome he was. White hair, blue eyes, profile like an eagle. He was always bringing her things—jam-centered candies, cuttings of begonias. Always telling her things. Once, he told her he had an organ at home and promised to play it for her someday. He expected her to believe, or act as if she believed, that an instrument of such occasion and size could fit into their modest units.

Still, she gave him what she could in return. Her docile attention. Half-smiles. A secret.

It had been right around the time that Jonathan was born, three years ago, that she had been diagnosed with a condition. She had left the doctor's office determined to tell no one, not even the children. *Especially* not the children. But on her way home, she had run into Mr. Sorenson. In his presence, she found herself seeking the exact name of her condition. She could only remember that the doctor had said something that sounded like "a tree."

"Atrial fibrillation," pronounced Mr. Sorenson. "Increases your chance of stroke by five."

Since then, it had become part of their routine. "How's that atria," he would ask, and she would become acutely aware that she had one. Actually, two. One on the right and one on the left side of the heart, according to Mr. Sorenson. It gave her a feeling of strangeness toward her body and all its functioning parts, as if they were not to be taken for granted.

Today, he handed her a medicinal brown bottle. "Take this," he commanded.

She took the bottle.

"No, not all of it," he said, seeming annoyed that she had not understood the precise measure of his generosity.

This embarrassed her. She was not a person who took more than her due. Even in her discomfort, she performed the small service of loosening the cap of the bottle before returning it to him so he would not have to ask.

ORGANIC INDIA HEART GUARD, the label read.

"Take some," said Mr. Sorenson. "Take ten." He shook some capsules into her palm and counted them, moving each pill across her palm with the stiff index finger of his stricken hand, 1, 2, 3, 4, 5, 6, 7, 8, 9, 10 times.

"Now," he said. "These are from the bark of the Arjun tree. Buddhists call it the tree of enlightenment. You know Buddha, of course. He's Oriental.

"See here," he continued, reading from the label without needing glasses. "Take with food. Take twice a day. Do not take if you're nursing or pregnant."

He looked at her with private amusement. His still-keen blue eyes. "Any chance you're pregnant?

"Come on. Smile."

When she returned home, Mo-Sae was in the living room, reading the *Chosun Daily*. He had a certain frowning expression when he was with a paper. She had once been fascinated by this look, had wanted to come under it herself: the look of a man exerting his personal opinion on the ways of the world, the movement of nations. Now she only snuck a glance at the front page to check the date of the paper he was reading.

The headlines referenced the historic summit between North and South Korea, the first such meeting since the country was divided. Could this be the start of reunification? Would there be an easing of military tensions? An opportunity for family reunions?

Last month's news.

She rubbed her hands, dislodging the sticky, warmed pills that Mr. Sorenson had given her. With that gesture, she reclaimed a kind of housekeeping competence over her mood.

Casting a brisk, efficient glance around, she noticed that the living room was neat and yet strangely occupied. Whatever had happened in her absence, it would never tell. All the toys that she normally swept into bins were categorized and lined up across the floor, some by size, some by type, some by color, some by fancy. It unnerved her, this carefully presented nonsense. The room was empty of the boy.

"Where is he!" she demanded.

"Who?"

"Don't say who! You know who! Jonathan! Where is he!"

"Jonathan?" asked Mo-Sae, half-rising from the chair. "Why he was here just a moment ago." He had started doing that: coming up with likely versions of the past that became fixed in his memory.

The boy was not inside the hall closet, hiding in the bedroom, the bathroom, the bedroom again, not crammed into the storage ottoman, suffocated in the front-load washer, splattered on the concrete from a five-story fall. She could not stand Mo-Sae's forbearing attitude as he trailed her on her frantic search. She whirled to face him. That uncharacteristically meek look. She wanted to beat it out of him. *You! No! How!*

But then, Jonathan simply appeared, in full view of the door through which she had just entered. She wondered that he hadn't called to her sooner.

Later that day, in the absence of tragedy, she and Mo-Sae sat in the living room with Jonathan lining up cars between them. The radio was turned to the Christian station, which played arrangements of hymns. "Just As I Am Without One Plea." "Rock of Ages." Mo-Sae sat in an armchair with no other occupation. She sat on the floor, with one knee hugged to her chest, snapping the scraggly ends of mung bean sprouts onto a spread section of the newspaper that Mo-Sae had been reading. All this talk of reunification. "Permanent peace." "Long road ahead." Her thoughts turned, with gentle reluctance, to the past.

That little room in Busan that she and her sisters had shared— so small that at night they had to sleep alternating heads and toes. They lived above a noodle shop, and day and night, as they went up or down the back staircase, they would pass the open kitchen door. Inside, the red-faced *ajuma* would work flour with water and a pinch of salt, cutting the dough into long ribbons, lowering the noodles into steaming vats—never once offering them a bowl.

How young she had been then, yet how like an old woman. Her work at the local rubber factory left her always tired, always short of breath, blisters between her fingers, curing fumes in her nose, a constant ringing in the deep cavities of her back teeth.

Once, she had come home from work to find her middle sister missing. The room could be swept in a glance. There was no trace of her. Only her youngest sister crouched in the corner. Her rising panic had felt almost euphoric, how her fatigue lifted, her aches vanished, and the spirit of drudgery and depression that accompanied her suddenly found clarity and purpose. She ran back into the streets, easily skirting the iron bicycles and slow oxen pulling hopeless carts of merchandise. The road beneath her pounding feet began to slope downhill, and she felt the easy momentum, the blood pumping into and out of her heart, her living body.

She realized that she had returned to the factory. There, in the last light, she could make out a humped form on the dusty road alongside the factory wall.

It breathed.

It slept.

Even now, she could feel between her thumb and forefinger, the tender curl of Young-Soo's ear as she gripped it, hard, right at the lobe, and yanked her to her feet. She could still see the look of distant amazement on her sister's face, lagging in dreams, emphasized by the dust in her eyebrows and lashes and hair. She had never struck Young-Soo before, but that night she discovered a taste for it. Nothing else could express so well her outrage, her longing for their mother, her need to connect again and again with something solid, resistant, and alive—shoulder, cheekbone, the open mouth that housed the teeth.

That was how it had been. She had forgotten. Her sisters had married and left her charge. They had emigrated—one to Germany, another to Australia. In later years, she had received news of them. One was divorced. The other unexpectedly died of a reaction to penicillin. Distant news, by the time it reached her. Here, in America, she had a different life, a different set of fighting instincts. When she had her own children, she never once laid a finger on them, no, not when they mouthed off or frankly and freely disobeyed. If anything, she was a little shy of them.

She glanced at Mo-Sae on his armchair, half-expecting to find him asleep, with the sense that here was her life. Yes, his eyes were closed. It was that time of day. What did the doctor call it? Sundowning. She had been told to expect increased confusion, even agitation. She had been told that the only way to respond was with patience and kindness. Patience. Kindness. What did they really mean between husband and wife? Sometimes she felt that patience and kindness could be stretched so far in a marriage as to become their opposites.

She studied the face tipped back on the armchair, unconscious yet holding fast to mystery. A face already given to absolution.

Did he know?

She could never directly ask him, never actually say the word Alzheimer's, *chimae*, in English or Korean. She would rather pacify, indulge, work around his nonsense. Perhaps this was patience and kindness. Or perhaps it was the worst possible way to be unkind.

Sometimes she wondered. Was it all an act? Would nothing really remain? In the middle of the night, did a dawning horror sometimes spread over his soul? Or did he really think, as it seemed when his defenses were up, that all the world was in error and he was its lone sentinel of truth and fact?

"Number 276," Mo-Sae suddenly said, as if responding to something she had said aloud. His eyes remained closed.

"Eh?"

"That hymn on the radio. 'Great Is Thy Faithfulness.' It's number 276 in the hymnal."

And then sometimes he could do that: remember something so far-fetched that she would be forced to admit, as the song said, that there was still strength for today and bright hope for tomorrow.

It was in this mood that Young-Ja took the call from Elder Lim's wife the next day.

"Mrs. Han," said Mrs. Lim, as if no time had passed. "Is Mr. Han aware that we have a new conductor at church?"

It was not such a big church. Everyone was aware. They had also been aware when Mo-Sae quit the choir in a show of outrage over the incompetence of the previous conductor.

So why was Mrs. Lim calling now?

Young-Ja listened as Mrs. Lim complained. That the new conductor wanted to do the entire *Messiah* for Christmas, not just the "Hallelujah" chorus. That he wanted to do it in *English*. That he wanted to hire professional soloists. She waited for Mrs. Lim to reach the point of her conversation.

"So-therefore," said Mrs. Lim.

There it was. That turn of phrase.

"Would Mr. Han consider re-joining the choir? At least for the Christmas cantata?"

Young-Ja had told no one at church about Mo-Sae's condition. She had only considered it a blessing that Mo-Sae quit the choir when he did instead of blundering on, forgetting lyrics and missing cues, until the truth became all too apparent.

And now he was being asked to return.

"Please," said Mrs. Lim. "We really could use some strength in the tenor section."

Young-Ja told Mrs. Lim that she would consult with Mo-Sae. But this was disingenuous. Even as she hung up the phone and approached him, she was almost certain that he would refuse, recalling past indignities.

As a matter of fact, he did not. Instead, he seemed gratified by the phrase "strength in the tenor section," savored it in a way that made her curious about his inner life.

So she took on this new worry.

Over the next few months, Young-Ja spent longer hours at church, waiting in the fellowship hall for Mo-Sae to finish rehearsals. Afterward, when the choir gathered to drink barley tea or Tang, she would watch Mo-Sae as he licked his lips and looked for conversation. When his conversations cycled back to certain themes, or grew incoherent, she would intervene, negotiating his annoyance as she set the listeners free.

October, November. As the holidays approached, Jonathan brought to their home a child's understanding of time. Pumpkins for Halloween. Turkeys for Thanksgiving. In the countdown to Christmas, rehearsals intensified and she had to take Mo-Sae to the church on certain weeknights. The days grew short and full. She rarely had time for her own errands now, busy as she was with the various tasks Mrs. Lim assigned her for the choir. She rescheduled her doctor's follow-up, and then rescheduled again. She hardly saw Mr. Sorenson, although once, as she was unloading dozens of binders in boxes from the elevator, he emerged from his unit. He did not offer to help. In fact, he did not even seem to notice the boxes, or her struggle to move them. Instead, he waited for a moment in her attention to present her with another cutting in a plastic bag, its roots swaddled in a wet paper towel.

The Christmas cactus, he began in his lecturing way, would bloom in late December with a biological sleight of hand. Every twelve hours, she was to take it out of a dark closet and give it full sun.

She nodded. But what she realized was that Mr. Sorenson's gifts were not free but finicky, and came with a burden of care. Indeed, when she remembered the cutting, days later, it had completely wilted.

As for Mo-Sae, no one complained of his behavior in the choir. If anything, they said that his voice was as youthful as ever.

Then it was December. The sanctuary was decorated for Christmas. The tree, the wreaths, the needlework banners of shepherds and trumpeting angels. The pulpit had been removed to make room for the risers, giving the sanctuary the look of a stage.

Earlier, Young-Ja had dropped off Mo-Sae in the choir room. She had helped him with his robe and positioned him beside Elder Lim. Now, as she sat in her pew and looked around at the Christmas decorations, she thought that she would lay her worries down. She saw her son, Timothy, come up the aisle with his wife. With his glasses and slightly irritated look, he reminded her strongly of a young Mo-Sae. And yet Timothy was now a father with children old enough to be left at home alone.

Then Christina entered the pew. Jonathan was at home with Sanjay, she said when Young-Ja asked.

The choir members started to file in. Young-Ja quickly identified Mo-Sae, but he maintained his stage presence and looked straight ahead. Next came the soloists, distinct in tuxedos or dresses, taking their seats behind four music stands. Young-Ja felt her children settle into a humoring attitude.

When the new conductor strode to his place, the audience didn't know whether to clap. As a congregation, they only ever said "Amen" after the choir sang on Sundays. But the conductor settled the matter by immediately turning his back. He gestured and the choir stood. He opened his palms and the choir opened matching black binders. The music began.

Young-Ja could not tell if the singing was good or bad, but she could see a new unison of attitude in the schooled faces, the binders that were kept open but hardly consulted. She noticed Christina and Timothy exchanging a glance but could not read its meaning. The music was long and wordy, with laughing scales—ha ha ha—sung soberly. Mo-Sae seemed to be keeping up. At times, she didn't hear the music at all but found herself mesmerized by the flashing lights of the Christmas tree. At times, she recognized certain passages of scripture: Comfort, comfort ye my people. For unto us a child is born.

At times she caught moments of tuneful beauty.

She noticed a pattern. One of the soloists would stand to introduce a change in the music. The choir would take up a response. The same phrase would be passed around for some time among the various voice parts, altered and yet the same. She saw Mo-Sae in compliance, his mouth opening and shutting with the mouths around him.

"He trusted in God . . ."

"That he deliver him . . ."

"Deliver him . . ."

"Delight in him . . ."

"Deli-ha-ha-ha-ight in him . . ."

The tenor soloist stood up.

"He looked for some to have pity on him," the tenor sang, "but there was no man . . ."

Then: movement in the risers.

Young-Ja was suddenly alert to the worry that had been pacified through the long listening. She felt that worry, which had been vague and formless, grow distinct as Mo-Sae sidled out of position on the top riser, setting off a wave of shirking among the choir members that blocked his path. With great seriousness of purpose, he came to the front of the stage. He took his place beside the tenor soloist, who had just launched into the melodic part of his solo. He opened his binder. He opened his mouth. He too began to sing.

Nothing could be read in the soloist's expression. Perhaps that was what made him a professional: the ability to keep singing, keep pretending. And no interpretation could be made of the choir director's turned back, from which a conducting arm continued to emerge and retreat in time. Or of the choir members who presented three rows of staunch faces.

But Mo-Sae's face was laid bare to scrutiny. The expression on it was high-minded and earnest, but also a little coy, as though he was struggling to disguise his basking pleasure.

What was he possibly singing? In which language? To which tune? Or had he somehow learned the tenor solo on his own? He was not behind the microphone so no one could hear. But anyone could see from the childish look of surprise that came over Mo-Sae's face that he was straining for the high notes that came forth in the soloist's voice.

So there it was. The spectacle.

Young-Ja could do nothing but watch, to feel that there in the spotlight that she had never once sought for herself, her private miseries had become manifest.

Ultimately, it was Christina who made her way to the stage; who waited, hands folded, until the tenor solo had ended; who took her father gently by the arm and led him down through the pews with no sense of apology in her posture or pace. There then seemed to spread through the congregation a spontaneous kindness, a collective will to look away, to appear absorbed in the musical performance so that Young-Ja, Timothy, and his wife could cast about for their things and make their escape.

Afterward, things were different. Better, almost. Now that the secret was out, the church members treated her like one of the New Testament widows. They saw her as devoted, praiseworthy. They never asked Mo-Sae to rejoin the choir or even take part in a real conversation. Thus she was free from the burden of his reputation.

And yet, sometimes she took the opposite view. She was not really a widow so she was not really free. While Mo-Sae was alive, she could not pretend that he did not exist in some real, sometimes inconveniencing way. Others might pretend, but she had to look squarely into the question of Mo-Sae's dignity. It was up to her to reclaim it from this point forward in a more complicated, arduous, thankless way.

At the start of the new year, she ran into Mr. Sorenson. He was leaning on a footed cane.

Just a fall, he told her. But his son (he had a son!) was convinced that he was too old to be living alone. Party time over. He was getting shipped out to a retirement community near Orlando. "You know Disney World? Mickey Mouse?"

He asked her, with new formality, whether she had a moment to step inside his house. He had something for her there.

Of course she did. Her life was once again full of such empty stretches, affordable moments.

The apartment was clean but smelled faintly of cooked cabbage and bleach. Over the recliner was a crocheted blanket in a classic granny-square, telling of some bygone female presence in his life. A few open boxes where he had started packing.

"Twenty medium-sized boxes," he said in a false, hearty tone. "That's what I get to take with me."

She noticed a handsome burnished instrument. It looked very much like an upright except it had two sets of keyboards and a variety of pedals. He caught her looking. "What you have there is a mint 1960s Hammond B3."

So it was true about the organ. She had only ever seen one in church, which had supplied her with an idea about *pipe* organs.

"I ask you," he said. "Can something like this be made to fit into twenty medium-sized boxes?"

She heard the bitter note enter his tone. She sympathized with it. But she also gently refused it. There was nothing she could do for him, that they could do for each other. They belonged to whom they belonged.

He seemed to understand this.

"There she is," he said, abruptly, drawing her attention to a large plant on a stand beside the organ. "Christmas cactus."

She dimly remembered he had given her a cutting of the same name. But it had never produced anything like this riotous display of flowers.

"All yours," he said. He wouldn't be able to take living things with him on the move either.

As he watched, she struggled to wrap her arms around the pot, the leaves coming right up to her face, into her nose, obscuring her vision. All the spiky, hot-pink, white-tongued flowers.

Afterward, she would sometimes meet him coming and going from the garbage disposal down the hall. Divesting, he said. He offered her useless things. Baseball cards, cassettes, souvenir spoons. He gave her some more full-grown plants but never anything that had yet to put down roots. He didn't give her a phone number or an address to reach him once he was gone, and she didn't think to ask.

One Sunday, shortly after the Christmas incident, her children had come to her. Something had to be done about Dad, they said, sternly, with loving intent.

Yes, said Young-Ja with gentle amusement. Who was disagreeing? Something had to be done. But what?

They had no solutions. They were all so smart and competent, so young in their conviction that they would not grow old. But who among them was prepared to take their father in? Or who would stand to see him in a home? Even so, who would pay?

She gazed at them, loving them with a freedom she had not felt since they were small. She was glad, so glad, that they did not know about her own ailing health. She knew that she would get up every morning and muscle through, as she always had. She had in her body the proof. The cancer in her kidney when the children were young, impossibly young. The alarming growth on her left eye, spreading toward her pupil. The aches in her joints, the stiffness in her back, the headaches from the Perc fumes. Each time, she had rallied, had made a habit of exceeding doctors' expectations.

Even now, she felt in herself a steadying of purpose, a long view opening up. Of course, she would be the one to provide a solution to the problem of Mo-Sae. That was why her children had come to her. To ask her to relieve them of this burden. And hadn't she known that this time would come? Hadn't she known from the moment she had taken his torn sock in hand with an offer to mend it?

She had offered other things as well: a way out from his hated degree program, a way to make a living. It had been her idea to purchase the dry cleaners from her old employer—the business through which they had bought their home, put their kids through college. They had bought it through her savings. Even so, she had known that at certain rocky junctures of their marriage, Mo-Sae would find in this a convenient source of blame. Indeed, she had seen this plainly on his face that night when he had taken the stage: the still vibrant longing for attention and applause.

Be that as it may.

She had borne him his children and set his tables. She had served him red ginseng in autumn, deer antlers in spring, marrow soup in winter, and medicinal chicken stuffed with licorice root in the summer seasons of his life. As things got worse, she had taken in his smell, coaxed him to bathe, clipped his thick yellow toenails, and boiled stains from his sheets. She had not neglected to bring him the plenteous pills—the regulators, inhibitors, uppers, and downers—that would perhaps prolong his life, with a glass of water set on a saucer.

And after all was said and done, after he had been laid to rest, she knew that she would not rest. She would put up his stern framed photo in the living room. Exhort the children and grandchildren. Make regular visits to the cemetery, where she would upkeep his memory with ammonia, an old toothbrush, and a handful of flowers.

Watch the boy, Young-Ja had said.

Now she is gone, swept out of the house on one of her errands.

Well, good. When she is around, she is always watching him, testing him, bringing as evidence the dry toothbrush or the empty candy wrapper.

The phone rings.

What! he shouts in Korean, then remembers to pick up the receiver. "Hello!" he shouts in English.

It is his daughter, his Christina. Young-Ja apparently isn't answering her cell.

Christina seems surprised, almost irritated, to hear that her mother is not home. She asks him where exactly Jonathan is, what exactly he is doing. She tells him to get a pen and write down precisely what she says: "Mom call Christina as soon as you get home."

He writes nothing. As soon as he hangs up the phone, he heads to the pantry, where he lords it over the products on the shelves. *His* good privilege. *His* bad choices.

He notices the boy watching him. "Come here, little one," he says, wooing.

They assess their choices. Beans, grains, glass noodles. Dark viscous liquids decanted into unlabeled glass jars. The faint smell of dried anchovies and sesame oil. Ingredients, not food.

Through the open window, they hear a distant mechanical melody. The boy identifies it. *Ice cream truck.*

"Grandpa has no money," says Mo-Sae, patting his pockets. "Nothing."

But the boy has a solution, bringing an old coffee can full of change. Mo-Sae picks up some coins, which have complicated pictures. Then he remembers that these are American coins. He returns them to the can, which is surprisingly heavy. "Aren't you rich!" he jokes to the boy. But what really stirs in him is sadness. This is his wife. This is the evidence of her life. A handful of small saving actions.

The boy tugs him toward the front door. He wants to go out. But Mo-Sae is deeply reluctant. He thinks that if he crosses this threshold without his wife, if he walks through the hallway with all its identical doors and goes out into the open world, he will lose all orientation. He will never find his way back. Still, when the child puts a hand in his, Mo-Sae is filled with belligerent affection. The belligerence briefly flares against Young-Ja, wherever she is, as though he will prove something to her.

He tells himself not to forget, not to forget, but by the time they reach the ground floor, he has forgotten why they are there. He looks out at the world beyond the lobby, the parked rows of cars and adjacent apartment buildings. What do they want from him? But the belligerent spirit warns him not to disappoint the boy. He notices a pool, gated and empty, and he tells his grandson in a rousing voice that when he is just a little older, Grandpa will teach him how to swim. They walk in that direction. At the gate, he fiddles with the fork latch. Surprisingly, the latch obliges and the gate swings open.

Mo-Sae and his grandson kneel beside the deep end of the pool. They lean over the water, which moves in dangerous fascination with sunlight. The boy has brought with him a can of coins. He drops a few into the water and watches them sink. As Mo-Sae takes in the boy—his absorbed, attentive attitude—he thinks it will be a pleasure to watch him grow. To teach him to swim or ride a bike; to eat spicy foods; to pour an older man's *soju* with both hands. For a moment he truly believes that he, Mo-Sae, will do this. That he will be permitted such responsibilities.

He does not stop the boy from tipping the entire can of coins into the pool, wondering himself what interesting consequence might result. It is only afterward, as he and the boy look down on the sunken heap, that he realizes that he has misjudged. He grows aware of the music of an ice cream truck, which had been making its rounds, and realizes that the simple act of buying a child ice cream has become absurdly complicated. The boy himself seems to realize this, setting off a howling show of disappointment. The sound puts Mo-Sae on high alert. He feels that if he cannot get that noise, that resistance, that blame to stop, he is in danger of losing all sense of judgment. He tries to seize the boy by the arm but the boy takes off, running through the parking lot, into the lobby. Mo-Sae spots him just as he enters the elevator, reaches him just as the doors slide shut on them.

Now that they are in that enclosed space, the boy cannot run. In frustration, he jabs at all the black numbered buttons on the panel, as high as he can reach, and turns to Mo-Sae in defiance. Whatever motion he has set off, Mo-Sae is powerless to stop it. He feels something engage, deep inside the elevator shaft, and the gears begin to shift. The elevator car begins to rise, but only for a moment. On the second floor, it stops. Its doors open and then close. On the next floor, it stops again. Open, close. The doors keep opening and closing on identical hallways, and Mo-Sae realizes that he has no idea which is his own. Still, he begins to find his panic subsiding. His breathing slows. This small space is manageable. Its lighting is plain, its corners exposed. The boy also becomes quiet.

On the fifth floor, the doors open onto a scene with a difference. An elderly man with a cane is waiting to enter, so Mo-Sae and the boy exit the elevator car. Glancing down the hall, Mo-Sae notices that a certain door has been left ajar. Could it be their own? Had they left it open? No matter. They will find out soon enough. They head toward the open door. Walking through it, they see themselves reflected in the entryway mirror. They see paired shoes lined up neatly on the floor. That is when Mo-Sae realizes that by happenstance or miracle, he has gotten home.

Time passes. The sun goes down.

Mo-Sae feels in himself a lengthening of the patience and waiting with which he occupies his days. He moves about the house, looking for helpful things to do. The fact that Young-Ja is not home does not particularly trouble him at the moment. He clears the kitchen table, wipes it down. *Shit,* he says softly to himself as he waters the plants. *Goddamn.* The phone rings from time to time. He lets it.

In the living room, he sees Jonathan, remembers Jonathan. The boy is asleep on the living room sofa. His open mouth, his sticky grasp. Mo-Sae brings a large towel from the bathroom and lays it over the boy, to make his sleep seem more intentional.

A knock on the door.

Opening it, Mo-Sae is momentarily surprised to find a dusky stranger in doctor's scrubs. But of course, it is the son-in-law. The son-in-law is apparently Indian. Mo-Sae suddenly feels a sharp sympathy for his wife: how she must struggle with this!

"Mr. Han? It's Sanjay? May I come in?"

Sanjay's manner is pleasant, suggestive. Crossing the threshold, he knows to remove his shoes. "Christina sent me over. She went straight to the hospital. She says you weren't answering the phone."

Hospital?

Mo-Sae isn't sure what to do with that information. It brings something deeply unwelcome to his sense of well-being, shows it as precarious. But he is also afraid, perhaps *more* afraid, to expose his confusion before a young man.

Sanjay moves deeper into the house. In the living room, he notices Jonathan lying on the sofa, lightly sweating under a towel. "Oh," he says. His face, beside the boy's face, suddenly seems inevitable. "He's sleeping."

Yes, sleeping.

The two stand over the boy, not knowing how to progress from there. Young-Ja would know. Mo-Sae wonders why she is not around.

Sanjay's cellphone vibrates in his pocket. He walks to the far side of the room and takes the call with his back turned. Mo-Sae watches and listens, newly aware of Sanjay's scrubs, the authority of his uniform, which seems bound up in the mysteries of his one-sided communication.

"Christina? I'm here. How's she doing?"

"So what's the whole story? They found her where? In front of which bank?

"How is it possible that nobody knew?"

"Okay, okay, I'm sorry.

"Who's the attending? Maybe I'll give him a ring . . .

"Jonathan? He's fine.

"I said he's fine. He's sleeping.

"You want me to stay with him? With them?

"Well, what do you want me to tell him?"

Sanjay hangs up and looks toward Mo-Sae. He puts on a professional, chummy guise, telling Mo-Sae not to worry, that Young-Ja is in good hands, that the attending physician is a buddy of his. But Mo-Sae senses something false in his execution. When Sanjay falls silent, it is a relief for both men.

Only, moments later, he is at it again. It seems this son-in-law of his can't keep still, can't keep quiet. He consults his phone. He looks around. "I see you grow spider plants!" Sanjay says, suddenly delighted. "Oh, and begonias! Christmas cactus!" He seems profoundly relieved to have stumbled on certain matters of fact.

You like plants?

"Just a hobby of mine," says Sanjay, walking toward a plant with flat, sword-shaped leaves. "The scientific name of this one," he tells Mo-Sae, "is 'Mother-in-Law's Tongue.'"

Mo-Sae notices that Sanjay has lost all his discomfort and re-sumed his jokey doctor act. Perhaps this is part of Sanjay's bag of tricks, to deliver bad news after his patients feel at ease. He watches Sanjay probe the soil in the pot with two diagnostic fingers. "Just don't over-water," Sanjay says. "Some plants thrive on neglect."

Once again, silence. There is a waiting quality to the silence.

Then it occurs to Mo-Sae that Sanjay might be waiting for him to provide the next direction. That he, Mo-Sae, occupies a certain position as the father-in-law. That he has a certain power of per-mission and refusal.

Go, says Mo-Sae.

"I'm sorry?"

You can go. Then come back. Just leave the boy. Let him sleep. I will keep watch.

"Oh, no," says Sanjay immediately. "Christina said I should stay."

But moments later, he relents. "Maybe I'll just run out and grab a bite? I noticed a Carl's Jr. on the way over. Haven't eaten since breakfast. In and out of surgeries all day."

Still, he wavers.

What, he doesn't trust Mo-Sae with the boy?

"Is okay," he says to Sanjay. "Go."

After Sanjay leaves, Mo-Sae goes out onto the balcony, bringing with him pieces of the mystery that he couldn't put together in his presence. Why was Sanjay here? What is the meaning of that phone conversation?

Warily, he circles the matter of Young-Ja's absence. But what can he make of it without her help? In all the ways that she is not what he had wanted—in her homeliness, her surprisingly conventional taste, her imperviousness to art or beauty, her stout resilience —she provides the resistance that distinguishes the reality from the dream.

Below, darkness. The headlights of cars pulling in and out of parking spots. There is some pattern to their coming and going. If only he can figure it out, he will be able to make sense of other things as well. But as he applies his concentration, he becomes distractingly aware of certain sounds.

No.

Yes.

The lights are tricky and misleading, but the sounds are actual sounds. They are coming from a nearby unit, perhaps through an open window. He senses the dawning of recognition, waits for it.

Of course. It is an organ.

An unseen musician is playing. Tentatively at first, as though it has been a while since he has been with an instrument. Chords, half-scales, just noodling around. Then, with growing conviction. The notes begin to come together, fall in place, mustering up to the start of a song. Yes. There's the tune, faintly ridiculous, jaunty yet nostalgic. And here are the words, right there in his memory like a gift time had bestowed:

> Take me out to the ballgame
> Take me out to the fair
> Buy me some peanuts and cracker jacks
> I don't care if I never get back

As it sometimes happens, he simply begins to remember. His name is Han Mo-Sae, born 1940, ten years before the start of the Korean War. His wife is Han Young-Ja. Born 1945. In 1960, they met in Philadelphia. They married, bought a dry cleaners, Kim's dry cleaning, and never bothered to change its name. They have two adult children.

Those very children have talked. He has heard them speak. In this very balcony he had sat, not so long ago, with his eyes closed, pretending not to hear as his wife and children gathered around the kitchen table to discuss the problem of his continued existence. Who should care for him? Who should take him?

If he feels an old flicker of indignation, a last assertion, it is easily extinguished. Oh, he doesn't blame them. He loves them. He gets the impression that he is already looking back on a life; a life divested of time, ego, and even regard; a life weary of its own argument.

A motion-sensor light momentarily illuminates the pool, then goes dark.

Once, he remembers, his father had taken him swimming in Sokcho Beach. He enters the memory. His mother sits on a blanket by the rocks, under the pine trees. She waves. His father is in the ocean, motioning for Mo-Sae to come deeper into the water. His father has taken off his stern black scholar's glasses, which he is never without. Mo-Sae sees him, framed against the sea and the sky; he can tell that his father's nearsighted eyes, squinting, are unaccustomed to taking in the long view. Still, his father beckons, tells him not to be afraid. Tells him that swimming is like singing. That there is a scary little moment of trust, and then . . . nothing. You find that inside you are made of lightness and air.

Mo-Sae wants to move toward that moment, to move deeper into its memory.

But not just yet.

He senses that there is still something for him in this place, holding him back, staking its claim. He goes back inside the apartment and walks from room to room. He turns on every light inside the house. A pull of the chain under the tasseled lampshade beside the sofa, and he notices the sleeping boy. The lamplight catches what is gold about his curls, his skin. There is nothing but innocence and conceit in those thin arms and legs. The expectation of tender-loving care.

Where are his father and his mother, Mo-Sae wonders as he picks up a fallen bath towel and places it over the boy. When will they be back? Who will keep watch until they return?

As the evening turns into night, Mo-Sae sits beside the front door, hugging his knees to his chest. He has angled his stance to keep the sleeping boy in his sights. He watches vigilantly so he will not forget.

Los Angeles

FROM *Granta*

IT WAS ONLY November but holiday decorations were already starting to creep into the store displays: cutouts of Santa wearing sunglasses, windows poxed with fake snow, as if cold was just another joke. It hadn't even rained since Alice moved here, the good weather holding. Back in her hometown, it was already grim and snowy, the sun behind her mother's house setting by 5 p.m. This new city seemed like a fine alternative, the ceaseless blue sky and bare arms, the days passing frictionless and lovely. Of course, in a few years, when the reservoirs were empty and the lawns turned brown, she'd realize that there was no such thing as unending sunshine.

The employee entrance was around the back of the store, in an alley. This was before the lawsuits, when the brand was still popular and opening new stores. They sold cheap, slutty clothes in primary colors, clothes invoking a low-level athleticism—tube socks, track shorts—as if sex was an alternative sport. Alice worked at a flagship store, which meant it was bigger and busier, on a high-visibility corner near the ocean. People tracked in sand and sometimes beach tar that the cleaners had to scrub off the floors at the end of the night.

Employees were only allowed to wear the brand's clothes, so Alice had gotten some for free when she started. Emptying the bag on her bed, she had been stirred by the pure abundance, but there was an awful caveat: her manager had picked them out, and everything was a little too tight, a size too small. The pants cut into her crotch and left red marks on her stomach in the exact outline of the zipper, the shirts creasing tight in her underarms. She left her pants undone on the drive to work, waiting until the last minute to suck in her stomach and button them up.

Inside, the store was bright white and shiny, a low-level hum in the background from the neon signs. It was like being inside a computer. She got there at 10 a.m. but already the lights and the music conjured a perpetual afternoon. On every wall were blown-up photographs in grainy black and white of women in the famous underpants, girls with knobby knees making eye contact with the camera, covering their small breasts with their hands. All the models' hair looked a little greasy, their faces a little shiny. Alice supposed that was to make sex with them seem more likely.

Only young women worked the floor—the guys stayed in the back room, folding, unpacking and tagging shipments from the warehouse, managing stock. They had nothing to offer beyond their plain labor. It was the girls that management wanted out in front, girls who acted as shorthand to the entire brand. They roamed the floor in quadrants, wedging fingers between hangers to make sure items were hung at an equal distance, kicking dropped shirts out from under the partitions, hiding a leotard smeared with lipstick.

Before they put the clothes on the racks, they had to steam them, trying to reanimate the sheen of value. The first time Alice had opened a box of T-shirts from the warehouse, seeing the clothes there, all stuffed and flattened together in a cube without tags or prices, made their real worth suddenly clear—this was junk, all of it.

At her interview, Alice had brought a résumé, which she'd made some effort to print out at a copy store. She had also purchased a folder to transport the résumé intact but no one ever asked to see it. John, the manager, had barely asked about her employment history. At the end of their five-minute conversation, he instructed her to stand against a blank wall and took her picture with a digital camera.

"If you could just smile a little," John said, and she did.

They sent the pictures to corporate for approval, Alice later discovered. If you made the cut, whoever did your interview got a $200 bonus.

Alice fell into an easy rhythm at her post. Feeding hanger after hanger onto the racks. Taking clothes from the hands of strangers, directing them to a fitting room that she had to open with a key on a lanyard around her wrist, the mildest of authorities. Her mind was glazing over, not unpleasantly, thoughts swimmy and hushed. She'd get paid tomorrow, which was good—rent was due in a week, plus a payment on her loans. Her room was cheap, at least, though the apartment, shared with four housemates, was disgusting. Alice's room wasn't so bad only because there was nothing in it—her mattress still on the floor, though she'd lived there for three months.

The store was empty for a while, one of the strange lulls that followed no logical pattern, until a father came in, pulled by his teenage daughter. He hovered at a wary distance while his daughter snatched up garment after garment. She handed him a sweatshirt, and the man read the price aloud, looking to Alice like it was her fault.

"It's just a plain sweatshirt," he said.

The daughter was embarrassed, Alice could tell, and she smiled at the father, bland but also forgiving, trying to communicate the sense that some things in this world were intractable. It was true that the clothes were overpriced. Alice could never have bought them herself. And the daughter's expression was recognizable from her own adolescence, her mother's constant commentary on the price of everything. The time they went to a restaurant for her brother's eighth-grade graduation, a restaurant with a menu illuminated with some kind of LED lights, and her mother couldn't help murmuring the prices aloud, trying to guess what the bill might be. Nothing could pass without being parsed and commented upon.

When the father relented and bought two pairs of leggings, the sweatshirt, and a metallic dress, Alice understood he had only been pretending to be put off by the prices. The daughter had never considered the possibility that she might not get what she wanted, and whatever solidarity Alice felt with the father dissipated as she watched the numbers add up on the register, the man handing her his credit card without even waiting to hear the total.

Oona worked Saturdays, too. She was seventeen, only a little younger than Alice's brother, but Henry seemed like he was from a different species. He was ruddy-cheeked, his beard trimmed to a skinny strap along his chin. A strange mix of perversity—the background on his phone a big-titted porn star—alongside a real boy-ishness. He made popcorn on the stove most nights, adored and replayed a song whose lyrics he happily chanted, "Build Me Up Buttercup," his face young and sweet.

Oona would eat Henry alive, Oona with her black chokers and lawyer parents, her private school where she played lacrosse and took a class in Islamic art. She was easy and confident, already well versed in her own beauty. It was strange how good-looking teenagers were these days, so much more attractive than the teenagers Alice and her friends had been. Somehow these new teenagers all knew how to groom their eyebrows. The pervs loved Oona—the men who came in alone, lured by the advertisements, the young women who worked the floor dressed in the promised leotards and skirts. The men lingered too long, performing a dramatic contemplation of a white T-shirt, carrying on loud phone calls. They wanted to be noticed.

The first time it seemed like one of those men had cornered Oona, Alice pulled her away for an imaginary task in the back. But Oona just laughed at Alice—she didn't mind the men, and they often bought armfuls of the clothes, Oona marching them to the cash register like a cheerful candy-striper. They got commission on everything.

Oona had been asked by corporate to shoot some ads, for which she would receive no money, only more free clothes. She really wanted to do it, she told Alice, but her mom wouldn't sign the release form. Oona wanted to be an actress. The sad fact of this city: the thousands of actresses with their thousands of efficiency apartments and teeth-whitening strips, the energy generated by thousands of treadmill hours and beach runs, energy dissipating into nothingness. Maybe Oona wanted to be an actress for the same reason Alice did: because other people told them they should be. It was one of the traditional possibilities for a pretty girl, everyone urging the pretty girl not to waste her prettiness, to put it to good use. As if prettiness was a natural resource, a responsibility you had to see all the way through.

Acting classes were the only thing Alice's mother had agreed to help pay for. Maybe it was important to her mother to feel Alice was achieving, moving forward, and completing classes had the sheen of building blocks, tokens being collected, no matter if they had no visible use. Her mother sent a check every month, and

sometimes there was a cartoon from the Sunday paper she'd torn
out and enclosed, though never any note.

Alice's teacher was a former actor now in his well-preserved fifties. Tony was blond and tan and required a brand of personal
devotion Alice found aggressive. The class was held in a big room
with hardwood floors, folding chairs stacked against the wall. The
students padded around in their socks, their feet giving off a humid, private smell. Tony set out different kinds of tea and the students studied the boxes, choosing one with great ceremony. Get
Calm, Nighty Night, Power Aid, teas whose very names implied
effort and virtue. They held their mugs with both hands, inhaling
in an obvious way; everyone wanted to enjoy their tea more than
anyone else enjoyed theirs. While they took turns acting out various scenes and engaging in various exercises, repeating nonsense
back and forth, Tony watched from a folding chair and ate his
lunch: stabbing at wet lettuce leaves in a plastic bowl, chasing an
edamame with his fork.

Every morning in Alice's email, an inspirational quote from
Tony popped up:

DO OR DO NOT. THERE IS NO TRY.
FRIENDS ARE GIFTS WE GIVE OURSELVES.

Alice had tried, multiple times, to get off the email list. Emailing
the studio manager, and finally Tony himself, but still the quotes
came. That morning's quote:

REACH FOR THE MOON. IF YOU FALL SHORT, YOU MAY JUST
LAND ON A STAR!

It seemed shameful that Alice recognized celebrities, but she did.
A stutter in her glance, a second look—she could identify them
almost right away as famous, even if she didn't know their names.
There was some familiarity in the way their features were put together, a gravitational pull. Alice could identify even the C-list ac-
tors, their faces taking up space in her brain without any effort on
her part.

A woman came into the store that afternoon who wasn't an actor, but was married to one: an actor who was very famous, be-

loved even though he was milk-faced and not attractive. The wife was plain, too. A jewelry designer. This fact came to Alice in the same sourceless way as the woman's name. She wore rings on most fingers, a silver chain with a slip of metal dangling between her breasts. Alice figured the jewelry was of her own design, and imagined this woman, this jewelry designer, driving in the afternoon sunshine, deciding to come into the store, the day just another asset available to her.

Alice moved toward the woman, even though she was technically in Oona's quadrant.

"Let me know if I can help you find anything," Alice said.

The woman looked up, her plain face searching Alice's. She seemed to understand that Alice recognized her, and that Alice's offer of help, already false, was doubly false. The woman said nothing. She just went back to idly flipping through the swimsuit separates. And Alice, still smiling, made a swift and unkind catalog of every unattractive thing about the woman—the dry skin around her nostrils, her weak chin, her sturdy legs in their expensive jeans.

Alice ate an apple for lunch, tilting her face up to feel the thin sun on her forehead and cheeks. She couldn't see the ocean, but she could see where the buildings started to dissipate along the coast, the spindly tops of the palms that lined the boardwalk. The apple was okay, bright and clean-fleshed, slightly sour. She threw the core into the hydrangea bushes below the deck. It was her whole lunch: there was something nice about the way her stomach would tighten around its own emptiness afterward, how it made the day slightly sharper.

Oona came out on the back porch for her break, smoking one of John's cigarettes. She had cadged one for Alice, too. Alice knew she was a little old to take this much pleasure in Oona, but she didn't care. There was an easy, mild rapport between them, a sense of resigned camaraderie, the shared limits of the job alleviating any larger concerns about where Alice's life was going. High school was probably the last time Alice had smoked cigarettes with any regularity. She didn't talk to any of those people anymore, beyond tracking the engagement photos that surfaced online, photos taken on the railroad tracks during the golden hour. Worse: the ones taken on the shores of a lake or in front of sunsets, photos name-dropping the natural world, the plain, dull beauty of the shore. Children followed soon after, babies curled like shrimp on fur rugs.

"It was the guy," Oona was telling her. "With the black hair."

Alice tried to remember if she'd noticed any particular man. None stood out.

He'd come in that afternoon, Oona said. Had tried to buy her underwear. Oona laughed when she saw Alice's face.

"It's hilarious," Oona said, dreamily combing her long bangs out of her eyes with her fingers. "You should look online, it's a whole thing."

"He asked you to email him or something?"

"Uh, no," Oona said. "More like, he said, 'I'll give you fifty bucks to go into the bathroom right now and take off your underwear and give them to me.'"

The upset that Alice expected to find in Oona's face wasn't there—not even a trace. If anything, she was giddy, and that's when Alice understood.

"You didn't do it?"

Oona smiled, darting a look at Alice, and Alice's stomach dropped with an odd mix of worry and jealousy, an uncertainty about who exactly had been tricked. Alice started to say something, then stopped. She moved a silver ring around her finger, the cigarette burning itself out.

"Why?" Alice said.

Oona laughed. "Come on, you've done these things. You know."

Alice settled back against the railing. "Aren't you worried he might do something weird? Follow you home or something?"

Oona seemed disappointed. "Oh, please," she said, and started doing a leg exercise, going briskly up on her toes. "I wish someone would stalk me."

Alice's mother didn't want to pay for acting classes anymore.

"But I'm getting better," Alice said to her mother over the phone.

Was she? She didn't know. Tony made them throw a ball back and forth as they said their lines. He made them walk around the room leading from their sternum, then from their pelvis. Alice had finished Level One, and Level Two was more expensive but it met twice a week plus a once-monthly private session with Tony.

"I don't see how this class is different than the one you just took."

"It's more advanced," Alice said. "It's more intensive."

"Maybe it's okay to take a break for a while," her mother said. "See how much you really want this."

How to explain—if Alice wasn't taking a class, if she wasn't otherwise engaged, that meant her terrible job, her terrible apartment, suddenly carried more weight, maybe started to matter. The thought was too much to consider squarely.

"I'm pulling into the driveway," her mother said. "Miss you."

"You too."

There was only a moment when all the confused, thwarted love locked up her throat. And then the moment passed, and Alice was alone again on her bed. Better to hurtle along, to quickly occupy her brain with something else. She went to the kitchen, opening a bag of frozen berries that she ate with steady effort until her fingers were numb, until a chill had penetrated deeply into her stomach and she had to get up and put on her winter coat. She moved to catch the sunshine where it warmed the kitchen chair.

There were countless ads online, Oona had been right, and that night Alice lost an hour clicking through them, thinking how ludicrous people were. You pressed slightly on the world and it showed its odd corners, revealed its dim and helpless desires. It seemed insane at first. And then, like other jokes, it became curiously possible the more she referred to it in her own mind, the uncomfortable edges softening into something innocuous.

The underwear was cotton and black and poorly made. Alice took them from work—easy enough to secrete away a stack from the warehouse shipment before it got entered into inventory or had any tags on. John was supposed to check everyone's bags on the way out, the whole line of employees shuffling past him with their purses gaping, but he usually just waved them through. Like most things, it was frightening the first time and then became rote.

It didn't happen all that often, maybe twice a week. The meetings were always in public places: a chain coffee shop, the parking lot of a gym. There was a young guy who bragged about having some kind of security clearance and wrote to her from multiple email accounts. A fat hippie with tinted glasses who brought her a copy of his self-published novel. A man in his sixties who shorted Alice ten bucks. She didn't have any interaction beyond handing them the underwear, sealed in a Ziploc and then stuffed in a paper bag, like someone's forgotten lunch. A few of the men lingered, but no one ever pushed. It wasn't so bad. It was that time of life when anytime something bad or strange or sordid happened, she could soothe herself with that forgiving promise: it's just that time of life. When you thought of it that way, whatever mess she was in seemed already sanctioned.

Oona invited her to the beach on their free Sunday. One of her friends had a house on the water and was having a barbecue. When Alice pushed open the door, the party was already going—music on the speakers and liquor bottles on the table, a girl feeding orange after orange into a whirring juicer. The house was sunny and big, the ocean below segmented by the windows into squares of mute glitter.

She was uncomfortable until she caught sight of Oona, in a one-piece swimsuit and cutoffs. Oona grabbed her by the hand. "Come meet everyone," she said, and Alice felt a wave of goodwill for Oona, the sweet girl.

Porter lived in the house, the son of some producer, and was older than everyone else—maybe even older than Alice. It seemed like he and Oona were together, his arm slung around her, Oona burrowing happily into his side. He had lank hair and a pitbull with a pink collar. He bent down to let the dog lick him on the mouth; Alice saw their tongues touch briefly.

When Oona held up her phone to take a picture, the girl who was manning the juicer lifted her shirt to flash one small breast. Alice blanched, and Oona laughed.

"You're embarrassing Alice," she said to the girl. "Stop being such a slut."

"I'm fine," Alice said, and willed it so.

When Oona handed her a glass of the orange-juice drink, she drained it fast, the acid brightening her mouth and her throat.

The ocean was too cold for swimming but the sun felt nice. Alice had eaten one greasy hamburger from the grill, some kind of fancy cheese on top that she scraped off and threw into an aloe plant. She stretched out on one of the towels from the house. Oona's towel was vacant—she was down by the water, kicking in the frigid waves. Music drifted from the patio. Alice didn't see Porter until he flopped down on Oona's towel. He was balancing a pack of cigarettes on a plastic container of green olives, a beer in his other hand.

"Can I have a cigarette?" she said.

The pack he handed to her had a cartoon character on it, some writing in Spanish.

"Is it even legal to have cartoon characters on cigarettes?" she said, but Porter was already on his stomach, his face pressed into the towel. She palmed the pack back and forth, eyeing Porter's pale back. He wasn't even a little handsome.

Alice adjusted her bikini straps. They were digging into her shoulders, leaving marks. She surveyed the indifferent group back on the patio, Porter's prone body, and decided to take her top off. She chickened her arms behind herself and unhooked her bikini, hunching over so that it fell off her breasts into her lap. She was having fun, wasn't she? She folded the top into her bag as calmly as she could, sinking back onto the towel. The air and heat on her breasts were even and constant, and she let herself feel pleased and languid, happy with the picture she made.

Alice woke with Porter grinning at her.

"European-style, huh?" he said.

How long had he been watching her?

Porter offered her his beer. "I barely had any, if you want it. I can get another."

She shook her head.

He shrugged and took a long drink. Oona was walking down by the shoreline, the ocean foaming thin around her ankles. "I hate those one-pieces she wears," Porter said.

"She looks great."

"She's embarrassed about her tits," Porter said.

Alice gave him a sickly smile, and pushed her sunglasses back up her nose, crossing her arms over her chest in the least obvious way she could manage. They both turned at a commotion further down the sand—some stranger had made his way to this private beach. The man seemed a little crazy, gray-haired, wearing a suit jacket. Probably homeless. She squinted: there was an iguana on his shoulder.

"What the fuck?" Porter said, laughing.

The man stopped one of Oona's friends and then moved on to another one.

Porter brushed sand from his palms. "I'm going inside."

The man was now approaching Oona.

Alice looked toward Porter but he was already heading back, unconcerned.

The man was saying something to Oona, something detailed. Alice didn't know if she was supposed to do something. But soon enough the man moved away from Oona and was now heading toward Alice. She hurried her bikini top back on.

"Want to take a picture?" the man asked. "One dollar." The iguana was ridged and ancient-looking and when the man shook his shoulder in a practiced way, the iguana bobbed up and down, its jowls beating like a heart.

The last time she ever did it, the man wanted to meet at 4 p.m. in the parking lot of the big grocery store in Alice's neighborhood. It was a peculiar time of day, that sad hour when the dark seems to rise up from the ground but the sky is still bright and blue. The shadows of the bushes against the houses were getting deeper and starting to merge with the shadows of the trees. She wore cotton shorts and a plain sweatshirt from work, not even bothering to look nice. Her eyes were a little pink from her contacts, a rosy wash on the whites that made it look like she'd been crying.

She walked the ten blocks to the parking lot, the light hovering in the tangle of blackberry vines that crawled up the alleyways. Even the cheapo apartment buildings were lovely at that hour, their faded colors subtle and European. She passed the nicer homes, catching slivers of their lush backyards through the slats of the high fences, the koi ponds swishy with fish. Some nights she walked around the neighborhood, near the humid rim of the reservoir. It was a pleasure to see inside those nighttime houses. Each one like a primer on being human, on what choices you might make. As if life might follow the course of your wishes. A piano lesson she had once watched, the repeated scales, a girl with a meaty braid down her back. The houses where TVs spooked the windows.

Alice checked her phone—she was a few minutes early. Other shoppers were pushing carts back into jangled place, the automatic doors sliding open and open. She lingered on an island in the lot, watching the cars. She checked her phone again. Her little brother had texted: a smiley face. He had never left their home state, which made her obliquely sad.

When a tan sedan pulled into the lot, she could tell by the way the car slowed and bypassed an open space that it was the man looking for her.

Alice waved, foolishly, and the man pulled up next to her. The passenger window was down so she could see his face, though she still had to stoop to make eye contact. The man was bland-looking, wearing a fleece half-zip pullover and khakis. Like someone's husband, though Alice noticed no ring. He had signed his emails *Mark* but hadn't realized or maybe didn't care that his email address identified him as Brian.

The car looked immaculate until she caught sight of clothes in the backseat and a mail carton and a few soda bottles tipped on their side. It occurred to her that perhaps this man lived in his car. He seemed impatient, no matter that they had both gotten here early. He sighed, performing his own inconvenience. She had a paper bag with the underwear inside the Ziploc.

"Should I just—" she started to hand the bag to him.

"Get in," he interrupted, reaching over to pop the passenger door. "Just for a second."

Alice hesitated but not as long as she should have. She ducked in, shutting the door behind her. Who would try to kidnap someone at 4 p.m.? In a busy parking lot? In the midst of all this unyielding sunshine?

"There," the man said when Alice was sitting beside him, like now he was satisfied. His hands landed briefly on the steering wheel, then hovered at his chest. He seemed afraid to look at her.

She tried to imagine how she would spin this story to Oona on Saturday. It was easy to predict—she would describe the man as older and uglier than he was, adopting a tone of incredulous contempt. She and Oona were used to telling each other stories like this, to dramatizing incidents so that everything took on an ironic, comical tone, their lives a series of encounters that happened to them but never really affected them, at least in the retelling, their personas unflappable and all-seeing. When she'd had sex with John that one time after work, she heard her future self narrating the whole thing to Oona—how his penis was thin and jumpy and how he couldn't come so he finally rolled out and worked his own dick with efficient, lonely habit. It had been bearable because it would become a story, something condensed and communicable. Even funny.

Alice put the bag on the console between herself and the man. He looked at the bag from the corner of his eye, a look that was maybe purposefully restrained, like he was proving he didn't care too much about its contents. No matter that he had found himself in a parking lot in the unforgiving clarity of midafternoon to buy someone's underwear.

The man took the bag but didn't, as she feared, open it in front of her. He tucked it in the pocket of his side door. When he turned back to her, she sensed his disgust—not for himself, but for her. She no longer served a purpose, and every moment she stayed in the car was just another moment that reminded him of his own weakness. It occurred to her that he might do some harm to her. Even here. She looked out the windshield at the cars beyond, the trees. It would be dinnertime at her mother's house. Her mother steaming rice in a bag and putting out placemats that easily wiped clean. Asking Henry if he had a good movie in mind for after dinner. Henry loved documentaries about Hitler or particularly exotic animals. It suddenly seemed nice to load the dishwasher and wish for small things.

"Can I have the money?" she said, her voice going too high.

A look of pain fleeted across his face. He took out his wallet with great effort.

"We said sixty?"

"Seventy-five," she said, "that's what you said in the email. Seventy-five."

His hesitation allowed her to hate him, fully, to watch with cold eyes as he counted out the bills. Why hadn't he done this ahead of time? He probably wanted her to witness this, Mark or Brian or whoever he was, believing that he was shaming or punishing her by prolonging the encounter, making sure she fully experienced the transaction, bill by bill. When he had seventy-five dollars, he held the money in her direction, just out of reach so Alice had to make an effort to grab for it. He smiled, like she had confirmed something.

When she told Oona the story on Saturday, Alice would leave this part out: how, when she tried to open the car door, the door was locked.

How the man said, "Whoops," his voice swerving high, "whoops-a-daisy." He went to press the unlock button, but Alice was still grabbing at the door handle, frantic, her heart clanging in her chest.

"Relax," he said. "Stop pulling or it won't unlock."

Alice was certain, suddenly, that she was trapped, that great violence was coming to her. Who would feel bad for her? She had done this to herself.

"Just stop," the man said. "You're only making it worse."

Unearth

FROM *Grain*

THEY FOUND HIM while laying the groundwork for a fast food restaurant. She forgot the name as soon as the officer said it—not McDonald's, not Wendy's. No, it was something new, something flashy and fleeting. Whatever it was, the thought made her sick. She couldn't shake the image of a child's tooth being pounded into beef patties, or tiny brown limbs being thrown into an industrial-size grinder. Sour fluids burned their way up her esophagus. She started to gag.

"Are you alright, ma'am?" the officer asked.

Henry's makeshift grave was on the grounds of the old residential school. Of course it was. Of course. What was that famous Sir John A. Macdonald quote? Kill the Indian, save the man? Turned out killing the Indian saved no one. It just killed Indians.

"Ma'am? I can call back if you want."

It had been 55 years since he went missing. Their mother had been dead for 20. What was there to even remember about him at this point? He was named after their alcoholic grandfather, then he was five, then he was gone. Not much to hang any misplaced nostalgia on.

She swallowed, found a tissue and wiped at her mouth.

"I'm fine. Please continue."

The officer was nice enough, if deceptive. All dirty details were declawed. How did they even know it was her brother? There were lots of kids that died at that school. Testing was still underway, of course, but they were pretty sure. The officer mentioned school records and death certificates and police reports (no doubt filed by her mother), then started talking about "closure" and "the ceremony Henry deserved." That very artlessly segued into the date the remains would be released, and referrals of some affordable funeral homes. What the officer really meant was that she, Beth T——, a widow on a fixed income, could now pay for the disposal of her brother's half-century-old remains. And no, the grave and empty casket her mother had spent the last of their grocery money on would not be acceptable for use. The law had problems with reusing those sorts of things, though strictly speaking it wasn't used in the first place. Beth should really get in touch with one of those funeral homes. They would have more information. And if she didn't claim the body? The officer's voice became clipped. If she didn't claim the body for whatever reason, the province would pay for a burial. Standard-issue, nothing personal. That was the kind of thing only family could provide.

"Do you need me to—" her stomach clenched, her palms sticky, "—identify the body?"

"I'd be surprised if you could identify anything at this point. But if you want . . ."

Beth's mouth suddenly filled with the taste of carbon—a taste she'd always associated with Henry's disappearance. Once he was gone her mother couldn't be bothered to pay attention to everyday things like cooking. Henry was all that mattered anymore. Everything Beth ate was burnt black.

Before, she used to help their mother pound roasted white corn into flour, sift it, mix it with lard and hot water and maple syrup. Henry was too small to help, too impatient, so it was just the two of them. Beth wasn't allowed to taste any while they were making it, though sometimes she'd sneak some when her mother turned away. She was hardly a clever thief—smacking her lips together luxuriously, sometimes letting out a little groan, but her mother, gracious as she was, pretended not to notice. Once the mush was ready Beth's mother still offered her a giant spoonful, smiling. It tasted better than any food she'd ever had. She remembered having the corn mush for breakfast and sometimes lunch or dinner, if she begged.

Then there was no more homemade mush. There were only blackened scones, then cold bread, then nothing at all, every culinary decline another rejection, another sign her family was hurtling toward disaster and nothing and no one could stop it.

*

This is what she remembered: her brother was taken first. Their mother had recently converted to the Anglican Church: a "saved" Indian, a prize. With the encouragement of Father Landry, her mother had traded their Mohawk names for those of English monarchs: her brother became Henry, she became Elizabeth. Her mother was now, naturally, Mary. But that wasn't enough. Father Landry suggested the kids go to the residential school to get saved properly. They needed "a good education in the Lord." Mary was hesitant to pull Beth out of school in the middle of the year; she had friends, she was doing well. Henry, on the other hand, was still at home, still susceptible, so he was hesitantly offered to Jesus and the Anglicans as a sort of down payment on salvation. Father Landry assured her that Henry would be back that summer, that he'd send letters thanking her. Summer arrived without a single letter, then departed much the same. Henry never came back.

When Mary went to the school and inquired, she was told Henry didn't go there. In fact, he'd never gone there. No records existed. She was mistaken. She went to the police, to the band council. They shrugged their shoulders and shook their heads.

She couldn't find Father Landry. Ironically enough, he'd gone to Quebec for a "family emergency." He was gone for a month, which turned into two, which turned into six. With each passing day her mother unraveled a little more. By the time Father Landry finally came back to do a guest sermon at his old parish three years later, Mary's nerves were tangled threads. She attacked him at Sunday mass: clawed at his black eyes, yanked out clumps of his white hair, slammed his head against the brick of God's walls. She was arrested and sentenced to ten years in prison.

After that, Beth was promptly deposited into the same school that ate her brother, then adopted by the T——s not long after that. They were Anglicans, friends of Father Landry. They liked her pale skin, her tragedy. They liked how she forced herself to smile. She excelled at school, excelled in her career, excelled at passing, at forgetting. Beth was saved after all.

Apart from the yellow police tape, the site looked ordinary. There was no evidence this Indian burial ground was a *Poltergeist* scene waiting to happen, much as she wished it was—no blood bubbling forth from the ground, no eerie lights or voices from beyond the grave. Just abandoned construction equipment and dirt. Somehow she expected more. After all, that soil did sap nourishment from her brother's body for half a century. It got more from him than she ever did.

She stood in front of the garish COMING SOON! sign, her whole body heavy and limp, though she was sure that had more to do with her 63-year-old frame than any latent trauma. It took two hours of driving in heavy traffic to get here. The houses around looked mostly the same. It even felt the same. Children were squealing and laughing and running. One could nearly hear the collective caps popping off so many post-dinner beers. There was a certain inherent trust here, the kind that lulled parents into letting their kids run around unsupervised because what was the worst that could happen? Beth hated neighborhoods this stupid.

She wondered if she were to knock on the doors today who would answer. Would it be the grandkids of the people who fed her when she went around begging with the other kids? Would it be other families entirely—ones who had no idea their children were running and playing and laughing on the bones of Native children? That COMING SOON! was a place their kids could gorge themselves on burgers and fries shiny with grease where she once gagged on stringy oatmeal crawling with worms? Easier to forget. It was always easier to forget when it didn't happen to you.

Beth had tried to forget Henry. The good memories went first. She had no rosy recollections of holding him or being in awe of his newborn beauty. He only ever came back in sharp, stabbing pangs. Whenever Beth misbehaved she was compared to him. Within days after Mary's visit to the school Henry seemed to have been eroded, his youthful imperfections buffed to a glossy sheen. At first this bothered Beth; she was a good daughter, a good student. Her mistakes were no more notable than any kid her age. But now that Henry was gone he never made any mistakes. His very absence invited imagined mythologies to crystallize into facts.

"Henry would have been on time." Nope. He was five.

"Henry would have eaten his whole plate." He hated everything but sugar.

The truth didn't matter. There was no competing with a memory.

It took 20 minutes to find her daughter's work number on her new cellphone, ten to work up the nerve to dial, then another ten to navigate the automated switchboard. She was both pleased and disappointed when Lindsay picked up on the first ring.

"Hey, Ma. What's up?"

"Was I a good mother?"

"What?"

"Did I love you enough?"

"You never got me that Teddy Ruxpin doll I wanted for Christmas, so I guess not."

"Lindsay, be serious for five minutes. It's important. Did I make you feel loved?"

"You were loving in your own way—"

"'In my own way'? What does that mean?"

"Calm down. Of course you made me feel loved. I still pick up the phone when you call me, don't I? I don't have to do that, you know."

"Then why didn't you have children?"

Lindsay let out a long, slow sigh. "Look, Mom, we've talked about this. My decision to not have kids has nothing to do with you. It's between me and my uterus."

"Maybe it does have something to do with me. I mean, I was thinking about it and I'm pretty sure I didn't have any more children after you because of my mother. She was always comparing me with my brother; she had these impossible standards. I didn't want you to feel . . . inadequate."

"You have no reason to feel inadequate, Mom. You had an amazing career. You were a nurse—you helped so many people. Uncle Chris is nice, but to be honest he mostly sits around reading conspiracy theories all day. It's not even close."

"I'm not talking about him."

"Then who are you talking about?"

"I had another brother. A biological brother. Henry. He disappeared when I was eight. I guess he died then, too."

"What? Are you serious?"

"The police called. They just found his body."

"Oh my god. I'm so sorry, Mom. Where did they find him?"

"The grounds of the Iroquois Residential School we went to. They're building a restaurant there now."

"Wait, you went to a residential school?"

"I barely went for a year. It doesn't count."

"It absolutely counts. Why didn't you ever tell me?"

Beth had no answer she was willing to give. She stared out her car window at the old school grounds, trying to imagine five-year-old Henry working the fields.

"I don't remember what Henry looked like. Isn't that strange? I keep imagining him as that white and blue baby on jars of mushed peas."

"The Gerber baby?"

"That's it, the Gerber baby. I think he looked kind of like that when he was an infant, only he wasn't white, obviously. Chubby cheeks, smiling and all that. But Henry was five when it happened. Five-year-olds look like themselves."

"Are you okay, Mom? Should I leave work and come over?"

"Of course not. I'm fine. Have a good day at work, honey."

The rez was a blur of green past her windows. Every so often there was a flurry of white: tiny trailers that had recently joined the increasing ranks of neon-signed smoke shops. BUY 10 GET 1 FREE. BUY 8 GET 1 FREE AND A LIGHTER. The further in she drove the more outrageous the deals became. It was like the Cold War of lung cancer. Nothing like the place she and her mother used to wander on weekends, gathering medicines and telling stories. She stopped at five smoke shops before she found one that could help her. ROLLIES 2 FOR 1 ON TUESDAYS. The cashier was surprisingly young. She told her exactly where she should go to buy white corn—lyed or dried, the cheapest place, the best place. Beth thanked her.

"You're welcome, Istha."

The word sounded vaguely familiar, like a song she'd heard long ago. "What did you say?"

"Sorry. I'm in the language-immersion program. Trying to practice. I just assumed you spoke Mohawk."

"I used to. When I was a kid. What does that mean again?"

The woman gave a small smile. "Auntie."

Beth nodded, then turned to leave. When she was at the door she turned back one more time, her eyes squinting behind her glasses. "How did you know I was Mohawk?"

She shrugged. "You've got that tough Mohawk look to you."

Beth went stiff. Her insides felt like a painting doused in turpentine. Even though she'd had her hair cut and her tongue tamed, even though she'd donned pantsuits and pearls and spoke English as well as either queen she was named for, even though she let people think she was Portuguese or Italian or Greek, even though she'd left the scarred memories of her childhood in a dark, unattended corner of her mind—her people still recognized her. It was like they'd been here, waiting, all this time.

That night, she took the white corn out of the food processor. Much easier than grinding with mortar and pestle; modernity had its benefits. As she mixed the flour gradually with boiling water, she wondered if Henry missed their corn mush while he was at school, this treat their mother prepared so lovingly. Maybe he tried to pretend the stringy gruel they were fed was this corn mush, as she had so many years ago. Beth added a dollop of maple syrup, stirred it, then brought it to her lips. It tasted just like she remembered.

DANIELLE EVANS

Boys Go to Jupiter

FROM *The Sewanee Review*

THE BIKINI ISN'T even Claire's thing. Before this winter, if you had said Confederate flag, Claire would have thought of high school beach trips: rows and rows of tacky souvenir shops along the Ocean City Boardwalk, her best friend Angela muttering *They know they lost, right?* while Claire tried to remember which side of the Mason-Dixon Line Maryland was on. The flag stuff is Jackson's, and she's mostly seeing Jackson to piss off Puppy. Puppy, Claire's almost-stepmother, is legally named Poppy; Puppy is supposedly a childhood nickname stemming from a baby sister's mispronunciation, but Claire suspects that Puppy has made the whole thing up. Puppy deemed it wasteful to pay twice as much for a direct flight in order for Claire to avoid a layover, and her father listens to Puppy now, so for the first half of her trip, Claire had to go the wrong direction—to Florida from Vermont via Detroit.

Jackson has a drawl and a pickup truck and, in spite of his lack of farming experience, a farmer's tan. Claire meets him at Burger Boy, the restaurant a few miles from her father's house. Its chipping red-and-white tiles and musk of grease give it all the glamour of a truck-stop bathroom, but it's a respite from the lemon-scented and pristine house that brought her father to St. Petersburg for retirement. At college, Claire mostly lives off of the salad bar, but here she picks up a burger and fries to go every afternoon. It is the kind of food Puppy says she can't eat since she turned thirty, and Puppy, having no job and, from what Claire gathers, limited ambitions beyond strolling the house in expensive loungewear, is always home to miserably watch her eat it. On her fourth Burger

Boy visit, Claire picks up Jackson too. They get high and make out in the pool house that afternoon, and the next and the next and the next.

At nineteen, Jackson is six months older than Claire, but still a senior in high school. They try hanging out at his house once, but Claire feels shamed by his mother's scrutiny, assumes she wants to know what's damaged or defective about Claire that has her screwing a high school boy. After that, when they cannot be alone at her house because her father is home (rarely) or Puppy is unbearable (frequently), they find places to park. He gives her the bikini at the end of the first week, after she complains that her father's move to Florida caught her off guard—she is used to winters that at least make an effort to be winter, but her father's new life in St. Pete is relentless sunshine, sunburn weather in December. Outside, by the pool, she has resigned herself to wearing T-shirts over one of Puppy's old suits, which is spangled with faded glitter and sags over Claire's bee-sting breasts. Jackson presents the bathing suit wadded up in a supermarket plastic bag, the sort of awkward non-gift you give someone in an awkward non-relationship—he bought it for five dollars on a spring-break trip, he says, for a girlfriend he subsequently found blowing one of his friends in their shared motel room and broke up with.

It isn't much—three triangles and some string—but the tag is still attached and Jackson is beaming at her.

"You'd look so hot in this," he says.

She does look pretty hot: like someone she is not, what with the stars and bars marking her tits and crotch, but a hot someone she is not.

"You look like white trash," Puppy says to her the first time she sees the bikini.

"You would know," Claire says back. The bathing suit becomes a habit, even after the temperature dips. Two days before she leaves town, she throws a pair of cutoffs and a T-shirt over it before she and Jackson leave the house, but when they get to the parking space—a clearing in a half-built, abandoned subdivision—she makes a show of stripping off the shorts and shirt. In the few minutes before he takes it off and fucks her in the truck's cab, Jackson snaps a picture of Claire, radiant and smiling and leaning against the crisp foil-flash of the bumper, the bikini's Xs making her body a tic-tac-toe board.

*

She's already forgotten about the picture when Jackson posts it on Facebook that night, tagged with her name and #mygirl. Claire doesn't have the heart to object. On her last night in town she doesn't even see Jackson—her father takes her out for a fancy dinner along the waterfront, just her, and then it's goodbye. At the gate awaiting her connecting flight, Claire drapes herself over two airport chairs and checks the messages on her phone. She has eighteen new texts, most from casual acquaintances, the closest thing she has to friends at Dennis College. The messages range from hostile to bewildered, and it takes her a few minutes to decipher what has prompted them: a tweet from the account of the black girl who lives across the hall from her, which features the photo of Claire in the bikini and the commentary *My hallmate just posted this picture of herself on vacation* :/.

Claire squints at the thumbnail photo of the tweet's author, the only black girl on their dorm's floor, and vaguely remembers her. In the frenzied first weeks at Dennis, full of getting-to-know-you games and welcomes, Claire accepted the girl's friend request, but she wasn't really aware that *hallmate* was a thing, a relationship carrying some expectation of trust or camaraderie. She is strangely embarrassed by the picture, the way it turns her into someone else. She wasn't wearing the bikini to bother black people—for Christ's sake, there were none in her father's new neighborhood to bother even if she wanted to—but to bother Puppy, who is half-racist anyway, which makes her aggrieved reaction doubly hilarious. Claire turns her phone off again, closes her eyes, and thinks to the mental picture of the girl whose name she cannot remember, if she has ever known it, *well fuck you too*.

In their old Virginia neighborhood, in the old house, the one Claire's father sold the second she graduated, they have black neighbors. The Halls move into Claire's subdivision the summer before she starts first grade, back when the neighborhood is still brand-new: tech money is paving western Fairfax on its way out to Reston, which will be malls and mini-mansions and glossy buildings soon. Claire's mother prefers the idea of a sprawling country house a little further out, but her father likes the idea of something you can build from the ground up, tinkering with room sizes and flooring types, and so her father gets his house and her mother gets to choose from seven different shades of granite for the counters and eight different types of wood for the floors, and everything is so new and shiny when they move in that Claire is afraid of her own house, afraid her presence will somehow dent or tarnish it.

Though Claire has always lived in Virginia, and Virginia, she knows, is technically the South, Angela is the first person Claire remembers meeting whose voice lilts: the Halls moved from South Carolina, and the whole family talks with drowsy vowels and an occasional drag that gives some words—her name, for example —a comforting dip in the middle. In Mrs. Hall's mouth, Claire's name is a tunnel from which a person can emerge on the other side. Claire is fascinated by their accents, and, yes, by the dark tint of their skin, but mostly she is anxious to be seen. In her own house, Claire is alone: her only sibling is a half brother, Sean, ten years older, from her father's first marriage. Her father keeps long hours, and her mother has a certain formality; Claire loves her, but feels, in her presence, like a miniature adult, embarrassed by the silliness of her six-year-old desires.

Mrs. Hall is an elementary school teacher and has a high tolerance for the frenetic energy of children's games. Angela's house also has Aaron, her brother, who is only a year older than the two of them. Claire's mother refers to Angela and Aaron as Irish twins, which confuses Claire because they are neither twins nor Irish, so she adopts Mrs. Hall's term: stairstep siblings, one right behind the other. At that age, they are the same size, Angela tall for her age and Aaron short for his. Aaron is skinny and quiet and wears glasses that dwarf his face; Angela is a whirlwind.

Since Claire has no brother at home to torment, she and Angela torment Aaron together, chasing him around the front lawn, menacing him with handfuls of glitter and other arts and crafts detritus, taking his shoes from the row by the front door and hiding them in cupboards, in the garage, in the laundry. Claire, not yet entirely clear on the rules of family, thinks of herself as having not a half brother, but half-a-brother, and shortly after meeting the Halls she thinks of herself as having half of Angela's too. The first summer, Angela teaches her that silly hand game, which starts *My mother your mother live across the street.* Though this isn't technically true of them, it's close enough, so they swear it is about them, and torment Aaron with its refrain—*Girls are dandy just like candy, boys are rotten just like cotton, girls go to college to get more knowledge, boys go to Jupiter to get more stupider.* In most aspects Aaron is indifferent to their teasing, but the Jupiter taunt seems to bother him for its failures of logic. Boys, he insists, would have to be smart to go to Jupiter, and would probably go to college first. The argument has merits that Claire and Angela ignore in favor of papering the door of his room with pictures of Jupiter: crayon-drawn, ripped out of magazines, snipped out of her parents' dusty encyclopedia set and once out of a children's book about the solar system, stolen from her pediatrician's office. *How is the weather on Jupiter,* they ask him, though he never answers. Even now Claire recognizes renderings of the planet on sight, cloud-spotted, big and bright and banded, unspectacular until you consider all it holds in orbit.

The girl across the hall doesn't look like Angela at all. She is lighter-skinned and heavier-framed and her hair is wilder, deliberately unkempt in a way that would have made Angela's mother raise an eyebrow. Her name, Claire eventually remembers, is Carmen. By the time Claire arrives at her dorm room, on the second floor of a row of flat brick buildings that house a third of the small college's freshmen, there are forty-seven responses to and twenty-three retweets of Carmen's post. Claire is surprised by the level of interest, then annoyed by it. She distrusts collective anger; Claire's anger has always been her own. Claire prints a photo of the Confederate flag and scrawls in loopy cursive on the back *Welcome back! I hope you had a great vacation.* When she slips the photo under her door, she means to tell Carmen-the-hallmate to fuck off.

The next morning, the voicemail on her phone is full. She has 354 new emails, most of them from strangers. Across the hall, campus movers are noisily carting Carmen off to a new dorm. A reporter from the student paper, unable to reach her by phone, has slipped a note under Claire's door asking for an interview. She gathers from his note that several bloggers have now picked up both the bikini photo and Carmen's photo of last night's postcard. She has a text from Jackson. The hashtag #badbikiniideas turns up 137 results, including one with a picture of swastikas photoshopped into palm trees. An email marked URGENT informs her that her academic counselor would like to speak to her. In a separate URGENT email, the Office of Diversity requests her presence. Someone using the email fuckyoufuckyoufuckyou@gmail.com thinks she is a cunt. Twenty-two different rednecks from around the country have sent her supportive pictures of their penises.

It seems clear to Claire that most of the hall has taken Carmen's side. Claire forgoes both showering and breakfast, opting instead to burrow in her room. Someone from the campus TV station has interviewed Carmen and put the clip online. In the video, Carmen stands in front of Bell Hall, one of the upperclassmen dorms, where she has apparently been relocated. She wears a Dennis College sweatshirt and wraps her arms around herself. "Up until this happened, I thought she was nice," Carmen says. "We always smiled at each other in the hallway. But she put a hate symbol where I sleep, and she thought it was funny." There is genuine fear in her eyes, which startles Claire.

Sean has left an angry voicemail asking her what she was thinking. Claire does not call him back. Jackson texts again to tell her he knows she's busy but he thinks she's awesome. Claire turns her phone off and shuts her inbox tab and spends the afternoon watching online videos of singing goats. She is on her tenth goat video when the president of the campus Libertarians shows up at her door and introduces himself. His name is Robert and he lives two floors down, where he is the RA. He smiles like someone who has just won second place.

"I'm here in support of your right to free expression," he says.

"Don't take this personally," Claire says, "but unless you're here in support of my right to go to bed early, I don't care. I don't care about any of this. It was just a stupid picture."

"And you shouldn't be punished for it, but you will be if you don't get ahead of this. My friend lives in your hall and hadn't seen you all day, so we figured you were hiding out. We made you a care package."

The care package consists of a foil-wrapped caramel apple from the dining hall, which has declared it carnival week at the dessert buffet, and a book on libertarian philosophy, in case she's bored. Claire considers the offering. She is unimpressed, but also hungry, so she lets him in before his presence in her doorway becomes a spectacle.

"For the record," he says, "I'm not a big fan of the Confederate flag myself. The Confederacy was an all-around failure of military strategy. Lost the battle when they lost the ports, if you ask me. But

I'm no one to judge anyone for their support of lost causes. As far as I'm concerned, you can wear anything you want."

Claire gathers that she is supposed to find this endearing, that she is supposed to bite the apple and lick the caramel off of her lips and ask him to tell her more about military strategy and let him plan her own response campaign, and that sometime several hours into this discussion she is supposed to end up naked out of awe or gratitude. Instead she sets the book and the apple on her desk, politely thanks him, tells him she is tired and, when he finally leaves, locks the door behind him. She eats the apple alone in bed, figuring it can cover her meals for today and maybe tomorrow—she's still got some Burger Boy calories stored up.

When she checks her mail again before bed, there are another hundred emails. Her student account's address has been posted on several message boards and #clairewilliamsvacation ideas is a locally trending topic (Auschwitz, My Lai, Wounded Knee). She is losing on Twitter, but a group called Heritage Defenders has picked up the story and distributed it to their members, so at this point she has more supporters than detractors in her inbox. Cliff from Tennessee writes that when he was in college, his fraternity hosted an annual plantation ball for their sister sorority and everyone dressed in their frilly historical finest. One year he and his frat brother decided to cover the house's front lawn in thousands of cotton balls, so that when they posed for pictures on its steps, the college's mostly black janitorial staff could be seen in the background of the shot, cleaning up. *PC police tried to shut down our chapter for it, but we stayed strong. Hang in there!* the email concludes. There is an attachment: a picture of a boy, smiling wide in khaki pants with a button-down and vest, his arm around a laughing redhead in a corset and frilly hoop skirt, cotton balls blanketing the ground beneath them, a stooped black man in a green uniform sweeping up cotton in the background. He has a broom and a plastic trash can on wheels and his uniform is crisp and synthetic-shiny—there's nothing historically authentic about his presence, other than his blackness. She cannot see the man's face, but she can imagine it, and the imagining comes with a twinge of shame. But she is not Cliff, Claire reminds herself; Cliff thinking they are the same doesn't make them the same. The next email is angry and anonymous; its writer threatens to find out where she lives and set her on fire. Claire decides she will tell anyone looking where to find her. She prints out a copy of the flag and tapes it to her dorm window. She calls the reporter from the student paper back and tells him she is simply celebrating her heritage, like any number of groups on campus encourage students to do. She affects a lilt to say so, but as soon as the words are out of her mouth she realizes that the effect is a mistake. She doesn't sound like herself. She sounds like Angela.

In the second grade, sometime after discovering that Angela is black, Claire writes a poem about their friendship for Martin Luther King Day. Most of the lines she has forgotten over time, the exception being the dubious couplet *I judge her for her character / and so I'm never mad at her.* Their teacher likes the poem so much that she stages it for the school's February assembly, assigning them costumes: Claire a stiff black and white "patriot" uniform, complete with tri-cornered hat, and Angela a kente cloth dress. For the next three years of elementary school they are dragged out to recite the poem every February, a performance that Angela's mother permits only after mandating a costume change.

Claire and Angela forever. By adolescence they have both lucked into beauty, but neither has really noticed yet; there is so little room for interlopers in the tight world of their friendship that they are often each other's only mirrors. When they are swarmed by boys at the mall, Angela will name the game, *Wiccans* or *airheads* or *runaways,* and they will play their roles until the boys catch on that they are being teased. The last good summer, they go to camp together at a college a few hours south of Fairfax. Other girls they know go to horse camp or dance camp or Paris, but they go to what Angela calls nerd camp. Technically they are not at camp together, because nerd camp is separated by discipline—Angela is there for poetry and Claire is there for language immersion—and most of the time all Claire can do is shout dirty words in French from across the quad when she sees Angela's group trouping to lunch like a line of maudlin ducks. But in the evenings everyone socializes together, and as the weeks accumulate the counselors, who are only college age themselves, become lackadaisical about chaperoning and enforcing rules.

The third week of camp, a group escapes the confines of the

awkward Saturday dance, flees the repurposed assembly room with its drooping crepe paper, the flailing girls on the dance floor ringed by a wall of scared boys who will not ask anyone to dance and are not cool enough to pretend not to want to. One of the photography campers has a water bottle full of vodka and someone else has a Tic Tac case full of pills and at some point on their way to the most private patch of lawn they have taken pills and shots and then they are running through lawn sprinklers. Everything sizzles. When they kitten-pile into the grass, Claire turns to Angela. It is a love that requires touch, and so Claire snuggles against her, nuzzles into her neck to say it out loud against her. *Love love love.* Angela is her best friend, her other self. Someday they will go to college together. The world will unravel for them, fall at their feet.

A year later both of their mothers are sick. It starts slow, with both of them, and then quick quick quick. With Angela's mother it is a lump, with Claire's a vague malaise. We should have caught it sooner, Angela and Claire say to each other, over and over again, as though their mothers' bodies are their own. At first it seems as if, even in its cruelty, the universe is being kind, giving Claire a person to suffer through this with. Who else knows the smells of hospitals, the best way to sleep in a hospital chair, the flushed shame of disgust at cleaning up your mother's vomit, the palpitating anxiety of waking each morning thinking that this is the day something will go terribly wrong, the wince every time the phone rings while your mother is out of sight? Claire doesn't even have to give Angela words.

Aaron knows too. He is two grades ahead of them and supposed to be gone by now, but when his mother gets sick he defers his college acceptance. "Guess you were right," he says to Claire one afternoon, all of them in the basement watching daytime TV. "It's Jupiter for me after all." On-screen, two men on a court show are declared not the father, but one of them throws a chair at the other anyway.

"Jupiter would be better than this," says Claire.

One afternoon when their mothers are miserable and weary from chemo, Aaron finds Claire jogging in the rain, and pulls over for her. She cannot explain why, in spite of the storm, she hasn't turned around and gone back to the house—why she is, in fact, running in the wrong direction. When she gets into his car she sobs and then dry heaves and then follows Aaron into his house, where she strips and wraps herself in a throw blanket on the basement sofa and he makes her what his mother always made when they were kids, peppermint hot chocolate. It is out of season but still the best thing that has happened to her recently, though when she reaches for his body, feels the first thing she has felt in months that isn't slow death, that isn't bad either. He is still skinny, his hips slimmer than hers, so she slides underneath him; the weight of her, it seems, might smother him, but the weight of him tethers her to something. He is too gentle with her even after she tells him not to be; after he is finished she has to fake an orgasm to get him to stop insisting he'll make her come too. They don't love each other that way, or pretend to, so it isn't weird afterward, just a thing that happened because everyone is closer now. Claire and Angela can complete each other's thoughts. Claire and Aaron can be naked. Their mothers, who have only ever been casually friendly, now speak an intimate language of supplements and painkillers and hospitals and wig shops. Even their fathers have taken to neighborly gestures of solidarity.

Mrs. Hall has been Claire's second mother most of her life, and Claire fears that she will lose both her mother and her other mother, but it turns out that it is worse to lose only one, when it's the one that counts. Claire knows as soon as she feels it the first time that there is cruelty in this sentiment, so much cruelty that it surprises her, but that doesn't change the feeling. Mrs. Hall walks out of the hospital in full remission. Not a trace of the cancer left. Her hair grows back, soft and downy. She takes up running to drop the steroid weight. She is working up to marathons. Angela trains with her.

Claire's mother dies in July. They bury her on a damp Tuesday when the ground is slimy from an afternoon thunderstorm. She does not hear a word the priest says, thinking of her mother down there, rotting. For weeks before the funeral she has nightmares in which she is the one being buried, alive, the sickening smell of earth always waking her. At the funeral, Angela holds her hand and Aaron puts an arm around her shoulder. He is a perfect gentleman, but one with a mother, and Angela is a friend with a mother, and already they are galaxies away from Claire, alone in her grief.

*

Robert is not easily dissuaded. He returns the next morning with a sandwich, a task list, and backup in the form of a short, freckled sophomore named Alan. By noon, Robert and Alan have sold Claire on their strategy. They tell her putting the flag up was brilliant, and that three other students have taped Confederate flags to their doors in solidarity. One of them, Robert confesses, is Alan. They have drafted a statement for her and agreed to a town hall meeting on her behalf.

"You're not breaking any rules," says Robert.

"You have a right to celebrate where you came from," Alan says. "Just stick to that and you'll be good. Don't let them make you sound like a racist. Don't let them turn you into your own worst enemy."

Claire's mother came from Connecticut. She found even the northernmost reaches of the South vaguely suspect. She missed New England seafood and would occasionally, when feeling extravagant, pay an exorbitant amount to express mail herself a live lobster. Claire's father was originally from Minnesota. Before he retired to Florida, Northern Virginia was the furthest south any relative of hers had ever lived. For the moment, it feels like a miracle to her that no one has to know any of that.

Claire has skipped her Monday and Tuesday classes, but the next morning is the occasion of her mandated appointment with the Dean of Student Affairs, the University ombudswoman, her adviser, and the Vice Dean of Diversity. She showers for the first time this week, blow-dries and teases her hair. She wears a horrible mint green dress Puppy bought her for an engagement event that Claire refused to attend. She puts on her mother's pearls, takes them off, puts them on again.

It is a short walk to the ombudswoman's office, but by the time she gets there Claire is freezing, despite her coat, and wishes she had stopped for hot coffee in the student center. The office is wood paneled, newly renovated in a bright but bland way that invites you to imagine it decades later and dingy. Behind its windows, Claire knows, is the grace of woods in winter, but this morning the blinds are drawn. Claire's adviser, a twenty-something brunette whom Claire has met twice so far, gives her a tentative smile. At their first advising meeting, Claire noted that some of her student files were tagged with Post-it tabs. Claire's was tagged with red. The adviser was sheepish about it when Claire asked her what the color system was about, and Claire realized later that red must mean exactly what it looked like, though which disaster the adviser intended to mark, Claire still isn't sure. She doesn't trust a woman who puts literal red flags on things and expects people not to catch on. The ombudswoman is a middle-aged Puerto Rican woman in a drab pantsuit and the Dean of Student Affairs is a middle-aged white man wearing what Claire can only presume is one in an ongoing series of wacky ties, this one featuring cartoon insects. Together the two of them look like someone's embarrassing parents. The Vice Dean of Diversity, a thirty-something black man with dreadlocks and skinny jeans, has taken his own couch. He has his notepad out and does not meet Claire's eye.

"We can't force you to take down the flag," says the ombudswoman, once Claire is seated. "I want to be clear that that's not what we're here to do. Your decor is not in violation of any official university policy. But we can *ask* you, in the interest of the campus community and the well-being of your peers, to remove the flag from your window, and apologize to Miss Wilson. You will face a peer disciplinary hearing on the subject of your harassment of Miss Wilson, and I can only imagine that having made some attempt to rectify things will make a good impression on the disciplinary board."

"What harassment?"

"The threat you slipped under Miss Wilson's door," says the Vice Dean of Diversity.

"I threatened her to enjoy her vacation and feel welcomed back?"

"You left a Confederate flag postcard under her door," says the ombudswoman. "Aside from the fact that the image itself, sent to a black student in the place where she lives, could be construed as a threat on its own, you knew already that Miss Wilson felt distressed by the image and was wary of your affinity for it. She reasonably construed it as a threat and requested that the university relocate her."

"A threat of what? That I was going to legally enslave her? Secede from the hallway, declare war on her, and then lose?"

"Please take this seriously," says her adviser.

"I only knew that she was *distressed* by the flag because she put a picture of me on the internet to harass me. When is her disciplinary hearing?"

"You, or your friend, put your picture on the internet," says her adviser, exasperation creeping into her voice. "We stress during orientation that nothing on the internet is private, and we wish more of you took that seriously. So far as we can tell, no one from campus had anything to do with publicizing your contact information."

"So a hundred people can send me death threats, but I can't put a flag in my window."

"No one can send you death threats," says the ombudswoman. "If any of them are traced to this community, those students will be dealt with. And I would advise you to speak to both campus safety officers and the local police about any and all threats you receive. You're not on trial here. No one is out to get you, and none of us are the disciplinary board. It is our job to ask you nicely to make this easier on everyone. What you do with that is up to you."

"The first thing I would do, if I were you, is take advantage of our excellent history department and talk to a professor about why the image you've chosen to go to bat for is so hostile," says the Vice Dean of Diversity.

Claire focuses on the window blinds and takes a breath.

"I am familiar with the Civil War and the student code of conduct," she says finally. "But bless your hearts for being so helpful."

Claire leaves for lunch feeling in control of the situation for the first time, and feeling in control of the situation is luxurious enough that she grabs lunch in the student center, not minding the stares. In an otherwise uneventful lit class, the professor seems confused by her accent, but Claire doesn't talk enough for anyone to be certain she didn't sound like that before. She heads back to her dorm giddy with relief.

When she first sees the photograph, it takes her a full minute to connect it to herself. One of the blogs that has taken to relentlessly covering the story and recommends she be expelled has posted a photo from the police file. There is her smashed-up car. There is a senior yearbook photo of Aaron. The article only has pieces of the story. Claire reads it to see if the Halls—any of them, all of them, Angela—have made any comment. The article says they cannot be reached.

It is November of senior year and Claire is hanging out with a girl named Seraphin, as in, that is her actual given name, which never stops being hilarious. Or, Claire was hanging out with Seraphin, but who knows where Seraphin is now—her ex-boyfriend is back in town for Thanksgiving weekend and invited them to this party. Claire is three? Four? Four drinks in to something bright pink that the host calls panty-dropper punch, one drink for every month her mother has been dead so far. She still thinks of it that way, as in: so far, her mother is still dead, but that could change any day now, any moment her mother could walk in and demand to know what she is doing, and what she has been doing, tonight, is drinking. Grief has a palpable quality, and it is all she can feel unless she's making an active effort to feel something else. Tonight she is feeling drunk—pink and punchy and panty-dropping, because all of those things mean she is not at home, where Puppy has already strutted into the space her mother left behind with such velocity that it's clear to Claire that her father checked out well before her mother did.

Claire is still wearing panties, so far; she has that going for her, though she has held on to them only barely after an aborted tryst with a boy she met in the laundry room. She is barefoot, which she realizes only when something sharp startles her, which she has already forgotten by the time she gets to the other side of the kitchen and braces herself against the counter, but remembers again when she lifts her head and sees a streak of blood on the kitchen floor. Shoes, she is thinking, when she hears her name.

It shouldn't surprise her that Aaron is there. He has finally gone to college, but it is Thanksgiving, and there is so much to be thankful for in that house, so of course Aaron is back. He looks well. The freshman fifteen suit him. There is a girl on his arm Claire has never seen before—she is curly haired and caramel colored, and he whispers something into her ear that causes her to reluctantly leave them alone in the kitchen. So now Claire doesn't know two things, where her shoes are or who this Aaron is who has a life she knows nothing about. It has been months since she has spoken to either sibling. There is so much she wouldn't know about Aaron now, and yet standing in front of her he is a flip book of all the other Aarons she has known, from *rotten rotten rotten Jupiter Jupiter Jupiter* through last year in the basement, the grip of his palm on her hip.

"Claire?" he says. "You okay?"

"I'm fucking amazing," says Claire.

"You don't look good. Do you need me to call Angela?"

"For what? We don't talk."

"She's upset about that, you know. She has no idea why you won't talk to her."

"Because every time I see her I want to tell her I'm sorry your mother is alive, because it reminds me that mine is dead."

Aaron winces. He takes a nervous sip from his red cup before looking at her again.

"That's fucked up, Claire. My mom misses you too. You're messed up right now, I get that, but at some point you're going to have to stop making it worse."

"I'm not making it worse. I'm looking for my shoes."

"Where did you leave them?"

"Maybe with Brendan. He's in the laundry room. Probably still putting his pants on."

"Who's Brendan?"

"Who is anybody, anyway? Who are *you?*"

"Claire, enough. I'm taking you home, okay?"

There is something firm and brotherly in his tone and it infuriates her. She shakes her head, but he ignores her and comes close enough that he could touch her if he stretched out his arm. Claire lets out a scream that startles him into momentary retreat, a bestial noise she has been holding in for months. While Aaron is deciding what to do next, she is around him and out the door, the grass cold and wet on her feet. By the time he catches up with her, she is climbing into the driver's seat of her car. Claire leans her head against the steering wheel, suddenly exhausted. Aaron sighs from outside her open door. He hesitates for a minute, then hoists her over his shoulder and carries her around to the passenger side.

"Let's go home," he says.

She doesn't know whether he means her home, or his home, but she is too tired to protest. Let him deliver her to her father's doorstep or the Halls' guest room, let someone who is still alive yell at her the way her mother is yelling in her head all the time. She presses her temple to the window and starts to fade out, only barely aware of Aaron digging through her purse for her keys and settling in behind the wheel, only barely hearing the yelling coming from somewhere nearby.

The person yelling is Seraphin's current boyfriend, who is pissed that Seraphin went to her ex's party and invited him as an afterthought. Claire knows him, but not well. He's a little buzzed from pregaming but mostly he's angry, so when he sees, as he tells the police later, *a huge black guy* pulling Claire out of her car and rummaging through her purse and driving her away, he is alarmed enough that he and his friends get back in their car and follow Claire's, alarmed enough to call the cops while they're driving.

Claire sleeps through it at the time: Aaron, unnerved by the car behind him, flooring the accelerator; Seraphin's boyfriend tailgating, flashing his brights, then the car full of boys pulling alongside them, his friends throwing a soda bottle and yelling at Aaron to stop. Aaron only goes faster, losing them for a moment, then, less than a mile from their houses, turning onto Cleveland Street at such speed that he spins out and the car flips into the trees. Claire wakes up, vaguely, to sirens, and then for real, in the hospital, where she has a concussion and a hangover and a starring role in someone else's rescue story.

Aaron is dead. By the time Claire is awake enough to be aware of this, it has already been determined that he was not a stranger, that he was just above the legal limit, that people saw him chase her out of the party after she screamed, that she was passed out in her own car. The people who give him the benefit of the doubt mostly feel themselves to be magnanimous.

"He should have just pulled over and explained," Seraphin will say sadly a few weeks later, and Claire will nod, and Seraphin will be quoted saying that in the paper when the *Post* runs an article about the accident's aftermath. Mrs. Hall will tell the reporter that a black boy doesn't get out of the car at night in the woods for a car full of angry white boys in Virginia. Claire's father will read the paper and say it's not the 1950s.

It isn't, it's the first decade of the new millennium, but Claire's father is a lawyer, and Seraphin's boyfriend's father is Claire's father's golf partner. No one is assigned any legal responsibility for the accident. The Halls' lawsuit is dismissed before Claire has to say anything in public. It's Angela who won't talk to her now, and the tenth time Mrs. Hall knocks on their front door and no one answers, Claire's father gets a restraining order. Claire tells the reporter Aaron was a friend, that she was drunk and he was taking her home, but the bones of that story don't convince anyone it wasn't all, at best, a tragic misunderstanding; at worst, a danger she didn't see coming. Claire tells the reporter some innocuous nice thing about Seraphin's boyfriend, and the paper calls him one of her best friends, after which she stops trying to explain.

The Halls rent out their house for the spring and Angela finishes her senior year at a private school closer to DC. When Claire sees them rolling their suitcases out to the car, preparing to follow their moving van, she feels shame and relief, in which order she cannot say. Claire rides to prom in a limo with Seraphin and her boyfriend and a date whose name she forgets soon after. A month later the house Claire grew up in is on the market and her father and Puppy are formally engaged. Three months after that she is gone, tucked away at a small liberal arts college where no one has ever met her and anything is possible.

Robert is at her dorm door again. She sees herself as he sees her, a problem to be solved. He is logic; she is x. The internet's discovery of the accident has driven the attention to a pitched furor. He wants to prepare her for the town hall that has been called regarding her continued presence on campus. Claire is not even sure she likes Robert, let alone trusts him, but she tells him everything. Someone has found a photograph of Aaron, the one that ran with his obituary. His smile melts into the part of Claire that still remembers when he was missing his two front teeth.

Aaron's favorite joke:

Knock Knock
Who's there?
Anticipation
Anticipation who?
. . .
Who?
. . . . . .

It takes Claire and Angela more than a year to stop falling for it, to realize that the joke is their own impatience, not a punchline he's been holding out on them. Even as teenagers, they sometimes take the bait; they don't put it past him to have been waiting years for the right moment of revelation, for the payoff they've been promised.

The town hall is held in the library's rotunda. The evening has been devised as an open mic, moderated by the Vice Dean of Diversity and the Dean of Students. People who do not wish to speak may make comments on notecards and drop them in boxes at the end of each row. The cards will be periodically collected and read aloud. Robert has provided Claire with an annotated list of episodes of Confederate valor or sacrifice, anything she might say the flag stands for, to her. She scans it for highlights: *Albert Johnson, who sent his personal doctors to treat the injured Union soldiers while he bled out on the battlefield—don't mention that he probably didn't know he was shot—the point is a crueler man might have lived. 3,200 African-American Confederate veterans. Such a young army; so many dead boys.*

Claire is wearing a dress marked with yellow flowers. The first person to speak is a weepy white sophomore boy, who expresses how distraught he is to be on a campus that has been touched by hate and personally apologizes to the black students on campus, which apology takes the full remaining three minutes of his allotted time. Claire watches Carmen, who does not look in her direction. Carmen is surrounded by two full rows of black students, more black people than Claire has ever seen on campus before —maybe, it occurs to her, more black people than Claire has ever seen at once in her life. None of them stand to speak. A boy in a vest and fedora approaches the microphone and dramatically reads the lyrics of "Sweet Home Alabama." No one can determine whether or not he is being ironic.

Robert has told Claire to wait for as close to the end as possible, to let everyone rage against her and then win with the last word. Claire waits.

She is only supposed to talk about Aaron if somebody asks. She is supposed to say accident as many times as she possibly can. She is supposed to say that he was one of her best friends and she is insulted by any speculation to the contrary. She has practiced saying these things as truths and saying them as lies. I killed someone. I loved him. I walked away. A warped version of that icebreaker game. Two truths and a lie, or two lies and a truth.

After the boy in the fedora finishes, two other white students speak, and then the microphone stands unattended. None of the black students move. At first Claire thinks their silence is hesitation, but everyone remains still long beyond awkwardness—ten minutes, exactly. One by one the black students stand. They hand their notecards to the Dean of Students, and then they leave. The Dean turns over card after card after card; all of them are blank.

Handfuls of white students begin to stand, gather their things, and file out behind them. Robert is scribbling a note.

Claire has come prepared for an argument. She does not know how to resist this enveloping silence. It is strategic. It hums in her head. But the room is still half full. The microphone is still on. There are three reporters from the student paper, and ten from national news outlets. There are still ten feet between her and the echoing sound of her own voice, telling her she can still be anybody she wants to.

A History of China

FROM *Ploughshares: Solos Omnibus*

Dixie

EVERY YEAR AT the family reunion—before Cousin Monique comes to your rescue—the uncles sit back in their folding chairs and napkin-necks and ask about your father. They take you in with age-soggy eyes, as you stand before them in a floppy blouson and skirt. You look different now than you did in 1970 or 1981 or 1997—though you still have what lyrical Aunt Vitrine calls your *swan quality*. Cousin Monique had wanted to ditch the reunion for the shopping mall in Auntsville; she has always been your wings and, as such, was born to ignore the uncles: in 1970, she set fire to the truck belonging to one uncle and claimed it was lightning; in 1981, she put Ex-Lax in their pound cake frosting. Now she is nowhere to be seen. There's no reason we can't have fun at the reunion, you told her the night before, when she picked you up at Raleigh Airport. You're right, Monique replied, grinning in the dark, the car pulling faster and faster along the blind curves of the road. Slave food and rockheads. I don't see why that would in any way be an obstacle to fun, cousin.

Your blouson sticks to your skin. The uncles lean forward as if to smell you—girls here only wear that kind of top if they are in trouble—but gradually their eyes drift over the dirt hills across the street, behind the Baptist church. They don't care if you're like every other girl down here: fast Monique and her sisters Mae and Wanita and Tarnisha and Lynette. Her cousins Meggie and Mercy and Shawnelle and Winsome. Their kids LaDonna and Kelly and

Juan and Quanasia and Cedric and Colin. Tons more. Monique's mom had given her a fancy name in the hopes that she would be better than the rest. But look what happened, your father once remarked. 1981? 1982?

The uncles want news about him. Word on the road is that their nephew wants to return to his roots in North Carolina. The prodigal son returning—what a laugh, the uncles concur.

You stretch your eyes across the property, exasperating because it is huge and small at the same time and fills you with a familiar hopelessness. Monique and a friend were supposed to meet you at dawn. You all were supposed to slip out of your respective houses (you are staying with Aunt Nephronia, and Monique and Kate are, of course, staying with Monique's mom, Vitrine, two houses down; as a child, this road of relatives fascinated you)—but you overslept, in part due to the brutally hot North Carolina night, in part due to your tears. Can a dead person ever change? Can time remove a tiger's stripes? Those foolish questions made you weep in your sleep last night; in the days before your father died, you'd been too stingy to say goodbye.

The uncles look at you and say, Your daddy ain't set foot here in near twenty years. But tell him we forgive him if he wants.

You need to tell them that he somehow finagled all the land from Great-Grandma Elldine and left it all to you in a will. Something about an unpaid loan, the land not being worth spit. The letter actually read, But why not enjoy it as your own, Sasha Jean. I utterly wish I could give you more.

The uncles are suddenly worked up in clammy anger.

How come he don't answer when Vitrine call? That ain't no way to be treating your one sister on this earth!

He always thought he was the best at checkers. Well, he got another thing coming.

If he thinking about parking that damn Cadillac in my yard again, he even crazier.

That sucker!

You'd had a dream, coming back to the folks in North Carolina: that you'd get a chance to talk smoothly after they all finished eating and were in good spirits; that you'd lay out everything Bobby Lee's scribbled will said, though in reality it was vague, not more than four sentences. The sun wouldn't be too hot and the children wouldn't be too unruly. Dogs, as they happened to wander

back and forth from each house, would not frighten you with their
larva-laden ears. This was your dream. In reality, you can't recall
a single time that the uncles, in their walking days, didn't eventually get smashed drunk and start fighting with the women. The
pig, burnt to a crisp on the outside but pink as a newborn on the
inside, would turn your stomach. The same gospel songs would be
sung, the same protests as to who would hold the mic, who would
gather the children from their hiding places and force them to
sing. It's not Sunday, one of them would say, relenting under a
smack upside the head. How could your dream stand up to these
details? Your dream was like a story that was told in the pages of
some huge, incomprehensible book, spread out on a lemon-wax
table in the only good part of someone's house or trailer. Everyone
sensed it was there but knew how to avoid it.

That and still: you want to find the right time to tell them—
what better place for sad family news than at a reunion?—and
you're hoping that since it didn't happen last night (your arrival at
Nephronia's, with glasses of Harveys Bristol Cream) or this morning (gluten-free breakfast crepes—à la the Food Network—with
Vitrine), a suitable moment will come today.

Everyone is in the backyard of Grandma Elldine's decrepit Victorian. Random picnic tables have been set out and on them, flies
chill over Tupperwares of mac salad and wings. Curlyhead, fever-
few, and false foxglove dot the perimeter but everyone treats them
like weeds. Already at eleven in the morning, it is 90 degrees; the
relatives fan themselves with their hands until someone drags out
a standing General Electric and plugs it (via two extension cords)
into an unseen outlet.

I hope my brother don't think we still in the prehistoric days,
Aunt Vitrine had said at the breakfast table, her gray wig toppling.
I'm learning to eat healthy, Sasha Jean. Buttermilk, no heavy
cream. You go back and tell my brother that for me. We all gone
live forever, like it or not.

In reality, it should be easy to tell everyone that your father died
(in his armchair, surrounded only by his home healthcare aide
and *General Hospital* playing on the tablet in her hands). Perhaps
they will expect you to cry, and then for you to expect them to
cry back. Ancient Hattie Mabel carries a mic (via three extension
cords) out to the middle of the yard, preparing to gospel. We can
forgive, the uncles say. But hell if we can forget.

You are silent; handed a plate of beans and rice by a young boy; pushed into a chair next to the uncles, in direct sunlight. You mention that your daddy plans on coming down to the reunion next year. That he misses everyone and longs for the red earth of his childhood. The uncles raise their brows and laugh. They tell you, don't lie. Ancient Hattie Mabel removes her hand from your shoulders and starts in with "The Old Rugged Cross." You notice that she still has on her overnight curlers, that her eyes are closed as she sways from side to side, as if in a godly stew. The fragrance of the beans and rice is heavy for this time of day, but still you lift a fork. The uncles say they've never known you to be untrue.

They have heard rumors all these years. Your father, the big gambler, every weekend in Las Vegas, thousands lost. Your father, owner of not one but two homes in Los Angeles. Your father, the lady's man. He never paid child support. He called himself a minister on his tax forms and got caught by the government people. He tried talking Grandma Elldine into selling him this property just before she went into Pine Haven Home but luckily she resisted his advances. He wanted to tear down the old Victorian the first chance he got.

He got called on by the cops one time for "untoward deviousness." He never said *I'm sorry* to anyone like he meant it.

The uncles tell you not to lie. Ain't no way he's coming back. Our Bobby Lee is gone for good.

Chinet

The will—scribbled on a yellow legal pad and witnessed by *Faith Akintola, Dept. of Aging Adult Services, Los Angeles County*—indicates that you're supposed to evict them. That you're supposed to raze everything and then build a real house here, with functioning plumbing and privacy windows. Sit on your newly built porch and look out over the chicken hills across the street and invite loads of educated folks over for drinks and perhaps to hear those "short stories" you've been publishing in graduate school—you can read them aloud (that is, your father last said, if they really want to sit around on a firefly night and listen to that crap). You're supposed to recall childhood summers here, laughing in Great-Grandma Elldine's post bed with Monique while the other children went to work tobacco. (Why not make a story out of that, he demanded. Monique and her slut self. Lazy, that's all. Monique's sisters and their slut selves—chasing men like firehouse dogs. Those girls belonged to nobody and look where that got them. Four kids apiece and no guardian in sight.) You're supposed to see why he turned out the way he did, and why you will never go down that particular path. Never ever. (You belong to me. My *favorite*. Forgive me. Forever and ever.)

Royalton Japan Blue

In 1961, your father stood outside a small white house on a street empty of trees. He was bowing his head, quite uncharacteristic. But his mind went like: Thank you, God, for this is not Carolina red dirt or Carolina sun. Trees can be planted if people need them, and churches can be fucking avoided by simply watching the ball game on TV.

Your father rocked a carriage with one hand while looking over a brochure handed to him by the real estate agent. *Pomegranate Estates*, it read. *Take a Bite of This Fruit.*

In 1961, the real estate agent had called this Long Island neighborhood a "colored development," shying away from words like *community* or *housing project*, as he didn't want your father—already coming across as uppity—to get the wrong idea. These were normal houses for normal people, the agent claimed—some even had wooden shingles. People watered lawns here, drove cars into proper driveways. There would be no fists here, no spirituals or arms linked in arms or fires or Jackson Five records or Aretha Franklin passion in this part of Pomegranate Village. The agent waved his hand over the sea of three-bedroom-plus-den Cape Cods (there were actually thirty-five on this cul-de-sac) and said, If you all want something to do, think about painting the shutters a different color, or planting a little garden or something. No vegetables, no livestock, no front yard clotheslines. Just a row of marigolds or begonias.

Tell your closest friends, the brochure encouraged.

In the yard of your soon-to-be new house, your father ignored the agent. His job at that particular moment was to keep his eye on the carriage in which you lay. The sun beamed straight into your

eyes, and you bawled; the carriage was a foot away from a struggling maple sapling, but your father made no attempt to wheel you
into that bit of shade. He was, instead, listening for your mother.

Who was walking around the yard, wringing her hands, not believing her luck. Not only did the house have more than one bedroom and a bathtub and basement, it had all this land. Nearly a
fifth of an acre. She imagined planting the gooseberries and potatoes she'd smuggled from her last trip home to Laboe. One patch
here, another here, near the culvert. There was that annoying maple sapling in the front yard by the curb, but in the backyard, there
was nothing. Plenty of room for German food.

In 1971, your mother announced that she hated trees.

Rosenthal

You struggle to eat the beans and rice, only to have Aunt Cathy
tuck a bowl of grits and eggs into your lap. For later, she says, wink-
ing. From the corner of your eye you notice Monique, her brown
skin glistening with baby oil, hurrying in a dress and bare feet.
There was that one time, in 1981, when she duct-taped shut the
door to the church and wouldn't let them out for over an hour.
In 1982, she stole seven dump cakes from the church basement
breakfast and threw them into the branches of the tall pines.

She is flying like a pterodactyl now, large brown wings out-
stretched in love. She is coming for you.

Corning Centura

I love it, your mother cried, walking away from the men and the
carriage toward the side of the house. There were huge lilac trees
and a gutsy chain-link fence running from front to back. When
can we move in, she cried, without once turning her head.

Just out of sight of the men, her hands went back into her coat
pocket; she, too, began a quiet prayer. The house was a miracle—it
would be *her miracle*. It was close to the others. It looked exactly
like the others. Likely, when you opened every door, you saw the
same walls, you noticed that the bathroom was in the same place,
the kitchen fan made the same noise. But how fantastic was that?

No useless standing out or drawing attention to the wrong things. Being the same meant being the same.

Your mother wandered back toward the front yard. I love this place, Bob, she whispered. Please say we never leave.

Elspeth, he murmured. His hand on the carriage, the baby that was you still bawling.

The real estate agent cleared his throat. It was not often that he saw a black man hold a white woman in his arms and live to tell about it. His own family was Connecticut stock by way of Georgia and New Mexico. We'll take it, your father announced. Bring me the papers.

The agent again looked at him funny; just what did this colored man think, using a phrase like that? *Bring me*—what was he, the fucking King of Siam?

But still, the agent didn't resist. That afternoon the three of them sat together in the office on Main Street in Pomegranate Village and signed the papers. In the carriage, you bawled even further.

Aztec Melmac

What your father has left you is a deed to these dusty thirty-seven acres, populated by fallen-down prefabs and trailers, at least seven in total, and at the end of the road, a rusted old church. Faith Akintola sent you a letter with a copy of the signed will you've carried in your purse; the letter (dictated, in fact, to the aide during commercials) continued:

> I'm sorry for
> any way you thought I might
> have hurt you. I love you, Daddy.
> With all my heart. Doesn't life go on?

Monique is scowling at the uncles. Why you talking to these old skunks? she asks, yanking you toward the road. Her face is riddled with egg white, remnants of an acne cure she'd applied earlier that morning. Unlike almost everyone here, she is as slim as a model. Her skin bakes underneath your hand into pure chocolate custard.

You tell her you were just making small talk.

Small talk, Monique sighs, wincing. Those suckers don't know nothing about no small talk. Try making BIG talk and see what happens.

Big talk?

They think they doing you a favor when in reality it's no way to treat a baby girl they supposed to be loving. They think they doing you a favor. I wish I could kill them all.

When you get to the roadside, you vomit in an echinacea bush.

Let it out, don't be afraid, Monique whispers, lifting your sweaty hair from your shoulder. She giggles, but the pulse of her hand is soothing. You knocked up, Sasha Jean? I would be so happy. You don't know how long I been waiting to say to you: JOIN THE CLUB.

(Re: the uncles: later she will claim what she was talking about was the time the uncles were asked to watch her oldest daughters —Monique was doing two shifts at Target—but then fell asleep and let the baby girls wander off down the road—almost two miles on their own. She wanted to kick them in the dick, hurt them so they'd stay awake forever, damn stupid talkers.)

What's going on? Monique asks, as you rest against an oak stump. She smiles. In 1981, she poured sugar in various gas tanks, and then told the uncles it was a case of ornery white men. Girl, it's nothing to be ashamed of, she whispers, clasping your face between her hands. You attempt to smile an answer, but then the bile comes back up. Monique looks into your eyes, unwavering. Exactly what kind of bun, she asks, do you have in your oven?

Melitta

There was a story before Long Island. In it, El boarded the plane with the Melitta in her suitcase.

She'd never been on a plane before, had never been spoken to by a stewardess bearing peanuts and napkins, had never left her home in the night like some common criminal. The stewardess brought around a cart of drinks, but El shook her head; all she could think of was Bobby, waiting for her at the end of the line, opening his arms to her so that she could melt inside. Liquor on the breath could possibly prevent that melting. The third time around, however, El gave in and said she would just adore a gin and tonic. She'd been gone from the Laboe farm for a little over

six hours. Though her suitcase—the one from her dead father—
was stowed solidly underneath her seat, she imagined she could
hear the Melitta dishes clinking softly against each other.

El had taken the dishes in the middle of the night as her mother
slept. She'd lifted the tea and coffee pots from the cabinet in the
basement kitchen and wrapped them in a cotton nightgown,
stowed the cake platter at the bottom of the suitcase, hoping the
cushioned lining would prevent it from breaking. During the
fourth gin and tonic, El gazed again out the window and imagined
she saw the chocolate-wafer edge of America.

They landed sometime in the early day. The waiting room was
loud, strewn with paper cups and newspapers. The sounds of
planes overhead rattled the chairs. She stood looking for help, for
Bobby, but there was nothing. Eventually, El slumped into a chair
attached to a miniature TV; she was hungry and thirsty and tired.
To watch the television cost two quarters per fifteen minutes, but
since Bob had told her she wouldn't need any money once she arrived, she'd only packed an emergency five-mark bill.

The clock on the wall moved slowly; next thing, it was eight and
the sky outside the plate glass was pure black. The janitor sweeping
at her feet told her it was time to close this waiting area, that she
would have to go to Arrivals. He showed her to the escalator. Good
luck, ma'am, don't let nothing happen to you.

But she nearly toppled down the moving stairs. Her suitcase
seemed heavier than before.

She felt tears form. This country, it was so loud, so ugly, so wildly
placid. She wanted to find a stewardess and ask how she could return to Germany—to Laboe on the Baltic—because was this how
they did things in America? The man who swore his devotion—
vanished like a ghost?

At the bottom of the moving stairs, she quickly saw Bob. *Now Elspeth.*

He looked much different than she'd imagined him since their
fifth meeting five months ago: gaunt, mustached, palpable. No
longer Bobby Lee—she saw immediately that he was to be called
Bob. *Now Elspeth.*

He reached out a hand to her. No embrace, no tongue in her
ear, no touch of her breasts. In her mind they were practically married, she'd run away to be with him, had taken her future wedding
dishes without permission. She expected Bob would at least put

his hand under her elbow, leading her the correct way into the future. But instead, he walked in front of her toward the luggage carousel; and when they got there and stood side by side, and she reached over to caress his cheek, Bob stepped back and frowned. *Now Elspeth.* Isn't it enough you made me look all over the damn airport for you? Don't you know I have better things to do? Plus, I had to get up and go to work this morning, unlike some people I know who spend their days drinking cocktails on Lufthansa jets.

His voice was so different from the voice he'd used in the aerograms, the one that began each letter with *Baby* or *Darling* or *Sugarpie* and ended with *Forever Yours*. His last letter, dated April 29, 1961, had begun *Dear Sugarpie, I saw you in my dreams last night.* As the luggage began to tumble onto the carousel, Bob took out a cigarette. Life in America was tough, he said, did she think she could make it? Did she bring any money? If she didn't think she could make it, she might as well get back on the plane.

El didn't know why they stood there; she already had the yellow suitcase in hand. As if reading her thoughts, Bob quickly tossed his cigarette. He led her to the exit by her hand. All the while never looking her directly in the face. Had she ever seen a cockroach, he asked, because his mother's apartment, it was a cockroach paradise. His mother's apartment—you couldn't call it a honeymoon suite unless you were crazy—was only one bedroom, with him on the couch, and collards and chicken-fried steak three times a week. Pork chops and gospel radio on Sunday. He hated it, sometimes. But that was what was on the table.

Did she think she could handle that—black life?

Baby, we will live off a love, the letter from April 29 insisted.

Bob wiped his forehead with his shoulder, and El then noticed the large perspiration stains in the armpits. He noticed her looking. Been hot as hell, he said. Here in America, summer's no joke. My mother has a Westinghouse fan, yes. But no air-conditioning, if that's what you're expecting.

The letter from April 29 had ended with the words *I don't know if you will want me once you are on these shores, but I will pray every day that you will. Forever Yours.*

They walked out to the parking lot under a half moon. Bob swung the suitcase into the trunk, and just then she thought she heard the platter crack, the little lids of the coffee and tea pots clatter together. What in the hell you got in there, Bob asked, laughing, as he started the car.

The drive was bland, a few lights sparkling over Jamaica Bay.

Corelle

Monique makes sure you can stand on your own (how no one else saw you throw up is a mystery) and then leans you against a pine tree, saying she has to go back inside for just a minute; she's afraid Kate (a white girl from Duke who has *forever and a day* wanted to experience *this kind* of family reunion) might have fallen prey to her cousin Stanley. You haven't seen Stanley in years, Monique whispers. But he's still the same. Thinks he's gone get his hands on Kate. But that'll only happen after I get *my* hands on her.

You'll love Kate, she says. You're different.

She hurries off in a cloud of roadside dust and pollen. You imagine Monique finding her white lover and kissing her under a pile of stale pillows, in a wrought-iron bed, under dozens of family photographs—the ancestors. Forgetting about you for whole hours. When you attend their commitment ceremony three years later—only one uncle will come to the church where two females are saying "I do"—you notice the same crystals of love in her eyes, the same spike of deliverance as you see on this day, the last reunion you'll ever attend.

Dime Savings Bank Account-Opener Bonus Set

You were ten years old when you told your mother about the nighttime touching. She rolled her eyes into her head, as if this were the straw that literally broke the camel's back. How could he do this to me? she blurted. Then: Oh, baby.

It was nothing more than a few weeks' worth of touching. The moon came out from your Mother Goose window and stared in shock. His finger didn't even make it in all the way. Do you like this, your father asked. No, you answered. It took another five and a half weeks for him to get that through his head.

Ach du meine Güte! Heaven, hear me.

Your mother said she would leave him, take you and your brothers back to Germany. There was no way she could stay with a child molester. A monster.

Heaven, don't stop hearing me!

But then weeks, more than a year passed.

Ovenware Brown Ten Piece

When they entered his mother's apartment on Hoyt Street, Bob set the suitcase down. The shower was running, and a woman's voice sang the sweetest melody El had ever heard. *The only way that we can survive, we need the Lord on our side!*

Bob kissed El on her forehead and said, More of this later; he pointed to his lips. The woman in the shower called out to Bob to make his girl comfortable.

Bob took the salami out of the suitcase, holding it to the ceiling. You know, he said, we got food over here too. No need to drag this sucker clear across the world. This here salami is Italian food. What's a German girl doing with Italian food?

El fell on the plastic slipcovered couch and rubbed her eyes. Her stomach growled. And she fell into a faint, a short deep sleep. No dreams whatsoever. Minutes later she woke up to Bob's mother applying a cold washcloth to her face. *What did you eat, baby? You bony as a bird.*

El slowly raised herself and shook her head; she didn't know enough English without her pocket dictionary to tell the woman that in fact the only thing she'd eaten all day was four gin and tonics. I got a pork chop in the icebox, his mother said. Let me go and heat it up, baby.

Bob turned away. But El could see the Army still left over in his bones and she felt his anger. Mama, he said. We don't want that country food. Let me show my girl what we got to offer in Brooklyn!

And despite his mother's protests, he lugged El back out in the car again; it was nearly 11. Her eyes were fully open as she rolled down the window. By now, her mother would probably be pulling her hair out, weeping with utter and relentless despair. That's how El liked to imagine her: writhing in regret. Her mother had once denied knowing that the Jewish girls who came by after the war were starving. They looked fine to me, she'd said, giving all the

crab apples to the horses. Bob pulled into a restaurant that had a
window on its side and a sullen girl stuck in that window. *Hello my
name is Maryann and welcome to Jack in the Box and can I take your order?* Bob grinned at the girl, then turned back to El; Dry your eyes,
girl, he said. You making me look bad.

They ate in the car while listening to Ray Charles on the radio.
When they got home, his mother greeted them at the door in a
caftan gown. El had never seen anyone so smart, a woman who
looked like a magazine. You will make my son very happy, Barbara
said. She kissed El's ears with lips that felt like firm pin cushions.
Bob's mother was thirty-six years old.

She served El a slice of sweet potato pie on a chipped plate
with cornflowers around the edge and spread out a blanket on the
couch. It's not a fold-out but I hope you will be comfortable, she
said. I don't believe in young folks pretending marriage. It's my
church upbringing, but don't even mention the word church to
Bob! Do, and he'll give you a mouthful.

She embraced her full-on, a mother's hug. Bob's told me only
a little about you, so tomorrow I hope you'll fill in all the blanks,
Barbara said. And that was the very last thing El heard.

She felt herself lifted into the air. She felt herself descending
into the ground. After so many years of no dreams, she was bom-
barded that night by pictures she hadn't seen for ages. Cows, fires,
birch trees, coins.

Dreams are nothing but random images, an elderly Polish doctor would tell her years later. This is how they do things in America.

Fiestaware

They want to be nice to you, all these relatives at the reunion in
Spring Hope. Cleopatra and Susie and Katrina and Shequanna
and Betty. Horace and Clotilda and Tanya and Dove. They want
to be nice, in spite of the way your eyes are your father's eyes,
your nose flat brown and wide as his. When you talk, even the
younger cousins say they can hear Cousin Bobby's voice come alive
in yours. You know these kids have never met him, that they only
know him from tall tales. Still, you laugh when they say that if he
were to step foot on Grandma Elldine's land, they would kill him
with a hatchet.

They can't imagine, these young cousins say, what it would be like to live in California and never see North Carolina again.

No, they will have to carry me out, one eight-year-old boy announces.

The sun is starting to set over the field. You breathe in this air: a hint of sulfuric chicken farm, a drying watering hole but evergreens as far as the nose can smell. A hint of thimbleweed out the corner of your eye.

You loom alone at the picnic tables like an unlit candle. The women and the uncles are discussing an evening service at the Baptist church. Ancient Hattie Mabel wonders if you'd like to come. It's about time you learned the words to all the songs they sing.

But then, deus ex machina, Cousin Meggie comes running from her pickup. A giant cross plops between her breasts.

Sasha Jean, she cries. I been praying you wouldn't forget me!

1964 World's Fair Commemorative

She is as round as the proverbial barrel, and yet she moves storklike from the truck between the fading aunts and uncles. You've thought about her for years but haven't picked up a pen or tapped on a keyboard. What would those hicks have to say to you? your father once asked. What would they have to say to anybody?

You stopped seeing him, despite his letters, his infrequent calls to your college dorm, your first apartment in Manhattan, your sublet in the Bronx. When you turned eighteen, you announced you were never going to see him again, and he laughed. Sasha, he said. People make mistakes. People get over things. It's the course of life. Grudges are about as real as cotton candy.

But you kept true to your word. Years passed—and then you received notice that he'd died in his sleep. Next to Faith Akintola. In front of her *favorite* show: Luke and Laura, escaping on foot over the top of a jetliner. In the middle of the ocean. During a lunar eclipse.

Meggie squashes you with treacly hugs, doesn't wait for any answers before immediately asking after your mom. Her skin is as light as a white person's; her eyes, round and small (Mongoloid, your father once said), literally sparkle as she talks. She says your mom's name, and her face is quickly awash in tears—she apologizes for not sending any kind of note when she heard of your mother's death. Victuals always heal a broken heart, she says, leading you to the table with the hot sauce steak and loading another plate high. Crispy kale and artichoke hearts. You want to tell Meggie that now you officially belong to her, to them—what use is a girl without a parent to stake her in the landscape? But she is eyeing you up and down; too skinny, she concludes. Your mama would not be happy.

When you shake your head, Meggie frowns. Your mama was the best thing that ever happened to this earth, she says, waving over Aunt Quincy and her bowl of spicy pork barbecue.

Hutschenreuther

El awoke the next Brooklyn morning not on the sofa but on a huge double bed. Striped sheets had crumpled under her armpits; a thin blanket straggled at her feet. El felt a terrible, lovely ache in her shoulders, in between her legs. Music sounded from the kitchen, from a radio on the table; later in the day someone would say, You mean you never heard gospel music before? Lord Have Mercy!

A car horn screeched the sunlight into her eyes. Bob, she called.

Royal Doulton Knock-Off

Later that day, El would sit in the front pew of the First Church of Christ on Avenue J and nod along as the choir sang, "Going Up Yonder." She would be next to her future mother-in-law; her husband was at home, looking out the window.

The church mothers would cast glances her way, happy that a white person had finally sat in the pews without looking over their shoulder. The pastor, Melvin K. Ritter, commanded the congregation to stand and be thankful; El liked this. She liked standing and begging, slowly, not too fast, the pure act of supplication, of asking things of someone who might just actually fulfill her deepest wishes. Just before his final sermon, he introduced Bob's bride-to-be to the entire congregation.

Child's too small, said one church mother in the pew behind El. Better put some meat on that skeleton, said another, smiling at Bob's mother. Them Krauts do indeed have it bad, after all this time.

When the sermons were done (there were five in all), the church people went to the basement and sat at a long table in front of several platters of minute steaks, cornbread stuffing, and okra; many wrinkled hands took hold of El's, wishing her the best with Bob. Lord knows other girls have tried to get him to change his ways, the hands told her. Hopefully, El would be the lucky one.

Sango

You and Meggie head to the watering hole—Monique has texted that she will get there as soon as "lovingly possible." Meggie blushes as she stuffs her phone into her bra. She says she's all right with two ladies in love even though there is something creepy about it.

You enter the woods—about a half mile in is the bluestone watering hole, the one that is said (by Aunt Vitrine and others) to contain healing liquids. The trees hang low, and you notice that it is dark but not pitch; you can still find your way. You'd hoped for complete darkness—what would they say when they learned you hadn't said a proper goodbye to the man? Down here, everyone deserves a proper goodbye, hated or no.

You hope for one of those legendary water moccasins to snake its way to your ankle and take out a huge chunk.

Would it be wrong to tell them that the last time you saw your father, you said nothing specific? That the words *forgive* and *forget* never made it past your lips? That you engaged the reams of selves who came before you—the little baby in the carriage, the kindergartner, the science project acolyte—and told them it was time to close up shop, as though your father had never ever existed? He once was alive, and was all things to those former selves. You, on the other hand, despise that idea. Was it wrong to turn your head away from the phone the last time he called? Was it wrong to crunch up the letter in which he explained he'd suffered a major heart attack and needed just a touch of kindness? You hate him for keeping your mother, and you hate your mother for having been kept. You have his last will and testament sewn into a seam of the blouson, sort of like the way slaves traveled with their papers. You'd read about slaves in the fifth grade. Your father tested you on their names for a social studies test. He patted your head when you got the answers correct.

This thirty-seven acres is yours.

Immediately as you step foot under the canopy of trees, you are eaten by mosquitoes. Meg has something in a small flask; she offers it to you, and you take it down fast, lemonade and something bathtubby. Meggie giggles uncontrollably and admits that she's always wanted to visit California and start herself all over again.

But dreams cost, she suddenly moans, her lips puffed out with fake citrus.

At the next clearing, she stops and puts her cheek against your arm. You had the best mom in the world, Meggie says.

You tell her you know.

Meggie ignores you, saying, She saw me on one of your visits —I think you were only seven at the time. Your mama saw me and marched straight to my mama—God rest Evangeline's soul but my mother was a dumbass—and told her I was having a quote unquote rough time of it. That I needed more taken care of. That she only had one Meggie in the world, and what was the sense in ignoring that?

Your mama, she says. She saw my belly bowling out like a sail in the wind. She saw my legs bow and the ringworm on my cheeks blossom like flowers. Your mama saw, Sasha Jean. And she said something. And at that point, my mama had no choice but to *look at me*.

You want to ask her what happened, but Meggie is already walking away. You remember Meggie's family, the father whose eyes were so outlined in whiskey they looked like huge beetles on his face, the mother whose cough shook every house on the road of relatives. Once they both took you to church and called you their adopted daughter—Look at this good skin, they'd said, almost in unison. You laughed when they did this—was it 1970 or even earlier?

You arrive at a grove of pear trees, tucked away neatly in this back wood against a small bluestone quarry. Vines everywhere come alive as snakes and then go back dead as plants. This is where

Grandma Elldine used to go for her canning fruit. You smell their fragrance, wish to reach for the fruit. Your mama, Meggie keeps saying, If it wasn't for her I wouldn't've been alive.

Your mother died on her way to the VFW nursing home where she was a volunteer. She'd been planning to visit her own ailing mother in Kiel, had even booked her tickets. But then her heart conked out, and she had to be placed in the nursing home morgue. The veterans went crazy, sliding their wheelchairs into walls, throwing food at each other. How could Mrs. Elspeth be gone? And so young?

Try as he might, the Polish doctor in charge could not get those men to calm down for weeks and weeks.

Dansk

You are ten and Fortunoff is the store of dreams. Like your Aunt Vitrine once said to you: don't let your eyes get bigger than your stomach! Well, this is your mother in Fortunoff. She wants everything; as our neighbor Miss Jerldean sometimes says behind her back, Fifth Avenue tastes on a Bowery budget. It is a Saturday when the two of you escape here; your father lies in the backyard with a cold compress on his forehead; it was only the day before that you told your mother about the nighttime touching. In Fortunoff, you and she can forget the world.

Your mother admires the blue onion pattern of the Wedgwood, the clean dullness of the Rosenthal. Are you in the market for bone today, the salesgirl asks. Her tag says EVIE. It's a bit early, but have you seen the Christmas Spode?

Your mother says as a matter of fact, she was in the Christmas mood right now. Who says you can't have Christmas in July?

Here, Evie says, Feel this. Villeroy and Boch, straight from the Manhattan showroom. Hold one of these cups up to the light and you can see clear through, like it's a veil.

Last spring, the Church Mothers of Pomegranate Baptist chipped in to get your mother a set of white coffee cups, a thank-you for being such an inspiration to the kids at Tuesday Teen Services. Who knew that hearing all that talk about life during the Big War would have made such a difference to these young folks?

Always mouthing off as if they knew life better than everybody else—thank God for Miss El and her tales of woe at the hands of that Nazi scum! (The Church Mothers were not above occasionally using a swear word in their speech.) Four white mugs, supposedly out of pure Japanese china, had been stuffed in a Christmas box and tied together with twine. I seen those very same mugs in White's Department Store, two for a dollar, said Bob. Why these females have to be so damn cheap? There isn't a damn thing for you in that church.

Evie goes in the back and brings out a soup tureen. This is my personal *favorite,* she announces happily. Her lips, your mother notices, are the color of strawberries.

For those women not afraid to spend a little more on themselves, Evie adds, a bit louder; perhaps she has noticed your mother's thick accent.

The trip to Fortunoff is a major departure. You both were supposed to go to the Fruit Tree, and then to White's for some tube socks, and then to the doctor, the one who will tell your mother that IUDs don't normally fail, and if she is in the family way, it is due to her own recklessness. Then on to the butcher for lamb chops, and finally to the dentist, where she would have that impacted wisdom tooth looked at.

So much to do.

But early this morning, when the dawn was sparkling with a few lights over Pomegranate treetops, something possessed your mother. She waited. She called Miss Jerldean and asked her to pick the boys up from school later—Johann from the first grade, little Keith from kindergarten; she pulled you from your bed and tossed you into the backseat; she drove at the speed limit to Westbury, where Fortunoff loomed like a Long Island Everest.

You've always wanted to come here. You've always wanted to go with your mother. But it would take until now, the day after you told your mother. In the store she doubles over the counter and begins to cry. To you she whispers that the word *finger* literally crushed her spine.

Ma'am, are you OK? Evie asks.

Utter exasperation. Your mother replies she's fine, all the while caressing the bottom of the dark blue salad bowl on the counter. It isn't the blue onion, but rather a blue fleur-de-lis. It is a pattern

she is gradually and quickly falling in love with. The small bowl
has a rounded bottom and soft, wavering edges. You touch your
mother's hand with your own.

Sorry, ma'am, you can't just buy one piece. It comes in a five-
piece place setting. Tureen, large cake platter, medium cake platter, teapot, coffee pot, creamer, sugar additional.

You look up and see the impatience in Evie's eyes.

And can hear your mother's thoughts, loud and clear, funneled
into your own head, the small bowl in her hands: how wonderful
it would be to run away, with just the girl. To come back in a few
weeks for the other kids. But just have this girl, all to myself. To
hear what the world has been saying all along.

The bowl is hard as a rock.

Your mother purchases an entire dinner service of the unnamed
pattern, twenty pieces in all, but says she'll have to come back at a
later date for the soup tureen and cake platter. She is, after all, not
made out of money.

Lenox

With the first light of her first morning in America, El felt the wind
blowing in from the open window. A train clanged by, as if the
track were close by. Bob, she called out again.

She found her suitcase in the front room of the apartment,
right where Bob had dropped it, and she immediately went for
the lock she'd snapped shut after tossing the cufflinks back inside.

The tea and coffee pots were fine, maybe a tiny chip on the
edge of one lid. The platter was broken in three places. With glue,
it could be restored. A bit of glue and some sun, some fresh New
York air. The skyline, the taxis, the restaurants, the department
stores. Gin and tonic flowing like a gulfstream toward Jamaica Bay,
and from there out to the beckoning Atlantic.

She laid the Melitta dishes—blue pansies etched on a white
background—back into the suitcase and went into the kitchen.
The radio played soft and loud at the same time. Outside this window, which was covered with an eyelet curtain, a woman and child
walked by, laughing.

El's hands felt damp. She smelled like Bob's hair, his chest.

Surely there was a tea kettle somewhere in this kitchen. Above the stove a small plaque bearing the face of a black man read: I'VE BEEN TO THE MOUNTAINTOP.

She would have to shower, she would have to wash her hair.

Pfaltzgraff

The swim was more delicious than food; afterward, you all rest on your backs on the slick bluestone shore, you and Monique and Kate (high as kites off some pills they borrowed from Stanley) and Meggie, who can't seem to stop crying. Her face has gone back to childhood, with its circles of ringworm and eye dirt. She says she will never get over the day your mother saved her life.

Once, she says, there was a family all living on top of each other in a double-wide but still there was no room. We ate Cap'n Crunch every day and felt hungry all the time. Then this lady appeared out of a cream-colored DeVille. She was wearing a blue scarf on her head, like a turban, and she smelled of lilacs.

Little girl, she said to me. Don't make such a sad face.

She lifted me into her arms, and I could smell baby roses over those lilacs. The powder blue ones, the kinds with the thorns that don't make any difference.

Little girl, she said, Would you like to come live with me?

And I was all set to drift asleep, let this fine lady take me with her, away from the smell of unwashed cereal bowls and all the feet of my brothers.

She was better than a fairy godmother. She was cleaner than a queen. There was a pot of summer rhubarb boiling somewhere. And just like that, I recall my mama having words with her. Saying some nonsense about how her daughter was not some African orphan in the desert.

The truth was, I would've gone to any desert.

My mama lived twenty years after that day. You know what happened to me. On her last day at Auntsville Rehabilitation, where she was fidgeting with her kidneys, she told me I looked like a million bucks. How was it I raised such a gorgeous gal, she asked. Her lips were like quarry silt.

You did such a good job, I told her. I didn't want to bring up the cream DeVille. I didn't want to talk about that blue scarf or the queen walking into every house like she owned it. I was afraid of seeing the last drop of my mama evaporate on the spot.

Anchor Hocking Homestead

Quit that bellyaching, Monique says, laughing. We all been there. We never look back, dummy.

What you need is a baby, says Kate, who is the only one — besides you — who is childless. She adds, A baby to love in the right way.

Monique swats her cheek gently and says, Lucky for us, there will never be a shortage of kids. Take your pick you want another one. Myself, I got three I'd love to give you. And I think Sasha Jean about ready to tell us of the newest addition, isn't that right?

No one waits for an answer: instead, they laugh faintly and remove their wet shirts and shorts. They are becoming mermaids, and for some reason, you can't stand to watch. Is it ever too late? Would swimming be better than a life of feathers? You know you're no different from the rest — so you get up and dive back into the hole, letting its blackness swallow you. Too late: at water's touch, your arms become fins and your legs fuse together. Your belly feels cold as you plow through the underground ripples; your neck has grown bright brown scales. The others don't seem to notice. But moments later, they call out to you, and then dive in themselves.

Do they change? You can't really tell. Eventually, you all swim, however, with the same ease, the same ruffled glide, to a mangrove tree, the roots of which sit like umbrella handles above the water. When you come up for air, you all look strangely bloodless. Tell us, Monique finally says, resting one arm on a root, What would you say, Sasha Jean, to some extra cash?

When you raise your eyebrows, she says, I plan to empty out the uncles' payday accounts tomorrow. I figured out a computer way.

Please don't name me accomplice after the fact, Kate says, swooping over to kiss Monique on the lips. Meggie blushes.

You are quiet, bobbing your head halfway into the water. And then you plunge as deep as you can to the bottom. You can hear the girls shout after you — *Rude Bitch, why can't you answer the question! You gone tell on us?*

It's lonely down below but also green. Pallid, alive. You wonder, as you open your eyes, where all the green has come from. There must be snakes here, you think, as you pull yourself—with fin arms —down farther into the hole.

He will never love you like he used to, your mother told you.

But he says I'm his *favorite*.

You are an angel, she replies, wincing. I have to live with that.

Down below, you believe you see your mother's bluestone eyes, feel her farm-toughened hand upon your forehead. In Laboe there is an authentic German submarine on display on the sand; you can read the plaque and you can wail but you can't go in. You look past the motionless sea plants and recognize a knife in your mother's apron pocket. If he ever says "finger" again, she warns, then lifts the knife to her breast. You reach out and she vanishes among the weeds—how could you tell her that he never once even uttered that word?

When you bubble up out from the depth—when you gasp for air and hold tightly to Meggie's arm—you hear Kate, speaking in a thick Southern accent, imitating someone back at the reunion. Hattie or Cathy or LaWanda or Ancient Hattie Mabel. Chris or Daquan or Malik or Harris. You think they've forgotten you when suddenly Monique nods toward the reunion noise in the distance and says, If Bobby Lee intends to take back Grandma Elldine's house, he's got another thing coming. Family is family. We got our own ideas.

You and what army, Kate asks. That house needs bulldozed, plain and simple.

It'll be a place for you and me one day, Monique announces, taking Kate's hand and pressing it against her neck. You and me.

Y'all better cut that shit out, says Meggie. But don't forget to make me bridesmaid.

They laugh. They touch. Sunbeams try hard to burst through the woods' canopy. You're supposed to evict them all.

Kate says, I like it here. I open my eyes and every day it's a new surprise.

Only a white girl would say that, Meggie laughs.

Why don't you say something, Monique suddenly asks.

But you're sure you *are* saying something, that words are actually exiting your mouth and penetrating their ears. You're pretty sure you're telling them that as of nine months ago, you inherited everything here, as far as the eye can see. Thirty-seven acres. You paid for it. You can't imagine ever wanting to set foot here again.

And perhaps they *have* heard. Monique flips her fins playfully in front of her. We'd miss you if you never came back, she says, not understanding. This is a sign. They hear what they want to hear. And that's fine with you. You can never really be free, but you're already there.

Crows and starlings screech through the landscape. In the distance there is the fragrance of the pig being roasted on the spit. You hear the old shingles peel off the Victorian and land in the elderberry hedge. The house will certainly die.

You clear your throat, make your way to the other side of the pond. The others release themselves from the umbrella handles and follow you, drifting on their backs. A child screams into the woods and waits for an answer. Ancient Hattie Mabel is shouting the words to "I'm Getting Ready."

You all dive again, this time not needing to come up for air. This is the world and there is no need for stealing, kissing, anger at past wounds. This world operates on scales and silt.

You expect it to end. For the fins to melt, the tails to finally recede, the women to call you all back to the tables. Hair will be quickly braided or wrapped into shirts, skin smoothed back into order. You expect that soon you will all tramp slowly and un-eagerly through the forest—Kate will suddenly squeal in horror as she steps upon a harmless worm—and then it will take forever for Meggie and Monique to tame her cries with their hands.

A fantasy arises in which you all continue your walk, even with the brays and hollers of the slave women in these woods, their feet smashing snakes, their arms tattered by thorned vines, their minds agape with the babies they could not afford to carry. The slave women are deafening, the slave women are worse than ghosts. You wonder if your parents are trapped here with the slave women. Would they torture your parents like ghosts in a cheap horror flick? Would that make you feel any better?

But this is all so conveniently stashed away. The world you're in now is all scales and silt. Meggie, Monique, and Kate dive deep, trail air bubbles behind them; their light and dark brown breasts hang over their bellies, not in perfect mermaid style, but in the style of girls who have longed to do this since the day they were born. Their hair floats in the depth like a series of snowballs. They remind you of Christmas. There is swimming, miles of it—and a surprise underground clearing, and giggles over mermaid nipples and moles, and promises, and some hope. Why ever resurface? Why not stay here for all time? Dandelion wine and nougat truffles. You could live like kings.

It's tempting, but not going to happen. *Land ho!* Meggie screams, laughing as she runs on ahead; she'll be the first one to fill up another plate and hug the kids. Kate and Monique touch fingers to lips behind every tree, vow to go to Stanley's room and steal the rest of his "raw material."

And over midnight margaritas on Aunt Nephronia's roof, you tell them (these girls now your girls) in clear, cement words, that you have no idea what your father is planning on doing to the land. But you promise it won't be anything bad.

Royal Copenhagen

El lifted her hand to her throat and felt the tiniest swell there, like a foamy wave bundling itself to the shore. She would have to go out and see Jamaica Bay up close. She would have to find that chocolate-wafer edge of the world, once again.

There in the afternoon sunlight of the kitchen table, El dared not move. She hated the feeling that life was a race—would it be possible to remain here like this, forever? She found a pack of cigarettes behind the toaster and took one out, a race to the finish.

Anyone there, called Bob, slamming open the front door to the apartment. He carried a bag of sweet rolls in his arm. I'm home. I'm home.

She rose from the table, allowing herself to swoon against the wall. Don't I get no sugar, he asked, and she felt oddly moved by his stingy smile.

He buried his face in her neck. I'm a changed man, he whispered. Do you believe?

But El wasn't listening. She was wondering, instead, if her mother had finally noticed that the dishes were gone. She kept seeing the old face, disappointed and yearning at the same time. Not at all the right punishment for the crime.

Come On, Silver

FROM *Tin House*

June 15

Dear Future Husband,

Please do not call me Josephine. I'm writing to you because that's what we're supposed to do right now in quiet hour. Captain Bev says I ought to tell you that I am waiting for you. My mother says it's rude to keep someone waiting. She also says that I am an impatient girl. She promised that this camp had horses but I have not seen the horses yet.

Cordially, Fin

June 16

Dear Future Husband,

I hope this letter finds you well. It is my second day here and already I am in trouble. Captain Bev says I ought to apologize for my handwriting, and for my impertinence. I am very sorry if I offended you. I look forward to meeting you one day, whoever and wherever you are. Today we were awoken at dawn and made to run east, toward the sun. I am fast for my cabin but not the fastest in the camp. I asked my bunkmate, Pita, about the horses and she laughed in my face. Pita seems like a real wisenheimer. Now I will share my hopes and dreams for us. I hope and dream you are handsome, with wavy hair and shining dark eyes and two distinct eyebrows. I hope and dream that you will not have a moustache, and that we will live in a mansion with horses in the stable. I do not know what exactly I am waiting for. No one will tell me.

Sincerely, Fin

*

June 17
Dear Future Husband,

The Beaver says my letters to you are a dereliction so now I am writing in my notebook, which is not a diary. I hide this small notebook in my trunk, at the bottom of a box of sanitary napkins. I don't see what's so derelict about what I wrote. I did exactly what the Beaver told us to. Today I wrote you a fake letter to get her off my back. The Beaver is what the campers call Captain Bev. Get it? Caroline, my cabinmate, is playing her flute despite the fact that this is supposed to be quiet hour. She isn't bad but she plays the same dumb Christmas song over and over again. That's why it's called *practicing*, she said to me, as if I were a literal idiot. She said, Bet you didn't know this song is about a hooker. I said, I *know*. I didn't know, but it was a necessary lie.

Everything here is a competition. Tampons versus sanitary napkins. Bras versus undershirts. On the first night, the Beav divided everyone into two teams: the Cubs versus the Colts. (I am, fortunately, a Colt.) Also, older girls versus younger girls, even though everyone at this camp *achieved menarche* in the past year. No one talks about the menstruation requirement. I only know because I found the brochure on Mother's desk. The older girls are called Evening Primroses. The younger girls are called Morning Glories. (The camp is called Camp Moonflower. I am a Morning Glory.) The camp motto is *Dignae et provisae iucundae,* which we are made to chant three times at the beginning of each meal.

Through our daily tasks we earn points for our team, and at the end of the week, one team will be named Queens of the Moonflower. The Beav says in a menacing voice that anyone who leaves the cabin at night unattended will get a zero for her team. This is meant to be a threat, but a zero is nothing. If you add zero to a number, the number doesn't change. I seem to be the only one to have figured this out.

Fin

June 18
Dear Future Husband,

This morning I met the horses. Jo, the white western mare, is my soulmate. We have basically the same name. The elitists are in love with Lady Diamond, who is sensitive and dark and English. I know about the elitists because my father said that summer camps were full of them. I put my hand on Jo's side and felt her muscles twitching hot under velvet. She smelled of maple syrup and pencil shavings. For a moment the trees and dirt and wooden fence of the pen and the horse noises and girl noises went blank and I was my breath and the horse breathing with me. The horse possibility. The horse my friend. The horse my wings. We did not get to ride the horses today.

Pita's not an elitist. She's a big-mouth pain in the ass. That's what her name literally means. Pain In The Ass. Caroline told me it's her nickname at school and even the teachers call her that. Pita says she is in love with Andrew the horse counselor, who looks like a Ken doll in a baseball cap, with a deep tan. Andrew is from the same town as Pita, so Pita won't stop talking about him, even though he's a senior in high school and they've never once seen each other before today. When Pita talks about Andrew, she squinches her eyes and stretches her lips tight across her teeth, because she is making a conscious effort to form apples with her cheeks. The Beaver taught us to do this yesterday in our Anatomy and Etiquette class.

The sun pressed down on me as we stood in the pen, Andrew lecturing us about horse safety and horse responsibilities. We'd run far this morning. I almost reached the woods on the other side of the field before the Beaver called us back. Then we'd spent an hour mixing mud for the earth oven before breakfast (shriveled sausages and dry scrambled eggs). Sweat popped out on my cheeks and shoulders and Caroline announced in front of all the elitists that I was going to faint. Andrew dug in his bag and offered me a bottle of warm water, which I drank. It did make me feel better. But Pita wouldn't leave me alone about it for literally hours. What if Andrew had put his lips on that bottle? What if I had put my lips where his lips had been? Did it smell like his cologne? What about his backwash? It's quiet hour and she was supposed to be up on the top bunk writing a letter to her Future Husband, but instead she knelt in the middle of the cabin floor, thrusting her canteen into her mouth, drooling and moaning, *Oh Andrew.* Everyone else laughed, confused. Then our counselor came in to announce that Caroline had been selected for the Sisterhood and Pita finally, finally, finally shut up.

Fin

*

June 18, again

Dear Future Husband,

Another competition, this time at the lake. I do not refer to
the canoe race (the Cubs won). I refer instead to the battle of the
bathing suits. Pita laughs at my one-piece Speedo, which I selected
for its bright yellow straps and its ability to somewhat restrain my
disproportionately large and unwieldy breasts. I am convinced that
my breasts are the reason I am an incompetent swimmer, but I will
not, for obvious reasons, articulate this to the swim counselor, who
repeatedly explains the forward crawl to me as though I am both
stupid and hard of hearing. Pita is built like a stick bug, and this
afternoon she strutted across the dock in a flimsy bikini, swatting
the sunbathing campers and counselors with a wooden oar. Andrew finally snatched the oar from her and threw it into the lake.
The Beaver was mad, but Caroline (also wearing a one-piece) and
I applauded. The way Pita tells it, of course, Andrew was declaring
his love to her by throwing the oar into the lake.

We just had our first mail call. I received a letter from my
mother. She hopes I'm learning what it means to be a woman.
Today I learned how to arrange flowers in a crescent shape while
forming apples with my cheeks. Pita asked me who my letter was
from, and I told her it was from my best friend. She looked disappointed.

If I were home right now, I would be sitting in the living room
with my grandmother, watching game shows and waiting for the
summer to end. *This basic swimming stroke was pioneered in Australia
during a rescue approach.* I used to learn things from the game shows
but they've run out of answers. My grandmother paid for me to
come to this camp after convincing my parents that I needed to be
around girls my own age. She'd caught me playing with Barbies.
(Last year when I gave up my diary I also relinquished most of my
Barbies, but I secretly retain a few for emergencies.) On this particular day, Ken and Skipper were naked, and Ken had tied Skipper up with a broken necklace that my grandmother had given
me from her junk drawer. I read a book once about a girl who was
raped and then she became best friends with a horse. The horse
was the only creature she could trust. I don't understand rape, but
I do understand loneliness.

Yesterday before supper, Caroline went to her first Sisterhood meeting. She had to wear her camp whites. To require an all-white uniform at a camp that caters to menstruating girls is, I am sure, a form of sadism. The Beav says that one of the members of the Sisterhood will be chosen at the end of camp to represent Woman, and her steadfastness will be tested in front of everyone. My cabin-mates and I have spent the afternoon wondering what this test of steadfastness could possibly be. Pita suggested that it will constitute a public examination of the chosen Woman's laundry for the purity of her camp whites. I told her she was confusing steadfastness with colorfastness. After the Sisterhood meeting Caroline sat down with us in the mess hall looking swollen, like she'd been crying, but she wouldn't tell us anything. She said it was a secret. *The secret of the Sisterhood,* Pita stage-whispered to me, *is that there is no secret.* Then we all clapped our hands and began our evening chant.

Fin

June 19
Dear Future Husband,
Caroline is sitting on her bunk bed playing the Christmas prostitute song. Pita says that at the end of camp, she is going to lead our cabin in a procession to the lake and hurl the flute into the water. We all (besides Caroline) agree that this is the first good idea Pita has ever had. The hurling will be either a milestone or a ceremony. Captain Beaver is big on Milestones and Ceremonies.

My personal milestone while I'm at camp will be to ride Jo at a gallop. In riding class we're only supposed to walk, but the elitists with experience are trotting already. Andrew should tell them to stop, but he doesn't. I try to encourage Jo to trot but she walks like she's waddling through molasses no matter what. I have less than a week left to reach my goal. You can't ride a horse by reading a book.

Today Andrew told me that Jo was so fat she probably couldn't even tell I was riding her. She probably didn't even know I existed. Struck dumb with fury, I was able only to glower at his carefully suntanned Ken-doll face. He slapped my thigh, hard. "Horsefly," he explained. He gave me a slow smile. "You wanna ride a different horse?" What different horse, I said sullenly. All the other horses were taken. He said if I really wanted to learn how to ride, he would give me a private lesson after taps. Then Pain In The Ass butted in to ask what we were talking about. "None of your

damn beeswax," I said, and turned back to Andrew to remind him
that we had the Black Night Ceremony after taps. He smirked and
touched the brim of his baseball cap in a gesture I have only ever
seen in *The Lone Ranger,* which I was forced to watch over many
long afternoons at my grandmother's house. I stared at him over
my shoulder as Jo bore me away to plod in a ponderous circle.

Fin

June 19, again
Dear Future Husband,

It's been raining hard since mail call. I heard the counselors
whispering at dinner about canceling the Black Night Ceremony.
They think the weather will make it too scary. Pita says they're playing it up to set the mood, because the whole point of the ceremony is to scare us. Same with the porno movies, she says. (Our
last activity before dinner was an hour-long Sexuality presentation
in the gym. I pretended to be bored. Caroline pretended to be
disturbed. Pita laughed and laughed.)

Fin

June 19, again
Dear Future Husband,

We're back in the cabin. They decided not to make us sleep
in the Temple (the lodge) after all. We had to put on our camp
whites for the ceremony, and before we went into the lodge the female counselors told us stories about menstruating girls who were
inhabited by demons. The demons could make the polish on our
nails turn rotten. The smell of blood could bring snakes slithering
into our cabins. We were forbidden from touching pickles and instructed to form an unbroken circle. The lodge was decorated with
moose heads and stuffed ducks and mounted antlers, and candles
lining the walls for maximum shadow effects. The male counselors
danced and hollered outside with burlap sacks over their heads.
They weren't very well disguised. Andrew still had on his cowboy
boots. Inside we sat on the floor in a clump. We weren't supposed
to talk, but Pita whispered dirty words from the porno movies to
needle us. After a crack of thunder Caroline started chanting *Dig-
nae et provisae iucundae,* and we all joined in. Finally the Beav came
in and turned on the lights, and that was the end of the Black
Night Ceremony.

Our counselor didn't come back to the cabin with us. She rarely spends time with us, so we hate her. Although I was not impressed by the ghost stories and pickle warnings at the ceremony, I confess that the thunder is loud, and the rain, and the wind pushing through the trees. I worry for the horses. Our cabin roof is leaking in two places. Caroline announced she's homesick and began to cry. Now everyone in the cabin is wailing.

Caroline asked her bunkmate to sleep in her bed, prompting all the top-bunk girls to climb down into the bottom bunks. Guess who got stuck with Pain In The Ass? I suggested that we sleep head to feet, but she said no, and she wrapped her spindly arms and legs around me. "Get off me, Pita," I said. "My name is Emily," she whispered in my ear, "and this is how we always sleep at slumber parties." I pushed her away so hard that she rolled onto the floor. Then I stood up and, as a distraction, loudly announced I would go in search of our counselor. Caroline reminded me, however, that I'll get a zero for the Colts if I leave the cabin. Pita (also a Colt) climbed back into her own bed and dangled her head over mine and threatened to spit on me if I tried to leave. She said I'd never find our counselor anyway, because she escapes nightly to the woods with the other counselors to participate in a vomiting ritual.

I have to tell you a secret. After I told Andrew that I couldn't meet him after taps tonight, I made plans to meet with him for a private lesson tomorrow.

Fin

June 20
Dear Future Husband (Andrew?),

This morning, like every morning, we rose at dawn and ran toward the sun. This morning, unlike every morning, I ran all the way to the woods and back, and I was fastest. Half awake and half dreaming of a gallop. The girls behind me a stampede of hooves. *Hi-yo, Silver! Away!* When I got back to the starting line, the Beav slapped me across the face and hung a medal around my neck. "Welcome to the Sisterhood, Josephine," she said. I was so startled that I bit my own tongue. Caroline plucked a buttercup from behind our cabin and smeared its pollen on my forehead as if she were a priest anointing a new baby, after which I upchucked last night's dinner (lasagna) into the weeds.

Instead of having a Sisterhood meeting today for the new members, the staff held a camp-wide emergency trunk inspection, and a girl in another Morning Glory cabin was sent home. She'd been caught faking her period. "But I bet her laundry was extra-steadfast," Pita said sullenly. She has been in a particularly sour mood all day. Caroline says she's just jealous that she hasn't gotten picked for the Sisterhood. Pita says she heard that the trunk inspection was really meant to make sure we weren't hiding any contraband. "Like candy bars?" Caroline asked pointedly. Contrary to her malnourished appearance, Pita is an actual pig for candy bars. She brings back armfuls from the canteen. "No," snapped Pita, "like a giant vibrating dildo." It's hard to tell sometimes if Pita is joking. Our counselor, both lazy and careless, didn't look in my sanitary-napkin box, so my notebook remains undiscovered.

The horse pen turned to mud after the hard rain last night. At the beginning of our class Andrew already looked like the Swamp Thing from the knees down. I squinted at him so that he went blurry and I could pretend he really was the Swamp Thing, and for one raw moment I missed my grandmother, her paisley sofa and her too-loud infinite TV. Summer used to be simple. I used to want simple things, like small marshmallows from the jar in my grandmother's kitchen. I would squish them into tiny pancakes between my thumb and forefinger and eat them one by one. I stopped squinting at Andrew and tried to tell him with my eyes to come talk to me. But he ignored me, and with each passing minute I felt my dream of horsewomanship slipping away. In the fifty-fifth and final minute of class, Jo waded nonchalantly back to the gate, carrying me powerless on her back. As we passed Andrew he reached up and touched my arm. "After taps," he said, in the same casual voice he uses to tell the elitists Nice Work Today! I looked down at the muddy streak his hand had left on my skin. *Speak in a low, soft, soothing voice. Be accommodating. Use your yes words.* I tried for apple cheeks. I had been practicing all morning. "Yeah," I said, apple-cheeked, to my own bare arm.

Fin

June 20, again
Dear Future Husband,

My cabinmates are away at the canteen. I stayed behind, claiming I had cramps and I wanted to take a hot shower. This is partially true. I don't have cramps, and no normal person wants to shower in our bathroom facility, inaccurately named the Pink Palace, which is infested with daddy longlegs and flying palmetto bugs. However, I understand that I am expected to be clean and pleasantly scented when I meet Andrew tonight for my private lesson. In lieu of my usual two-in-one Pert Plus—what Pita refers to as my *dandruff lotion*—I have borrowed from Caroline, by virtue of my Sisterhood status, miniature bottles of vitamin-enhanced shampoo and conditioner that smell like exotic fruit. In my efforts to be perceived as a warm, thoughtful, and generous hostess, I have also secured, in Pita's absence, two king-sized candy bars from her elaborate under-mattress stash. These will serve as our midlesson snack.

While rummaging through Pita's stockpile, I encountered what is either a giant vibrating dildo or an extraordinarily complex flashlight. I wish it were a flashlight, and a waterproof one at that. I am off to contend with the cockroaches.

Fin

June 20, late

A zero. A zero. I chanted it to myself all the way to the horse pen, alone. Lights out in the cabin, our counselor gone, and a zero is nothing. My mission nothing short of revelation. I was prepared. No longer would I bumble through my life in a perpetual state of impotence and bewilderment. I took the box of sanitary napkins with me in case anyone lying awake in the cabin wondered where I was going.

Tonight he took off his hat. He asked me to call him Drew, but he didn't introduce me to the horse. Then something broke in the dark pen. He was fiddling with the saddle, the moon our only light, and I could barely make out his face. "Shoot," he said. "You want to try riding bareback? I'll ride with you." He said it would improve my balance. "Plus it's natural," he said. "Think about it."

It was not possible for me to think about it. My mind was full of Pita and pornos, backwash and cologne, how I was supposed to act, what I was supposed to want. "Yes," I told him. My cheeks were perfectly round, not that he could see them. He hoisted me onto the horse.

Then we were moving fast and it didn't feel like flying. I sat in front and his arms around me and his thighs pinning me and

my back slamming against his chest and my butt slamming against
the horse and all of it hurt. The horse was not fat like Jo. I tried
to communicate telepathically with the horse, but she was blank
silent running. And Andrew rocking and grunting behind me. Finally it ended. He helped me dismount. We were both breathing
hard. I stood still in the muddy pen and felt all the sweat pour out
of me. I doubted it smelled of exotic fruit. Then Andrew bent his
face down toward my face. "You're not like the other girls," he
said. "I knew right away." I could see his eyes, finally. They were
glassy blue and strange. "Did you feel anything?" he asked.

"Yes," I said, sweating, silently counting my bruises. He did not
ask me to specify but wrapped his arms around me and pressed
his hands into my backside. I jumped away. "My butt hurts," I told
him. "Grow up," he said, snorting exactly like a horse. "You got
just what you wanted." He turned away to tend to the horse, and I
walked back to the cabin the way I came, alone. I didn't even tell
him about the candy. The candy is a zero. My apple cheeks are a
zero. The horse is a zero. They change nothing.

Fin

June 21

Tomorrow is the last day of camp. The other girls in the cabin
have been whistling cheerfully all morning. As predicted, Caroline's flute song has fully penetrated their brains. Pita claims she
overheard the counselors saying that the Colts are going to be
named Queens of the Moonflower. I am glad for my team but I
cannot bring myself to celebrate. I reflect on Captain Beaver's first
directive of the summer: to wait. Perhaps she was right. Perhaps
I could not achieve my milestone because I was not patient. I am
left only with these small physical traumas, tender to the touch but
invisible to the eye, and my own confounding shame.

Fin

June 21, again

Something terrible has happened. I have been accompanied by
whistling all day long. The same Christmas song, ad nauseam, and
not just from the girls in my cabin. I thought it strange, but the
significance of the tune was lost on me. Finally, on my way back
from our afternoon Stain Removal class, I saw the letter taped to

the front door of the mess hall. It was handwritten, addressed to Andrew, and signed with my name.

Obviously I didn't write the letter. The penmanship was curly and fat, a cartoon of a girl's handwriting, not like mine at all, and my name was misspelled at the end. The letter mentioned how *I liked it when you touched my butt* and *all the guys like my big tits* and *Andrew won't you touch them too.* It occurred to me, the way that pitch-black water occurs to someone falling down a deep well, that someone had been reading my private notebook, and that this letter was intended as a public indictment. But I had failed, in fact, to like or want these things. I had failed, in front of Andrew, and I had been made to feel embarrassed for failing. Now this forged document revealed at last what no Anatomy and Etiquette lesson could illustrate, no amount of bone-rattling horse sprint could knock into me: I was supposed to want, and not to want, simultaneously. Those were the rules. There was no winning. I would fail either way.

I fled to the cabin, a handful of Evening Primroses running after me, humming loudly. My own galloping pulse was not powerful enough to drown out the sound of their accusation. Whore song. In the cabin everyone was somehow already in their bunks, fake nonchalant, early for quiet hour. No one was whistling now. It was their silence that betrayed them.

I flung open my trunk. It appeared undisturbed. I grabbed the sanitary-napkin box and dumped the contents on the floor and my notebook was there as usual. But Pita in the top bunk was laughing. I looked up at her. She had her fist wrapped around her dildo flashlight. She met my eyes, then brought the dildo flashlight slowly to her mouth and ran her tongue down the length of it. Pita, the prophet of my revelation. I experienced in that moment a naked rage that caused my head to lift and separate from my body. A new vocabulary sprung incandescent from my lips. *Cock-faced pervert,* I heard myself shriek, *I will fuck your hair right off.* My next move was to take Caroline's flute and bludgeon Pita's face with it.

Before I had the chance, however, our counselor appeared in the doorway. "Josephine," she said. "Come with me." I was surprised she knew my name. She escorted me in silence to the office, where Captain Beaver sat behind a scabby wooden desk. On the desk was the letter. "What do you have to say for yourself, Josephine?" the Beaver asked. I looked down at the letter, then up at her worn, lumpy face. The proof of my innocence—the dilettante forgery—was right in front of her. It was self-evident. But to my horror, instead of answering, I burst into tears.

"That's all I needed to see," the Beaver said firmly. I was taken away, not back to the cabin but to the infirmary at the edge of the camp. My trunk and bedroll have been delivered to me. I will spend the night on a cot, in isolation. Even the nurse is gone. She mumbled something about chiggers and departed in apparent disgust. Tomorrow is the last day of Camp Moonflower, but if the Beaver tells my parents about the letter, I will be forced to endure this humiliation forever.

Fin

June 22

Though Captain Beaver's intent behind her letter-writing assignments remains mysterious to me, I now understand that I must retain these letters as a record of the truth. Whether or not the Beaver reports this incident to my parents, whether or not the letter was an obvious fake. I have learned a great lesson: just as Pita is Pita wherever she goes, this story will follow me.

I regret that I can no longer document my current location. I expected my parents to pick me up from the infirmary in the morning, but the Beaver came to me instead. She instructed me to leave my possessions behind and follow her. Because I am not a complete idiot, I asked for permission to change my sanitary napkin. In the infirmary bathroom, I unwrapped a fresh pad, discarded it, folded my notebook carefully into the plastic wrapper, and stuck the notebook into the back of my underwear for safe-keeping.

The Beaver led me to the lake. Everyone was there, dressed in their camp whites, presumably for some kind of closing ceremony where the winning team—Queens of the Moonflower—would be announced. Caroline was sobbing. Pita sat beside her with her knotty knees folded to her chest. At the end of the dock, a male counselor, his head concealed in a burlap sack, held a wooden oar. Beside him was a canoe. "Go on, Josephine," the Beaver said, nodding toward the canoe. I walked down the dock alone, forcing my chin up like an elitist, pretending like I knew what I was doing, feeling a hundred traitor eyes on my body. The male counselor steadied the boat as I stepped inside. Then, to my surprise, he entered the canoe after me and took the bow position. I didn't have an oar, so I sat with my arms crossed, staring down the lake horizon, waiting for whatever came next. He pushed off and directed the canoe through the water with strong, precise strokes. The girls of Camp Moonflower applauded politely.

"Fin," Caroline shouted. I didn't want to look back, with all of them watching. But Caroline called my name again, as if she had to tell me something very important, and I couldn't help myself. I twisted around in the stern seat. A long piece of metal glinted in her hand. She waved it violently in the air: her stupid cornball flute. When she was satisfied that I'd seen it, she pitched it into the lake. Another milestone. I turned back around and closed my eyes and imagined the flute sinking slowly to the bottom of the lake, where it would torment the undeserving fish.

The male counselor kept rowing, despite the sack over his head. He wore sneakers, not boots, but he was sporting a fastidious suntan, and by the time Camp Moonflower was nothing but tiny dots on the shore, I had worked up the nerve to say his name. "Drew?" He shook his head. I didn't know if that meant *Not Drew* or *No talking*, so I asked another question, which was "Can you see with that sack on your head?" He didn't respond at all. By this point I was feeling very antsy, so I kept on. I asked him, "Do you know what the Camp Moonflower motto means?"

Then I said every swear word that I know. I'd learned eighteen new swear words since arriving at Camp Moonflower. When I ran out of known swear words, I made some up. When I couldn't make up any more, I began to scream. No words. Just noises. He kept rowing. The lake was a lot bigger than I'd realized. I knew which direction the camp was, but I couldn't see it. And I still couldn't see the other shore. Finally he stopped rowing. I stopped screaming. My throat felt like it'd been hacked to pieces. We drifted in silence for a minute. Then he spoke from inside the burlap sack.

"You gotta get out," he said. "You gotta get out and swim all the way back to shore." Why, I demanded hoarsely. "That's the test," he said. This was the test. This was the Test of Steadfastness. I had been chosen, out of all the Sisterhood, to represent Woman, and I wasn't even wearing a bathing suit. The swimming counselor had ceaselessly mocked my floundering attempts at the forward crawl. How long would it take for me to dog-paddle steadfastly back to camp? He shrugged. "They're all standing out there wait-ing for you."

I took in a deep breath and let it out and felt the full force of the sun on the water. I was so tired, and so hot. I did not want *dig-nae* or a *provisae iucundae*. I wanted the man in the burlap sack to go away. I squinted at him until I could imagine him gone. Then, shameless, I stripped down to my underwear and kicked off my shoes and dropped myself into the lake. The water burned up the inside of my nose like crying. I imagined not the bottom of a well. I imagined the lake all briny. My body buoyant. What is the Great Salt Lake. What is the Dead Sea. What is a girl in repose, floating on her back, making up her mind. The sky stared at me, metal-bright and blank, without any answers.

I knew the way back. Instead I put my head down and I crawled forward, riding the salt in the water of every queen's tears.

JACOB GUAJARDO

What Got Into Us

FROM *Passages North*

RIO IS THE bravest boy I know the summer we are fourteen. The beach is ours and all its coves and sandcastles. I have bug bites like beads of sap on my legs. It is June in Michigan and we giggle like princesses as we pull dresses on in the bedroom our single mothers share. We clip on earrings and hate their heaviness. We imagine our lives as women and say the things we think they would say. We tuck our penises between our skinny legs and walk with our thighs together. When we are through we hang the dresses up and put the earrings back inside their cedar boxes at his mother's bedside. We promise not to tell anyone. There is a handshake, a promise with our bodies that I will not remember until years later when I see the neighbor boys slapping hands before they part for dinner.

The summer we are fourteen Rio kisses me for the first time as he zips me into a dress. The dress is blue and white polka dotted and the zipper snags on my tighty-whiteys. The kiss feels like a bug landing on my shoulder. He kisses my lips after he kisses my shoulder. The smell of his teeth is the smell of our shared lunch, fried bologna sandwiches and rice and beans. We made the sandwiches ourselves, the rice and beans we heated up in the microwave. He does not zip the dress up all the way. My shoulder will sting later —like it had been a bee on my shoulder, not the harmless fly I'd felt. It will not always feel like stinging. When my husband kisses my shoulder it will feel good.

We kiss when we think we are alone. We flip paddleboats on the beach and kiss beneath them, the seats dripping water on us. We kiss at the playground where there are secret places in the wooden infrastructure of the jungle gym. We get away with too much this summer.

We grow up on Marlin Street in swim-trunks. Our mothers drive their Chevy with every window down. The wind ruffles our hair like pages in a book. Years from now I will move away from Marlin Street. Not far—a few streets. Close enough that our mothers can walk, thumbing their rosaries, to my house and sip mimosas on the porch, where they will laugh like Spanish witches.

But we grow up on Marlin Street in a beach house. The beach house is blue and has a screened-in porch. On the porch there are two white plastic chairs and a second-hand end-table between them where our mothers sit with their sangrias. We sit on the splintered wood beside them or sit inside on the couch. Our mothers cannot afford to own two houses—will never be able to afford to own two houses. They sleep on two twin-beds in the master and Rio and I sleep together in our room on one queen size. We never have friends over from school.

Families rent out the beach houses for brief Michigan summers, but our mothers own a taquería on the boardwalk. We own our vacation home. Our mothers are known by locals as the Taco Sisters. They are not sisters. They are not sisters the way Rio and I are not brothers. They are childhood friends—immigrants' daughters who grew up translating for their mothers and fathers. They asked for what their parents could not. They are not sisters but they shared beds and sleeping bags on the floors of dirty shacks.

They tell us we washed up on the shores of Lake Michigan. They say they spotted us lit up by the lighthouse against the rocky shoreline. They say gulls carried us to their doorstep. They fit us with seafarers' names. Mine is Delmar, his is Rio. Both our mothers' names are Maria—Maria Carmen and Maria Blanca.

We will never know our fathers. We know that they were light-skinned and fair of hair. Rio's hair looks like bleached coral. My hair is black but my skin might as well be butterscotch pudding. The only way we look like our mothers is our eyes. When we ask about our fathers they tell us, in English, that they are no longer a park of the picture—an idiom they've grown up saying wrong. We imagine our fathers must have been small men to leave such boisterous women. Our mothers never complained, never cursed men and their unwieldy cocks. I will ask about my father again when I

am leaving Marlin Street for college and my mother will ask if they
were not enough.

The locals gave the taquería the unofficial name Authentico.
Our mothers had bought a neon sign to advertise their authentic
Mexican cuisine: tacos el pescado, camarones rebozados, paella
de marisco, arroz con pollo. The gaudy neon sign flickered over
the walk-up window. They'd meant to name the place El Lago, but
the loan from the bank bought them just one sign. We made fun
of the unofficial name. We warned that someday a couple herma-
nos could open up a place called Genuino and ruin them. We sit
outside the taquería on picnic tables and pick gum off the seats.
We watch our mothers fry tortillas and wipe their hands on grease-
licked aprons. Our mothers shoo us off the picnic table when the
stand is busy. Years from now, when our mothers can't spend every
day making tacos for tourists anymore, and I tell them I am too
busy to run the place, Authentico will close up. I will buy the sign
from them and hang it in my garage.

The vacation families drive their cars too fast down Marlin
Street. They are on their porches smoking sausages, or taking
boats out on the lake. They are fucking on the beach inside murky
coves. We hear them and call them monsters. We call anything we
cannot explain that June monsters. In Michigan, summer is only
a few months in the middle of the year, but our mothers love the
beach year round. It means every winter we have to hear about
some gringo trying to walk on the lake and drowning. One year
the gringo will be a boy from our high school that we hate and
they will never pull his body from the lake and we will feel bad for
having hated the boy. Our mothers make the holy triangle up and
down and side to side.

We break into the empty summer houses. We scare the spiders
out and play house. We spend the night in the empty beds after
our mothers pass out drunk from rum and Cokes. We make the
beds every morning, fluffing up the pillows. We take things that
do not belong to us. Things we think no one will miss. I take cards
from Euchre decks and tape them inside a lined paper journal.
Rio cuts buttons from Sunday bests and carries them around in
a velvet bag like they are marbles. We are monsters. We carve our
initials into the underbellies of the summer homes' expensive
wood furniture. We lie under the giant oak frames of the summer-

time beds with a set of keys and cut away at the bed flesh. We find out that if the wood has not cured long enough the furniture will bleed. When I am twenty-eight and expecting my first child I will wonder what had gotten into us that summer and hope my child is not a monster.

When I am twenty-eight and expecting my first child, my husband and I will drive up Marlin Street to show my mothers the first sonogram. The child will be growing inside a woman we have paid through an agency. The surrogate will be a healthy, Latina woman getting her PhD in women's studies at the college in Kalamazoo. I will believe that this detail will make my mothers proud. I will struggle to find the best way to tell them. I will expect that they will not understand. I will expect that they will have questions I will not know the answers to. I will bring them a flyer from the agency complete with illustrations and a number to call should they have any questions. They will make the holy triangle, up and down and side to side.

Rio and his mother fly to Texas for the month of July to visit familia. My mother and I take them to the airport. Carmen has to stand on her toes to kiss my forehead. She holds my face in her hands and says, "We'll be back before you can say Tenochtitlan." My mother spends July harvesting the garden in our backyard. She does other things too, but mostly she is outside on her knees where she can pray in the dirt. I hear her say Carmen's name to the tomatillos once. The tomatillos' papery husks crack and flake when they are ready to be harvested. I watch my body do the same. I spend July under the paddleboats in the dark where I press my fingers to my lips and put my other hand down my shorts and say Rio's name.

Rio comes back taller and darker. Beside me in our bed his skin is still hot from Texas. He kisses me, like we had so many times before. Then he takes my pants off and pulls my cock out and licks his hand and gets my cock wet and puts me inside of him. After that we are fucking everywhere. We are naked when our mothers are at work in the taco stand. We fumble around in the darkness for each other, like moths to the only light in a room. Our sex life will never again be as exciting as when we are fourteen and sharing a bed.

In August there is a summer camp in the city at the Baptist church. The campers are new every week. We are too poor to go to summer camp. The campers swim on a private beach. We think maybe they can walk on water. We see them splashing out by the buoys. We start to call the boys buoys. We walk up the shore and get as close as we can. They wave sometimes and others push their noses flat with their fingers and stick their tongues out. I have not said out loud what I am but I think about it all the time. Especially the summer when we are fourteen and watching the buoys throw footballs on the church's private beach. I want to pick each mole from their pink backs and eat them like Raisinets. We walk ten minutes into Grand Haven to sit outside the chapel and listen to the Bible lessons. The pastor's sermons scare us out from under the paddleboats for a few days. I think I am more scared than Rio. Rio is brave. Rio is the bravest boy I know the summer we are fourteen.

There are days I'm not up for cove crawling, buoy watching, kissing inside the belly of the yellow slide at the park. I stay inside and read instead. Rio is not much of a reader and heads out to adventure without me. He calls me a faggot first, and then the screen door slams.

We will not always get along. When we start high school he will start to play varsity baseball. Our mothers will go to every game. I will love the way he looks in a jockstrap. He will be trying too hard. I will tell him he is trying too hard and that nobody believes him and he will hate me. He will have the chance to be popular and he will take it. He will run away from home the summer he is fifteen. My tio, Valentino, will be visiting from Arizona. He will have rented a car. One night, when they are out walking the pier, Rio will take Tio Valentino's rented car and drive it as far as Tennessee where a state trooper will pull him over. Rio will have just picked a car and followed. We will all drive down to Tennessee to pick him up from jail. Carmen will be furious. I will think he's so fucking cool.

We are subscribed to *Michigan Animal Magazine* this summer. Really we are taking them from the Johnsons' mailbox, reading them, and then putting them back. We learn that cougars used to be native to Michigan but we drove them out. We learn that the feral swine are a problem. We already know that the state bird is a robin, but we learn that cranes fly necks extended—herons fly necks drawn back. We learn that what we thought were owls are mourning doves hooting in the trees. We learn that a monarch's

wings are orange with black veins, not orange with black stripes. I
look at my veins, blue beneath my skin, and wish I could fly.

Late August we are caught, giggling and naked, fucking in the
preacher's bed. From his house we'd collected sheets of cardstock
paper with his parish's name embossed along the top. He will tell
the police officers hours later as we are being loaded into the back-
seats of the cop cars that he'd left a pair of good shoes at the lake
house. This explained his unexpected visit. The preacher opens
the door to the beach house and Rio and I jump from the bed,
pulling on our swim-trunks. He grabs Rio by the hair and slams
him into the wall. He thunders like a sermon. We get away and run
and hide down in our spot by the paddleboats.

Before we go home and before the cops arrive we are walking
the shoreline, panting. Rio sees something and points. "Look," he
tells me. I see a brown mass—fur and antlers. It doesn't move.
I am scared to get closer. He runs ahead, kicking up sand. The
beach looks so big, like he could get lost in it. I do not want to lose
him. I follow, my ankles buckling to the uncertainty of the sand.
The brown mass is huge. It is a monster—it could rear its ugly
head and tear us limb from limb. It looks dead for weeks, stinking
and bloated, its blood has turned the sand and water black. We
know from *Michigan Animal Magazine* that this is a moose. Standing next to it Rio looks so small, but he is fourteen and taller and
darker with skin still hot from Texas. He covers his mouth. We
know from *Michigan Animal Magazine* that moose are only found in
small numbers in the Upper Peninsula. We figure that the moose
died up north and the water carried him here.

Rio crouches, covering his nose. He says we have to do something. "What can we do?" I ask. He starts to gather twigs and shells,
leaves and driftwood. He uses what we have: scattered branches,
pebbles, brittle shells. He scatters them around the moose, creates
a perimeter of earthly discharge to sanction off this bit of beach
for the moose. I help him. I pull bentgrass up and pick flowers
from the beach trees. We sit away from the moose and lean our
heads on one another. We watch the shoreline for Wisconsin. The
moose's antlers have already begun to bleach clean in the sun.

Our mothers will struggle through the winter. They will rely on
second jobs cleaning houses. They won't trust us alone in the same
room together. The cop had been able to speak Spanish and had

told our mothers what we'd been doing. The preacher dropped the charges. Rio will start to sleep with his mother and I will sleep with mine. Rio will crawl the coves without me. He is the gringo who falls through the ice that winter, but he will pull himself out and walk, shivering, back to our house where I will tell him how fucking stupid he is. I will take his clothes off and take my clothes off and press myself against him inside a scratchy mohair blanket.

He will flunk out of college and move back home. Carmen will put him to work in the taquería. We will barely talk for months. He will become the kind of brave that says yes to everything. When I graduate college he will be in rehab fighting a heroin addiction. He will call saying that one of the steps is making amends and a week later we will end up fucking against the walls of the apartment I share with my boyfriend. He will break off in me like shells. I will meet my husband, Fisher, when I am twenty-six and he will meet Rio that same year at Thanksgiving and Rio will not be happy about it. In the kitchen, while Fisher is trying his best to speak with our mothers, Rio will tell me that no one can love me as hard and as real as he has every year since we were fourteen. I will say something to destroy him: "It took this long to find someone that could love the rest of you out of me." Fisher will hear our voices rising and will step into the kitchen as Rio slams his fist against the laminate countertop. Fisher will ask if everything is all right. I will have to explain that night on the drive home about Rio and I.

The summer we are fourteen and playing dress-up with our mothers' clothes in their bedroom with Jesus hanging on a cross on the wall, we talk about getting older. We sit on my mother's bed, the dresses zipped up halfway and pooling around our waists. We have not become monsters yet. We have not stolen the Euchre cards and buttons. We have not called the boys buoys. The boy from school that we hate has not drowned in the lake. The moose has not washed up on the banks of Lake Michigan. We do not know that we will never know our fathers. We will wonder what got into us. Outside, though the curtains are closed tight and all we can see are the curtains' stitches in the sun, we know the beach is clean because summer is just getting started and the summer families haven't moved in. Rio has just kissed me for the first time.

"I'll get a sex change," Rio says. He gathers the dress up around his hips and clips at his penis with two fingers.

"I like you as a boy," I tell him.

"Then you're gay," he says.

"Don't you like me?" I ask.

"I love you," he says. "It's wrong though. We have to stop or something bad will happen."

We take off the dresses and hang them in the closet.

CRISTINA HENRÍQUEZ

Everything Is Far from Here

FROM *The New Yorker*

ON THE FIRST day, there's a sense of relief. There are other feelings, too, but relief is among them. She has arrived, at least. After three weeks. After a broken sandal strap, sunburn on her cheeks, mud in her ears, bugs in her hair, blisters around her ankles, bruises on her hips, boiled eggs, bottled water, sour berries, pickup trucks and train cars and footsteps through the dirt, sunrises and sunsets, nagging doubt and crackling hope—she has arrived.

They tell her to sleep, but that can't be right. First she has to find her son, who is supposed to be here, too. They were separated along the way, overnight, a few days ago. The man who was leading them here divided the group. Twelve people drew too much attention, he claimed. He had sectioned off the women, silencing any protest with the back of his hand, swift to the jaw. "Do you want to get there or not?" They did. "Trust me," he said.

He sent a friend to escort them. When she glanced back, she felt a shove between her shoulder blades. "It's only for a few miles," he hissed in her ear. "Walk."

By morning, the men were gone, the children gone. The friend, a man with sunglasses and a chipped front tooth, said, "I am here to take care of you." What he meant was that they were there to take care of him. Four women. Which they did. Which they were made to do.

"Where is my son?" she asks a guard who speaks Spanish. He shrugs in reply. "*¿Mi hijo?*" she asks anyone who will listen and many who won't. "He's five years old. He has black hair, parted on one side, and a freckle, right here, under his eye. He was wearing a Spider-Man shirt." People just shake their heads.

"There's a family unit," one woman says, pointing down the hall. "They have cribs," she adds, as if that's something.

In the family unit, which is one large room, she searches every crib. She gazes down at infants and eight-year-olds curled against the bars. She scans the faces of the children watching *Dora the Explorer* on a television set mounted to the wall.

"He's coming," a young mother sitting in the corner assures her. She has a child on her lap. "The same thing happened to me. The kids just take longer. They don't walk as fast. Mine got here a whole week after I did. Everyone makes it eventually."

She wants to believe that's true.

The first night, she lies in a bed and listens to the noises of the women in the room with her. Dozens of them. They're stacked neatly in bunk beds, like bodies in a morgue, and she stares at the bowing mattress above her, the straining metal coils, worried that they will not hold. She considers the possibility that the gray-haired woman who clambered up there earlier and who is snoring there now might fall through and crush her to death. She begins to laugh. What if? After everything? What if that's how it ends? The sound of her laughter blooms in the dark. From across the room, a voice asks, "What the fuck is so funny?"

They let her store: her clothes, her broken leather sandals, a plastic comb, an elastic hair band. They let her keep: the silver wedding ring she still wears even though her husband died four years ago. They take: her pocketknife (no weapons), a sleeve of Maria cookies (no food), a tin of Vaseline (no reason).

In the morning, there's a count. In the evening, there will be another. The guards yank the beige sheet off her bed, balloon it dramatically in the air. "Forty-eighteen, clear!" They move down the line.

It's a warehouse, this place: cement floors, fluorescent tube lights in the ceiling, flyers taped to the painted cinder-block walls —ads for phone services, for immigration attorneys, for psychologists. She takes it all in.

After the inspection, she returns to the processing desk, near the front of the facility. Through the windows she can see a chain-link fence topped with a confection of barbed wire and, just beyond it, an open field speckled with wildflowers and long grass and a few broad trees.

"My son?" she asks the woman sitting at the desk. "Gabriel Rivas? Did he get here yet?"

The woman consults her computer. "Sorry," she says. "No one by that name."

She stares at the woman, unsure of what to say.

"Did you check the family area?" the woman asks.

They get one hour to eat. Hash browns and syrup for breakfast. Chicken broth and French fries for lunch. Turkey cutlets and potato dumplings for dinner. So many potatoes. It's a world made of potatoes. There is water to drink, but it tastes like chlorine, and it makes her nauseous.

They take showers in the trailers. The guards control when the water turns on and when it turns off. Soap bubbles skim across the floor.

In the bathroom, which is in a separate trailer, she wads up toilet paper and stuffs it into her underwear. A woman next to her notices.

"Talk to Esme," she says. "She'll hook you up."

She finds Esme in the dayroom, watching TV. Esme offers to sell her a tampon for a dollar, money she doesn't have.

Esme is unsympathetic. She purses her lips. "At least you got your period," she says. "Many of us don't, you know, after what they do. We get pregnant instead."

She marks the days on her arm. A small dot on the inside of her wrist becomes a trail, then a winding chain.

Periodically, new people arrive, escorted by border-patrol agents. A few every week. She watches them with their tattered backpacks, the children with stuffed animals in their arms. When the weather turns cold, people are wrapped in foil blankets as they trudge up the walk.

"Did you see a little boy?" she asks every new arrival. "A boy who looks like me?"

The people glance at her with weary, red-rimmed eyes. Some of them shake their heads. One after the other, none of them him.

What if she's forgotten what he looks like? What if she's gone crazy? What if he's here, lying in one of those cribs, and she sees him every single day without realizing he's her son? What if it's been too long? What if memory fails? What if everything fails, and getting through life is simply learning to cope with the failure? No, she scolds herself. Don't think like that. Don't let yourself give way.

A woman named Alicia arrives from El Salvador with her six-year-old daughter in tow. They sleep in the bed together. They shower together. The girl won't leave her mother's side.

"She's nervous," Alicia says, as if there's a need to explain. "It was a terrible trip."

"Yes."

"We're going to find her father in Minnesota."

"But this is Texas."

"Is it far?"

And how, she wonders, does she answer a question like that. Is it far? Everything is far from here, even if it's only across the street.

She meets with a lawyer, a man in a stained tan sports coat. She asks him how long she'll be here. She asks him what happens after this. "*Eso depende*" is his answer to both. Then: "Tell me everything. They'll need to determine if you qualify for asylum, if you have credible fear." And though she doesn't want to relive it, she tells him about the day, a few months ago now, that the boys—boys whose mothers she knew from the neighborhood—pushed her off a moving bus and dragged her across a busy intersection, how she kept scrabbling her legs under her to try to stand, and how they kicked her to keep her down. How nobody helped her, how nobody stopped them because nobody knows how to stop boys like that. How they made her kneel in the alley behind the fruit store while they held a gun to her head and all took turns, how they put the gun in her mouth and made her suck that, too, and how when they were finished they said, "You're in the family now, bitch," and laughed.

"Why do you think they targeted you?" the lawyer asks.

"I was alone."

"You're not married?"

"Not anymore."

"And you're pretty."

She narrows her eyes.

"And men—"

"They were boys."

"Even more so. We have an expression here: Boys will be boys."

She feels a rising anger.

"If we go back," she says evenly, "they will do it again."

"We?" he asks. "Is there someone else?"

"My son," she starts, but her voice breaks. She clenches her fists. She digs her nails into her palms, determined not to cry.

At night, lying in her bunk atop the beige sheet, she imagines running back the way she came, retracing her steps through the dirt and the weeds until she finds him standing in the overgrowth somewhere, hungry and cold. She wants to gather him up, to hold him close, to smell the apricot-sweetness of his skin, to feel the fuzz of his ear against her cheek, to say I'm sorry I'm sorry I'm sorry—for what? Had she wanted too much? Safety for herself and for him? Was that too much? It hadn't seemed like it at the time, but if she hadn't wanted it they never would have left, and if they had never left she never would have lost him. She wouldn't have lost everything.

Often now, she wants to scream. Sometimes she does, and then the guards come to restrain her. They hold her arms behind her back. They drag her down the hall and put her in a room, a colorless box with spiders in the corners, until she calms down. But that's going in the wrong direction. The scream is for help, not for hindrance. Why don't they understand? The woman in the box next to hers is there because she threw up. To throw up is to disobey orders. You disobey, you get the box. The guards think: The smaller the box, the more we can control them. But everyone else knows: The smaller the box, the more out of control people become.

One day, when the air is damp and the sky is mottled and gray, there's a protest. People outside hold signs that say ILLEGAL IS A CRIME and SEND THEM BACK WITH BIRTH CONTROL. People hold American flags over their shoulders like capes. Superhero

Americans. She imagines them at home in their living rooms, a bowl of dog food by the door, a cup of cold tea that has steeped too long on the counter. She imagines them laying the poster board on the floor, uncapping markers, drawing the letters, coloring them in.

Esme lost her baby. She left that part out.

"She had a miscarriage a few weeks after she got here," a woman named Marta tells her. "*Gracias a Dios* that she didn't have to carry it to term. Her body released its own pain." Marta stops and shakes her head. "They don't take care of nobody in here, see. They don't care who we are. It's easier to fuck somebody than to give a fuck, you know?"

One morning, a woman in a pale-pink T-shirt approaches her in the cafeteria while she's getting a tray.

"I heard you were looking for your son," she says quietly.

She looks at the woman—she can't help it—with delirious hope.

"I might know something," the woman says.

"Like what?" Her heart pounds. She can hear the echo of it deep in her ears, even amid the clatter and scrape of silverware, the grumble of voices around them.

"Your ring," the woman says.

For a moment, she's confused, but then she understands. "Tell me," she says.

The woman nods at the ring.

"Tell me first."

A smile spreads like an oil slick across the woman's face, but she doesn't speak.

She keeps her eyes on the woman, her round face and her widow's peak, as she touches the ring on her finger. It's looser now than when she arrived. She twists it gently and slides it off. She closes her hand around it. When she gives it to the woman, she feels part of herself go numb.

"Tell me," she says again.

The woman fits the ring over the tip of her thumb. "I heard about a boy they found on the side of the road," she says. "They took him to a hospital in Laredo."

"How old?"

"Ten?"

She forces herself to swallow. "No," she says weakly. "My son is younger."

"Oh, is he?"

She nods.

"Sorry," the woman says. "I thought maybe it was him."

She loses track of the dots. She loses track of herself.

Alicia and her daughter are released. Marta is sent back. She doesn't see Esme again.

And yet. Every day she waits for him by the front door. She sits on the floor, knitting her fingers in her lap.

And then—

"Gabriel!"

She scrambles to her feet. Mixed up in a tangle of people, there he is. His dark, combed hair, the freckle beneath his eye. God in Heaven! It's him! She lunges forward and wrests him from the crowd. She falls to her knees and pulls him into her arms. She's so flooded with shock and gratitude that she can hardly breathe. Her nose in his hair, the smell of him almost unbearably sweet. Her hands cupping his shoulders, those same slight shoulders, as small and breakable as eggs. "Gabriel," she whispers again and again. She can feel him shuddering. "It's O.K.," she tells him through tears.

Around her there is cheering. Or is it shouting? Why is everyone shouting? A woman's voice saying, "Don't touch my boy! Mateo!" And why does she feel hands on her now, prying her away, tugging her back as she reaches for him—isn't it him? isn't it? but it looked so much like him!—hands that carry her down the hall, hands that shove her into a room, hands that turn the key in the lock.

She crumples to the floor and blinks in the dark. From inside the box, she screams.

And then one day there are leaves on the trees, and wild-magnolia blossoms on the branches, bobbing gently in the breeze. She will stay in this place, she tells herself, until he comes. Through the window in the dayroom, she watches the white petals tremble, and, in a gust, a single blossom is torn off a branch. The petals blow apart, swirling, and drift to the ground.

She closes her eyes. Where has she gone and what has she become? The blisters have healed, the bruises have faded, the evidence has vanished—everything dissolves like sugar in water. It's easy to let that happen, so much easier to give in, to be who they want you to be: a thing that flares apart in the tumult, a thing that surrenders to the wind.

Good with Boys

FROM *ZYZZYVA*

I WAS GOING to sleep in a museum—with any luck, next to Esau Abraham, a boy so gorgeously Jewish he held the entire Old Testament in his name, in the perfect contours of his face. I had this theory about boys, that if they just got close enough to me, and sort of focused in, they would forget about the obvious deterrents, the glasses, the frizzy hair, the underdeveloped body. I was zany, I really went for it, I knew all the good dick jokes. Everyone talks about personality like it's a bad thing but the fact is, without one, you've got nowhere to go but ugly.

It's the beautiful people, isn't it, who most often wind up dead or alone.

We took a bus, not a yellow school bus but one of those real ones, with plush red seats and TVs, although we weren't allowed to turn the TVs on. Esau Abraham's mom, Mrs. Abraham, was on the bus, one of the parent chaperones. This was a problem but not necessarily a dealbreaker. She loved her son. She wanted what was best for him. We could be allies.

Someone opened up a giant bag of Cheetos. We were going to have dinner in the museum cafeteria but a bus ride demanded snacks. The bag got passed around, and soon the smell of powdered cheese was upon us all like a pollen. I knew even as a kid that kids were disgusting, the constant hand to mouth, the reckless tactility. Most of us did not wash our hands after we used the bathroom—a fact I'd empirically uncovered by spending a lot of time in the bathroom. I hid in stalls to avoid certain things, which was my right, which was all of our right.

The bus driver was a middle-aged woman who clipped her turns close. The second time we bounced off a curb, Mrs. Abraham jostled up to the front and rapped on the Plexiglas. "Hey," she said. "This is a bus full of kids you're driving. Can you please be more careful?"

"Lady, I been driving kids a long time. They love it rough."

She wasn't wrong. We did like it rough. The higher we bounced, the better.

The year before we'd gone to the planetarium. Esau Abraham wasn't at our school then. I had big plans for Sam Bell—got behind him in line so that I could sit next to him—but as we entered the darkened room, Allison nudged ahead of me. "Sam," she'd said. "Sam, you dropped this," and handed him a VISITOR button. His VISITOR button was fastened to his shirt, so we all knew it was a big fat lie. But I gained a lot of admiration for her just then.

We hit a pothole and I flew a couple inches into the air. "Take it easy!" yelled Mrs. Abraham.

"Not much I can do about the roads!" the bus driver called back gleefully.

There was a rumor that the local news team would be at the museum when we got there, since this was the first time an elementary school class—or any class—had been invited to spend the night. As an event, it was just hitting all the right chords for me: a sleepover, not at my house, at the museum of natural history, with boys.

I just loved boys so much, it was a sickness, it was a secret. I had to pretend I didn't love them as much as I actually did. I didn't want to be boy crazy. Once boy craziness became your signifier you couldn't be taken seriously. Your art would be ignored. I worked so hard on mine, I fully expected to have a gallery showing of my gouaches and charcoal sketches within the year. Esau Abraham was a really good drawer and I looked forward to our future collaborations, the font of mutual encouragement we would fill together.

When we pulled up to the museum and the bus came to an especially jarring stop, I slung my overnight bag over my shoulder, tucked my sleeping bag under my arm, and squeezed into the aisle behind Mrs. Abraham. I leaned in and breathed in to see if I could learn anything additional about Esau. She smelled like Vicks Vapo-Rub and faintly, confusingly, bacon. In the dusk, we gathered on the wide sidewalk in front of the museum. Sure enough, a newsman was talking to Ms. Green, our teacher. What a moment for her, for all of us. She was smiling and talking with her hands, her rosy face exuberant. I could tell she felt famous, and honestly, I think we all did.

Once inside, we were led to the Discovery Room, where we were told to find a place for our bags and sleeping bags. I was startled; I did not expect this to happen so soon. The Discovery Room had a hodgepodge of hands-on exhibits, some insects and fish, a family of stuffed wolves behind glass, and an enormous sculpture of the human brain that you could walk inside. Each of the four lobes was a different color and came with a mini audio tour.

Obviously, the Discovery Room would also be where I "discovered" more about Esau Abraham, if you catch my drift.

Esau followed his mother to a small enclave created by an aquarium flanked by two bookshelves.

"Here, Esau, this is a good spot for us," she said, taking his navy blue sleeping bag from him and laying it on the floor. "We can look at the fish while we fall asleep!" She unrolled hers—red with a tartan print on the inside—right next to his.

My unsinkable heart sank. I had to be strategic. I put my things down on the other side of the bookshelf closest to Esau. I quickly tested the space and realized that if I stretched all the way out, my head would be more or less in line with his, about four feet apart. Three feet and eleven and three-quarters inches too many.

What could I do but wait, which was of course the one thing I was terrible at. My great aunt told me once, when you dislike doing something, you have to do it more, do it over and over, any chance you got, until you not necessarily liked it—liking wasn't the goal—but just felt neutral toward it. Neutrality, she said, was the whole purpose. Real Buddhist talk for a woman—my namesake —with a severe QVC addiction. But I thought of her now, and tried to make this situation apply. How to wait more? How to wait over and over? Impossible. Thanks for nothing, Aunt Jill.

Most of the other girls in the class had spread their stuff out in a long rectangle on the other side of the room, closer to the brain. Coyness was never a virtue I cared very much about. Once it was lights out, once Ms. Green and the other chaperones were asleep, those girls would have twice as much work to do, with twice as much risk. Me, I was staying right here, close to my target.

Mrs. Abraham was squeezing hand sanitizer onto Esau's open

palms. I had to be careful not to watch him too much when he was with his mother. It was a turn-off. I took off my glasses and cleaned them on the bottom of my shirt. The only thing worse than a girl with glasses, I reasoned, was a girl with dirty glasses.

I was good with boys because I knew what they wanted. I could enter the simple machines of their minds and see how their gears turned. Most of them needed a lot of oil. To be told, a lot, how correct their opinions were, because most of them believed that opinions were like facts—provable and true. *Thinking* something, for a boy, meant not-thinking all other things. When two even vaguely conflicting ideas rubbed together, they either quickly chose one and discarded the other, or abandoned them both for a new and better topic, often something they felt absolutely certain about, like a cool video game, or whose bra was visible beneath her shirt, or what was I even doing there anyway. Over time, I could make them talk to me, just by simply existing. I occupied a genderless place where I neither quickened the blood like the obvious girls, nor inspired the bravado often necessary around other boys. Around me, they got to take five. Being a safe harbor may seem dull and sexless (so to speak—nobody's having sex) but it's actually a place of power. Deep, hard, penetrating power.

(That's the kind of riffing I had access to, for example.)

Mrs. Abraham went off to use the bathroom.

"Hi, Esau," I said casually, coming from around the bookshelf.

"Hi," he said. "Aren't you supposed to be over there, with the other girls? It's just boys over here."

"Oh really? I didn't even notice. It looks pretty crowded over there. I might just stay put."

Esau rubbed his hands on his jeans. "I wish we could sleep in the brain."

"Are we not allowed to?" This was a possibility I hadn't considered.

"I don't think so. There's not really a lot of room in there."

Mrs. Abraham came back from the bathroom. "Who's this?" she asked brightly, glancing from Esau to me.

"Hi Mrs. Abraham," I stuck out my hand. "I'm Jill."

"Well hi, sweetie. Did you find a spot for your stuff? Looks like the girls are going to be on the other side of the room tonight. Probably a good idea, right?" Her eyes were roving over my shoulder to where I'd painstakingly placed my things. I noticed from this close distance that the majority of her eyebrows were drawn on. I was a mothers' favorite and a grandmothers' favorite and I had to decide whether I would risk my reputation and stay put, or oblige her and move. But before I could say or do anything, Ms. Green was summoning all of us to the doors. It was time to eat dinner, she said—pizzas had arrived—after which we had forty-five minutes to spend as we wished, in approved areas of the museum.

I got my two slices of pizza and fruit punch juice box and sat with a table of girls. My best friend Sarah was dabbing her pizza with a napkin.

"Why did you put your stuff on the boys' side?" she asked.

I punctured the foil circle with my straw. "I didn't actually realize there were 'sides,'" I said. "Seems like the whole point of being here is to, you know, mix it up."

Sarah chewed carefully. She was a very careful chewer. She told me once that you were supposed to chew every bite thirty-five times before swallowing it. "Well, I don't think we're allowed to sleep on the same side. They were supposed to put us in separate rooms but the other rooms have to be kept really cold or something, that's what I heard."

A girl named Caroline tossed her long, pretty hair. "They'll probably come to our side after everyone's asleep, and try to be gross. I heard Nick say he was going to steal our underwear."

"Nick's an idiot," I said. "Who even brought underwear? It's not like we're staying here for a week."

Caroline shrugged. "I brought extra, just in case. My mom always says to pack extra underwear, because you never know."

"Yeah, like, you could pee your pants or something!" Lauren shouted out, and everyone laughed.

I didn't laugh. I tried not to roll my eyes. Caroline definitely wanted her underwear to be stolen. I could see right through her. I didn't like this kind of game-playing. I didn't like silliness, the silliness so often ascribed to our sex. I was constantly trying to get out from under it, kill it as savagely as possible, like a slug you pour salt on even after it's dead.

If you wanted a boy's attention, you had to get it. You had to take it.

After dinner, I kept my eye on Esau. His mother was talking to Ms. Green and the two other parent chaperones. With a few other boys he headed toward Ornithology, which was fortunate, since it was adjacent to the Mineralogy wing, where I wanted to spend my time. I had some money to spend in the gift shop tomorrow and I was definitely going to get a few new polished rocks and minerals for my collection. Some agate, maybe. I did not want to lose sight of the educational purpose of this trip. I knew, deep in my bedrock layer, that Esau Abraham would come and Esau Abraham would go. I knew I had to keep a firm hold on my interests outside of boys. I stood looking at an exhibit containing necklaces of jade, peridot, and pink topaz, right next to the clusters of Mississippi pearls so creamy they seemed edible, and I felt stirred, filled with longing.

My desire for boys and my desire for certain other things—often inexplicable, sometimes beautiful, frequently plain, occasionally attainable, like a tiny plastic fifty-cent notebook charm complete with even tinier pencil, for my charm bracelet; sometimes not, like these exquisite jewels that came from places in the earth that no longer even exist—were knotted together as intricately as a DNA double helix. I wanted and wanted and wanted. I believed, like my Great Aunt Jill, that objects had the power to protect me from harm—the harm of loneliness and my own impermanence—and I believed that boys had the same power.

My little voice told me, take what you want. Take what you can. Heal in the long shadows of the taking. My little voice and Aunt Jill's little voice, maybe, were the same.

I realized I was standing with my hands and forehead pressed to the glass. I heard a few people enter the room and then Esau's voice, "Adam—wait up!"

"Where are you guys going?" I asked, straightening up.

"Adam wants to go to the dinosaur room, right?" Esau asked. Adam was a shy boy, shyer than Esau, and obsessed with Abraham Lincoln.

"I'm not sure we're allowed upstairs. I think we're supposed to stay just on this floor," I said, unsure of why I was taking the rule-abiding position, especially since I was planning on breaking a few unspoken rules later that night.

Esau looked at Adam. "I could ask my mom," he said.

"Let's just go," I said. Being alone with Esau plus Adam was better than being alone without Esau. And it was fun to take the lead, exciting. "We can pretend we didn't know."

The three of us walked quickly to the lighted exit sign. I opened the heavy door to the stairwell and held it for Adam and Esau. I saw Mrs. Abraham craning her neck behind a few kids wandering between Botany and Mineralogy, looking, surely, for her son.

We hurried up a flight of stairs, laughing, which was the sound of our nervous bodies trying to expel their nervousness.

The Vertebrate Paleontology wing was cold and very dimly lit. We fell silent immediately upon entering, tiny insects beneath the impossibly tall ceilings. The air smelled like stone—no, like bone. For a minute we stood there without moving, just inside the entrance. I felt a tingle in my body like a sustained high note, like I myself was an echo chamber for our collective giddiness. This would be a double trespass, I thought to myself. Once for being a forbidden area, twice for being an ancient era. We were moving through time in two directions, forward and backward. I wanted to be in charge of this moment, of being in this ideal place alone with two boys, like some better version of *From the Mixed-up Files of Mrs. Basil E. Frankweiler,* one of my all-time favorite books. Surely it wasn't too much to ask, to believe, that here under the spell of these skeletons and this flattering lighting they would both fall in love with me, and that although I would choose Esau, we would all remain friends and vow to undertake future adventures together. What good was a relationship, after all, with nobody around to witness it?

Adam broke off, breaking my trance, and hastened toward the crown jewel of the entire wing: the seventy-two-foot long *Haplocanthosaurus delfsi.* His footsteps were loud and sloppy.

Esau started to follow.

"Wait, Esau," I said, putting a hand on his arm. "Wanna see the T. rex's cousin?"

I actually didn't know anything about dinosaurs, but I had seen a sign earlier: the Late Cretaceous *Nanotyrannus lancensis,* for which the museum had recently acquired a skull.

Esau glanced over at Adam. "Sure—I just want to check out whatever-that-is real quick."

"Oh—yeah. Definitely. Me, too." I followed him, suddenly feeling less in charge. Esau stood close to Adam, his striking cheekbones slightly pink.

Adam reached with his index finger toward one of the dinosaur's tail bones. He reached and reached, but was still at least a foot off. He hoisted himself up to kneel on the platform and tried again, giggling, reaching. When he started to lose his balance, Esau caught his arm, pulling him down. The two of them in a heap on the floor, their laughter eddying through the room like ink in water. I stood above them, surprised by my anger, which felt like a betrayal to all of us, the same kind of massive bummer that happens when an adult walks into a youth situation.

"Ha ha," I joined in weakly, wanting them to get up off the floor.

Finally, they did. I tried not to look at how Esau was looking at Adam, tried not to register it as anything but boyish camaraderie. I felt a pang of something—sadness, but also panic, and desperation, like I'd been given the chance to re-enter a good dream and had messed it up somehow. I would do anything to get back in, is how I felt. I studied Adam, trying to memorize him so that I could be more like him, look more like him.

He started to say something, but was cut off by the jarring click of an intercom, a loud voice coming from the walls: *All students please report to the Discovery Room. Once again, all students please report to the Discovery Room.*

"Crap," I said.

Esau's face clouded over, exactly the way clouds cloud over the sky. "Let's go," he said.

We followed him quickly, wordlessly. When we got back down to the main floor, Mrs. Abraham was waiting outside the Discovery Room.

"Where were you?" she said. She grabbed Esau in a hug and cast a disapproving look toward Adam and me. "I was really starting to worry!"

"We just," Esau mumbled, "we wanted to see the dinosaurs real quick. Sorry, Mom."

Maybe I could win him back with righteousness, maybe I could get his mom on my side. "Yeah, I'm really sorry too, Mrs. Abraham. It was actually my idea."

"I see," she said. Her face did something I couldn't decipher. "Well, you're here now. Go get in line with the girls, Jill. It's time for all of us to get ready for bed. Tomorrow morning they're going to release the monarch butterflies, bright and early."

Reluctantly, I moved my stuff across the room. I followed the other girls into the bathroom, where we changed into our pajamas and brushed our teeth.

"Where'd you go?" Sarah asked, when we were side by side at the sink. She was wearing a soft pink pajama set with satin trim.

"Just, upstairs. To the dinosaurs." I spit. I was wearing a giant Snoopy nightshirt.

"Esau's mom was freaking out. It was kind of funny," she said, dabbing her mouth on a paper towel. "And, P.S., could you be any more obvious?"

We got in our sleeping bags. Ms. Green gave us one final lecture on good conduct, standing there in the center of the room wearing some kind of a sweatsuit. I lay and looked at the ceiling, listening to the whispers and giggles around me, and felt anxious. Across the way, the boys were mostly quiet. Someone let out an enormous belch, and there were staggered titters around the room. In less time than you would imagine, there was absolute silence, the climax of this much-anticipated day folding noiselessly into itself.

I was awake and grew more and more alert. I thought about Esau, I prickled with Esau. I needed his undivided attention. What was this broken mirror inside of me, that showed me I was ugly, showed me I was wrong, but persisted in its reflection that I was better than other people? Could low self-esteem loop all the way around and become narcissism?

I heard breathing, a body intermittently shifting, rolling over. I felt like I was part of the museum, part of an exhibit, the control group of an experiment—proximity to sleep as a kind of stimulant, maybe, since my head buzzed as if from caffeine. Surrounded by bodies, bones, all the inert matter proffered by our tiny planet, I felt neon.

I don't know what time it was when I knelt cautiously on my sleeping bag, and then stood, and then tiptoed soundlessly to where Esau was lying. It seemed as though the darkness itself was carrying me. I squatted against the bookshelf and could just barely see him, his face wholly at rest, his lips slightly parted. If I could just get him away from his mother, if I could somehow communicate through the thick silence—

"Get back to bed, missy." Mrs. Abraham's voice was a sharp whisper.

I fled. I tried not to cry. I didn't cry. I slept, a hideous sleep of humiliating dreams.

The next morning, we stood shivering in the damp grass of the museum courtyard, squinting at the early sun streaming into our faces. One of the other parent chaperones had lightly slapped my arm to wake me—apparently she and Sarah and several others had tried over the course of twenty minutes, but I wouldn't budge, and now I was holding up the rest of the class—so I'd thrown on my clothes and rolled up my sleeping bag and raced to meet the line. My mouth felt mossy and the chilly, bright air made me feel extra exposed.

Predictably, Esau stood close to Adam. I watched them openly; I didn't care about butterflies. Esau looked as though he had slept at a spa, his pretty skin glowing, his eyes fresh. Adam was oblivious, infuriatingly unremarkable—if this were a play he'd be chorus, back row—but what did my opinions matter? I wasn't in charge of anything. I leaned a little against Sarah, whose tallness usually got on my nerves, and watched three men from the museum set down covered cages on the long table we were standing around. I leaned on Sarah a bit more, bracing myself for a long boring lecture about butterflies and their dumb habits. But the three men merely counted to three and unlatched the doors, and all of us were made to forget for a second, as wings filled the air, what was hurting.

JOCELYN NICOLE JOHNSON

Control Negro

FROM *Guernica*

BY THE TIME you read this, you may have figured it out. Perhaps your mother told you, though she was only privy to my timeworn thesis—never my aim or full intention. Still, maybe the truth of it breached your insides:

That I am your father, that you are *my* son.

In these typewritten pages, I mean to make manifest the truth, the whole. But please do not mistake this letter for some manner of veiled confession. I cannot afford to be sorry, not for any of it. I hope you'll come to understand, it was all for a grander good.

You see, I needed a Control Negro, grotesque as that may sound—

You should know I was there on the day you were born, a reflection behind the nursery glass. I laid eyes on you while your mother rested, along with her husband—that man you must have accepted, at least for a time, as your father. You seemed to see me too, my blurred silhouette. Your birth (natural, vaginal) took place at the university's teaching hospital. I noted your weight (7 lb., 7 oz.), your color (dark and florid), your temperament (outwardly placid) like mine.

I assisted with payment for your daycare as well, when you were so small, still in those plush, white Pampers. The facility sat at the edge of campus. So graduate students, like your mother, could enroll their young children while they worked or studied. And faculty, like me, could take guided tours and observe through mirrored one-way glass. I took mental notes on the room of children, a rainbow of faces, but my eyes hung on you: your mahogany skin and dark, keen eyes. Your fat, curled fingers grasping at blocks, try-ing to build something sturdy and true. I grew skilled at enduring the feeling you inspired, a seeping pride that filled my chest, then spilled into a painful ache.

Remember your season of Little League games, the ones at Washington Park, just down from the bus stop? I could always spot you, especially at a distance. You'd be standing at the plate, arms angled, aiming for the bright white ball, determined to hit it past every boundary we could see.

What I mean to say is that all this time I've watched you, or else had others watch in my stead. My TA did a practicum with your sixth-grade civics teacher. One of my graduate students tutored you in middle school at my suggestion that he "give something back." He shared anecdotes of your progress, never suspecting that you were mine. Your sophomore year, I hired a college stu-dent, a young man of legal age but slight enough to pass for sev-enteen. You knew him as "David" from the neighboring county. Under my direction he befriended you, prodded you toward swim-ming (and away from the fraught cliché of basketball). He ferried me printouts of your correspondence, revealing your vernacular speech, the slant of your smile in cellphone pictures. Hearing this now, you might feel manipulated, violated, even. But I am almost certain that my determination to shape and groom, my attempts and failures to protect, aren't terribly different from those of any other parent.

Everyone has an origin story and this is yours: you began as a thought fully formed and sprung from my head. No, you were more like a determined line of questions marching altogether to-ward a momentous thrashing. It was 1985, years before you were born, and I'd just come to work here on this campus. Mother died at the start of fall semester, her body inundated with cancer, un-diagnosed until she had passed. Still numb, I traveled south to bury her, missing the initiation of my own first classes, returning as promptly as I could. I was only away for a week and a day, still a cold snap had scattered leaves onto the great lawn. My first af-ternoon back, I walked over to my office and was straightening the objects on my desk, my shirtsleeves rolled up, my back to the door. A man walked in and he startled when I turned to face him, so I startled too. He was—I learned a few minutes later—a senior colleague from my own department: history. He'd been away on sabbatical, and had come to my office to welcome me. "Sorry," he said. "I'm looking for a Professor Adams. Do you know where I can find him, buddy?" I realized what was happening a moment before he did, and forced myself to laugh, to try to put him at ease, though I fear my laughter came out as a strangled sound. You see, he'd mistaken me for one of the evening janitors.

But then, the next week, I stood before all of my bright young students. For the first time in a long time, I felt, if not settled, then at least situated. Soon afterward, in a morning seminar, I remember feeling hopeful as I collected an early set of in-class writings, our topic, nineteenth-century thinkers. I discovered a hand-drawn cartoon among the shuffle, no name in the corner, passed in on purpose or by accident—it was hard to tell which. It was nothing really, just a single frame of itchy graphite titled "Irony." Within its borders, a history professor leaned over a lectern, looking quite like me—same jacket and bow tie—except with something primitive about his face. A thought bubble hovered over the room of students: "Darwin Taught to Men by an Ape."

It's nothing, I told myself again, walking back to my apartment that evening, though, in truth, I felt tired. *What does it matter,* I remember thinking. What does it matter how much I achieve, or how clearly I speak, or how carefully I conduct myself, if the brutal misjudgments remain regardless? What if, even here, they cannot bring themselves to see me, and instead see something oblique reflected where I thought I stood? Mother always told me, "Work hard, Cornelius. Work twice as hard and you can have something." But there I was, a grown man, wondering what it was I could have, and what would forever be withheld.

What I needed, it occurred to me then, was to watch another man's life unfold: a black boy not unlike me, but better than me—an African American who was otherwise equivalent to those broods of average American Caucasian Males who scudded through my classrooms. ACMs, I came to call them, and I wondered how they would measure up with this flawless young man as a watermark. No, it wasn't them exactly—I wanted to test my own beloved country: given the right conditions, could America extend her promise of Life and Liberty to me too, to someone like me? What I needed was a control, a Control Negro. And given what I teach, it wasn't lost on me, the agitation of those two words linked together, that archaic descriptor clanking off the end like a rusted shackle.

Those words struck in me and, from them, you grew.

That was the start of my true research, a secret second job hidden inside of the rigors of my first one. Evenings and weekends I searched library stacks, scoured journals and published studies. I focused on contemporary ACMs, looking for patterns, for cause and effect. An ACM's access to adequate childhood nutrition up against disciplinary referrals resulting in primary-school suspensions. An ACM's expected time with his father (watching the game, I imagined, practicing catch), versus police reports of petty vandalism, of said balls careening through a neighbor's window. I was determined to measure the relationship of support, to action, to *re*-action, to autonomy in these young men. At some point it occurred to me to work backwards. I gathered a more intimate sample: twenty-five case files borrowed from the university's records, culled from a larger random pool. These ACMs came from families of high-middle income, had average or slightly above average IQs, had faces that approached symmetry as determined by their student ID photos. In my pursuit to better understand them, I called suburban high schools, interviewed teachers, coaches, parents, even, always over the phone, under less than forthright pretenses, I concede. My ACMs were all "good" promising young men, but they were flawed too if you scratched the surface. My dredging uncovered attention deficit disorder, depression, vandalism, drug and alcohol abuse. In several cases, I found evidence of more serious transgressions: assault and battery, accusations of sexual misconduct. Not one of these young men was perfect, yet each held promise, and this promise, on balance, was enough to protect them and to buoy their young lives into the future. Five years of my life spent marveling at the resiliency of theirs.

Now all I had to do was monitor a boy who enjoyed, on average, the same lifted circumstances that my ACMs had experienced. Prenatal care and regular visits to the dentist. An educated mother and father (or father figure). Well-funded schools and a residence situated in a "good," safe neighborhood. For his part, this young man would have to keep his grades up, have clear diction, wear his pants at an average perch on his waist. He would have to present a moderate temperament, maybe twice as moderate—just to be safe —as those bright boys he'd be buffed so hard to mirror.

What I aimed to do was to painstakingly mark the route of this black child, one whom I could *prove* was so strikingly decent and true that America could not find fault in him unless we as a nation had projected it there.

About this time, I met your mother.

What can I say—she was, in her own way, a force of nature, and the sole woman of color in the graduate program for environmental studies that year. I spotted her one rainy afternoon in a dimly lit classroom. The door half open, she stood at the lectern rehearsing, her PowerPoint blinking furiously behind her, projecting light and shadow on her face. Slide after slide of washed-out shores and water rising. She looked up at me but did not lose her place. It would be only one more year before you were born.

Our first night together, your mother informed me she was married—she intended to *remain* married—which came as a relief. Those early years of struggle and I'd become a solitary sort of man. Nonetheless we continued to see one another, sporadically, into the spring. She wanted a child, I knew, and although her husband was likely the source of her childlessness, to protect his pride she alone bore the blame between them. That winter, when I found out you were growing inside her, part mine and a boy, we both agreed. I would contribute financially and keep silent about my paternity. She would keep you nearby and take my requests regarding you to heart. She knew about my ACMs, but never that I needed a boy to balance them. Right then and there, I realized who you would be.

There are many studies now about the cost of race in this great nation. Most convincing is the work from other departments: sociology, cultural anthropology. Researchers send out identical résumés or home loan applications, half of which are headed with "ethnic-sounding" names. They instruct black and white individuals to watch other black and white individuals receive a painful-looking shot. The needle digs into muscle and the researchers mark how much sweat leaks from the pores of the watchers. They measure who gets the job, the loan, who gets the lion's share of salted, dank empathy. They mark which human-shaped targets get shot at by police, in study after study, no matter how innocuous the silhouetted objects they cradle. All these studies, I concede, are good, great work, but I wonder if there isn't something flawed in them that makes the findings too easy to dismiss.

My research, by contrast, has been more personal, challenging me, at times, to re-examine my history. How different my life has been from the lives of my ACMs, and from your life. You grew up on that tree-lined cul-de-sac, while I was born in the backroom of a two-room house, in the sand hills of South Carolina. I was a dark-skinned bookish child—we both are only sons. My own mother didn't have much money, but then again, no one had much. Certainly not any of the colored folks we knew, the only point of comparison one dared in those days. Most of my schoolmates had fathers, though, and mine had gone north, to Chicago, for work, and not come back. He was essentially a stranger. Even so, growing up, I felt his abandonment acutely, like hunger. I filled that hunger with reading.

Like you, I played baseball, if briefly. The summer I turned ten I joined the Negro Youth League. I went for the promised uniforms, which turned out to be sweat-stained cast-offs salvaged from a white church's collection. Even so, thick patches had been sewn onto the chests, and underneath mine, my heart felt sanctioned. Our very first practice, I managed a decent hit, a satisfying thwack like an axe cleaving wood. Afterward, I should have walked back with the others, but instead I set off on my own, replaying my minuscule victory in my head until it felt epic and novel-worthy. I wandered down behind White Knoll, crossing Main, still dreaming. I didn't realize where I was until I heard car doors slap shut behind me, felt the chilled shadows of strangers. Three young white men had gathered around me, their bodies blocking each path of escape I darted toward. "Where does this boy believe he's going?" the one in the work boots said.

As they knocked and beat me to the ground, I couldn't help but think of a boy we all knew of—Tully Jones—whose body had been found some summer before, floating in the river, his head bashed in. *When these men finish killing me, they'll drag my body down to the water too,* I remember thinking. Please, don't hold me down under that murky water—I can't even swim! Why hadn't I learned to swim? And how would Mother even find my body? What if she thought I'd run off, like my father had? Up close, the men reeked of peach brandy, the kind my schoolmates' fathers would nurse Friday nights under the sycamores. When those men finished doing what they did to me, I lay chest and cheek in the sand, playing dead, as they staggered back to their car, breathless. Even after they pulled off, sending up a sharp spray of gravel over my body, I kept on playing dead, as if I were sunk down under that endless water, my skin a wrinkled softness that would soon scrape away or be eaten by crawfish, by those microscopic creatures that troubled the silted bottom, until no one could tell or else it didn't matter what color I was.

The following fall, Mother insisted I attend a private boarding school, miles out of town. I wasn't to live in the dormitory with the others. Instead, I woke before sunrise, walked out to the highway, and caught a ride with a deacon from our church, an elderly man who smelled of polishing oil. He was the boarding school's custodian and the only other brown face to grace those halls besides mine. During the school day, we never looked at one another. I was always aware when he was in the same room, but I never let my eyes rest on his, not until we were far away from that place, and even then it was with a kind of shame.

The school's headmaster—the man who had agreed to my admittance—had gone "up north" for some number of years. His surname was the name of the school, and everyone knew it was his family's money that kept that dying boarding school from going under. At school assemblies, this headmaster would find excuses to parade me across the stage—my improbably strong elocution, the sharp crease in my uniform—defiant or oblivious to the contempt my visibility inspired. Even the dimmest boys were clever in their cruelty. Mother had been hired to cook and clean at the headmaster's residence in town, and for this, the others mocked her mercilessly. What could I do, it was true—my scholarship was her bowed back, her bleach-bitten hands. Enrolling me there must have been an act of faith or desperation, like pressing a message into a bottle and floating it onto turbulent waters.

Even so I clung to my formal education, setting off at seventeen to a small all-black college, then going far north for graduate school. The boys I'd grown up with mostly stayed rooted. They married girls from church, worked hard to scrape together a living or get ahead. Some were shipped off to Vietnam, a few marched in bigger towns, facing police dogs and fire hoses. I devoted my life to scholarly truth, spending the majority of my adult life here at this esteemed institution. After you were born, I purchased my own home, just a two-bedroom bungalow, but in a good neighborhood not far from campus. I can walk to work, and sometimes I do. Whenever I walk my mind wanders. Occasionally I worry that I've been self-indulgent in my research, somehow selfish in my secret fatherhood. Walking, I think the world is surely a better place now than it used to be for people of color. Aren't I myself living proof against my theories? Can't I be satisfied?

But then, like current, I'll feel it again, even now. It might be the guard at the campus market who follows me when I walk in to buy a carton of milk for my tea. Or a pair of young mothers who push their strollers widely around me on the great lawn. Mostly it's a growing unease about my career. Yes, I was hired. Yes, I've managed to keep my head above water, but in these final years, they've burdened me with the lowliest committee assignments, filled my schedule with 100-level classes, as if I were an adjunct. Of course this might be a reflection of some defect in my performance — a failure to publish as well as some colleague down the hall, my secret research obscuring my official work. But how can I know for sure? How does anyone know if they are getting more or less than they deserve? All I know for certain is that, last September, a police car trailed me when I was walking home one brisk evening. Me, Professor Cornelius Adams, in my sixties, in my overcoat and loafers, my briefcase clutched beneath my arm. As you well know, cruisers often patrol the edges of campus, quieting fraternity parties, corralling drunken freshmen back onto grounds. They only pulsed their lights at me. When I turned, the one on the passenger side — a black officer — shouted from his window. Where was I going, he wanted to know. Before I could gather words to answer, a more urgent call must have come in. They turned on lights and sirens in earnest and sped away.

Here are our lives laid out together: At ten, while I flailed beneath the blows of work boots, you flew down a zip line at a well-rated day camp. At twelve, while I reread tattered spy novels on the bumpy ride back home from that boarding school, your baseball team placed second in the region. You brought home a trophy. Your mother took a photo of you lifting it. Eventually she sent it to me.

As you grew older, I continued to make certain wishes clear to your mother — about your friends, your schooling, about the crop and length of your hair. Only once did she truly bristle at my intervention, when I insisted you leave swim team your senior year. The swimming had been good at first, but then you placed at state, a dive so graceful a big-league coach courted you. For a season, you took private lessons, shearing your hair, waking before dawn. You excelled in the water, your mother said—you might get a scholarship or more, so why not let you continue? I could feel her picturing you, her black son, draped in red, white, and blue, holding gold. In truth, I entertained this vision too, but in the end, I couldn't allow such a glaring deviation. When you were small, I'd worried you would sink below my ACMs, that you would be dragged down. But here you were, soaring too high for a fair comparison instead. Of course I did not say any of this to your mother. All I could do was remind her of my unwavering discretion: Hadn't I held up my side of the bargain all those years? When I said this, she hung up on me, and for a long time we did not speak, though I soon found out that the swimming had stopped.

And so I was surprised when your mother called last August to inform me that you were transferring here to finish your degree. I was only startled to hear her voice. I already knew you were coming, of course—I'd seen it on your social media. Perhaps your return was an act of muscle memory: all the years spent here at daycare, then later, in the back offices with your mother. It's possible too that you were persuaded by the slick recruiting packets I mailed to your PO box each semester. Two years you'd attended that out-of-state school, and while you were away, I followed you as best as I could, though less closely than felt comfortable. Like any parent whose child leaves for college, I was forced to let go of some of my sway—though this gap depressed me. Were you drinking too much? I wondered. Had you gotten in a fistfight, or fallen in love with somebody? I drove up to your campus once, but found the whole layout disconcerting—and never did set eyes on you. After that, I watched from a safer distance, monitoring arrest reports, subscribing to your local and school media sites. I hoped to catch a glimpse of your life. Did it resemble the lives of my ACMs, those boys I'd watched so ardently years earlier—their drunken escapades, their fearless hearts?

All I know is, when I spotted you here, you looked tall, so lithe. I did the math—your age against mine—and you'd just turned twenty-one. Whatever else had happened in the intervening years, you'd also become a man. Your visible ease in your own skin awakened something in me. Never mind those tragic stories from other towns and cities, young men lost and taken—they were not *you,* they were not mine. Your ascendance was a glimpse of what could be and their deaths felt submerged. I realized you had never been average: you were more like a line of poetry too lofty for me to decipher. With you here, I convinced myself that you'd made it out past an invisible trip wire, out to some safe and boundless future. Even if I could not be part of that future, I might still be able to revel in its promise. I was nearly ready to give up on my questions, or claim that they'd been answered favorably—those questions of mine, which had always been about hope.

But then—we both know what happened then.

As soon as I heard what they'd done to you, I wrote through that first long night and cancelled my next day's classes. Decades of research became a single anguished letter detailing the difference I could now measure on your face. I wrote about the burden of Race—how it warps the lives of black and white people. I did not speak of my experiment directly. Instead I used what happened to you as an anchor for my findings. I could never have predicted that my essay would spread so widely, that inside of a week I'd be invited to appear on several networks and a handful of national radio shows. In studio after sound stage, I laid out my meticulous argument, supported by data and by true stories I'd witnessed with my own eyes. I thought they'd be convinced, but instead they interrupted with other stories, opposing conclusions. I thought they might believe me, but instead they held up a few undisciplined lines from my essay as proof that I was angry and absurd. Death threats flooded my inbox, along with crooning love letters from mothers and sisters, from fathers and sons. Still, last night, I was contacted with an offer of publication—not from a prestigious university press, as I'd always envisioned, but rather a two-book deal from a large, traditional publisher best known for true crime stories. Maybe there I can finally write what I want—if it's all right by you—about what's been done to me, about the things I've done.

As far as what happened to you: I saw the pictures like everyone else, I read every account. I studied the cellphone video, frame by bloody frame. Here is your face, in which I have always recognized fragments of my own.

Here is your blood, too bright and pouring. Even as you lie stock-still, pinned to the pavement, the police shout staccato commands, which they seem desperate for you to follow. The camera veers and I see them too, sauntering by in spotless sneakers, their ball caps askew. They look relieved that it's you there on the ground, or else they flash faux gang signs at a camera only they seem to appreciate. The police made a statement before the video surfaced, in defiance of the fact that there is always a video nowadays. You seemed dangerous, they said, and I think of you as a swaddled newborn. They feared for their safety, they said, and perhaps this is true. Later, in a press conference, they admitted you had an ID, but there was some discrepancy. It was from a neighboring state and unfamiliar. You did not appear to be who you said you were.

Beyond all of this, I understood a separate truth, one not yet found in any publication. I knew that they had *chosen* you out of all those wasted students partying on the strip of college bars. I knew this because I'd worked late that night, the first warm evening of spring. I'd decided to walk home through the carnival of youth, and only by chance spotted you out front of that bar on the corner. You were right there in the fray of students, half swaying to music that spilled from an open patio. You tilted your head toward me. Did you see me, too? Did you recognize me? I can't adequately explain it, but I must tell you now that *I* was the one who called the precinct, claiming to have seen a "suspicious young man" at the corner of University and Second. I called but I did not specify your height, your *color*. Afterward, I hurried home, reassuring myself. Nothing will come of this, I tried to tell myself—and I will finally be able to let it go, or be let go by it. Son, please believe this, if you believe nothing else I've written: this was a test for *them*—for the world!—not for you.

But here, again, we must take a step back, and remind ourselves that this has all been in service to something bigger—that someday our sons' sons might be spared. Your mother used to say to me, "The seas are rising, whatever you believe. Soon we will all be wet together, and together we will gasp for air . . ."

I saw you again the other day, out on the lawn at the student-led protests. At first I didn't recognize you, with that white bandage plastered across your head and the new bowed way you hold your body. But then they delivered you to the front and the small crowd swelled in support. I've read there have been other demonstrations on other campuses along the East Coast. A rainbow of faces chanting and wailing as if there are multitudes of watchers now.

When I saw you, I knew that you would recover, and it felt like I could breathe again for the first time in a very long while. But even closer to the bone was a feeling of grace that may well soon release me. I mean, look at you—look at all *you've* accomplished, in spite of everything. You made it here, just like *they* did. And I saw you, Son, turning and wild—free, even—for a moment at least.

The Brothers Brujo

FROM *Tough*

THE FUNERAL IS a Day of the Dead fever dream, all crowns and skeletons and robes and icons burning in the shimmering, dying light of the west. Women in face paint urge the icon down the street as mourners come and pin slips of green paper to his bedazzled robes, their faces slashed with tears. Men beat their chests and howl like apes, women offer up quiet prayers. Children dressed like mutilated angels kiss foreheads and pass out cardboard blessings. The air is thick and cloying with the cheap sugar of dollarstore candles and cigar smoke. This will last all day and deep into the denial of night, carried by songs of redemption and resurrection.

The mayor is dead, and the town, a part of it at least, dies with him and screams to be reborn.

Skeet's down by the rivermark, cutting symbols into the spackly mud with a stick when his brother crests the hill past the fence and calls down to him.

"Dad's looking for you."

Skeet keeps cutting in the dirt. He decides that one of the symbols means ribbon. He draws it again, just to make sure he's got it. Above him, Leonel skids down the crumbly hill, knocking sheets of dirt loose and tumbling down ahead of him.

"You have to come home."

"Who says?"

"I told you. Dad."

"He can come and get me himself then."

"Don't be a dick. He says the mayor's dead."

"I know he is."

"How? You've been out here all morning."

"Listen."

The two of them go silent. At first, Leonel can't hear anything, but then, a moment later, it's there. A shaking, dissonant clanging, like three bands playing different dirges against each other. A three-way car crash of notes and melody, metallic and reedy and ugly.

"They've been going for hours now. They only play like that when somebody important dies." Skeet keeps carving in the mud. He doesn't turn around to face the other boy. Not yet. He knows his bigger brother doesn't like to see the marks unless he has to, and right now, he doesn't.

A silence passes between the two boys, brittle and porous, like dry bones. Skeet threads one long-nailed hand through his scrubby short hair, Leonel kicks at the mud.

"He's waiting, Skeet."

"Let him wait. I don't want to go just yet and neither of you can make me."

"He's just gonna get madder."

"He's always mad."

"He's not."

Fine, fuck it.

Skeet turns to look at his brother, gets in real close, so Leonel has to look at the thick black X tattoos carved on the thin skin under his eyes. His earliest memory, his father buzzing the needle-gun into his face with cold, meth-head determination. The pain, the way it lit his brain on fire. The way he sobbed, like he was never going to breathe again. Red tears cutting down and pooling along the line of his jaw, dribbling on his bare chest and collarbone.

"He is, Leo."

Skeet studies his brother's face, somehow left unscarred by the old man's cruelties, shaped more by neglect and self-reliance than anything else. Agaju's damages are clever, left in places hard to find. Scars webbed under the hair, bruises punched in under his arms, belt lashes striped along his back and thighs. Skeet's suffered too at Dad's hands, but they both know Skeet's the favorite, a fact that neither of them will ever give voice to. To Leonel, Agaju's an empty temple housing a withered, sadistic god. To Agaju, Leonel's a first draft, a failed attempt. Something to send out for beer and cigarettes and to fetch his brother. Groceries. Bets at the horse track. A warm, crying body to smack the shit out of when he gets in the depths of his booze-rages. School, if there's time, and if Leo's not too marked up to go.

Skeet hasn't ever been to school.

Agaju hasn't left the house in seven years.

"You know he is."

Leonel's eyes are already wetting up from staring at the tattoos. He finally draws a breath, sharp and sudden, and tears himself away from his little brother. When he speaks again, it's with a voice that shouldn't be his yet, weary and haggard and worn threadbare.

"It's just going to be worse for everyone if you don't come with."

Skeet turns and cuts another few symbols into the ground—still, time, death—then throws the stick into the dried-up crick. Smiles at his brother.

"Okay. Let's go."

"Okay."

"Okay. You first."

"Okay."

They climb the hill single file, hop the fence, and disappear from the little wild for the edge of town. They don't talk as they go. They don't talk at all, unless they have to.

Down the VA they call Agaju Threefer, or at least they used to, back when he went. Shorthand for Three-for-Four on account of his no legs and one arm. Blame Vietnam. Still enough life left in his ruined mutilation to fuck two sons into two different beer hall cheaps, though. Even married one of them for almost a year. Long enough to saddle him with one of the boys. Nobody remembers which one, though. Doesn't exactly matter. Bastards. All fucking bastards.

Around town, most people butcher his name, pronounce it Aggie-you or Aggie-jew, else they just call him the priest. They don't come out to the house 'less they have to. They don't know what he does the rest of the time inside the shitty clapboard trailer-and-a-half just outside the city limits, they're content to clank and drink and fuck their lives away, whispering rumors to each other and living in fear of his boys, the marked one and the one with the serial killer stare. Something wrong with the whole genetic line, half-buried out there in the dust.

Still, they need them. Don't mean they have to like it.

The boys pretend not to notice.

Agaju's hunched at the altar when they walk in, folded over in his chair and grunting and cranking on himself among the candles and incense. Skeet and Leonel wait quietly in the kitchen until he's finished. The hot smell of it, sour and musky, stains the air and he yells for fucko to bring him the rag.

Always fucko. Never Leonel.

Fucko forever.

The older boy stalks through the house, looking for the embroidered handkerchief that his dad calls the rag, stained and blackened from dozens of rituals past. When he brings it, his father snatches it out of his hand, then waves him off. He can do the cleaning himself. Soaks up the filth with the silk, then folds it and sets it on the altar. Pulls on his stitched-shut pants with his one arm, hard as oiled ship rope from years of solo work, then glowers at his older son from behind his patchy scrub of beard.

"You bring him?"

Leonel nods. Knows better than to actually try and speak to the old man.

"Then go get him. Bring him in here. Fuck you waiting for?"

Leonel shuffles off. Whispers from the kitchen. Skeet wanders in, hands deep in his pockets.

"Fuck you been, huh?"

Skeet stares at his shoes, still caked in muck. "Down the crick."

"Doing what?"

"Just, I don't know. Drawing. Stuff."

"Drawing and stuff? What the fuck is drawing and stuff?"

"Like drawing in the mud and stuff. Throwing rocks. Just stuff."

"Drawing what?"

"Just pictures."

"Pictures like what?"

"Just pictures."

"Pictures like the old language?"

"No. No. Promise."

"You sure?"

"Yes, Dad."

"You wouldn't lie to me, would you, boy?"

"No, Dad."

"Shit's not to be fucked with. S'bad old magic, you hear?"

"I hear."

"What?"

"I said I hear."

"Good. You know what happened?"

"The mayor?"

"Good. Yeah. Look at me, boy. Said look at me."

Skeet looks. The sight of his gnarled stumps and raw, home-done tattoos makes his stomach twist and crawl in living tangles, a basket of pregnant snakes. Agaju sticks a Marlboro between his bloody, chapped lips and lights it, the Bic so buried in his knotty paw that it almost looks as if he's summoning the fire from nothing. Skeet's pretty sure that his dad can't actually do that, but he's not a hundred percent. Agaju blows a grubby cloud in his son's face. It stings his lungs with a familiar buzzing that he's almost learned to enjoy.

"You know this one's important."

"I know, Dad."

"Can't have anybody fuckin' it up for us."

"I know, Dad."

"Not you, not anybody out there, and 'specially not that fuck-tard brother of yours."

"Yes, Dad."

"We pull this one off, we get to eat for the next few years. This isn't parlor trick shit, a few bucks here and there from strangers. This is real work, and real work means we eat. You wanna eat, right?"

"Right."

"So don't fuck up. And keep that retard far out of it. Got it?"

"Got it."

"Good. Go wash up and get ready. Imma prep the altar. Gonna give these hicks a hell of a show. That's what they're expecting, right?"

"Right."

"You're motherfuckin' right, right. Go."

Skeet goes. Agaju stays. Sits still until he hears the rickety shower start up. Starts pulling together the rest of the ingredients he needs—fresh blood, mezcal, sage. A few bullets, a couple small

amethyst daggers of scante. Teeth. Hair. A little glass phial of gaso-
line, another one of holy water. A straight razor, a box of matches.
And the soppy rag.

American magic is brutal, and ugly, and messy, but goddamn it
fuckin' works.

Happy with the collected mojo, the old man slowly creaks to
the garage, and his homebaked tattoo gun. Strips his pants off and
picks out a bare spot on top of his left stump. Dips the sharp end
of the rig in the ink and starts drawing. Rides the needle deep, 'til
red seeps out around the wet black. He relishes the hurt, drinks it
in. The ritual demands sacrifice. When it gets too much, he starts
to groan and growl and then he's coming again.

Leonel's out in the back lot breaking bottles against the rocks and
fence when everything goes quiet. It's not one of those strange
moments when synchronicity descends on the world for a perfect
breath of shared silence, nothing like that. More like all the noise
gets sucked out of reality. He can't even hear the ringing in his
ears that sings him to sleep every night, a memento from one of
Agaju's cerveza-and-meth-fueled hurricanes. The scar on the far
side of his head tells the same story in a different language.

The silence is perfect, absolute. Crushing. It presses the air out
of him, throbs the inside of his head in hot swells of blood. He
tries to battle back the nothing, but he can't even scream. He tries
and tries, feeling his face turning red, sweat breaking out in thick
lines across his forehead. Futility. Gives him the spins. Not long
before he hits the dirt, but it doesn't help. Just feels like he's being pestled into the side of the planet. He throws up a little in
his mouth.

Then he rolls over and sees.

There, behind the bathroom glass door. Skeet, staring at him
from over those fucked-up, ratty X's like drunk crosses. He doesn't
blink. Doesn't move. He's the one doing this. It's him, it's always
him. Except when it's not.

Leonel grabs for one of the beer bottles and whips it at his
brother. It cartwheels through the air and bursts against the glass,
exploding the window inwards in a razor spray. The sound is catastrophic, a gale sucked through a pinhole. There's a terrible wet
ripping just beyond the inside of his eardrums and the first thing

he hears when it stops is his own useless shrieking. Agaju's impotent yawling from inside, mush-mouthed rage like fuckenshit's wrong with you fucko. An insistent low-frequency hissing that he thinks is snakes until he remembers that Agaju made him kill all the snakes.

What is that?

He gets to his feet and follows the sound, shaky and a little bit painful still. There's a raggy hole in the side of the house where the sliding glass door used to be. Beyond it, Agaju bellows, the sound carried on the back of the hissing. Blades of glass blanket the bathroom floor tile, some rimmed with thin red. Steam rolls across the tops of them and out into the sunlight and Leonel understands. His brother's showering.

Which means the ritual isn't far off, now.

I won't watch this time. You can't make me.

He turns and runs deeper into the back lot, a maze of junked cars and corrugated metal, wire and bone and oil. He runs until he can't breathe and his legs quake and threaten collapse from beating against the earth. His face boils hot under his skin and his eyes well and blink.

Over ruined rusty sedans and towers of broken old TVs, he winds a path to his safe room, a gutted-out station wagon filled with books and a camp light and a sleeping bag and a couple porno magazines he swiped from Agaju's collection. He tells himself that he likes the pictures, but the truth is they make him feel funny and uncomfortable inside. The women are all hairy and misshapen and stare at him from the glossy paper with something dead and gross in their eyes. Some of the girls have dicks.

This is his real home, where he keeps his things, precious and obscene. His sanctuary from the strange hell that is his father's home. Out here, he can be alone. Out here, he can be himself. With all of his stolen things.

Under the hood of the station wagon, though. That's where he keeps his real treasure.

He vaults over the top of the station wagon and looks around, making sure no one's spying. Satisfied, he pops the catch and lifts the hood. Inside, where there should be an engine is a half-rotted, splintery wooden box. Inside that, the treasure, wrapped in a towel. Leonel pulls it out, slams the hood, then climbs into the wagon. Nestles down on the bunched-up sleeping bag and lays the bundle across his knees. Unwraps it carefully, as if he were handling a sick infant. Feels his guts curl up with something almost like arousal once it's in his hands.

Sleek and heavy and cold, black-blued and cut with walnut. The Henry .45-70 Government. Lever action. Pretty much the most perfect weapon ever devised by man or god.

One of Agaju's, but he's not good with rifles anymore. Obvious reasons. Still buys them, though. The old man buys all sorts of guns. Hides them around the house like he's expecting a revolution or a siege. He didn't even notice when this one went away. Leonel snuck it out of the house one night with a few boxes of bullets, kept it out here ever since.

He practices shooting when Skeet's away and the old man's drunk himself entirely under. The gun barks like a dog trying to rupture its own throat, spits bullets bigger than his fingers. It kicks purple blotches into his shoulder, grinds the second knuckle of his first finger into callused sausage. He's gotten a lot better at hitting all the targets.

In the secret places deep away in his heart, he likes to call the gun Ochosi.

He loads the weapon—four in—and snaps the lever shut. Slides the barrel out of one of the wagon's windows, toward the house. Imagines putting holes in the walls until metal hits meat. Either of them, both. Let their holy wounds fill the house with blood and drown their attendants. He and Ochosi alchemizing living things into empty objects.

Skeet and Agaju and their bullshit magic.

This is real magic right here, motherfuckers.

He sets the rifle down next to the bag and turns toward the other side of the car, face to the sun. The warmth is radiant and sets his insides glowing. He stares until the burned-out afterimage of the sun eclipses the real thing. He doesn't think he's blind, but still clenches his eyes and basks in the liquid, fluttering nothing dark until the pain dismounts.

When he opens his eyes again, he sees the note.

Hermano, written across the top in his brother's clumsy script.

He unfolds it, holds it up to read. Goes through it twice. He even signed with his real name. Not that bullshit nickname Agaju makes them use because he's scared of the real one. Skeet. Agaju's own personal joke, his sons little more than wasted cum-shots to him, outside the utility of the rituals.

Leonel reads the note again, and again.

He likes what he reads.

Steam climbs the mirror and blurs out the blood, leaks out the hole in the wall. Through the churning fog, the marks under his eyes look different now. Like ampersands, or pound signs. Skeet can still hear his brother wailing when he climbs in the shower and starts rinsing off the blood. The water darkens as it licks along his new cuts. The heat stings. Makes it feel like his whole body's on fire.

Soap's only gonna make it worse.

Still, he reaches for the bar of dollar-store Kleenscrub and tries to get the thin, gritty pulp to lather. The hurt gets worse and worse. Alcohol in the soap. Makes him want to scream, but he doesn't, saves it for later. Gonna need all that air, all that power for the ritual. So he soaks the pain and swipes a finger through the cheap suds. Starts writing on the Plexiglas with one finger.

C
H
A
N

Two more letters and he's done. Admires his name, clear against the steam, then wipes it away. Gonna need that for later, too. A quarter of a mile away, in the rusted depths of the lot, his brother should be finding the letter. No way to tell if it worked until later. But he believes. And that might be enough.

The warmth in the water starts to gutter. Skeet turns it up as high as it will go and burns the chemical sting away. Lost in the steam.

Agaju rolls the bottom of his lighter over another piece of glass. Relishes the brittle crunch of it, no other sound like that in the world. Empties the crumbles into the bulb of the pipe, fires up the lighter, the flame a steady blue dagger of heat. Rolls the pipe over the fire until little lizard tongues of smoke appear inside and tangle around themselves. Puts the other end to his raw, chappy lips and hits it.

Chemical biters cut with sweet decay fill his mouth and lungs and spark hectic at his nerves and fillings. Like smoking wet garbage on fire. The rush is a demon whistling through his veins on a supersonic jet. For a moment, he forgets just how much of himself he's missing. For a moment, he's whole again. Restored masterfully by a loving god, the shine back on the apple here at the bottom of the world.

Then it fades and the old familiar wells around the emptiness like blood from a wound. Useless, alone. A heart filled with rotting pink vapor.

He's still got time. He's got plenty of time.

He takes a heavy slug from the bottle of mezcal and fires up the pipe again.

Come back. Please.

For the love of god, please just come back.

All around the house, there's nothing.

A grand empty washed in sand and mottled with vegetal scrub under the unchanging, unforgiving dome of the desert sky. Their house, a lone outpost built up against the edge of a wasteland, fortified with rust and steel and magic and blood and hate. Night falls in a heap and Leonel can see for miles. Lights stud the horizon, the town in the distance, a cluster of lives burning electric.

Soon they'll come, bearing the light as they wade through the darkness, draped in their strangest finery and all their desperate cruelties. Pressed under the cold livestock weight of the mayor on slab. Come to pay witness to the sermon, Agaju's ritual. Come to see real magic.

Leonel clutches Ochosi in both hands and nestles down in his tower of scrap and broken glass. Closes his eyes. Waits for the sounds of them to rusk and clatter up the empty miles between the house and the town. There'll be no mistaking it—Leonel is the only one who walks the dirt road, and he's already here. They only come for the ritual, and discourage the curious. Agaju shoots at the curious from behind broken-out windows. You only have to kill someone once before they learn. Only a few townies bear the marks of Agaju's education, treated as heretic plague. Examples of the priest's wrath, for all to see. Hasn't been a new one in years.

Sleep tugs at him from beyond the walls of perception and he begins to sink. His eyes are still already closed. It's so easy. He disappears, and he waits, and he listens, and in his dreams, he is not himself.

Then, the parade. Leonel grinds the fuzz from his eyes and rises, watching them cross the glass eye of Ochosi's scope. One by one by one by one. Men in tailcoats, women in ballgowns. They all wear masks, brutally rendered in exacting detail that turns his stomach. Wolves and coyotes with slavering jaws, birds with glassy, bloody eyes, insects with mandibles that click-click-clack in time with their steps. Some wear masks not of animals but of vile caricatures of human beings, faces Leonel knows from town, their features all mutant and obscene, artificial deformity.

They wear these clothes to make the ritual auspicious. They wear the masks to hide their faces from the old man and each other. As if their supposed anonymity absolved them from colluding with the local necromancer. They hide in their masks, believing that they're safe from Agaju and God and each other and themselves. Formality coupled with idiot superstition. As if they could keep him from seeing anything he wanted to. They listen to their fear and their confusion. They play futile coward. Agaju always laughs about it after they leave.

There, in the middle, on a stretcher bedecked in fake jewels and sugar skulls and roses and cakes, lies the mayor. Carried by the four strongest men in the town. Fishbelly white and sloppy red, dressed in a white baptismal gown with his hands laced together over his prodigious gut. Eyes closed and held sealed with two heavy silver coins. Washed and trimmed and shaved leather-smooth. Brought unto the edges of the known world to be made whole again, their very own Hillbilly Christ.

Leonel's sure he died like he always does—too much crank and booze and pussy and doughnuts for his overworked heart to handle. Wonder who found him this time. Suppose it doesn't really matter. Agaju will do what he always does, and behind their masks, they'll all quietly thank their dead god that it worked. And everything will go back to running the way it always does. No cops. No law. No government eye. No consequences. A tiny kingdom with none but one rule.

Until the next time he dies. And the next. Again and again into the depths of vulgar infinity.

Leonel lowers Ochosi and lays it across his lap. Shuts his eyes and listens to the sound of the crowd's hushed jabbering as it carries over his wreck of a home.

"—freaks—"

"—think it really works—"

"—must be some kind of sin—"

"—Threefer's mad, always been that way—"

"—those boys getting to be a problem, I don't give a fuck what they can—"

"—You haven't seen him do what I have—"

"—public nuisance—"

"—freaks—"

He hears them all. They say his name. They mangle it with hate and fear and too many teeth. Maybe they've never heard it said right. Something wrong with their hearing, something wrong with their brains. Leonel thinks about him and Ochosi cleaning the wax out of their heads.

Electric candles light their way from behind, but he doesn't see them. He just lies in his self-made cage and lets the blood bubble out of his brain.

The limbs are cracked and splintery and uneven and don't fit over his mangled stumps the way they used to. Had them made years back, when he was thinner, less gruesome. He hasn't worn them in almost two years, and in the time between they've started to grit and rot. They grind wooden needles into his scars and his bones and he cinches the leather belts tighter to distract from the hurt. The skin underneath goes pallid and squeezed-stiff and he punches his misbehaving flesh in toward the bone until it learns to do what it's told. He secures the buckles and, swallowing back tears and yelps, heaves himself up.

Agaju totters over to the dresser on driftwood legs and uncaps a pint of Yukon Jack, presses the mouth to his lips and drains it. Honey and spice and battery acid snarl into flame in his belly like a torch held to a ball of crude oil. It aggravates his ulcers and for a moment, he feels as if he's going to belch blood, but it passes and settles into a manageable, coiled pain.

Then there's a knock at the front door and it's time.

He creaks and clicks into the living room and shows them all to the altar. The four biggest ones set the mayor down on the marble slab and step back. All the masks turn slowly to leer at him with plastic imitations. Nobody makes a sound. They know how this works. After seeing it so many times, they'd better. He basks in the silence. Owns it.

For a moment—just a moment—he thinks of his boys. Skeet, out in the hallway in his ritual raiments, the X's under his eyes pulsing with power. He doesn't know where the other one is. Wherever fucko got to, he'd best stay there, not fuck this up.

Agaju takes a deep breath, and begins. The sound is like a clap of thunder.

Skeet slips into the altar room as his dad shows the townies to their places. He's small, so it's not hard to hide behind adult legs and skirts, staying out of sight. They're all wearing masks anyway, so of course they can't see. Agaju's too concerned with staying upright to see anything else, but Skeet sees him. All that pride cut across his face like carved from wood. Severe and ugly darks and lights burned into his flesh.

Power gathers around the altar, makes the air feel puffy electric. Skeet's lower eyelids hurt and the crowd goes silent. Blood pools heavy in his fingertips as if drawn there by some alien gravity. It's close, now. He wonders if Agaju can really feel it or if he's just faking it.

In the middle of the room, a crease opens in the altar and none of them see it. Not even the old man has eyes to understand. Beyond the crease, Skeet can see shapes, impossibly massive and drowned in shadow, writhing in the light. His mind recoils at first, but he makes himself look into this strange bright dark beyond, to call to them, these dark things. Teeth the size of houses, tongues like highways. He leers into the strange void and when a colossal yellow and black eye rolls toward him, he has to force himself to not scream. It's coming. The ritual is already underway—just not the one Agaju thought.

The crease splits wider and light begins to spill out, laying heavy on the crowd, a blinding, tangible thing. It renders the expensive horrors pulled over their faces cheap and artificial, exposed for mummery. Skeet wonders if, underneath their costumes, they're squinting without knowing why. He hopes so, likes to think so.

He leans into the power and the light and the presence of that terrible, lake-sized eye, makes himself a conduit.

He whispers his true name against the crushing silence and that's when the quiet's blown apart.

Something fucked up happens to a normal person's brain the first time they see real magic. It's like a disconnect. Because real magic isn't like people imagine in the movies.

Real magic is so much better, and so much worse.

Most people can't comprehend it, really. It's too much, too sudden, too vulgar. So the brain only lets in little pieces, flashes of light and color and salvos of sound from far off and not much more. It edits the rest out, cuts lacunae in itself, leaving little more than pitty cigarette burns behind. Metaphysical self-mutilation at its finest, the limited human mind hurting itself in little ways in order to distract from the bigger, uglier damage. To make the truth a little more manageable, because undiluted, it isn't.

The truth is that magic's a beast, enormous and lumbering and starving. It's powerful, and it's violent, and it makes a fuck-awful mess that people don't want to see, or if they see, they don't want to remember. So their minds compartmentalize and let them remember the lights and the pretty colors and the temporary suspension of the laws of physics. They hear thunder instead of screaming. They forget the blood and the shock and the stink and the explosions of teeth and hair that seem to come out of nowhere.

They forget that magic's like watching someone get shot in the head.

Even when they're watching someone get shot in the head.

The finger-thick bullet rips through brain and bone and Agaju's face bursts in a bright red poppy.

He hits the floor in slow motion and everyone starts screaming.

In the corner, his marked eyes glowing in the shadows, Skeet forces the crease the rest of the way open and lets the magic do the rest.

Say fucko now, you stumpy shit.

Ochosi barks again and mule-kicks the soft of Leonel's shoulder. A cloud of smoke rises from the muzzle, and through the blown-out window, he sees a sheet of blood skate off a lady's head before atomizing into thin nothing. Behind the smell of burned powder, there's the ozone electricity of his brother's ritual seeping out of the house in vaporous waves. Almost at its saturation point. Seconds away.

Skeet'll handle his part, Leonel just has to handle his own. Crowd control, that's what his little brother called it in the letter. He had the whole thing planned out. Freedom from the gimp and his abuses and his bullshit in a few easy steps. All it would take was a whole lot of dead people, and that wasn't going to be a problem.

Leonel knocks another empty brass from the rifle and looks down the scope at another scared masked someone, crouching and hiding from the madness they've found themselves in.

Breathes, in, then out, slow.

Pop.

Another spray of hand-tooled foam rubber and chunks like rose petals floats into the dark.

The air inside catches fire and resolves itself into a spiderweb of characters from a language that doesn't exist. They swirl and lick and flood into each other, a wave of orange and red and black descending on the gathered heads as they're trying to escape. It's no good. The doors are lodged shut, or locked, or blocked. The result's the same. The manimals start clawing at each other, kicking and punching to try and find another escape that doesn't exist. The smell of burning pork mingles with the rank fog filling up the room.

Then, finally, thankfully, they start to die.

They breathe and swallow scalding oxygen, they catch flame and fall to the ground next to what's left of the old man. They roll around. They scream. They beg. In the middle of the room, the mayor's anointed carcass swells and blackens and erupts, spilling over with a phalanx of rotten meat and insects and unidentifiable effluvium that immediately catches fire. The burning spillage runs over everything, seeps into eyes and noses and throats. Living napalm burns the life from them.

Then they go quiet, all at once. The magic drains all out of the room, and then Skeet's alone in an abattoir. He's exhausted and sweaty and sort, but he's smiling wider than he has in maybe his whole life. It splits his face in half, a white calcium zipper spotted with red and black. Something moves under his skin, something gargantuan and heinous and ancient. His tattoos knit themselves into another shape, and beneath his feet, the house is collapsing. He unlocks the doors and leaves to wait for his brother.

Wood bows and cracks, siding warps and gets stripped away. Glass bubbles out for the briefest of moments before shattering entire. The house crumples in on itself as if pressed by a compactor, or crushed by the invisible hands of some pissed-off elder god. Leonel watches it happen from atop his tower of ruin, Ochosi still warm in his white-knuckled fists. It doesn't make any sense.

When the house is good and flattened and gone and the smoke's cleared, he looks down the scope again, just in time to see Skeet's small form walking off, away from the crash and massacre.

Down to the rivermark.

"Are they all dead?"

"Yes."

"All of them?"

"Yes. All of them."

"What happened to the house?"

"Gone."

"I saw."

"Then why'd you ask?"

Skeet's floating in the river, arms out like a drowned Christ. Black water that wasn't here before laps at him and drags the edges of his clothes out in white streamers. Leonel can see that his little brother's tattoos aren't X's anymore, they're stars, infinitely black. He has the sudden vertiginous sensation that he's not just talking to his brother. The twin stars look up at the empty night, seeing more than Skeet's other eyes ever could. Ochosi is heavy in Leonel's hands, but he holds it close all the same.

"Did you do that to the house?"

"Maybe."

"How?"

"I can do anything."

As if to illustrate his point, Skeet raises one hand from the water and all around him, slithering red and white coils surface and dive and surface again. Leonel sees long blades of fin, and pocks of bright black eyes. Eels. Dozens of streaky, albino eels. He shudders, suppresses his gag reflex, but doesn't look away. There's a pattern to it, some horrible symmetry in their thralled ballet. He doesn't want to see how it's beautiful, but he can't help it. The eels froth around Skeet for another moment, then vanish underneath the sputile waves.

"How did it feel?"

He almost lies, then he doesn't.

"Good."

"Good."

Thunder trundles overhead, uneven percussion beyond the clouds. Leonel's shoes sink into the wet loam of the rivermark. Grubby dirtwater splashes his laces. It takes him a minute to realize, the river is rising. Slow at first, but now steadily. He steps back onto the dead grass to stay dry. It crisps under his feet, a whisper against the chatter of the water. He turns away and doesn't see the thing that became his brother sinking in.

Over the ridge, the lights are flickering and going out. The wakes rumbling to rest, the townies passing out drunk and stoned for the night or maybe just dying. Maybe the fog of his brother's magic reached that far, snuffing lives out as it rolled along the wastes, chilly and indifferent. By morning, whoever was left would come looking for their friends and mothers and brothers, and when they came, they would come with teeth and knives and bullets and heads brimming with weird, spoiled hate. They'd cut the boys apart and eat the pieces. Screaming and jacking off to their own delusional self-righteousness as they did. They would have their revenge.

Or at least they'd try.

Better that they never get the chance. Leonel turns back to tell the brother-thing that he understands, but it's gone. Only the waves remain as the black, oily river rises nearer the ridge that blocks it from the rest of the valley. Not long before it spills over, blackens and drowns everything in its path. Heedless.

Leonel watches the opaque water rushing over everything for a moment more, then returns to the remains of the compound and fetches his boxes of bullets before turning his attention back to the distant town. He sets off on foot. He takes his time, no need to rush. The walk is cold and dusty and he pays it no mind. They get closer and closer and Ochosi grows warmer against his palms, as if excited. He purrs to the gun as he reloads it and walks the path. He tells it secrets and the gun whispers back.

At the edge of the town, next to the first house, they stop and listen to the nothing of locked doors and drunk sleep. The stillness of playhouses and rust-blackened barbecues and empty, distant highways. Not long for this world.

There are lights left to extinguish and he still has a little magic of his own left to dispense.

A Big True

FROM *The Southern Review*

STANDING OUTSIDE HER locked door, he scanned his memory for places Yasmine might have gone—a drink? A day-trip? He walked the forty blocks back to Port Authority, spending most of it knotted in regrets and daydreams. He adjusted his earbuds, turning up the sound on the 1970s Turkish folk player he had found, his late father's colleague. The ragged old hippie droned in Rahad's ear as he walked, the sound crossing oceans and decades. Every time he heard this song, he remembered the singer's thick moustache, the way he seemed to sing through it. He missed Yas. Against all reason and recent memory, he had imagined her delighted to spend an afternoon together, indulging in a bottle of smoky red. If he had taught her nothing else, at least she had kept this: an hour isn't squandered if you taste a good wine, if you fill your ears with good music. He had convinced himself that such a visit would be possible, if he could just survive her initial surprise and anger—he hadn't considered that she may be spending the day elsewhere.

The last time he showed up unannounced, his welcome was a long, dramatic sigh. "I called, *azizam*," he said, deflecting the lecture he knew was brewing in her head. He didn't set down his overnight bag or sitar case for fear of her anger, but in the end, she invited him in. "I called many times," he said and moved past her. "You don't check your messages. I got tired of waiting." That was months ago.

Today he had rung her doorbell again and again, shifted his bag and case to his left shoulder, and glanced up at her girlish,

sea-green curtains, before turning north to catch a bus to Wilmington. His cheeks flushed—he had believed she would invite
him to stay for a night or two. He had believed with such force.
Never mind, he thought; that afternoon he would move into the
Wilmington YMCA, his fourteenth in six years, but better not to
make a spectacle of it. Since the death of her mother when she was
six, Yasmine suffered from a kind of hysteria triggered only by his
various superficial prospects.

He shook his phone for a new song, losing himself in one by
Thom Yorke—oh, how he loved Western music. How glorious,
whatever the style. Secretly, he liked it far more than the Iranian
sitar classics he had played to spellbound crowds in Tehran. Maybe
later he would post this song and collect the likes, lucky amulets to
carry on the road. This meager attention helped him fend off the
suffering over Yasmine and Iran, his vanished self, his music. His
father, the elder *ustad* Sokouti, had been a world-renowned master
of seven string instruments, and Rahad a celebrated sitarist and
music teacher—but no *ustad,* no master. Still, he had a voice. But
by the time the blood reached his daughter, it seemed all artistry
had been strained out. Who, then, would remember those heady
Tehran nights?

On the bus, he posted and waited. The song was bad bait—only
four likes. He felt ashamed for the display: a serious Iranian musician, in his fifties no less, posting the songs of American teenagers
who have no musical education. No, no, Yorke was good, and not
even an American.

Now Yasmine appeared at the top of his feed. Ah. She was
spending the weekend in Connecticut. He was tempted to like
it, but refrained. She blocked so willy-nilly lately, and since he re-
opened his account, she had liked nothing of his. Where was the
dignity of fatherhood? Yesterday, fifteen people had liked his post;
but from her, nothing.

In Wilmington, the April air was crackling and fresh—none of
the wet, cold residue of winter that covered New York—and the
walk from the bus station revived him. Before long he saw it, the
brown brick, the blue sign: YOUNG MEN'S CHRISTIAN ASSOCIA-
TION. He was neither a young man nor a Christian, though he was
willing to pretend—in fact, he enjoyed it; there was great peace
in disappearing. In Iran he had pretended to be a Muslim while
spending every night in underground clubs. Once, in an Afghan

village he had pretended to be his own father—all this in service of hunting the next great fog of music in which to disappear, a rhythm to shape that month or that year.

The facade of the YMCA building was graying in parts, blotched like the face of a pretty woman who has spent the day crying; he could see that it had recently been presentable. He entered and signed in, paid his twenty-five dollars, and accepted his key, nodding thanks to the receptionist, a young black woman with a tight, old-fashioned bun at the nape of her neck. Looking him up and down with almond eyes (almost Persian, like his), she licked her gleaming teeth in momentary confusion. What was he doing there, in his long black trench coat that might have cost something in better days, his elegantly battered leather shoulder bag and sitar case? He wanted to say to her, *Surely, young lady, respectable people pass over rough soil now and then?* But if he said this, he would likely botch the English, draining the words of their poetry. Besides, she must already know it; she offered rooms for twenty-five dollars a night.

"No needles, weed, or weapons in your room," she said, her voice flat. "There's a shared kitchen and bathroom, but you need your own dishes and soap."

He walked through the dark corridor, past the communal bathroom and kitchenette, to his first-floor room. Before turning the key, he said a word in prayer (these days he said his prayers to Bob Marley, though the recipient changed often). Each new YMCA rekindled his dread of what that first swing of the door would reveal: in some states, he was met with a room as nice as a countryside motel, with a clean white duvet and a quaint photo on the wall; in others a hovel, hospital sheets and burned patches on factory carpets. Inside, he removed the trench, folded it twice, and placed it carefully on the twin bed. Eyeing the shadows on the crimson bedspread, he thought better of it, and placed the coat on the chair instead. He pulled back the bedding, lifted the mattress, and checked every seam and corner for insects. From his leather satchel, he removed a wrinkled garbage bag and a box of baking soda and peeled back the duct tape on the box's mouth. He placed his folded coat in the bag, sprinkled it with baking soda, and tied the end in a knot. He shook the package a little and left it on a shelf, the only available surface besides the chair and the bed. Then, he began the work of examining his sitar, polishing it,

tuning it. He mourned his lack of funds, as the sitar needed new
strings. When he was finished, he put away the instrument and
turned his chair toward the window. The curtains were thick, a fading floral pattern, and smelled of long-extinguished cigarettes. He
didn't want to touch them. Instead, he watched the cars disappear
from the parking lot outside—the teenagers going home after basketball, mothers leaving a yoga class.

He craved a coffee but thought it better to wait until dinnertime, when he could have his coffee with a meal and perhaps find
a cluster of computers nearby so he could check what the Internet
was saying about him today. He regretted breaking his laptop. But
things break; this is a reality of life. He didn't want to waste his
days puttering around online as Yasmine did, no matter what her
job title. And yet, he had to admit, as he watched the basketball
players and yogis rush home, their hours bound by routine but
also simplified by it, that he did waste a precious lot of hours just
surviving. Looking for a new neighborhood, beginning from zero
for the fifth time in a year, coordinating his meals around Internet
locations, finding Laundromats, hunting teaching gigs and motels
outside of town, visiting friends and hoping they would invite him
to stay for the night. This, every day for weeks, including winters.
Then, always, back to the YMCA.

As a matter of habit, he spent most of his daytime hours at the
public library looking up music, always remembering to check the
three big websites dedicated to his own career that the Internet
had created in the past few years. He admired the artful arrangement of his photos and videos; his biography in both languages;
the muffled, sorrowful tune (his own composition) that played
when he clicked on the first page. Finding the sites had been a
welcome surprise. For so long, when the Internet thought of "ustad Sokouti," they thought of his father, who already had dozens
of websites to himself. They must be witnessing a resurgence of interest in more modern renditions of classic songs, Rahad thought
when he first came upon the sites. He considered showing them to
Yasmine, since they might give her a feeling of security. He longed
to be an asset to her, like American parents. Not a burden. But he
never spoke of it; such topics always turned into fights.

To Yasmine, it seemed that Rahad had stopped journeying
along with the rest of society somewhere around 1998. He had
given up, sat in the road, and fiddled with his sitar until the oth-

ers were far out of sight. Progress was not his talent—he liked the 1960s, even the '70s, but beyond that, he had to be dragged. He had no health insurance, no acumen for anything technical, and was apparently an Internet bumbler. He had an outdated, off-line smartphone for his music, an old flip phone that held fifteen text messages at a time, no voicemail, and an email address Yasmine had set up that he checked every few days. Even so, he succumbed to some kind of scam almost monthly, each time thinking that the Web must have its rules and standards. "I wish you'd be more savvy online, Baba *joon*. It's full of con artists looking for someone just like you," she'd say. "I want you to be safe." He didn't know what safety had to do with it. Still, he made promises. "I promise you, Yasi *joon*," he wrote in an email, "I will acquire Internet skills and general American savvy."

The next morning, after a deep but troubled sleep, Rahad spent an hour disinfecting every surface, rechecking the pillows for bedbugs, and spraying every corner with insect repellant. When he was finished, he lit a sandalwood candle and put the Abyssinians on his portable CD player. The sound barely reached the four corners of his room, but it took all of a minute for someone to knock.

"What you are hearing there, neighbor?" a cheerful voice with a mixed-up Indian accent traveled through the flimsy wooden door. Rahad clicked his travel broom back into its plastic casing. He opened the door and said a muted greeting, trying hard not to react to the overpowering scent of patchouli and citrus that assaulted his nose. A dark man around his own age but more weathered, with thick gray stubble and a T-shirt that seemed to be made from an American flag, was smiling widely, displaying three yellow teeth that alternated with his white ones, like piano keys. He stepped inside, slapped Rahad on the back, and said, "Bro, do one thing. Please be putting on 'Forward Jah.' That is my favorite of this album by ten thousand percent." His mouth made wide, deliberate motions.

He introduced himself as Wyatt, wandered to Rahad's bed, and sat without invitation. He asked about Rahad's origins in a way that suggested he saw himself as the more American of the two.

"Tehran," said Rahad as he flipped to the song Wyatt had requested. "And you?"

"I am coming from DC," said Wyatt, rubbing his knees with his

palm. "An agreeable city. A first-class city. But bitch work to be surviving there, you know?"

Rahad tried not to chuckle. He had known many Indians. Most
had accents with a hint of British, dulled after decades abroad.
This man sounded American, but forcibly so, as if he had left Cal-
cutta last week and, afraid of sounding "fresh off the boat," as they
say, was trying to compel his accent to fit the patterns and rhythms
of natives through a heavy regimen of mangled Americanisms and
mouth exercises. "And the name Wyatt? How did you get it, sahib?"

"What you are meaning?" he said, eyes wide.

"I mean, tell me your good name," Rahad said. He wanted this
Wyatt to know that he had traveled to India, that he knew the
world this man had left behind, and that the only way to be Rahad's friend was to own up to the real story.

"My good name?" said Wyatt, making a twisting gesture with his
hand—as if plucking a ripe fruit from the tree—that absolutely
gave away his origins. He grinned toothily. "I have not the least
good idea what you are meaning. What finds you in this establishment, brother? Here is only down in the lucks, immigrants, some
pot smokers, and that sort. You seem like nice old Irani gentleman, no disrespect."

Rahad coughed into his fist. "We are same age, I think. Fifty-
four, fifty-five?"

"Oh no, no, sir," Wyatt laughed, flashing his yellow teeth again.
"I am just turning forty only. I am here temporarily. Who knows
what is coming next for anyone."

Having decided that the man suffered from some kind of mental illness, Rahad grew eager to expel him from his room. He
wanted to gather his things and find an Internet café or library,
but couldn't overcome his Iranian manners—he would not kick
out a fellow traveler. He nodded a few times and waited. But Wyatt
only smiled and shook his head to the music. "Forward Jah!" he
sang, not making the slightest motion to leave.

The next day Wyatt arrived at his door before breakfast. Apparently he had found naan, the soft, stretchy bread that Iranians and
Indians share. "Do one thing. Eat this naan, Mr. Rahad, because
you are surely missing your home."

He hadn't been *home* for two decades, but he didn't mention
this to Wyatt. Instead he focused on whether he should eat food
offered by a crazy man. Would it be tainted? But what can you

put in a chunk of plain naan? He ate some and agreed that it was good, freshly made like home. "You find *tanoor* around here? Where you buy this?"

Through a mouthful of bread Wyatt said, "No, no, is brick ovens here only. No *tanoor.* I am making dough in bathroom sink here, extra one I can be using all night for rising dough, then onward to my colleague at pizza joint for baking. Nice and fresher, cheaper breakfast than bagel or doughnut."

"Clever," Rahad muttered, giving the wet lump in his mouth a hard swallow.

Then Wyatt's gaze fell on Rahad's sitar in the corner of the room and his mouth hung open as if he had just seen a minor deity. "You have sitar? Holy shits!"

Rahad smiled. "And what does born-in-seventies DC native know about sitar?"

"I know every music, my friend," said Wyatt, now bent at the waist, nose-to-nose with the instrument, struggling not to pluck a string. "Shall we be having jam sesh today later perhaps? I have familiarity on tambour, which is make-doable using large bucket. You play from Viguen. I order for brick oven. It will be first class."

Rahad knew how to play Viguen. His father never played those songs, of course, since the legendary singer was his rival, and the old man felt obliged to dislike Viguen's Westernized music and pop-star image. The elder *ustad* Sokouti was a classical sitarist of the most traditional school. He excelled on every ancient string instrument, but would never touch a modern guitar. "Yes, a nice idea," he said.

He wasted the rest of the morning staring at parked cars, remembering those difficult months after Yas found out he had given up his house and become a drifter, an *avareh,* and he found out that she had put down her colored pencils (her last creative thread) and taken a tougher job at Google. One day he visited, and they paced her tiny apartment and shouted at each other.

"Did you want to stay the night?" She glanced over her blow-dryer. She was getting ready for a date. What did she hope for, he wondered, as she scrutinized these men over plates of oysters and fish tacos and bone marrow? The truth was almost certainly something he had failed to give her: a family, perhaps, or a home.

"I want to spend some time with you, yes," he said. Such skill she had at shaming.

"Where did you park?" she asked, eyes fixed on the mirror. He patted some baking soda from his pant leg, hoping she didn't see —every time he began a stint as a nomad, he found it clinging to him wherever he went, dustings of it on his shirt, in his jacket lining, in his sheets. The white powder was familiar and it amused him, but Yasmine would judge . . . if she could look away from her own reflection. Where did his daughter get this marble-hard vanity? Her mother had been a distracted scientist who memorized songs and didn't bother with appearances—sometimes she left the house with crumbs in her hair. Once, she went out with only one eye made up, and that night Rahad loved her more than all the days before. Now here was her American daughter, free to imagine and create and trust the universe, but instead she slathered on a second layer like a veil. In that, she was no different than those caged-in Tehrani girls he saw during his long sessions on the Internet, the ones with high hair under a scarf, big sunglasses and nose-job plasters, desperate to show their creative spirit in whatever way possible, but, in the end, masking themselves in another way.

Oh, the Internet, that mystical hand, that unseen eye, a marvel! It was a captivation he tried to hide from Yas. She would only say, *You don't understand it,* and conjure past arguments about art, vocation, legacy, and technological skill. Besides, who wants to admit to wasting their hours that way? He reached into his shoulder bag for the pistachios he had brought for her; the blushing, leathery bulbs, still in their outer skin, were every bit old Iran.

"Bus is easier," he said. In fact, Rahad's driver's license had expired and he wanted to ask to use her address to renew it, since his PO box—his one remaining fiber of a root—had lapsed. He busied his hands skinning the fresh pistachios with his thumbnail. He had found them in a nearby Eastern market that he browsed before each visit, steered there by an inexplicable banner at the edge of his screen—maybe the Internet knew that Yas had been ten when they left Iran and that she missed it more than she understood.

She shut off the dryer and stared at him, all angry eyes and perilous heels, and he felt like a boy on a scorching Tehrani school yard, again caught drumming on three upturned buckets instead of playing soccer or running the perimeter as instructed. "I can't believe this," she whispered.

"I like my life," he shot back. "No mortgage or bills. Everything easy and new. You might consider something more inspiring for yourself. You were so creative—"

"Jesus, Baba. Stop!" She slammed the blow-dryer on her dresser.

"Don't call me Jesus," he said, trying to lighten her mood with silly *bazi*, but her face grew colder and he had to look away, nodding to himself—no fun Yas tonight.

"Life isn't these quixotic fantasies!" she continued. "Yeah, Iran was all long boozy dinners and guitars in the garden, but that was a different universe. And even there it was possible . . . look at your *baba*. He had music *and* a big house with a courtyard—"

Such marksmanship. He interrupted in English that slipped in anger. "Why I have to be like others? You say this insult words, except than . . . is lies. Is not quick-exotic fantasy." No Iranian child would dare judge her parent this way. He had never spoken such words to his father, even as the old man napped away the mornings under a mosquito net and squandered hours on the veranda with his students, strumming three strings and ignoring everyone else. "Anybody can have black-and-white life by following some instructions. I choose colorful life. I want only to walk earth, find music, think . . ."

She turned and muttered in accented Farsi, "You're fifty-four. Maybe it's time to grow your own hands and feet." The familiar Persian expression stung. Where had she learned it? It was the sort of thing that frightened, unimaginative parents said to their children before prodding and elbowing them into medicine or real estate, and he had taken care not to be that kind of parent. Every day when she was young, he had read poems to her. Every day they had drawn castles, plucked notes, and trained her imagination through daydreams. Had he relied on other people? He never stayed more than two nights, always left behind skillfully curated CDs, washed every sheet and towel, replaced any milk or food he had eaten with organic milk and homemade bread. But to American children words are cheap, effortlessly learned and quickly dispatched. They strike fast with the tongue, offering instruction on every small thing. How can words you don't understand humiliate, they think, muttering their wisdom in low voices only to quench themselves.

Like the day he had arrived in New York to meet with his daughter in a café. She had time for only a coffee and she spent it telling him that he had disgraced himself online.

"Baba *joon*, it was creepy!" she had said. *Creepy* was a word with which he was familiar, but the connotations changed from moment to moment, and so it frightened him. She could have meant so many things. "If you like a photo, you click *like*. You don't tag yourself. You especially don't tag yourself on top of a picture of my friend in a bikini."

"What is you mean?" he had said, unable to hold in his anger. "I only click like. I click like for photo of my daughter enjoying beach. You make everything dirty and horrible."

"No, you *tagged* yourself," she had sighed, trying to sound sympathetic, an instinct that made him all the more angry. "You have to learn Facebook."

"In Iran," he snapped, getting up from the table, "no child says to father, *You have to learn*. No one. I never say to my father, *You have to learn guitar*, even though he refuses out of pride, even though no one wants to hear sitar anymore. I never say this to him. You and your computer *bazi*. Is big waste of life, these Facebooks."

Amid the hundreds of promises he had made to her on the day they left Iran, he had offered only one to himself: if exile was to demean and bruise him, fine; but it wouldn't clip his wings, replacing his craving for music with drudgery and fears of risk. And yet, the fates are crafty and they had inflicted his daughter with the very disease he despised. Yasmine, who had an American accent, who never mixed up her idioms and knew an insult from a joke and exactly what to say next, a girl who had every opportunity, had taken to taking root—a provincial instinct. At ten years old, she had set down her little suitcase, sharpened her pencils, and, like many good Iranian immigrants, set to work on her sensible American life: study, then do something joyless and technical with a steady paycheck.

After their argument at the café, he had thrown his laptop across the room (the guestroom of an old friend, a composer), shattering the screen. He quit Facebook from a library desktop. He didn't need a computer. If he didn't have one, Yasmine could never humiliate him with another explanation. She would just stick to complaining about his distracted, itinerant ways. And how could he make her see how life had unfolded for him?

Bringing her out of Iran with two suitcases and a sitar between them, stumbling from place to place, always at the mercy of chance, until he found their home in Baltimore. There he had stayed, teaching music to the children of rich Iranians and Turks all over Maryland and Delaware. Then Yas went off to college — Harvard, he was proud to say. He had begged her (a humiliating act, particularly in Farsi) to study music or art. "Computer science is the same at U of M or D or anywhere," he had said. "Please, *azizam*, Harvard has an art library that would wake Rumi from his grave." She had moaned. "You know, other Iranian dads would be proud." So he watched her graduate, move to New York, and start her first job. Then he set off into the world again, treading the unknown, always aching for stories, songs, adventure. Yes, he wanted a home, but purpose, inspiration, art: those are the soul's truest needs.

The night of their big fight in her apartment, after her date, Rahad sat up, watching his daughter sleep. The couch faced her bed, and the lights of the iron-and-fog city streamed in through gauze-thin curtains, so that he could watch her chest rise and fall. He followed its rhythms like a slow song, a ritual he had invented when she was a girl, in the days after her mother died and he worried that his daughter, too, would simply neglect to wake up one morning. Yasmine thought he had no dreams, but he had big dreams. He didn't escape the daily terrors of working in Tehran's creative underground to live a dull life, to be a clone of everyone else, to freely relinquish all imagination. Maybe Yasmine thought he was a disappointment to his own father, but she knew nothing of the old man. He had named him Rahad. *Rahad,* traveler. *Rahad,* a musical note.

He was glad he hadn't confessed to needing her address — the driver's license would sort itself, as small things always do.

In the afternoon Yasmine called. Surely her neighbor had seen him linger outside her door, knocking and waiting. But she only said, "Got anything new for me?"

He was already on his feet, unzipping his leather bag. "I stumbled onto an old man in Kenya who's been singing in the same village for fifty years. The Internet has put up five pages for him — lots of respect from the world. Let me see what I have here." He rifled through his bag for effect; he had already chosen the four songs he would send her. He added in English, "Poor Baba *joon* would roll in grave knowing we listen to Kenyan man . . . He would roll right onto antique sitar he should have left to me."

Yasmine laughed. "Baba *joon*, stop that silly *bazi*," she said, her code since childhood that he should continue. "The Internet isn't a person." He imagined her head thrown back, scratching the spot on her chin where she had a careless habit of resting her pencil tip. Ever since grade school, she wondered aloud where the spot came from, and to this day she thought it was a mole. He loved dreamy, distracted Yasmine; not the eyeliner tech jockey, but a girl who was human and original and full of absurdities.

"If Internet is not person," he said in English, "then why you work for him?"

She giggled. He recalled that on the day the Internet had put up his websites, the ones honoring his career, he went to a café, ordered an espresso, and read every page, nostalgia quickening and stinging his heart. Did Yasmine remember those glorious days? Apparently the Internet did. He marveled at this vital force in the world, one that hadn't existed when his dying father had lamented his legacy, pleading, *Who will play my songs?* Here, two decades later, was an answer from the cosmos, an unseen deity that recognizes you, remembers you, commemorates you when your daughter won't.

"Do you notice ever how much time is spent just in logistical doing?" Wyatt asked. They were in the Laundromat down the street from the Y, and he was carefully folding his Statue of Liberty T-shirt, which, by Rahad's count, was one of twelve America-themed shirts he owned, every last one permanently soaked in imitation Acqua di Giò. In Rahad's two weeks at this YMCA, Wyatt had visited every day. They had held four kitchenette jam sessions, with steadily growing attendance. Last time they even had a singer, a graying Vietnamese woman with a reedy voice like a parakeet. Often, Rahad had heard her crying in her room, her voice unmistakable. But that day, she had wandered into the kitchenette at the first sounds of music and sat on a stool, unmoving. With faraway eyes she watched Rahad play a classic Viguen tune, then she simply started to sing in her own tongue, stumbling now and then to follow the music, creating something broken and lovely. The heroin addict scavenging for food in the cupboards stopped muttering and turned to listen. Wyatt grinned with sad pleasure and quieted the rhythm of his bucket to make room for her small voice.

"I notice that, yes," said Rahad, as he packed the last of his own shirts into a mesh bag. "You try to live simple and free but you still need place to do washing, place to cook food, to rinse a dish. Is all automatic in old life, but now just being awake takes up all the time." Each morning Rahad locked his door and carried all his toiletries and towel back and forth to the shared bathroom. He undressed in his room, put on his clean clothes, and hung them up on a hook near his shower stall, hoping they wouldn't be stolen. He carried his bowl and spoon to the kitchen for every meal, washed them immediately after eating, and carried them back. No food was safe there, and he had no fridge, so he ate in diners often and shopped daily based on that morning's cravings. If he still had a car, he would keep his cash and papers in the trunk along with a cooler of water—a relief in summer, but mostly an excuse to fetch cash from the car without drawing attention. It seemed that something vital, a certain dignity perhaps, was lost in all this carrying of things.

"For damn sure, my friend," said Wyatt, nodding and shaking his head at the same time. "That is a true. A big, big true. You empty out, and life refills itself with shit."

"Then suddenly you're in your car with all your clothes like an *avareh*," Rahad joked. Wyatt laughed at this Farsi word they now shared. Vagrant. Itinerant. Drifter.

"And sons don't see this," said Wyatt, suddenly sad. Wyatt, Rahad now knew, had a grown son in Houston, an engineer and family man. "They see only what you don't do. They say you do nothing. They don't see the thousand CV papers you sent to this director and that director, the ten thousand doors you knocked on. You think, 'I must get these things quick.' Only you can't control the getting."

"Your English is improving, sahib," said Rahad, hoping to cheer up his friend.

After a moment Wyatt returned to his usual happy tone, his singsong affectation, which by now Rahad was convinced had a purpose, even if it was buried too deep even for Wyatt to know. Was he a DC native as he claimed, or a new immigrant as he seemed? He never spoke of India, avoiding the topic and insisting

that he was American born. Yet the posturing was comically pronounced. Rahad didn't ask what demon made the man muddle
his past. When asked about such things, he had long known, most
people lie, and even if they aim for honesty, they only ever hit near
the mark. "World is no respect," said Wyatt, "until nosy neighbor
sees you have own oven. Now you can make sandwich, now you're
OK. Now only—not before—they come to say, 'If ever something
is needful, you must ask.' Funny backward business." He chuckled
and flung his laundry bag over his shoulder.

For three weeks, Rahad watched the Vietnamese woman drag herself in and out of the kitchenette, her loneliness like iron boots.
Late in the second week, after a night of sharing music, she had
left a pot of spiced soup outside his door. He found out from Wyatt
that she had lived there for years, received food stamps, and always
found someone to whom she might offer her soup. She spent her
days reading her own diaries in the local mall and carefully sorting
through mail from Publishers Clearing House. Her downturned
eyes and drooping eyelids, like wilted petals, made Rahad want to
have a drink with someone new, to talk.

In the local library's computer cluster, he joined a dating website for older singles. He uploaded a photo of himself from three
years before, holding his sitar, not quite smiling, but not looking
grim either. All in all, he thought the photo captured his personality and mood. In his description he wrote:

> Iranian music man, 54, seeking liberal musical woman with educated
> children. I can cook Iranian food. I can play all music. I will be kind. I
> have a little money.

That should capture it, and it seemed savvy, too; Yasmine had
warned him that the Internet was full of people looking for free
money. He read the profile to Wyatt, who gave several hearty nods
before becoming distracted by an email from his son.

The first woman who caught Rahad's eye was a pretty, fifty-
something widow named Susan. She had bright blue eyes, a gray
bob, and one front tooth that overlapped the other as if in fifty
years she hadn't thought to fix it, a quality that reminded him of
his late wife. But before he could write to her, he had his first message. At the chime of the messenger, Wyatt rolled his chair toward
Rahad and began reading over his shoulder.

"Aha, a beauteous one," he said. "Do one thing, scoot your chair. Read, read."

Rahad shifted over. The message was from a thirty-year-old woman with fire-red hair, posing in a small orange skirt beside an enormous pool. It said:

> Hello sweetie. How is your day going and wats going on with you? Your profile much attracted me and I believe we can work something out between each other. I'm Elizabeth, 30 years old, from Carolina, much looking for man of my life. You have such a beautiful spirit, and you are so handsome. Tell me about yourself. What do you do? Write me at sexyliz@yahoo.com

"Oh my goodness," said Wyatt, "I am pissing myself. You caught such a good catch so quick into it! Say to her she looks like angel of light fallen from firmament."

"She is same age like Yasmine," said Rahad, trying to hide his shock for Wyatt's sake. "Why she ask what I do? I already say music man."

"Who gives the fucks?" said Wyatt, who seemed on the verge of ripping out his own beard. "Maybe she's being busy fighting men off with stick! Write her."

Rahad kicked away Wyatt's chair and replied:

> Hello young lady. Why you are writing the old men? I am from Iran with daughter your age. You are very kind. Good luck finding man of life. —Rahad

"Oh, you fool!" Wyatt slapped both hands on his face and leaned back in his chair. "You big, big Iranian fool. I cannot be enduring this not one small bit. I cannot."

Two minutes later, Elizabeth wrote again:

> Rahad, what a nice name. I can see you are very soulful. I'm so much glad you wrote back. In your answer I can see you could be the kind of person I can spend my life with. Age is nothing. Love is all that matters. I am Liz, and I'm 30 from Carolina, but I have degree from Harvard. I need older man to keep me intellectually satisfied. You seem like a good man. What do you do? Please write me at sexyliz@yahoo.com

"Oh holy gods, she is not giving up, this one," said Wyatt. "Write to her that she is a flower. Say, 'World has no first-class creation better than beautiful woman.'"

Rahad batted away his friend's hand, which was dancing between Rahad's nose and the computer screen. He had to admit, he
felt encouraged by the attention. As a young man in Iran, he had
enjoyed the attention of many women. He had fans. Now, he took
a moment to reread Elizabeth's words before he replied: "I am
musician from Iran." Succumbing to a tinge of vanity, he added:

> I was famous there in old days. Is very impressive that you go to Har-
> vard. What you study? My daughter is your age and she goes there for
> university! She is Eliot House and computer science. You are same year
> maybe? You know her? What house? She is Yasmine Sokouti.

"Excellent response," said Wyatt with a smack of his lips. "You
wised up very much. First-class message."

Moments later, his computer pinged: "Rahad, I see online that
you have nice history in Iranian music." Here Wyatt interrupted.
"What she is meaning?" he said, his bunched fingers in Rahad's
face as if he were offering him a plum. "Do one thing, be googling
yourself for me right now, right this second." Rahad waved away
the request and continued reading:

> I won't lie, I thought you were some scammer. But I didn't have enough
> trust. You must have trust too. Asking me about what year and what I
> studied and if I know your daughter shows no trust. I so much wish you
> would believe when I say so about Harvard. Now I am not sure if I wish
> to read back from you, unless you are serious about finding a Trusting,
> Loving, Cherishing, Mutual relationship based on TRUST.

"Ohhh. Crazy, crazy bitch," whispered Wyatt. "Was too good
from beginning."

Rahad laughed. "We are too much the dreamers, Wyatt *joon*."

"Maybe she's not fully, totally crazy in real life," muttered Wyatt,
leaning on his hand as he continued staring at Elizabeth's photo.

Rahad shook his head. "When Yasmine says word *trust* a hundred times in one talk, is because she lies by skin of teeth. And no
mention that real Harvard people wear details on forehead like
war paint." He typed Elizabeth's email address into a search engine that Yasmine had shown him. "Shame," he muttered. "Is on
list of scam."

He logged out of the computer and gathered his things while
Wyatt cursed their luck. "What cluster of fucks. Bitches always have
surprise in sleeves, I tell you."

"What if tonight we cook our own food?" said Rahad, suddenly eager to eat a Persian meal again. "Maybe we cook a nice kabob or a stew with rice."

"Oh yes," said Wyatt. "They have best Punjabi food in DC. We make with DC method, uses more turmeric than cumin, much nicer."

When Rahad finished packing his bag, he saw that Wyatt had googled his name and was shaking his head at the photos on one of the three big websites dedicated to Rahad's work. Wyatt clicked on a snapshot of Rahad with his head hung, cradling his favorite sitar, the instrument mostly obscured by his longish black hair. Rahad remembered that night and that photo. Yasmine had taken it from atop the shoulders of a distant uncle during Rahad's final concert in Tehran, just before they left the country. "I cannot read these Farsi writings, bro, but you are being modest before. Very modest."

"Internet does what it wants with informations," said Rahad, trying not to smile.

They strolled to a local discount market. In the produce aisle, Wyatt rushed ahead to find this and that, while Rahad checked items off a list. "Look at sea of onions people throw to floor," Wyatt groaned, craning his neck to see under the vegetable racks.

Rahad asked, "Do you think perhaps I am more Internet savvy after today?"

"Back in slum this is big, big crime!" said Wyatt to the onions. He added quickly, "Back in slum of DC." Rahad just stared at his list. "Oh yes, yes," Wyatt finally replied. "For sure. We thwarted lady romance scammer right in her tracks. Or maybe we have turned down super-delicious young redhead with Harvard degree. Either way, we most definitely did *not* do something *not* savvy. So, well done, sir."

The next morning, Wyatt brought him naan from his sink again, and Rahad offered him a story—an even trade in both their cultures. He told his neighbor about his broken computer, the sleepless nights he had spent on Yas's couch. He told Wyatt about the Thanksgivings Yasmine had spent as a guest of her friends or classmates, and about the famous *ustad* Sokouti and his palatial home wrapped around a Moroccan-style courtyard. He described the wash pool shaded by persimmon and plum trees, the vines that trimmed the high walls, the array of shapely string instruments lined up against the brick, tall or dainty or rotund, like bandmates waiting to play, and the pretty maid washing spoons and bowls and kitchen towels among the goldfish. In summer days, his *baba joon* walked around the garden in loose pants and a large straw hat, picking sour plums from the trees, sucking them through his gray moustache and shaking his head with pleasure. He was a large man with a full face and a wrestler's gait, but gentle, always humming, and his house was full of delicious smells and sitar music. Lost now, all that.

Wyatt murmured, "American children always are wanting more."

Later in the week, Wyatt waved two bus passes like they were winning lottery tickets and announced that they were going to New York. Rahad accepted, and when Wyatt told him to bring his sitar, he shrugged—his sitar was always with him. Maybe Yasmine had time for a coffee. He left her a message at work. At the bus stop, he sat quietly, hands on knees. Wyatt chatted on, almost to himself. "In DC, you know, they are putting fake bus bench outside old folks' home. Very realistic. You know why? So Alzheimer folks don't get on real bus thinking they are going to who knows where. Is that not brilliant? Sometimes I am sitting here, and I am thinking, Maybe I finally made it to Alzheimer bus bench. Maybe I am ninety, imagining myself sitting here with you, new friend, Irani music man, but really I am sitting next to a toy sign made of flimsy paper."

In Times Square, though the stench of piss and car exhaust and roadside hot dogs sickened Rahad, he followed dutifully behind his friend, clutching his sitar a little closer each time someone bumped into him. They stopped at a loud corner near a subway stop and Wyatt turned. "You will be playing here."

Rahad laughed. Then he saw that his friend was serious.

"Who knows who will be walking by and hearing you," said Wyatt, eyes alight. "Internet is nothing: this is the absolute very center of New York! You play. You get discovered. Done and dusted."

What harm could come of it? Rahad thought. He situated himself on a YMCA blanket his friend had brought, took out his sitar, and though the sounds of taxis, tourists, vendors, and fellow architects of harebrained stunts drowned him out, he began to enjoy the adventure. He could now say that he had played in Times Square. What Tehrani musician could say that? Maybe the Internet would catch wind of it and post a photo. Briefly the world felt as it had in his younger days, when he strummed and others snapped photos of him that would appear in unknown parts of the city.

Rahad and Wyatt played for an hour to small crowds overflowing from the popular Chinese restaurant next door and a few stragglers who drifted over from a nearby hot dog cart. Eastern men, like themselves, on breaks from their restaurant jobs. Most wandered away after a few seconds, realizing that they couldn't enjoy the music for the commotion of the street. Others recognized a melody and nudged each other. *Do you remember this?* they murmured in languages he didn't understand. But Rahad understood that you always know—if yours are the fingers that strum the strings—when someone recognizes your sound. And isn't that all there is to want?

Some gave money, and at first Rahad stopped to explain that this wasn't their purpose. Finally he gave up, but made sure that his sitar case was closed and stowed behind him and that his jacket was nowhere in sight. If he offered no place to drop money, the people would understand his intentions. Most didn't, throwing coins onto the blanket instead.

"Where are your music big shots then, agha?" said Rahad, grinning at his friend. He didn't mind if none of the promised record executives appeared. He enjoyed playing in this great cavity of noise, alone in a human swarm. He was doing something worth remembering, even if it was foolish and self-indulgent. And he was in New York.

"We must be patient," said Wyatt.

"Come, I buy you Starbuck," said Rahad, packing up his instrument. He was desperate for a coffee, a feeling that always reminded him to text Yasmine.

In the café, Wyatt ordered a foamy latte. When the barista muttered, "So you want a cappuccino, then," he shook his head sadly at Rahad. "These young generations think we are all terribly stupid, always in risk of poking out an eye if not for their instruction."

They sat down at a table near the window, watching their corner in case their record producer exited the subway at just that moment.

"I hoped to have coffee with Yasmine," said Rahad, checking his phone. "Especially this time that we come by bus. Twice before I came by car and she chose café with no parking spot and I got ticket. Then drove back in dark because I'm not welcome even on her couch. This treatment is normal for American parents, I think. After that, I sell the car. I only kept it for visiting often. But who wants to be burden?"

"My son is same. I am borrowing car, driving hours, and last minute, poof, canceled." Wyatt shook his head and stared into his latte, the foaminess of which obviously irritated him. "My son, he is thinking I am stupid. Where he gets this?"

"Is problem of generation," said Rahad. "We come to West, suffer in learning language in adulthood, which we can never lose accent or get joke and so on. But kids go to school and learn in a normal route with other first citizens, and later they think we are dumb or at least considering us lower than themselves. My daughter asks always, 'Did you google this or that like I tell you?' She thinks she is my teacher."

Wyatt's hands flew up in agreement, so that his spoon splattered foam on the table. "My son wants me to do video online instead of telephone," he said. "I tell my son, 'Oh, good try, good try. Next time, can you tell me something? Do you speak Urdu, Punjabi, Hindi? Can you write in these language? Can you change yourself every hour according to situation? Can you keep your American pride in foreign city? You can upload videos on social sites, nothing else. But Indian people can speak in minimum four languages. And we know when to put away all four and listen sometimes, too.'" Wyatt chuckled a little maniacally, scooped some foam out of his coffee, and stared at Rahad. "Did you ever read *Pnin?*" he said. Rahad shook his head. "Is about bumbling immigrant, but lovable because he is arriving new, learning, missing home. My son brings this book one day from school," he paused, as if wondering why he had mentioned it. "New arrivals, they have reason to be confuse, they must be missing home. But I say, fuck old country —I don't miss it. Is whole world that changed too quick! I am exile from my own child. It's like I try to jump gorge and got foot permanently stuck."

"Yes," Rahad laughed. "Is like pushing against an unbrokable wall."

"But we have music, right?" said Wyatt, tapping his paper cup against Rahad's as if to toast. "Music from the world."

Rahad watched his friend as he lifted his cup to his lips. Again, something was wrong with the way Wyatt spoke. "Your English is improving, my friend," he said. "*Gorge* is not word I know."

Wyatt wiped his mouth and let out a breathy, tittering sigh. "Nothing is improving, sahib," Wyatt said, his tone changing, his eyes emptying of the eager joy he seemed to carry in abundance. "Life is easier if people think you just arrived, you know? They expect, twenty years here and you should have made it." It took a moment for Rahad to realize, given his own troubles with English, that his friend was speaking without his unmistakable lilt. Now Wyatt sounded like the Indians Rahad had known in Baltimore and Tehran. "There are things you need," Wyatt continued, "things to survive, and you don't have it yet. Why not? You must be stupid. You must not have studied the culture hard enough. You must be hostile to it. Who needs that, brother? I'd rather be a lovable FOB than a failure whose story has grown stale."

What careful thought his friend must have put into every sentence he uttered. This new voice struck Rahad hard and he was quiet for some time. A proud look passed over Wyatt's face, like a person who had written a moving melody. He raised both eyebrows, sucked something out of his teeth. "See, twenty years ago when we were new, the new ones were invisible, too. Now everyone's read *Pnin* and those FOB-y bastards are loved, and us who lived here for twenty years, we're fucked again. Who has a kind word for someone who can't find their foot after that long? See? Fucked from both directions."

"So not born in DC then?" Rahad asked, feeling duped and a little angry. How had he grown so close to this man?

"All FOBs say they're born in DC," said Wyatt, then added, stroking his salt-and-pepper chin and reprising his phony accent, "That is a big, big true."

"You give me headache," said Rahad, touching his temple. He remembered the day they had met, thinking Wyatt was a crazy man. Now Rahad thought he might be a disturbed scholar, or a mystic, or a traumatized poet. How did he talk to his son? Rahad wondered. Did he put on the same new-immigrant act, hoping for a glimmer of sympathy? It would be misguided, Rahad knew; displays of foreignness were the children's greatest irritation. "I need another coffee. Too much Wyatt thinking for today."

"Vadhi," mumbled his friend as he emptied his cup. He rose and gestured toward the counter. "Vadhi is my good name. I'll buy as a sorry for lying. You buy next one."

Rahad spent the rest of the night playing melancholy songs in the corner by the subway entrance. During prime theater hours, Times Square was slightly less manic, and he enjoyed hearing his own songs under the feverish lights of a New York evening. They ate at the last open hot dog stand before the owner packed up and left. Late that evening, as they rode the last bus back to Wilmington, he phoned Yasmine again. He started to tell her about Wyatt and the Vietnamese woman, about the spicy soup and the naan from the brick oven, wanting her to share in his astonishment at the gifts of the universe — these scattered foreigners sharing from their food stamps and loose change, finding joy in music. He wanted to say, *Azizam, trust the universe. Life can be easy if you let it be.* But Yasmine's breath grew quicker. "Baba *joon*, are you in trouble?" she said. "Why are people giving you food? If you're in trouble —"

He cut her off, "Oh Yasmine, hush!" he said. "It was potluck dinner. I call for another reason: Did you go online today?"

She breathed out, relief kneading every syllable. "Of course I did. It's my job."

"Will you go to a page that I say? I give you address if you have pen."

"Don't need a pen." He could hear the fast clicks of her keyboard. "Go ahead."

He recited from memory the addresses of the three websites, the ones the Internet had granted to his former career. She was silent, and he didn't ask if she had finished typing. "Lately these appear on Internet," he said. "I want to tell you, I think they are good. Of highest creative quality. Maybe later I post them on Facebook."

"Oh yeah?" she said. She cleared her throat, as if responding would cost her something. Where had she inherited this pride? From the elder *ustad* Sokouti, perhaps.

"Well?" he said. "I'm famous. Aren't you impressed?" She laughed and said that she was. He wanted to tell her that he knew more about the Internet than she thought. Maybe not the codes and formulas and shortcuts, but he knew its spirit, its sweeping reach. This entity that granted a measure of justice—*Trust the universe,* he had always told Yasmine—it had circled the air above them, coloring their relationship from the time she was a student. He wanted to say, *Yas, I know the Internet isn't some deity. I know it's made up of people trying to inscribe the void, to mark the very ether with what they've lived and what they know. Thank you for etching me a corner in that vast, unfathomable place.* He wanted to tell his daughter that he knew she respected him, or some former, more essential version of him. But enough had been said for one phone call. "I find it very artistic, Yasi *joon,*" he said. "It captures the years."

All through the bus ride home, Wyatt sat silently, his head slumped against the window. Rahad was glad for the quiet, unsure of what to expect the next time his friend opened his mouth. Did it matter? When had he ever anticipated anyone's next syllable? His daughter's, least of all. Maybe such harmony wasn't needed to enjoy a drink with someone. Maybe the earth wouldn't collapse on itself if a person you love didn't cosign your every move, or you theirs. "A big true," he said to himself and chuckled.

The two men walked from the station back to their rooms at the YMCA. They parted ways in the corridor, each saying a few words about the next day's plans, the possibility of a warm naan from a pizza oven, the other residents who might join them in a song or two, the whereabouts of that reedy Vietnamese voice they had come to enjoy. Rahad dug into his pocket for his keys, and when he pulled his fingers out they were covered in a white dusting of baking soda. He glanced back at Wyatt entering his own room, hunched from fatigue, looking a decade older, an accustomed sort of quiet surrounding his steps. In their short friendship, Rahad had overlooked so much that had been hidden in the artificial cracks of this man's speech. And yet Wyatt had knocked on Rahad's door every day, hoping that, after enough afternoons together, Rahad—a true and verified musician of Tehran, a traveler and student of the world's many strange rhythms—might say, *Stop pretending now, my brother. I know your sound.*

But Rahad hadn't heard; maybe he was no master at all.

He unlocked his own door and turned on the lights. In all these years, what other voices had he only half heard? Maybe he still needed a more practiced ear. He sat on his bed, looked out onto the parking lot, and listened: to the low roar of a passing car, to stoned men talking in the corridor, to the mattress creaking under his weight. He thought of his wife with her glorious unwashed hair, the artful websites their daughter had made, and Baba with his students on the veranda, all their idle talk of sitar songs and why one should never touch a Western guitar, of how to listen for music amid the human noise.

Items Awaiting Protective Enclosure

FROM *Zoetrope: All-Story*

ONE EVENING ALMOST thirty years later, a call from an unknown number. The ringing brings your husband out of the kitchen, ladle still in hand. This is the prelude to the only scenario that keeps him up at night: some stranger, a kelp-rig medic perhaps, interrupting dinner to notify you that your son has been killed, washed overboard somewhere off the coast of Cambria amid the gray roil and boom of the Pacific.

To flaunt your immunity to these catastrophic fantasies, you let the phone ring and ring.

Tom's smiling, but he doesn't find it funny. "Pick up, Syl." Then, after a moment: "Fine. Why don't I just cancel our anniversary picnic and volunteer us for roadside cleanup instead? I know how you love scraping those possums off the freeway."

When you finally lift the phone to your ear to deliver the usual greeting—"Rayles-Brennan residence, home of the Arbor Cottages in scenic Grey's County!"—you get the wind knocked out of you. It's not a medic. Not a telemarketer. Not the Mammalian Gene Bank of the Rocky Mountains inquiring if you'd like to increase your annual donation.

It's Wade. *Your* Wade. So long-lost that his name overcomes you as first a sensation and then a smell before finally taking lettered form. Wade Dufrane. Calling from some other lifetime, his voice as familiar as your own, saying: "Syl?" And then: "I knew you'd sound exactly the same."

In a minute, it will hit you that of course you sound the same. But for now—for this particular second—there's just that one-note whiff of Fell Gulch in January, of pine and woodsmoke, of you at twenty, assisting your father up the narrow stairs to the office of Serenity Pods overlooking Main Street. Through his coat sleeve, Dad's elbow feels like a bag of bolts. Somewhere outside, the Rendezvous Trio is fiddling an overzealous two-step for the benefit of the tourists.

Serenity Pods occupies the attic above the Well Digger's Wallet Saloon, where your childhood friend Kenny Kostic tends bar. In the six years you've been helping him oust inebriates, you've never thought to investigate where the back stairwell leads.

Dad's monstrous shirt hides the black threads of more than a dozen mole excisions. Six foot three and down to 140 pounds, he's taken pale frailty to another level. And now here's Wade Dufrane, tall and ginger-stubbled, good-looking in the way of people who don't know it, manning the front desk in a white linen getup.

The place looks like a celestial break-room. Everything hums: the bare bulbs, the sleek computer panel, the wall painted up like a field of tree-brindled snow. At its center stands a thick black elm. Its roots twist around a subterranean teardrop, in which a glyphic body lies folded.

Wade maneuvers you both to the sofa with pamphlets and rank gray tea, then carefully sits between you.

"So—which of you is looking forward to reabsorption?"

While Wade talks your father through the marketing collateral, you try to smother your irritation. Let Dad get the reassurance he needs: that he's doing the right thing, that pod burial restores soil nutrients, that you just don't get this kind of solace from a coffin.

"Something about committing to reabsorption just gives folks a sense of peace," Wade says. "I know it did for me."

Conveniently, Wade's own father had signed the entire family up for pod burial back when the process was still new. "Not to mention far more expensive," Wade says, skirting around the price, "but I figured: if it could offset some of my parents' debts to our world, worth every penny."

You can't help yourself: "Yet here you are, sucking air and drinking water—I guess that means your folks are still in arrears."

Dad says: "Syl. Please."

Wade, as it happens, came dangerously close to reabsorption

when he was a teenager. Some vague cardiac incident briefly killed him en route to the hospital. He perceived himself floating up, above the gurney, above the bald EMT trying to resuscitate him. Of his three remaining sensations—besides filial love and the strange, sulfuric odor of his chest hair frying under the paddles —what stood out most was how complete he felt, knowing that he would soon give sustenance to a new tree. Even his miraculous return to his body, and the continuation of his life, haven't dispelled the strength of that feeling.

Dad nods gravely. As if Wade's story has firmed the legs of a newborn notion.

"We want to take a couple of days," you say, standing to leave. "Consult with the rest of the family."

The rest of the family consists of an uncle in Cleveland who hasn't returned your father's calls in years and the dog who's been underfoot ever since the combined chaos of veterinary school and bartending forced Kenny to abandon her at your house.

Wade insists you take all the time you need. "It's a tough mindshift. In the end, we're all just items awaiting protective enclosure. Most of us have a vision of what that is—a coffin, an urn. Not everyone can get used to the idea of a tree. But remember that with a Serenity Pod, the whole world is your memorial."

The trouble is, he really means it. The spell is cast. All the way home, Dad rests his head dreamily against the window. The tram winds past the Refuge boundary, past Highness Park, with its cocoa stands and skate rentals and brightly bundled husks of winter tourists, and then up Painter's Knoll, where the constellated hillside mansions recall the Fell Gulch of twenty years ago, when people were still able to convince themselves that everything would work itself out somehow, as it always had before.

Your father had been one of those people. Then came the Posterity Initiative, and a complete 180. He spent your entire childhood collecting prairie grasses for the Rocky Mountain Seed Vault, tallying pollinators, teaching you to culture penicillin. All the while bewailing what was lost: bacon and air travel and elephants. Things you would never have, thanks to his generation's excesses.

You could never see the point of his retrospective hand-wringing.

At home, Dad fans the pamphlets out on the dining table. He shouts pull quotes over the crack of your knife on the cutting

board: "Did you know that the average Serenity Pod offsets two
peoples' worth of carbon dioxide a year?"

"If it's so clean, they should be paying you to commit to it. Not
the other way around."

"Ha."

"Don't you think this is all a bit premature?" He looks up from
the blue columns of numbers on his napkin. "We haven't got the
biopsy results back. You're probably not even dying."

"Well," he shrugs, "someday."

The prospect of this "someday"—whose advent he's attempted
to accelerate at least twice—sends you back to Serenity Pods one
cloudy afternoon a few days later. Alone this time.

Wade, still in his diaconal finest, tries to bring you around. "Tell
me what's giving you pause."

"Guilt rules my father's life. And now he's got it in his head that
putting twelve grand down on a burial he might not even need
—knock wood—is the best way to square his ecological debts."

"It's not a bad place to start."

"Yeah, well. We run a housekeeping service. It's about all we can
do to keep the lights on."

Serenity Pods, it turns out, offers a payment plan. Wade pivots
to show you the literature on making reabsorption accessible to everyone.

You tell him you have all the pamphlets at home. "I didn't come
here for more of the company line."

He tilts his head a little, and says, "All right"—which is when
you go all warm. You sit there, blowing ripples across the smoggy
surface of your tea.

"How did you die?"

"Well, I guess in the end I didn't."

As he resumes his pitch about soil renewal and generational
duty, you're disappointed in his failure to intuit what you really
want to know: whether there's a crack of light and an eventual
shore to dying, or just darkness like you suspect. When the time
comes, will trenching your father in a shawl full of seeds, so that
filaments and roots can suck away everything that made him who
he was, somehow render the former more likely? You can't bring
yourself to say: *I'm afraid my father will simply cease to exist.*

"I'd like to hear more about burial from someone who doesn't
get commission selling it to me."

Wade laughs outright—a real laugh, earnest enough to furrow his whole nose. "Believe it or not, there's fuck-all money in pod sales."

"Yeah? What about this?" You hook a finger under his tunic collar to reveal the strap of his FieldSight 5000s—the latest model, the one you've been eyeing for months—and you're instantly embarrassed. Is it wrong to touch a man who dresses like a monk?

"Those are an oversight." Somehow, he's managed to catch your wrist. "They're for my other job. I usually remember not to wear them here."

"I didn't think revenant pod people needed side gigs."

He smiles that smile. Huge white teeth from here to doomsday. "If anything, this is the side gig. The other's more of a calling."

Which is how you get your start shed-hunting with Wade Dufrane.

All winter you drift along trails and fire roads together in the blue hours before sunrise. Geese vault overhead. Thick mists leave the Bitterroot peaks and come coursing down into the Refuge. You grow to love the cold walk from your porch to the corner where Wade picks you up, the bitterness of his whiskey-laced coffee, the way the snowpack warps your bulky shadows. Together, you scout tracks, cut and climb fence, disable cameras, dodge patrols, sift through acres of deadfall in your pursuit of the shed antlers of bull elk.

Most of the sheds have spent a decade or more underground, a vestige of the days of the great herds that once wintered around Fell Gulch. Generations of cast bone. Brittle scimitars snared in tree roots, or forking up where occasional mudslides have overturned the hills. You dig for them in gullies and creek beds below south-facing slopes, and along old game trails Wade first prospected with his father as a boy.

You're wary of encroaching on what was once a Dufrane family enterprise, but Wade has a lot of sympathy for your current predicament. He, too, grew up in West Gulch with a renter in the attic and a father prone to rash, costly decisions. He's surprised your families don't know one another: like yours, the Dufranes would let their house to snowies every Christmas and drive south to winter on the parched shores of Lenny Lake. Wade even supports an arthritic mother somewhere in Minnesota.

All this is nominally why he sees fit to cut you in on his shed hunts. Of course, you suspect there may be something more to it. Something warm and visceral and conspicuously unspoken.

On a good day, the two of you haul twenty or thirty pounds of bone back to Wade's place, a converted garage behind Zeke's Antiques. Between shots of whiskey, you lay the antlers out like kindling and sort them into pairs. Wade can read the life in them: tridents of bone notched with a hidden legacy of battles and famines and narrow escapes. He teaches you the criteria of appraisal: straight or crooked tines, spreads, points.

Elk sheds sell by weight, and come out to about two hundred dollars a pound. This is for hard white, the stale stuff, probably older than you are. Fresh brown—newly fallen, dark with recent life—is a thing of the past. Wade hasn't seen fresh brown sheds, or any other evidence of living elk, in years. He can't begin to guess what they might be worth.

Your dealer, a scrambled voice who goes by the moniker "Antlerdam," communes with Wade once a week by telephone. He wraps your money in turn-of-the-century plastic bags, which he leaves in a broken toilet tank at the Carter County Library. He is responsible for shipping your plunder to lavish and remote destinations: Canada, where bone smiths work in secret to carve the antlers into walking sticks and knife handles and door knockers; or California, where black-market apothecaries grind them into powder, measure them into tinctures and compounds.

On radio broadcasts and reward flyers, the Forest Service calls you poachers; yet in his more winsome moments, Wade likes to say you're nothing but vernal custodians.

Never mind that your exploits carry a $25,000 fine, and a maximum sentence of five years in prison.

"Prison, Syl," Kenny says, when you finally admit what you've been up to.

His disgust is pretty righteous. Elk sheds, like everything on the Refuge, are protected under Posterity. They're supposed to stay where they fall, reintegrate with the undergrowth. None of this is news to you.

Luckily, you've got a line for just this moment: Wade knows what he's doing, been at this for years. Besides, it's not ivory. It's not hurting anyone. "What am I supposed to do if Dad does turn out to have cancer, and I have to sell the house so he can come back as a tree?"

Kenny's having none of it. "I'm sure you'll be a lot of help to him in prison."

His resolution not to speak to you lasts about a week. Your father, meanwhile, is too busy convincing himself of his imminent death to suspect that you're flouting your entire upbringing. If he realizes that your agreed-upon eight-month hiatus from college has turned into two years, he doesn't show it. He won't interview new hires for Rayles Management, or let you teach him how to balance the budget by himself. Most days, he just ghouls around the house, checking for new skin lesions and comparing snowfall reports from down-valley towns. "Erlton only got twenty inches this year," he says by way of good morning. "Twenty inches. I remember when they had to shell the pass all night to loose avalanches. Now I doubt they'll get another real winter."

But it's still real winter in Fell Gulch. The snowies keep coming: keep sledding, skating, building legions of snowmen. Zambonis chug back and forth across Highness Lake. Curtains of icicles rim the Main Street gables. Christmas lights twinkle well into March, like the whole place is some antique snow globe.

You start picking up cleaning shifts whenever a staff member calls in sick. Changing sheets, staging ski compounds so you can visit the big mansions on Painter's Knoll and study the handiwork of your clandestine life: antlers twisted up in huge chandeliers, trophy tips meeting neatly over stone fireplaces.

"Nice twelve-point," you say to the lady of a house on Ridge Street one afternoon, gazing at a mount above a mantel littered with pictures of towheaded kids. The elk's eyes are dark and stygian. A tendril of cobweb drifts from one of his crowns.

"Oh." She pauses at the bottom of the banister, one sapling leg braced on the first stair. You can't help thinking of her heating bill, what it must cost to be able to willow around in such a thin nightie this time of year. "I don't really know. Somebody shot it a while back, I guess."

"Well, if we ever go bust, at least you know what to auction off first."

"Mm."

"That's probably fifty inches of beam on each side."

Knowing more about her own possessions than she does thrills
you. So does every corner of this new, secret world you've staked
with Wade: the coded cuts on the trees, the white silence of the
Refuge, the alpenglow gilding the rumpled chevrons of the Bitter-
roots, the black breaks of runoff ribboning the snow.

For all Wade's precautions, his lifework is hardly unknown. January through May, when the doors swing for him at Caviston's Road-
house, shots line the bar.

Growing up, you were made to understand that Dad would skin
you alive if you ever set foot inside Caviston's. It's out on Route
29, a lopsided cabin where the fur-trapper great-grandfathers of
the current regulars would rendezvous back in the days before the
chili pepper lights and neon signs and shamrocks that now disgrace it. You feel a little out of place among all the pretty women
and their black-marketeers: James Muldoon, who still harvests
wood out near Silver Pass; Roy Fitzgerald, who charges Painter's
Knoll–types two thousand a head for an underground quail feast
every fall. But once Wade announces that "Sylvia Rayles is no fucking waster," you're as welcome among them as anyone.

And all assembled are eager to supplement what you know
about Wade. There's an ex-girlfriend he's been hung up on, and a
litany of hilarious entanglements with park rangers. They tell you
not to worry about his vague idea of moving to his mother's place
in Minnesota—he always fails to follow through on his best intentions.

Listening, you're warmed as their stories fail to breach your
own trove of hard-won intimacies: Before moving to Minnesota,
his mother sang with the Silver Banshees down in Miller's Hole.
The night his father emptied his pill bottle he gave Wade twenty
dollars, which still sits, untouched, in a tobacco tin under the sycamore at the old Dufrane house; passing on Pinedale Road, Wade
reflexively pulls into the driveway sometimes. He's never cooked a
dish without burning it, or made it all the way through "Shenan-
doah" without his voice breaking.

April brings mud season, and Antlerfest with it. Fell Gulch goes
full cervine. Rangers scatter a modest haul of confiscated sheds all
over Highness Park, and the whole town turns up to honor this last
shred of heritage: ursine dads shouldering winter-swaddled daugh-

ters, reluctant teenagers milling around the parking lot, grandparents reminiscing about the days when you could hunt a whole elk, goddammit, and not just the antlers.

A whistle-blow at sunup sends four hundred citizens charging out into the field. Aware that your absence might raise suspicion, you and Wade make a point of being seen. You overturn logs and comb through bushes, right in the thick of it with all the grannies. You watch the kids hauling back their finds—nothing but spikes, straight and thin and practically worthless, but borne along as tenderly as sacrificial offerings. And all the while you recognize that you are the villains in this scene; you are responsible for this dearth.

You finally wind your way over to Kenny's pickle stand to bridge the two sides of your life. Kenny grips Wade's hand, then upsells him on a jar of beets and turnips.

"Twelve dollars?" you say through gritted teeth. "Really?"

Kenny shrugs. "They're award-winning."

He makes no attempt to mask his dead-eyeing of Wade, who wanders the parking lot inspecting the Antlerfest auction lots laid out on the tarmac like shot-down chandeliers. A chinless, brown-eyed ranger touches your elbow, keen to tell you more about the sheds. Did you know that elk cast their antlers every year? That once upon a time, pretty much anybody could just scoop them right off the ground?

You can hardly decide what thrills you more viscerally: knowing a man has underestimated you so profoundly, or flirting with a loathed enemy right in front of Wade.

The prize set of antlers—with an atypically considerable fifty-two-inch spread—sells handily for four grand. Afterward, Wade boosts you into the truck bed. The matter-of-factness of his presumption is stunning. As he continues to stand there, scraping a gob of mud off your knee, it hits you.

Still, you take a full week to say it aloud. "I think I might be in love with Wade."

"Well, fuck," says Kenny, without looking up from his textbook. "Just give me a moment to absorb this completely unexpected piece of news."

Apart from marooning you in a constant state of impatience, the realization changes very little of your daily life. Maybe you sleep a little less, rotate your more flattering clothes to the top drawers. But most nights Wade just picks you up, and the two of you drive the long, pine-ribbed highway to the Serbian diner over in Gentry. You share burek and fries and tease out where you'll land when Fell Gulch finally goes bust. You revisit the humor in familiar things: tourist tat shops, people who stand on ceremony, the daily reenactment of Crazy Jim Collins's murder at the Wallet, in which you briefly appeared as Dolly Dove, the shrill whorehouse madam.

Before your limited run, Wade had played Bertrand Stills, shooting ol' Jim right in the heart every Tuesday and Thursday.

"I'd have paid to see you in that white Stetson and bolo."

His fork dimples the top of your hand. "Those were mandatory."

He decides that if the need for aliases should ever arise, the two of you will be "Stills" and "Dove."

On the drive home, Wade cracks a window to let in the smell of pine. His fingers drum the console between you. The truck feels too small to contain this electric haze of possibility. Your first kiss is imminent, a single dram of courage away. There's safety in the knowledge that either of you could choose it anytime, a kind of chemical understanding. It's a world beyond the high school boys who used to hold you down.

Midnight, however, usually finds you on opposite ends of Wade's sofa, reading aloud to one another. By two thirty, you're home.

Fielding your reports of the lack of consummation exasperates Kenny. "What's taking him so long?"

You've spent hours puzzling this out. Maybe you've overestimated your appeal. Maybe if you were more delicate, more serious. More feminine. Maybe if every meal didn't stick to your ribs, if your body had any corners at all.

Kenny doesn't see the point of speculation. "You'll never know unless you confront him, Syl; and the faster you get on with it, the better. Go for broke."

You will yourself to courage. But it's easier to imagine almost anything—your father absolved, Fell Gulch parched—than that kiss and its aftermath. You can't even slip your hand past your waistband in the darkness of your room for the sheer mortification of having to face Wade afterward.

Again and again, you return to the same reality: a declaration of love will change things, one way or another. Better to linger in doubt than to lose your only source of joy, better to preserve the veil of promise. Like that shed hunt in mid-April, when you and Wade split up to cover more ground. He sends you down to Bitterroot Creek, a bottomland bearded with red-twig dogwoods. The day is warm and blindingly bright. You're enjoying the solitude, the *ftt-ftt* of your steps mashing the snow, when there's a whistle behind you. A rising note that could peel the enamel off your teeth. You twist around to find the source. A red flare explodes over the woods to your left, about a half mile away.

It's one thing to memorize protocol in case of a ranger encounter. Another thing entirely to follow it. You take off mindlessly into the trees, spraying snow everywhere, losing a snowshoe in the loamy creek bed. Finally you drop down in a stand of cottonwoods and wait. A line of melt drips beneath your collar. Through all that panting and hammering, you're a long while in returning to silence.

It's dark by the time you hear Wade calling. He's empty-handed, hatless, quietly infuriated by a wasted day, but relieved you're in one piece—which is definitely something.

The stars are out in their whorled millions. Eventually you give up arguing about where the road might be. Wade unpacks his winter hammock, strings it between two oaks, piles deadfall for insulation, while laughing periodically at your chattering teeth.

"At least we're together," he says. "If it grows too cold, we can just get to fucking." Then, after he sees your face: "Calm down, Syl. I'm joking."

The hammock sags with your combined weight, though your stomach is so empty it hurts. And even as the wind leaches all the heat from your back, there's a higher order of warmth between you, knees clicking, ribs grazing, the white purl of your breath massing in the clear air.

All night you commune over the truly celestial questions: What meat would you have most enjoyed, if you'd been born before Posterity? Wade thinks bacon; you say beef. How much nose could a person lose to frostbite and still look respectable? It apparently depends on the nose. "I could probably lose a good inch and be fine," Wade says. He butts his forehead against yours. "But you'd be doomed with one tenth of that."

If ever there was a moment to ask. "How did you die?"

"Briefly and stupidly." His long silence makes you hopeful.

Then he says: "When people measure distance by 'a cunt hair,' do you think they mean length or breadth?"

You manage to reply: "Breadth."

The next morning, during your postmortem of the evening's unrealized romantic potential, Kenny snaps. "I don't care how long he lingers over his good-nights or how many Yeats poems he knows by heart: no guy breathes the words *cunt hair* to a woman he cares about."

"I don't think I'm describing the moment properly."

He shakes his head. "You can take that to the bank, Syl."

You take it nowhere. You crumple it up and hurl it into the void that devours all evidence of Wade's ambivalence toward you.

Dad meets you in the doorway, floating around in a beloved tartan nightgown that refashions him as a junkie Ebenezer Scrooge. "Just getting in?"

"You know I am."

He watches you unlace your boots. "I almost called the police."

You glance up at him. How to explain you can't be officially unaccounted for the same night poachers are spotted on the Refuge?

"Well? Did you?"

"Kenny said you were out with that Wade fella from the mortuary. You could have called to check on me." He gives you a dubious once-over. "You look like you slept in a ditch."

In late April you find a cast antler out by Willow Fort. Just lying there, sharp as a scythe, half-buried by last night's snowfall. Fresh brown. Wade glasses it from across the field and starts running. By the time you get there, Wade is standing it up. It's taller than you, so big your hand can't fit around its knotty stem. The burr is pink with blood.

Ice encrusts Wade's nostrils, and in the morning sun his laughter courses out in shining eddies.

"It'll be a grand a pound if we can find the matching one."

"To hell with the matching one," you say. "If there's a live elk around, I want to see him."

Wade indulges your frantic search for the bull's tracks. The few hoofprints evident disappear into a bluestem grove. He isn't surprised.

"You're chasing ghosts," he says.

All the way back to the road, you let him rhapsodize about the living elk of his childhood. The disheveled bulls, with their flat, dark eyes, mean-mugging like he owed them money. Riled as hell in winter as they shed and looked utterly robbed. Often a single antler would linger, listing the head, the empty pedicle raw and leprous. The cows, with their accusatory stares, distinguishable from one another only by the tick trails in their coats.

That night, emboldened by tequila, the two of you try the door of Zeke's Antiques. Cones of light fall through the hangar windows. You trail your fingers delicately along racks of empty dresses. Wade won't quit with conjectures about where Zeke's old partner might be rotting. The steamer trunk is the obvious choice—but there's room enough for a body in the old roll-top desk, too.

"Jesus," you say as he swipes a feather boa along the nape of your neck. "Stop that."

A chance intimacy arises when a mannequin tips over while you're unspooling its collar of pearls. Of your clumsiness, Wade says only, "Oops"—but softly, as though your mishap is predictably endearing. As though he's grown accustomed to telling you to watch yourself. His hand lingers on the small of your back as you right the dummy. Flushed with booze and the thrill of the break-in, you will him to lean in and close the final distance between you. Maybe get to it right there on the old card table where Crazy Jim Collins allegedly played his last hand of poker, amid the mining lanterns and a century's worth of license plates from the forty-five states neither of you will ever see.

Instead, he sinks a plug hat onto your head. You force a laugh while he pries open the roll-top. Its dark insides smell like the woods after a rain.

In the morning you offer Kenny a ride to work. He bids his latest paramour for her address, and you find yourself winding up a familiar aspen-lined drive on Painter's Knoll, past bison topiaries and frosted ponds. You slink around the house before finding Kenny hunched over a breakfast counter, pectorals roiling in an undershirt you'd mock were it not for the similarly clad waif charring pancakes within earshot. She calls you "honey" without raising her eyes and spoons three more puddles of batter onto the griddle.

Kenny slides his coffee over to you. "How's your sad little heart?"

"Beat up."

He squeezes the waif's hips as he gets another mug, taking an age to select one. His movements are oddly, infuriatingly labored whenever he's choosing his next words with caution.

"Why isn't it enough just to be in love with him, Syl? I mean —what'll happen if the feeling turns out to be mutual? You gonna give up on college, move back here for good? Wait around till the place goes bust?"

This enrages you. It's meant to. "Maybe."

Kenny shakes his head. "I doubt you've even thought that far."

At dawn you climb into Wade's truck fully intending to lay it all out in the open. His unwitting grin convinces you to leave it until after the hunt—no point in ruining the day. Your plan, however, doesn't anticipate the phone call from your neighbor, whose breathless words all run together over the roar of the engine: "They took your father! They took your father!"

By the time you determine that *they* are the paramedics, you're back in town and Wade is racing daylight on his way to the Refuge alone. You finally track Dad down at St. Luke's. Laid up in urgent care, he's pale and sallow, with a brown plash of blood on his sleeve where the nurse made a failed run at his veins.

"I got a little out of breath," is all he offers as explanation.

You expect his chest scans to resemble an alien invasion. Bright orbs roaring out from the darkness between his ribs. But Dr. Miller only admonishes him for failing to take proper care of himself: "More protein, Mr. Rayles, more sleep." Nodding and smiling, he looks exactly as a doctor should, which makes you wonder why he has yet to leave Carter County. He rifles through a chart as thick as a cornerstone. "I see you recently got some very good news about your biopsies—but that's no excuse to get complacent about lifestyle."

In the hallway outside, Dr. Miller spells it out for you: the pathologist gave your father the all-clear weeks ago. He squeezes your shoulder and hands you a pamphlet on panic disorder.

Your call goes straight to Wade's voicemail. "You won't believe this shit," you say. "Come back and get me."

From the foot of Dad's bed, you read the pamphlet aloud: "Do you experience jolts of fear that make you think you are sick, dying, or losing your mind?"

"I know you're angry," he says, "but still, this is nice." His fingers on your hand are so light they feel deboned.

An hour later, returning from a coffee run, you find him hyperventilating again. "I can't stop thinking about all those water bottles I threw away."

"Jesus," you say. "Please don't start."

"How many gallons of water you think I just tossed into trash cans, back when I was a trucker?"

"I really don't know, Dad."

"Think it's more than a hundred?"

"Probably. So what now? You want to moonlight as a capper? Dig through landfills for trapped water?"

He takes a hit of oxygen to steady himself. "When I was a teen-ager, I used to run the tub every time I went to the bathroom. And I mean *every time*. We lived in such a small house—I couldn't stand the thought of anyone hearing."

Your venom slips away from you. "Well, don't worry," you say. "Once we get you into that Serenity Pod, you'll be square with the world, and everything will revert to the way it was."

By the time you realize his eyes are wet, it's too late. "When'd you get to be so cruel?" he says, without looking at you, which makes it worse. "Can't you be a little gentler to me? Don't I deserve to make amends? Aren't I worthy of the things I want?"

Perhaps to break this weird, sour sadness, Dad turns on the TV. He flips between aerial shots of a dry riverbed and close-ups of manicured fingers pressing eggplant slices into a lasagna pan, before stumbling on the breaking news of a raid on the Refuge. Hovering above the trees, the chopper's camera zooms in on rangers escorting a man toward waiting squad cars, while the chyron announces: *Shed Poacher Caught!*

"Syl," Dad says, "isn't that the guy from the mortuary?"

At Caviston's the next morning, the barroom is clenched in a gallows hush. Wade's compatriots fort up below the TV, as Channel Four loops footage of him getting pinned to the hood of a cruiser. There are no new details.

From behind the bar, Alfred, the owner, finally notices you and says: "Hey, ain't you Wade's girl?"

Suddenly drinks are on the house, and everyone's trading Wade stories again and treating you like the widow: reassuring you while you all wait for the bail jar to top up.

"Ever wonder why he's such a legend at shed-hunting?" Luckily, Alfred's not the kind of man who asks questions to have them answered. He leans over the counter toward you. "He's got elk in his blood." In a whisper intended to carry to the far corners of the room, he tells you the secret you've been longing to hear.

On a shed hunt about twelve years back, Wade was caught out in a blizzard up near Brake Creek; and after stumbling around in the drifts for hours, he chanced on an old hunting bunker. The Caviston's crowd argues about whether his entry was through a door or a ceiling. Inside were all the trappings of fonder days: meat cooler, bone boiler, rusted hooks. And in a corner, miraculously, an elk hung up for dressing. Alfred insists that the hunter's body was there, too, but most agree it was just the elk, dangling with open eyes, as if its blood had run only hours before. So Wade hunkered down to outlast the weather as the snow piled up, burying any point of exit.

"He got to chewing the rawhide string of the dead hunter's bow before he'd touch that elk," Alfred continues, shaking his head. "A true child of Posterity. Not like Fitzy here. Wade would have done damn near anything to keep himself from putting teeth to flesh."

But by the third day he had to square with the hard realities of his predicament, and he peeled hide off haunch and dug his knife tip into the blue gloss of muscle there.

"And you know what, Syl? It was so perfectly preserved by the cold that it was fine: raw and sweet, right down to the marrow."

It kept Wade alive for three more days, until the rescue party dug him out. And it wasn't bad meat that killed him, like some people said, or the cold. No, it was the warming-up that put him into cardiac arrest in the ambulance on the way to St. Luke's.

"Because you're one person before something like that," Alfred says. "And another after it. And it's a great shock for the body to switch between."

Solemn faces fill your vision. The ensuing silence is giving you away. Wouldn't he have told you by now, if you were really his girl?

You say the only thing that comes into your head: "I tell you what—after all that, if he's the kind of person who can find a fresh brown shed out by Willow Fort when no one's seen a live elk in a decade-plus, I'd say it's worth the freeze."

That earns you another shot of Brimminger's, an inquest about the shed, and an earful about how Posterity is either our salvation or the single greatest disaster the country has ever faced.

The following morning, Wade makes his phone call—to Alfred, of all people—and it's decided at Caviston's by unanimous vote that you alone should go post his bail. You drive over to Moreland County, guts thudding with all your intended declarations.

Wade emerges looking tough as a two-dollar boot. A scruff of beard softens his jaw. He slings an arm around you and gives you a squeeze, and then sits quietly, looking out the window at the blur of trees. Whatever you say now won't end the way you want it to.

"My dad got the all-clear."

"That's great," Wade says, "he must be so relieved."

You can't seem to keep the car off the shoulder. "He's never put too much stock in doctors' opinions. Doubt it'll talk him out of a Pod."

You roll down the window as Wade slopes up the driveway to his place and call after him: "I should have been there with you."

"So we could both get stung?" he says, without turning around. "Don't be ridiculous."

You don't hear from him for days. His truck stays tarped under the big elm guarding his house, and by Wednesday is covered in a thick, neat coating of snow. On Friday, the driver's side window and the margin of the door are clear, but then a cold snap glazes the exposed panels with ice well into the following week.

You ride the tram home from Painter's Knoll most evenings, help Kenny with inventory at the Wallet. It feels like trying to remember a native language you haven't spoken in years. One half-hearted morning, you wake up to a smell that reminds you of January so much it hurts, and you decide Wade is incidental to your happiness. You even make it out to the Refuge, probing ingress after boarded-off ingress until you're scraping through the trees way north of Miller's Hole, before the hopelessness of it all overwhelms you, and you give up and go home.

You're driving by Zeke's Antiques again a few days later when you see the bright glare of Wade's taillights. You park at the corner and wait. Soon enough he appears, looking almost like the Wade you remember. Knowing he's all right should be enough—but the sight of snowshoes hung over his shoulder finds you trailing a quarter mile behind him on Route 29, rehearsing your admonition of his silence: it's cruel, it's unnecessary. To avoid detection, you pass the Willow Fort turnout when he takes a left, and then double back a few minutes later to find his truck parked in the ditch.

Wade's tracks start just beyond the fir trees, where the May sun

has yet to breach the snowpack. Clouds hurry overhead, plunging
the valley in and out of shadow. You keep the bald, brown domes
of the Blacktooth Hills to your right and press on.

In a final insult to all your efforts, Wade is waiting for you at the
far edge of the tree line. "Goddamn it, Syl."

"Goddamn yourself."

His pants are torn, and a small spot of blood blooms near his
right knee. "Go home. You can't be here." Neither can he, you
point out—and what's he after anyway, a felony conviction? Is a
couple thousand dollars worth getting stung again? He lets you
go on for a while. Then he says: "I'm here to give Antlerdam the
Judas kiss."

"What do you mean?"

"He's meeting me just over the pass, and then we're going up
to Bitterroot Creek, where there's about a dozen rangers hiding
in the fucking bushes. After which I get off for giving him up. Still
wanna come along?"

You stand there in the full glare of ruin. Eventually find your
way to what feels like an acceptably sedate response: "What about
my father?"

"If I've put away enough to move to Minnesota, you probably
have enough to take care of the Pod."

"Minnesota." It's supposed to be a question, but it lands as
ridicule. As if he's just told you that the earth is flat, or that the
icecaps are intact. Minnesota. Impossibly absurd. "When did you
decide this?"

"Right around the time I decided against three to five in county."

There is no alternate version to this, no hidden meaning. You've
waited too long, and now anything you can think to say rises to
your mouth in some reduced form.

"You must realize I'd want to know something like that."

"Syl," he says. "Come on."

And that's it. The evening light purples the last dregs of winter
all across the field, to the lodgepoles on the opposite hill. A shiver
of movement catches your eye. A shadow leaving the shelter of
the trees.

"There's Antlerdam," you say.

You don't argue when Wade tells you to cover your face. The
man raises both arms and waves. His gear is so new and tight you
can practically hear it squeaking even at this distance, and he falls

once or twice as he struggles through the snow, gouging a huge wake in the hillside. By the time he reaches the bottom, you're following Wade to meet him. Up close, his face is battered and blood-plashed. His eyes are wild.

"Jesus," Wade says.

"Oh, thank God," the man says. "Rangers, thank God. I thought I'd have to spend the night for sure."

Not Antlerdam, then—just some lost greenhorn bumbling his way toward nightfall.

Wade doesn't miss a beat. "Do you realize you're trespassing, sir?"

The guy's nose is red and peeling, and you get the sense that he could throw himself into your arms at any moment. You lead him to a stump and sit him down.

"Got any water?" he says. "I'm so damn thirsty."

It dawns on you both that he didn't think to eat snow. Wade hides a smile. He hands the greenhorn his water pack, and turns to nudge your shoulder with his chin. Cold with sorrow, you edge away from him.

This is when you see the antler. Fresh brown, the bole stiffly cabled to the greenhorn's backpack. "What the hell is this?"

"Oh, God." The greenhorn twists around, clawing at his straps. "I forgot. Oh, God, please don't arrest me—it's my first time, I swear."

Wade drives his voice real low. "What's your name, sir?"

He says it's Gavin—except that's a lie, and all three of you know it. Wade takes out his notebook and writes it down anyway. You watch it materialize slowly—*Gavin*—right under the bloated consonants of Wade's previous note to himself: *Tell Syl.*

"Where did you get this, sir?"

"I found it. Heard from some guys over at Caviston's there might be new brown around."

"Fresh brown," you say, a little dizzily.

Wade grasps the greenhorn's pack and squeezes the burr. "This can't have cast more than a few hours ago. Were you trailing this bull?"

"No." Then: "All right, yes—I trailed him. But only because I knew it was just a matter of time." He turns to you confidentially. "So late in the season."

"You understand that's wildlife harassment?"

He understands, he'll never do it again, it's his first and only
time—but if the two of you had seen that bull, the sheer size of
him, the way this single antler weighed down his head, just magnificent. Well, it would have got the better of you, too.

Wade's balaclava is smoking like an incinerator. "Where's the
bull now?"

The greenhorn points. "There's a slope up behind that stand
of trees. I ran at him, just a bit to get him to drop it, and he went
down the far side."

For weeks, this elk's other antler has been wrapped in newspaper under Wade's bed. You've built joy on knowing it's there
—but in the end it was this amateur who got to see him, this idiot
who doesn't even know to eat snow when he's thirsty, this snowie
bastard with the doleful eyes who's now emptying his wallet into
Wade's hands and uncoupling the antler from his pack and saying,
"Can I go now?" while the light fades.

Wade points him toward the road with a ranger-like warning:
"Try to avoid the thin ice." Then he looks at you and says, "Come
on, Officer Dove, let's get a look at that bull."

For a moment it feels like Wade may be extending his hand
—but the point is, he's not. Not really.

"What for?" you say. "He doesn't even have his antlers anymore." You help the greenhorn to his feet. "Come on, Gavin, let's
get you home."

By the time you reach the road and see the greenhorn shakily
off, you've imagined it all differently. You've imagined the climb
up the hill in the bitter cold, a furrowed track near the summit, a
glimpse of hide through the trees.

By the time the newspapers are detailing Antlerdam's arrest,
this is no longer imagination, but memory.

And by the time your husband is moving toward you with the
ladle, asking, "What's wrong? Who is it, Syl?" it's no longer memory, but truth: the great, unrealized love of your youth ends with a
sighting of the last bull elk in Fell Gulch, his huge, black head in
full sylvan splendor.

So of course, of course you sound exactly the same. So does
Wade. And it shouldn't really surprise you that even after everything—after the bust; and Kenny's move to Michigan; and your
return to ecology; and your years on the same kelp rigs that will
eventually lure at least one of your sons; and the great, wild-easy

love of your marriage; and life here in Grey's County; and the eventual death of your father (not from cancer, but pneumonia, of all things, at the age of eighty-three); and so many iterations of disappointment and hope—all it takes is the sound of Wade's voice to unearth that other part of you: clenched around your guttering twenty-year-old heart, intact, still and always in that moment, in that clearing, raw and sweet, right down to the marrow.

RON RASH

The Baptism

FROM *The Southern Review*

REVEREND YATES HAD awaited his coming, first for hours, then
days and weeks. Now it was December and as cold as any in memory. When he'd lowered the metal well bucket, it clanged as if hitting iron. It took a leashed pitchfork, cast like a harpoon, to finally
break the ice. He was bringing the water back to the manse when
Jason Gunter came out of the woods on horseback. Reverend Yates
took the water inside and returned with a shotgun that, until this
moment, had never been aimed at anything other than a squirrel
or rabbit.

Gunter saw the weapon but did not turn the horse. Even in the
saddle the younger man swaggered, the reins loosely held, body
rocking side to side. Not yet thirty, but already responsible for one
wife's death, nearly a second.

"That's a mighty unneighborly way to be greeted," Gunter said,
smiling as he dismounted, "especially by a man of the cloth."

"I figured it would be one you understood," Reverend Yates replied.

Gunter opened his frock coat to show the absence of knife
or pistol.

"I didn't come for a tussle, Preacher."

Gunter was dressed in much the same attire he'd arrived in
four years ago—leather boots and wool breeches, white linen shirt
and frogged gray coat. As then, his black hair was slicked back
and glistening with oil, his fingernails trimmed, undarkened by
dirt. A dandy, people had assumed, which caused many to expect
Gunter to fail miserably when he'd bought the farm adjoining

Eliza Vaughn's property. But that hadn't been the case at all. He had brought his wife with him, a woman clearly once attractive but now hunch-shouldered. Her eyes were striking, the color of wisteria, though she seldom raised them when in town. A month after they had come, she'd hanged herself from a crossbeam in the barn, or so the county sheriff concluded.

Reverend Yates lowered the shotgun so it rested in the crook of his arm, but the barrel still pointed in Gunter's direction.

"If it's about where Susanna is . . ."

"It ain't about knowing where she is," Gunter answered. "That's over and done with."

"What is it then?"

"I got need to be baptized."

When Reverend Yates didn't respond, the younger man quit smiling. For a few moments they stared at each other.

"If you want someone to baptize you," Reverend Yates said, "there are plenty of other preachers who can do it."

"Who said *I* wanted it?"

Gunter turned and placed two fingers in his mouth and gave a sharp whistle. Eliza Vaughn and her fourteen-year-old daughter Pearl came out of the woods and stood silently beside the horse's haunches. Reverend Yates stared at her questioningly but she would not meet his gaze. Beneath a coat once worn by her husband, the woman shivered, and perhaps not just from the cold. He had warned her not to let Susanna marry Gunter, but despite what had happened to Gunter's first wife, Eliza did not stop the marriage. Widowed, she'd been forced to raise her daughters on her own. Gunter was a broad-shouldered man strong enough to keep the farm running. The first wife's death hadn't been Gunter's doing, Eliza claimed. *He ain't never drank a drop of liquor,* she'd said, as if all men needed alcohol to summon their perfidy. After the marriage, Gunter helped support Eliza and Pearl, keeping them in firewood, helping plant and harvest crops, digging a new well.

But there had been a price. First a pumpknot swelling Susanna's left brow, then two weeks later an arm so wrenched out of the socket that it hung useless at her side for weeks. Susanna did not claim she'd bumped her head entering a root cellar or twisted her arm restraining a rambunctious cow. She offered no explanation, nor did her mother or sister, even after several women in the congregation, out of curiosity or compassion, inquired. Her lot in life was to suffer, Susanna appeared to believe. But on that Sunday, watching her wince each time she moved the arm, Reverend Yates told her it was not her duty to suffer. Even then, Susanna had said nothing. She'd turned and walked back through town, past the manse and up the wooded path to where Gunter waited.

"Is this about your daughter, Eliza?" Reverend Yates asked sharply, "because if it is, I swore I'd never tell where she went, and I'll honor that, even with her own mother."

"It ain't about that hussy that you helped run off from me," Gunter said, looking at Eliza. "You tell him. You're the one says I got to do it."

"I want you to baptize Mr. Gunter," Eliza said.

"Why would you want that, Eliza?" Reverend Yates asked.

"To marry Pearl," the widow answered softly.

"She's of a mind it'll wash any devilment right out of me," Gunter said. "I don't think much is in me but it seems some folks do. Anyway, if getting doused puts a mother's mind at ease I'll abide it."

"Pearl is a child," Reverend Yates said. He looked at the girl, wrapped in a quilt she cinched tight around her neck. Like her mother, she stared at the ground.

"There's many been married at her age, Preacher," Gunter said. "There's one in your own congregation."

Reverend Yates looked at Pearl. She was not shivering but her cheeks glowed from the cold. He had baptized her and Susanna on the same July Sunday five years ago. A thin, delicate child, one often sick. He remembered how light she'd felt as he took her in his arms and lowered her into the river.

"You and your mother come into the house, child."

"Nah," Gunter said. "We need to be getting back. Some of us has to work more than just on Sundays."

"Eliza," Reverend Yates said.

She looked at him now, her pale face blank.

"This Sunday, Preacher," Gunter said. "Douse me in the morning and me and Pearl will get the justice of the peace to marry us right after. I done got that set up."

"Our baptisms are held in warmer weather."

"I know for a fact you baptized Henry Cope last winter," Gunter challenged.

"He was dying," Reverend Yates answered. "Even then it wasn't this cold."

"I know that water will be cold," Gunter said, grinning now, "but I figure Pearl will warm me up real good later."

"It isn't just the water that cleanses a man," Reverend Yates answered. "It's what is in the heart."

"I know that, Preacher."

"What if I won't do it?"

"We'll go to Boone," Gunter answered. "There's more than one preacher in this county. Of course that's a mighty long walk for Eliza and Pearl, especially with the chance of more snow coming." Gunter turned and nodded at Eliza and Pearl. "Go on now," he said.

Reverend Yates watched mother and child walk out of the yard and into the woods, stepping in their earlier footprints as if in Gunter's presence they dare not even disturb the snow.

"We'll be seeing you Sunday, Preacher," Gunter said, raising finger and thumb to tip his hat. He nodded at the shotgun. "I'm a forgiving man, maybe you ought be the same, especially since I wouldn't be needing a wife if you'd not meddled in another man's business."

"I know my business, Gunter," Reverend Yates replied, but the words sounded feeble.

"Good," Gunter replied. "Do it come Sunday."

Gunter jerked the reins and the horse turned. He kicked a bootheel against its flank and went back up the path. Even when Gunter was out of sight, Reverend Yates heard the crunching of snow under the horse's hooves. He stared at the woods, the bare gray branches reaching upward like wailing women.

Susanna had come in the middle of night, knocking frantically on the front door. Looking out the manse's window, he'd seen her silhouetted behind a lantern's glow. When Reverend Yates ushered her in, he saw she was barefoot and dressed only in a shift. Susanna raised the lantern to show the red and purple marks where his fingers had grasped.

"All I done was be late fixing his bath," Susanna pleaded, terror in her eyes. "He said next time it'd be a rope around my neck, not a hand. He'd do it, Reverend. You know he would."

"What would you have me do?"

"Get me away from here, someplace he'll never find me."

"What of your mother and sister?"

The fear in Susanna's eyes dimmed.

"They ain't able to stop him from killing me," she answered, a sudden coldness in her voice.

Whether she had or had not understood the intent of his question, Reverend Yates would never know. She'd asked for his help, he told himself, so how could he not give it? Was there a relative who could take her in, he asked, one not close by but that she could get to by train. Susanna nodded. He'd put a quilt around her and they walked down the street to Marvin Birch's house. The three of them had gone to Marvin's dry goods to purchase Susanna shoes, clothes, and undergarments, enough to wear and also fill a carpetbag. Marvin was known as a skinflint, but he refused any money. Which was all to the good, because it left twenty dollars to give her after Reverend Yates paid for the ticket to Johnson City. She could get to her final destination from there, he'd told her.

Afterward, he'd returned to the manse and waited for Gunter to show up, the shotgun by the door, unloaded but Gunter would not know that. But it was Eliza who'd come on that October morning. Reverend Yates told her he didn't know where Susanna was and would swear so on a Bible if need be. Without another word Eliza walked back up the path to her farm. Except for some glares when they'd passed each other in the street, Gunter did nothing. Perhaps he believed, as Reverend Yates feared, Susanna would return on her own. He'd seen it before, women or children fleeing and then returning not out of corporal need but some darker necessity. At such times, he feared some malevolent counterpoint to grace operated in the world. But Susanna had not returned. Gunter obtained a divorce on grounds of abandonment.

A polite knock interrupted Reverend Yates's reverie. Opening the door, he found four congregation members on his porch, in the forefront Marvin Birch. He invited them in. Birch seemed reluctant but the others eagerly left the cold, though no one sat when offered a chair.

"We have heard about Gunter's latest outrage," Birch said. "If I had known this was the purpose of his divorce I would have ensured Judge Lingard did not grant it. What Gunter proposes, surely you will not allow?"

"If you mean the marriage itself, I have no part in it. He says he will go to the justice of the peace."

"But the baptism," Birch said. "What of it?"

"If I don't, Gunter told me he'll go elsewhere," Reverend Yates answered.

"But if you do so," Birch sputtered, "it would mean the community condones this abomination."

"It was Eliza, a member of our congregation, not Gunter, who asked this of me."

"That is of no importance, Reverend." The storekeeper bristled. "Let them go elsewhere."

"He will make them walk there, Marvin, and in this weather such a trek could give a girl with her delicate constitution the whooping cough or influenza. Would you want that on your conscience?"

"Doubtful, I say," Birch answered. "And if so, might not death be better for the child than being wedded to that blackguard?"

"There is something else," Reverend Yates said, his voice more reflective. "What if the act itself, despite Gunter's lack of sincerity, were to truly cleanse the man?"

For a few moments the only sound was the crackle and hiss of the hearth's burning wood.

"You believe Gunter capable of such change?"

"No," Reverend Yates answered, "but God is capable. It is the mystery of grace. I cannot be true to my responsibilities if I doubt the possibility."

"But our responsibility as town elders is different, Reverend. We cannot permit this."

"So you question God's wisdom in worldly matters?"

"God allows us the ability to discern evil, Reverend, and the strength to defy it."

"Yet not in this matter," Reverend Yates replied, with less certainty than he would have wished. "Be assured, I have not made my decision lightly, gentlemen. I appreciate and understand your concern, but the baptism must be allowed."

The next morning at the service, Gunter sat with Eliza and Pearl on the back pew. Reverend Yates had contemplated altering the

sermon he'd written out Thursday night, but found himself too
vexed to do so. As planned, he spoke of Moses, and how he'd
led his people to the Promised Land though unable to enter that
place himself. He read the sermon with as little attentiveness as his
congregation offered in their listening, Gunter's presence casting
a pall over the whole church.

Reverend Yates did not announce the baptism. Instead, he
waited until the church emptied but for Gunter, Eliza, Pearl,
and himself.

"This weather, surely . . ."

"We got quilts and dry clothes, even a sheet if you ain't got me
a gown," Gunter said. "I'm going to have a fire on the bank, too.
Got my wood and kindling and flint rock already waiting. So we'll
go on out there, Preacher. Have you a fire going so you don't
catch cold."

Reverend Yates went to the manse and changed into the cotton
trousers and white linen shirt he always wore for baptisms. He put
on a wool scarf and his heaviest overcoat. The water might rise
to his hips but the pants would dry quickly by the fire, so he took
no change of clothes, only a drying cloth. The baptism pool was a
quarter mile away. Reverend Yates saddled his horse and followed
Eliza's and Pearl's footprints in the snow, unsurprised when the
hoofprints of Gunter's mount, which preceded the woman and
child, merged with those of other horses.

The trail curved and the river lay before him. A man-high fire
blazed at the forest's edge, stoked with enough wood to burn for
hours. Pearl and Eliza huddled beside it, Gunter close by. Reverend Yates dismounted and tethered his horse to a dogwood branch
sleeved with ice. The elders stood on the riverbank. In the crook
of Marvin Birch's right arm was a rifle.

As Reverend Yates approached, Birch stepped aside so he could
see the river.

"Tell me that ain't a sign from God, Reverend," the store owner
said, facing the river as well.

The river's deep bend that served as the baptism pool was completely iced over, the snow-limned surface unmarked but for the
tracks of a single raccoon. Had Reverend Yates not known otherwise, he'd have thought a meadow or pasture lay before him.

"When have you ever seen it covered like this?" Birch asked, his thumb on the rifle's trigger guard. "Never a one of us has. It's a sign to us all and I'll abide no man to profane it."

Reverend Yates turned and looked at Gunter, who appeared in deep reflection as he, too, stared at the frozen river.

"Marvin's right," another elder said. "It's surely a sign from God, Reverend."

The other elders nodded their assent. For a few moments the only sound was the crackle of the fire.

"There will be no baptism today," Reverend Yates finally said.

Only then did Gunter rouse himself. He shook his shoulders as if to cast off some burden.

"It's just ice," he said, and walked to the river's edge. He placed a foot on the ice, pressed his bootheel more firmly until his full weight was upon it.

"Fetch me a stout tree limb, woman," Gunter said to Eliza.

As Eliza turned from the fire, Marvin Birch stepped close to Gunter. He gripped the rifle on the upper stock and held it out.

"God won't let you break that ice even with this, Gunter," the store owner announced, nodding at the butt end, "and it made of hickory."

"We'll see about that, damn you," the younger man replied, grabbing the rifle barrel with both hands and thrusting the butt downward.

The sharp report of shattered ice was instantly followed by a louder crack. The sounds crossed the river, echoed back. Gunter still gripped the iron barrel. He appeared to stare down at it intently as skeins of gray smoke encircled his head. He gave a violent shudder and fell forward, the webbed ice opening to accept the body. Gunter slowly sank. Soon the only sign of him was the water's pinkish tinge.

In the months following Gunter's death, the community made certain that Eliza and Pearl were cared for. Spring crops were planted and harvested, wood for winter set by. At sixteen, Pearl married Lewis Hampton, whose father owned the valley's best bottomland, ensuring Eliza as well as her daughter would never again go wanting. Susanna learned of Gunter's death through relatives and returned for Pearl's wedding, though she did not stay, having made a life elsewhere. But Susanna and her family visited yearly even after

Eliza died. On such Sundays, the sisters and their husbands and children filled a pew.

To look upon such a sight from his pulpit was surely a sign of God's grace, Reverend Yates told himself, but on late nights he sometimes contemplated his silence when Marvin Birch offered the cocked weapon. Had his refusal to warn Gunter been a furtherance of God's will or his own desire to be rid of the man? On such nights the parlor became nothing more than shadows and silence. The manse's stillness widened beyond the walls into the vastness of the whole valley.

Suburbia!

FROM *The Southern Review*

"LET'S MAKE A BET," my father said, on my fifteenth birthday. I remember very clearly being fifteen; or rather, I remember what fifteen feels like to a fifteen-year-old. The age is a diving board, a box half-opened.

We were sitting in stiff wooden chairs on the porch, watching the evening settle over the neighborhood, all of that harmless diffuse light softening the world.

"I bet you'll leave here at eighteen and you'll never come back," he said. "Not once."

We lived two hours outside of Los Angeles, in a suburb attached to a string of other suburbs, where the days rarely distinguished themselves unless you did it for them.

"You don't even think I'll come back and visit?" I said.

"No," he said. "I don't." My father was a reasonable man. He did not generalize. He was not prone to big, grandiose statements, and he rarely gambled. I felt hurt and excited by the suggestion.

"What about Mom?" I asked.

"What about her?"

I shrugged. It seemed she had little to do with his prediction.

"And James?" I asked.

"Not sure about James," he said. "I can't bet on that one."

James was—and still is—my younger brother. I felt little responsibility to him. At ten, he was brilliant and anxious and very much my parents' problem. My mother adored him, though she thought she had fooled me into thinking we were equal. Make no mistake: we were equally loved but not equally preferred. If parents don't have favorites, they do have allies.

Inside, my mother was cooking dinner while James followed her around the kitchen, handing her bits of paper he'd folded into unusual shapes. Even then, he had a knack for geometry.

"Where will I go?" I asked my father. My grades were aggressively mediocre. I'd planned—vaguely, at fifteen—to transfer somewhere after a few years at the local junior college.

"It doesn't matter where," he said, waving away a fly circling his nose.

Next door, the quiet neighbor kid, Carl, walked his miniature pinscher, also called Carl, back and forth across his lawn. The weather was balmy.

"What happens if I do come back?" I asked.

"You'll lose," he said. "You'll automatically forfeit the bet."

I hated to lose, and my father knew it.

"Will I see you again?" I asked. I felt nostalgic in a way that felt new, at fifteen, as though the day had already turned shadowy and distant, a predetermined memory. I felt nostalgic for my father and his partly bald head and his toothpaste breath, even as he sat next to me, running his palms over his hairy knees.

"Of course," he said. "Your mother and I will visit."

My mother appeared on the porch with my brother, his finger slung into the back pocket of her jeans. "Dinnertime," she said, and I kissed my father's cheek as though I were standing on a train platform. I spent all of dinner feeling that way too, staring at him from across the table, mouthing goodbye.

My eighteenth birthday arrived the summer after I'd graduated from high school. To celebrate, I saw the musical *Wicked* at a theater in Los Angeles with four of my friends. The seats were deep and velvety feeling. My parents drove us, and my father gave us each a glass of champagne in the parking lot before we entered the theater. We used small plastic cups he must have bought especially for the occasion. I pictured him browsing the plastics aisle, looking at all the cups, deciding.

A week after my birthday, my father woke me up, quieter than usual. He seemed solemn. I still had my graduation cap tacked up on the wall, its yellow tassel hanging jauntily. My mother had taken the dress I'd worn that day to the dry cleaner, and it still lay pooled on the floor in its plastic.

"Are you ready to go?" he asked.

"Where are you taking me?" I wanted to know.

"To the train station," he said. "It's time for you to go."

My father had always liked the idea of traveling. Even just walking through an airport gave him a thrill—it made him buoyant, seeing all those people hurrying through the world on their way to somewhere else. He had a deep interest in history, and the architecture of places he'd never seen in person. It was the great tragedy of his life that he became a real estate agent. As for my mother, it was the great tragedy of her life that her husband was unhappy and didn't take any pains to hide it. I can see that now, even if I didn't see it then.

"Where's Mom?" I asked. "And where's James?"

"The grocery store," my father said. James loved the grocery store—the order of things, all neat in their rows. "Don't cry," Dad said then, smoothing my pillowcase, still warm with sleep. He had a pained look on his face. "Don't cry," he said again. I hadn't noticed it had started. My whole body felt emotional in those days, like I was an egg balanced on a spoon.

"You'll be good," he said. "You'll do good."

"But what about junior college?" I asked. "What about plans?" I'd already received a stack of glossy school pamphlets in the mail. True, I didn't know what to do with them yet, but I had them just the same.

"No time," my father said, and the urgency in his voice made me hurry.

We stood on the platform at the train station—just as I'd pictured at fifteen, like I were a character in a history book, *Manifesting My Own Destiny!* He held my face in both palms and squeezed, a gentle vise. The sky was bright blue and wide open, as though it had been shelled from a duller sky.

"You'll miss me," I said. I said it like a question.

"Of course," he said.

"Will I do OK?"

"Of course," he said. "Of course, of course, of course." The series of "of courses" worried me, as though he were trying to convince us both of something.

"Doth protest too much," I said.

"Ha!" My father pointed at a pigeon pecking its head in an odd little dance.

We hugged for a long time. My dad was tall, and he rested his chin against the top of my head. "Don't forget to shake my hand," he whispered into my hair. "We have an agreement, after all." He made a choking noise—a sob?—and ruffled my too-long bangs. He stuffed a sweaty wad of money into my palm. I put it in my purse. He handed me another.

"That's it," he said. "I wish I had more."

"Where will I go?"

"I don't know," he said. "Wherever you want, I guess! You can buy a ticket when you get on the train. You used to talk about New York all the time." That's true, I did—but in an abstract, watercolor way. I knew nothing about living on my own, especially in a city that "stayed up all night." I was usually in bed by eleven, quick to fall asleep, books always splitting open onto my chest after I'd only read a few paragraphs. In fact, I'd only just started doing my own laundry last week, and I had to keep calling upstairs to my mother, about the separation of darks and lights, and when to put in the detergent. When?!

I could hardly manage to think about my mother, who was very pretty, I realized all of the sudden, and maybe always had been. (My mother had red hair, and I once heard a man at the post office tell her that from far away she looked like she was on fire. He had an odd look on his face, a half smile, as if he'd won something.)

"Shouldn't I wait to say bye?" I asked. "Won't Mom be mad?"

"It's for the best," my father said. "She'll only try to convince you to stay."

"But what about my friends," I said. "I haven't said bye to anyone!" I started thinking of odd people—our neighbor Carl and his miniature pinscher, my debate coach Mrs. Swanson who told me I touched my face too much when I talked, the boy with the unusually deep voice who worked the counter at CVS. "And James?"

"You'll see them again," he said.

"OK," I said, turning away from him. I hoped my back looked brave. From the train, I watched him through the window until

I couldn't see him anymore, and the hand he'd been waving became like the minute hand of a clock—tiny—and then nothing at all.

After all that, I only went to LA. I didn't have enough money to get to New York, and anyway, that would have taken a long time on the train. On the ride, I met my first adult friend. He was sloshing down the aisles like he was drunk. He wasn't drunk though, just prone to motion sickness. His name was Charlie.

Charlie came with questions, I could tell. They animated his face before he spoke. He had just graduated from college, he told me. He had had three beers in the dining car, he volunteered, but was not drunk, just prone to motion sickness.

"Are you on your way back to school?" was his first question.

"No," I said, "I'm just leaving home. I might not even go to college."

He leaned forward. I wasn't scared, just curious. He had a harmless face—too round for murder. My mom was a big believer in physiognomy, and it had stuck with me. *Your long limbs,* she would say, *means you'll always be efficient. I'll always be awkward,* I'd say, but she assured me I was misreading my own body.

"Are you a runaway?" he asked.

"No," I said, "not exactly." I didn't want him to get the wrong idea about my family, that it was bad somehow, damaged. But then I wondered what sort of value that might have, the wrong idea about me—that I'd withstood something traumatic, that I was wise or strong. I decided the fewer words I said, the better. I'd be a person who spoke very little, but when I spoke, it would be especially important.

"I just left," I said, "I got up one day and left. Didn't even say bye to my mom."

"That's terrible," he said. "I'm sorry."

A silence fell over the two of us, one that made my pulse bang in all the wrong places—my wrist, my throat—and I asked him to tell me more about college. He'd studied political science, he said, "a stupid major, because it only made me cynical." That's what I wanted to be, too, I decided right then: cynical. It seemed fitting for the new personality I was cultivating.

"So," he said, leaning closer. "What were your parents *like?*"

I understood where this question was leading. "Terrible," I said.

I felt the pinprick of tears somewhere behind my eyes. "Scary-aw-ful."

Just then the slot of air between us lessened. He was leaning even closer. He had very nice teeth, prep-school teeth. I, too, leaned closer. "I'm so sorry," he said.

"Don't worry. I'm on my own now."

"Geez, I should never complain about my parents," he said. "They really are nice to me. I mean my dad asks stupid questions all the time, and never listens to what I tell him, but geez, nothing like you went through."

I nodded. Maybe I would be an actress. Why not?

Charlie said I could stay at his place until I found something more permanent. He lived off of Pico in a brown stucco apartment with palm trees cemented in the sidewalk. Someone had scrawled the words *Here fur good* on one of the garage doors. Charlie had two roommates who were rarely there, and when they were there, they were always on their way out. I only ever saw them in motion— dashes of solid-colored T-shirts, streaks of floppy, surfer-boy hair. They seemed used to having a visitor.

"Hey, Boss," they'd say, like it had always been my nickname.

"Maria," I'd correct them.

"Right," they'd say. "Cool." Or, in a singsong voice, "Maria, Maria, how do you solve a problem like Maria," before closing the front door.

I was always worried about becoming a problem.

I'd spoken to my father a few times. "You're doing great," he assured me. My mother got on the phone, tearful sounding some-times, but mostly relegated to curt sentences with her voice all choked up, like the sadness was lodged in her throat. I thought their voices sounded different, higher pitched somehow, or smaller. I wondered if my mother knew about the bet, but I couldn't tell her; I couldn't sell out my father. Regardless, she never told me to come home, just asked if I was happy. "Are you?" "Yes," I'd say, "I'm pretty sure I am."

After a few months, James started writing me emails. He was thirteen now, and had become suddenly articulate. When we were living together I hadn't realized it, or else, he had kept it from me. Maybe he was just better on paper. I started to rethink his and my mother's relationship—maybe they were true confidants, as young as he was, and as mom-like as she was.

The boys I lived with all loved horror films, and I would write James long movie reviews about whatever we'd just watched. He seemed to like it. I was getting to know the boys better—though they still usually called me Boss—and I would write to James about them, too.

"How are Mom and Dad," I'd write. "How's school?"

"I'm writing poetry," James wrote, "and I no longer care much for math."

"And Mom and Dad? What about them?"

"I'm thinking of going to boarding school," he said. "In fact, I'm sure I'll go." Sometimes he'd only respond with poetry: "I have perceived that to be with those I like is enough . . . I do not ask any more delight, I swim in it as in a sea," and so on.

"What is that?" I wrote back. "Some kind of prayer? That's not an answer! How are Mom and Dad?!?"

"Walt Whitman," he wrote, "and you really should read more."

The seasons changed. I moved into a small studio apartment by myself, and I did laundry remarkably often at a Laundromat down the street. Charlie said he was sad to see me go. I'd gotten a job as a waitress and I took classes at Santa Monica College in accounting and studio art. Eventually, I even managed to buy myself a used Jetta. "Wow," my father said when I told him about it over the phone, "that all sounds amazing." He kept telling me I was bohemian, that I was following my own path. He said it in a weird, far-off voice like he must have been sitting on the porch again, looking into the distance, at the purplish foothills.

Often, customers at the restaurant asked if I was an actress. All the waitresses in LA were actresses, and I had straight teeth and too-long legs, so sometimes I said yes. That was very meta, I thought—acting if only by telling people I was an actress. *Meta* was a new word I'd learned in community college, in the accounting class, of all things. Still, sometimes, at night, I'd rub my eyes and the tips of my fingers would be wet. I'd been crying and hadn't known it. I was quick to cry, but I wasn't sure if it was connected to any particular emotion. Like my mother said, sometimes I misread my own body. That hadn't changed.

After a while, I got a promotion at the restaurant, and suddenly I was a manager, telling the other actress-waitresses which territory of tables to serve. Sometimes, in the kitchen, they'd talk about their auditions—how often they were told to say, "Hi, welcome to Applebee's!" over and over—but more cheerful this time; no, more intense. "A waitress playing a waitress," I'd say. "Very meta!"

I started seeing Charlie every weekend. There was something about him I liked, a familiarity. We'd run errands—the grocery store, the comic book shop—so that the time we spent together passed easily. Being with him felt similar to being alone, only better, heightened. That's the best way I can describe it—we glided right alongside each other.

I started asking my father when he would come visit. "I'm no longer adjusting to my new life!" I said. "I'm adjusted. I'm an adult. I'm living an adult life, as an adult person." He started piling up excuses and handing them over one by one. Even over the phone, I knew they were stacked up, like plates—I can't explain it. I felt angry and gypped. "You're not holding up your end of the bargain," I said. "You told me we'd see each other!"

"It's complicated," my dad said, "but I love you and miss you. We all do. It's not what you think." After a while, I started wondering why I shouldn't just go home. What did I even stand to lose?

"You can't," my father would say when I asked about it, and something about the weight of his words held me in place.

Still, I became resentful. I started noticing all of the things I'd inherited from my father that I didn't like. My mother, too! She was not exempt. I listed these things in my emails to James: passive-aggressiveness, knobby knees, indecision, weak ankles that made ice-skating difficult, an allergy to shrimp . . . the list went on. "Dad chose to be a real estate agent," I wrote in one email, "what sort of job is that?!"

"You're saying that out of anger," my brother wrote. Then, he'd include another poem. He'd moved on to a life I couldn't begin to imagine, in which he made his own lattes and collected vintage typewriters. "Mom's into poetry now," he wrote. Of course she is, I thought. "But you still want to go to boarding school?" I asked. "I'm already packing," he wrote.

Charlie loved movies, and there was a line he liked to quote whenever I complained about not understanding my family: "The awful thing about life is this: everybody has their reasons." "I'm paraphrasing," he'd say. Meanwhile, I'd built my own kind of life for myself. Whatever it was, I knew it was distinctly mine. One week I ate every meal at the Russian deli across from my apartment. The next week, I called in sick to work and went out for a lobster dinner. The week after that, I spent the day in Venice Beach, watching the musclemen and skateboarders greet each other on the boardwalk. Still, my freedom made me restless. I saw Charlie almost every day now, usually after long shifts at the restaurant that made my clothes smell smoky like barbecue. He said my freedom made me brave. I never told him the truth about my parents, that they weren't awful, only strange. Actually, they had always been kind.

"I'm tied down," Charlie said, "by my parents' expectations. You just get to do whatever you want." Charlie worked at a law firm. He was rarely able to do what he wanted. "With you," he said, "I feel the rope around me slacken." By now, I knew he was subtly trying to sleep with me, and maybe always had been. We'd watch movies on the couch, and we'd start on opposite ends, and when the movie finished, he'd be right up against me, like we were two blocks getting ready to build.

"You're so brave," he said one night, after we'd eaten SpaghettiOs from a can. We were sitting at my small Formica kitchen table, and he kept dipping his head toward me, like he was trying to close the gap between our mouths. It's not that I didn't want to. The shape of his lips told me it would be good, and though I hadn't kissed that many people, I'd kissed enough to know shape mattered. It was the lie that kept me from pressing my lips to his.

"I haven't been honest about my parents," I said.

"Oh?" he said. "You can tell me anything. Anything they did to you—"

"I'm not as brave or as cynical as you think." Then I told him the whole story of the bet with my father.

"Well, you should go home and see them," he said.

"But then I'd lose."

"Who cares?" he shouted, and smacked the table. And maybe he was right. But I *did* care. I hated to lose. What's more, I hated to disappoint my father.

"I'll go with you," he said.

We took the train. "Remember when we met?" he asked. And of course I did. This time, he talked about his job at the law firm as

we rode out of LA, buildings flipping by like cards in a deck. He
hated his job.

"Then quit it," I said. It was a simple answer, and I said it simply. He looked like he wanted to kiss me, and this time I let him,
or I kissed him, and he let me. It was one of those kisses that felt
equal—where you're giving as much as you take. Also, I was right
about how the shape of his mouth would feel, and happy that I'd
read my body correctly. There was pleasure in knowing what you
wanted and acting accordingly. It was a different kind of freedom.

We kissed for most of the train ride, so that by the time we arrived at my stop, I felt dizzy and short of breath, as though I'd run
the whole way. Once we reached the platform, we took an Uber to
my house, debating the entire time whether or not I should have
told my parents I was coming—prepared my dad at least. I had
decided not to; I wanted to catch them off guard. Charlie thought
I should have told them. He thought it would have been more
considerate. "Consideration?" I scoffed. "I've already outgrown it."

When we drove up the familiar street toward my cul-de-sac, I
didn't realize I was nervous until I felt my insides twist up. Still,
the neighborhood looked like you might expect it to—neat, prim,
safe.

"Why are you nervous?" Charlie asked. "To see them?"

"No," I said. "Nervous to lose the bet." More so, I couldn't remember the last time I'd so blatantly gone against my father's
wishes, if I ever had before.

"Is this it?" the driver asked, looking at his GPS again, and then
at the empty lot. The curb was still painted with the numbers of
my address, but the land was filled with grass and dandelions and
other unnameable weeds.

"This can't be right," I said.

I saw a glimmer of something in the empty lot. Where were
my parents? My brother? From afar, the something shone in the
sun like a tin can. When I came upon it, though, I saw that it
was an exact replica of the house I grew up in, just tiny, a little
smaller than a toaster. I got down on my knees, then lowered my
body to the ground as though I were preparing to do push-ups.
"Hello!" I shouted through the windows. I flicked open the front
door with my fingernail. "Hello?" The tiny curtains blew with my
breath. The mailbox I remembered from my childhood was still

there—sponge-painted red, a task I had completed when I was in elementary school—only teeny now.

I thought I heard something coming from inside the tiny house: a tiny, high-pitched voice. I saw my tiny father in the tiny foyer, shaking his head at me.

"I told you not to come," he said. "You didn't listen!"

Charlie was behind me. "What is it?" he asked. "What's that little box?"

"My house," I said. The way he stood, the shadow he produced made it difficult to see anything else. "Back up," I said.

"I didn't want you to see us like this," my father said. My mother appeared alongside him.

"It's OK," I told him, "don't worry." Still lying flat, I talked to my parents through the tiny doorway, and told them a few details about my life, mostly about junior college and waitressing and Charlie. My mother was trying not to cry. I could see her red hair, like the tip of a match now.

"How are you?" I asked. I wanted to reach out and stroke the top of her head with the pad of my finger.

"OK," she said. Her voice was soft, a faint whistle, and I had to lean close to hear it. "Dad and I are seeing a couples' therapist," she told me, and I wondered if the therapist was also miniature. My dad turned away, embarrassed.

"That's great," I said. "And James likes boarding school?"

"Loves it," my dad said, brightening again. "You should see him now. We hardly recognize him."

I looked around for Charlie, wanting him to get down on his knees at my parents' tiny door and introduce himself. But no, he was waiting in the car, giving us our privacy. From where I crouched, he also looked smaller. I thought this was a funny thing, the way the past and the future could both shrink down to a manageable size, like a pill to be swallowed, or the head of a match.

The Prairie Wife

FROM *The New Yorker*

THE UNDERSTANDING IS THAT, after Casey's iPhone alarm goes off at 6:15 a.m., Kirsten wakes the boys, nudges them to get dressed, and herds them downstairs, all while Casey is showering. The four of them eat breakfast as a family, deal with teeth-brushing and backpacks, and Casey, who is the principal of the middle school in the same district as the elementary school Jack and Ian attend, drives the boys to drop-off. Kirsten then takes her shower in the newly quiet house before leaving for work.

The reality is that, at 6:17, as soon as Casey shuts the bathroom door, Kirsten grabs her own iPhone from her nightstand and looks at Lucy Headrick's Twitter feed. Clearly, Kirsten is not alone: Lucy has 3.1 million followers. (She follows a mere 533 accounts, many of which belong to fellow-celebrities.) Almost all of Lucy's vast social-media empire, which of course is an extension of her life-style-brand empire (whatever the fuck a life-style brand is), drives Kirsten crazy. Its content is fake and pandering and boring and repetitive—how many times will Lucy post variations on the same recipe for buttermilk biscuits?—and Kirsten devours all of it, every day: Facebook and Instagram, Tumblr and Pinterest, the blog, the vlog, the TV show. Every night, Kirsten swears that she won't devote another minute to Lucy, and every day she squanders hours. The reason that things go wrong so early in the morning, she has realized, is this: she's pretty sure Twitter is the only place where real, actual Lucy is posting, Lucy whom Kirsten once knew. Lucy has insomnia, and, while all the other posts on all the other sites might be written by Lucy's minions, Kirsten is certain that it was

Lucy herself who, at 1:22 a.m., wrote, "Watching Splash on cable, oops I forgot to name one of my daughters Madison!" Or, at 3:14 a.m., accompanied by a photo of an organic candy bar: "Hmm could habit of eating chocolate in middle of night be part of reason I can't sleep LOL!"

Morning, therefore, is when there's new, genuine Lucy sustenance. So how can Kirsten resist? And then the day is Lucy-contaminated already, and there's little incentive for Kirsten not to keep polluting it for the sixteen hours until she goes to bed with the bull-shitty folksiness in Lucy's life: the acquisition of an Alpine goat, the canning of green beans, the baby shower that Lucy is planning for her young friend Jocelyn, who lives on a neighboring farm.

As it happens, Lucy has written (or "written"? Right? There's no way) a memoir, with recipes—*Dishin' with the Prairie Wife*—that is being published today, so Kirsten's latest vow is that she'll buy the book (she tried to reserve it from the library and learned that she was 305th in line), read it, and then be done with Lucy. Completely. Forever.

The memoir has been "embargoed"—as if Lucy is, like, Henry Kissinger—and, to promote it, Lucy traveled yesterday from her farm in Missouri to Los Angeles. (As she told Twitter, "BUMMM-PEE flyin over the mountains!!") Today, she will appear on a hugely popular TV talk show on which she has been a guest more than once. Among last night's tweets, posted while Kirsten was sleeping, was the following: "Omigosh you guys I'm so nervous + excited for Mariana!!! Wonder what she will ask . . ." The pseudo-nervousness, along with the "Omigosh"—never "Omigod," or even "OMG"—galls Kirsten. Twenty years ago, Lucy swore like a normal person; but the Lucy of now, Kirsten thinks, resembles Casey, who, when their sons were younger, respectfully asked Kirsten to stop cursing in front of them. Indeed, the Lucy of now—beloved by evangelicals, homeschooler of her three daughters, wife of a man she refers to as the Stud in Overalls, who is a deacon in their church—uses such substitutes as "Jiminy Crickets!" and "Fudge Nuggets!" Once, while making a custard on-air, Lucy dropped a bit of eggshell into the mix and exclaimed, "Shnookerdookies!" Kirsten assumed that it was staged, or maybe not originally staged but definitely not edited out when it could have been. This made Kirsten feel such rage at Lucy that it was almost like lust.

Kirsten sees that, last night, Lucy, as she usually does, replied to a few dozen tweets sent to her by nobodies: Nicole in Seattle, who has thirty-one followers; Tara in Jacksonville, who's a mom of two awesome boys. (Aren't we all? Kirsten thinks.) Most of the fans' tweets say some variation of "You're so great!" or "It's my birthday pretty please wish me a happy birthday?!" Most of Lucy's responses say some variation of "Thank you for the kind words!" or "Happy Birthday!" Kirsten has never tweeted at Lucy; in fact, Kirsten has never tweeted. Her Twitter handle is not her name but "Minneap" plus the last three digits of her zip code, and, instead of uploading a photo of herself, she's kept the generic egg avatar. She has three followers, all of whom appear to be bots.

Through the bathroom door, Kirsten can hear the shower running, and the minute that Casey turns it off—by this point, Kirsten is, as she also does daily, reading an article about how smartphones are destroying people's ability to concentrate—she springs from bed, flicking on light switches in the master bedroom, the hall, and the boys' rooms. When Casey appears, wet hair combed, completely dressed, and finds Ian still under the covers and Kirsten standing by his bureau, Kirsten frowns and says that both boys seem really tired this morning. Casey nods somberly, even though it's what Kirsten says every morning. Is Casey clueless, inordinately patient, or both?

At breakfast, Jack, who is six, asks, "Do doctors ever get sick?"

"Of course," Casey says. "Everyone gets sick."

While packing the boys' lunches, Kirsten says to Ian, who is nine, "I'm giving you Oreos again today, but you need to eat your cucumber slices, and if they're still in your lunchbox when you come home you don't get Oreos tomorrow."

She kisses the three of them goodbye, and as soon as the door closes, even before she climbs the stairs, Kirsten knows that she's going to get herself off using the handheld showerhead. She doesn't consider getting herself off using the handheld showerhead morally problematic, but it presents two logistical complications, the first of which is that, the more often she does it, the more difficult it is for Casey to bring her to orgasm on the occasions when they're feeling ambitious enough to have sex. The second complication is that it makes her late for work. If Kirsten leaves the house at 7:45, she has a fifteen-minute drive; if she leaves at or after 7:55, the drive is twice as long. But, seriously, what else is she supposed to do with her Lucy rage?

Kirsten's commute is when she really focuses on whether she has the power to destroy Lucy Headrick's life. Yes, the question hums in the background at other moments, like when Kirsten is at the grocery store and sees a cooking magazine with Lucy on the cover —it's just so fucking weird how famous Lucy is—but it's in the car that Kirsten thinks through, in a realistic way, which steps she'd take. She's figured out where she could leak the news, and narrowed it down to two gossip websites, both based in Manhattan; she's even found the "Got tips?" link on one. If she met somebody who worked for such a site, and if the person promised she could remain anonymous, it would be tempting. But, living in Minneapolis, Kirsten will never meet anyone who works for a Manhattan gossip website.

Kirsten's coworker Frank has volunteered to leak the news for her; indeed, he's so eager that she fears he might do it without her blessing, except that he knows she knows he pads his expense reports when he travels. And it's Frank's joyous loathing of Lucy that reins in Kirsten's own antipathy. Frank has never met the woman, so what reason does he have to hate her? Because she's successful? This, in Kirsten's opinion, isn't sufficient. Kirsten hates Lucy Headrick because she's a hypocrite.

In 1994, the summer after their freshman year in college, Kirsten and Lucy were counselors at a camp in northern Minnesota. It was coed, and Kirsten was assigned to the Redbirds cabin, girls age nine, while Lucy was with the Bluejays, age eleven. Back then, Lucy weighed probably twenty-five pounds more than she does now, had very short light-brown hair, and had affixed a triangle-shaped rainbow pin to her backpack. The first night, at the counselors' orientation before the campers arrived, she said, "As a lesbian, one of my goals this summer is to make sure all the kids feel comfortable being who they are." Kirsten knew a few gay students at her Jesuit college, but not well, and Lucy was the first peer she'd heard use the word "lesbian" other than as a slur. Although Kirsten took a mild prurient interest in Lucy's disclosure, she was mostly preoccupied with the hotness of a counselor named Sean, who was very tall and could play "Welcome to the Jungle" on the guitar. Sean never reciprocated Kirsten's interest; instead, and this felt extra-insulting, he soon took up with the other counselor in the Redbirds cabin.

Kirsten became conscious of Lucy's crush on her without paying much attention to it. Having given the subject a great deal of thought since, Kirsten now believes that she was inattentive partly because of her vague discomfort and partly because she was busy wondering if Sean and Renee would break up and, if they did, how she, Kirsten, would make her move.

Lucy often approached Kirsten, chattily, at all-camp events or when the counselors drank and played cards at night in the mess hall, and, more than once, she tried to initiate deep conversations Kirsten had no interest in. ("Do you believe in soulmates?" or "Do you usually have more regrets about things you've done or things you haven't done?") When Kirsten and Lucy ran into each other on the fourth-to-last night of camp, on the path behind the arts-and-crafts shed, when they were both drunk, it was maybe not as random or spontaneous as it seemed, at least on Lucy's part. Kirsten had never kissed a girl, though she'd had sex with one boy in high school and another in college, and she's wondered if she'd have kissed just about anyone she ran into behind the shed. She was nineteen, it was August, she was drunk, and she felt like taking off her clothes. That it all seemed especially hot with Lucy didn't strike her then as that meaningful. They hooked up in the dark, on a ratty red couch, in a room that smelled like the kiln and tempera paint. Kirsten was definitely aware of the variables of there being more than one set of boobs smashed together and the peculiarly untroubling absence of an erection, but there were things she heard later about two girls—about how soft the female body was and how good another girl smelled—that seemed to her like nonsense. She and Lucy rolled around a lot, and jammed their fingers up inside each other, and, though both of them had probably swum in the lake that day, neither was freshly showered. There really wasn't much in the way of softness or fragrant scents about the encounter. What she liked was how close they could be, almost fused, with nothing between them.

The next morning, while Kirsten was standing by the orange-juice dispenser in the mess hall, Lucy approached her, set a hand on her forearm, and said, softly, "Hey."

Kirsten, who was intensely hungover and sleep-deprived, recoiled, and she saw Lucy see her recoil. Under her breath, in a hiss, Kirsten said, "I'm not gay."

If Lucy had done anything other than laugh lightheartedly, that might have halted things. But Lucy's willingness to act as if neither their hookup nor Kirsten's homophobia were a big deal—it made it seem O.K. to keep going. The whole whatever-it-was was so clearly short-lived, so arbitrary.

During the next five nights—the counselors stayed an extra forty-eight hours to clean the grounds after the kids went home —Kirsten and Lucy were naked together a lot. The second night was both the first time someone went down on Kirsten and the first time she had an orgasm; the orgasm part happened more than once. She was less drunk than the night before, and at one point, while Lucy was lapping away at her, she thought that, all things considered, it was good that it was happening with a girl first, because then when a guy went down on her, when it mattered, Kirsten would know what she was doing.

After Kirsten had basically spasmed in ecstasy into Lucy's face, she said, "Could you tell I'd never done that?"

It was less that Kirsten was confiding than that, with Lucy, she didn't feel the need to feign competence. Lucy was lying on top of her, propped up on her elbows, and she seemed amused—flirtatious-amused, not mean-amused—as she said, "Seriously? Never?"

Kirsten said, "Well, I've given blow jobs."

"Then that *really* doesn't seem fair."

The sureness of Lucy's hooking-up personality, the way it might even have been more confident than her regular personality, impressed Kirsten; the nearest Kirsten got to such confidence was when things felt so good that she forgot herself.

Lucy added, "Just in case none of the recipients of your blow jobs ever mentioned it, you're very, very fun to have sex with," and Kirsten said, "This isn't sex."

As she had by the juice dispenser, Lucy laughed.

"I mean, it's fooling around," Kirsten said. "I'm not denying that."

"You think if there's no penis it doesn't count?"

Lucy's apparent lack of anger surprises Kirsten more in retrospect than it did at the time. Lucy explained that she was a gold-star lesbian, which meant one who'd never had sex with a guy; in fact, Lucy added proudly, she'd never even kissed a guy. Kirsten asked how she'd known she was gay, and Lucy said, "Because, even when I was in grade school, the people I always thought about before I fell asleep at night were girls."

That what was transpiring between them would be kept secret was both understood and probably not very realistic. Before they lay down on the red couch, Kirsten would block the door with a chair, but sometimes dim figures, other couples in search of privacy, opened the door partway. When this happened, Kirsten would freeze, and Lucy would call out sharply, "There are people in here," and a retreat would occur. Once, someone very tall opened the door all the way and just stood there, not moving, someone else behind him, and Kirsten realized, with one of her nipples in Lucy's mouth, that the person in front was Sean, and Kirsten's fixation with him, a fixation that had lasted until just a few days before, seemed distant. Lucy lifted her head and said in a firm voice, "Can you please leave?" Sean and Renee did go away, but the next morning Renee asked, with what seemed more like curiosity than disapproval, "Was that you with Lucy?"

All these years later, while driving to work and considering ruining Lucy's life, Kirsten thinks that Renee would be her corroboration, and maybe Sean, too. Conveniently, Kirsten is Facebook friends with both of them, privy to the extremely tedious details of their separate suburban lives.

At the time, fake-casually, fake-confusedly, Kirsten said, "With who?"

That fall, back at school, Kirsten opened her mailbox in the student union one day to find a small padded envelope, the return address Lucy's, the contents a brief, unremarkable note ("Hope you're having a good semester . . .") and a mixtape. Kirsten was surprised and very happy, which made her inability to listen to the mixtape perplexing; the first song was "I Melt with You," and the second line of the song was "Making love to you was never second best," and though she tried several times not to, Kirsten always had to turn off her cassette player after that line. She never acknowledged Lucy's gift.

The next summer, Kirsten returned to the camp, and Lucy didn't; someone said that she was volunteering at a health clinic in Haiti. Kirsten had a boyfriend then, a guy named Ryan, who was working in the admissions office of their college and to whom she hadn't mentioned Lucy.

After that summer, Kirsten's only source of camp updates was a winter newsletter that she read less and less thoroughly as the years passed. She became aware of the Prairie Wife, in the amorphous way one becomes aware of celebrities, without having any idea that Lucy Headrick was Lucy from camp, whose surname had been Nilsson. But, last December, Kirsten read the newsletter in its entirety. It was the day after Christmas, and she was trying to get Jack to take a nap, which he didn't do much anymore, but he'd been cranky, and they were due at a potluck in the evening. She was sitting halfway up the steps of their house so as to intercept Jack whenever he tried to escape from his room; she'd pulled the newsletter from a stack of mail by the front door to occupy herself between interceptions.

The camp had been owned by the same family for several generations, and an eccentric great-uncle who taught archery wrote the newsletter. The item about Lucy was just a paragraph and not particularly fawning—"It's always fun to see what former camper and counselor Lucy 'the Prairie Wife' Headrick née Lucy Nilsson is up to"—but Kirsten couldn't believe it. Though she didn't own any of Lucy Headrick's cookbooks and had never seen her television show, she knew enough about her to find it hilarious. She knew that Lucy Headrick was gorgeous (she had long blond hair and magnificent cheekbones), was married to a man, and was, in some conservative-flavored way, religious. Kirsten was so excited to tell Casey that she let Jack get out of bed. They went into the den, where Casey and Ian were watching football, Kirsten carrying the camp newsletter. But it turned out that, although Kirsten *had* mentioned Lucy to Casey, Casey had never heard of the Prairie Wife, so Kirsten's ostensible bombshell was less satisfying to drop than she'd anticipated.

That might have been that—a funny coincidence—except that a week later, at the digital-map-data company where she works, Kirsten passed Frank's office while he was watching Lucy Headrick make chicken-and-dumpling soup online. "I'm decompressing," Frank said. "I just turned in a test tally."

Kirsten held up her palms and said, "Hey, no judgment." She almost didn't say it, but then, pointing at the computer screen, she did. "I kind of know her."

Frank raised one eyebrow, which was a gesture Kirsten suspected that he had, in his adolescence, practiced at great length as part of shaping his persona. Frank was her age, the son of Thai immigrants, and he was married to a white guy who was a dermatologist. Kirsten liked Frank O.K.—she respected his attention to detail—but she didn't really trust him.

Frank said, "Do go on."

She tried to think of reasons that not trusting Frank mattered and couldn't come up with any. Once, she had considered her interactions with Lucy to be her most damning secret, but now, ironically, they were probably the most interesting thing about her, even if Casey had been underwhelmed.

"I haven't seen her since the mid-nineties, but we worked at a camp a few hours north of here," Kirsten said, then added, "We slept together a bunch of times."

"No. Fucking. Way." Frank looked elated. He made a lascivious "Mm-mm-mm" sound, and said, "You and the Prairie Wife as baby dykes. I love it."

"Actually," Kirsten said, "I looked it up, and I'm pretty sure Lucy lives about forty-five minutes west of St. Louis. Which, for one thing, that's not exactly the rural farmlands, right? And, also, it's been a while since I took social studies, but is Missouri even a prairie state?"

"She's a fraud," Frank said happily. "A fraudulent butter-churning bitch."

That was three months ago, and, since then, without really meaning to, Kirsten is pretty sure that she and Frank have become close friends. The reassuring part is that, if anything, he monitors Lucy's activities more avidly than Kirsten does—surely his avidity has egged on her own—and Lucy represents ninety percent of all discussions between them. The unsettling part is that Frank also follows several other celebrities as enthusiastically yet spitefully; Kirsten isn't sure where he finds the time.

When Kirsten arrives at work twenty-five minutes late, Frank appears on the threshold of her office and gleefully whispers, "There. Is. A. Shit. Storm. Brewing."

Calmly, Kirsten says, "Oh?" This is the way Frank greets her approximately twice a week. But it turns out that a shit storm *is* brewing: someone on Kirsten's team stored sample data, data belonging to a national courier company, in the area of the server where production can access it, even though the agreement with the courier company hasn't yet been formalized. Their boss, Sheila, is trying to figure out who messed up, whether anyone from production has used the data, and, if so, how to remove it.

As Kirsten steels herself to speak with Sheila, Frank, who is still standing there, says, "Has your copy of your girlfriend's book arrived?"

"I didn't pre-order it. I'm stopping at the store on the way home."

"Well, as soon as you finish give it to me. Because I am not putting *one penny* in the coffers of that whore."

"Yeah, so you've said." Kirsten squeezes past him.

She definitely isn't the one who failed to sequester the sample data, but it's unclear if Sheila believes her. They have a forty-minute conversation that contains about two minutes' worth of relevant information and instruction and thirty-eight minutes of Sheila venting about how at best they've embarrassed themselves and at worst they're facing a copyright lawsuit. When Kirsten has a chance to check Lucy's various websites, she finds that they're all filled with book promotions. On Twitter and elsewhere is a selfie of Lucy and the host of *The Mariana Show* in the greenroom; their heads are pressed together, and they're beaming.

After two meetings and a conference call, Kirsten gets lunch from a sandwich place around the corner, and it's while she's waiting in line for turkey and Swiss cheese on multigrain bread that she receives Frank's text: a screenshot from the website of a weekly celebrity magazine, with a headline that reads, "Prairie Wife Comes Out as Bisexual." The first one and a half sentences of the article, which is all that's visible, read, "Sources confirm that cookbook writer and television personality Lucy Headrick, known to fans as the Prairie Wife, revealed during today's taping of *The Mariana Show* that she has dated multiple women. The married mother of three, who—"

Another text arrives from Frank. It reads, "OMFG!"

Back in the office, Frank says, "Do you think she mentioned you?"

"No," Kirsten says, though, since receiving Frank's text, she has felt very weird, almost nauseated.

"What if she's carried a torch for you all this time and she looks directly at the camera and says, 'Kirsten, please make haste to my quaint rural farmstead, pull off my muslin knickers, and lick my evangelical pussy'?"

"Jesus, Frank," Kirsten says. "Not like there's anything private about what I told you."

Her phone rings, and she can see on the caller ID that it's Casey. To Frank, she says, "I need to answer this."

"Ian has strings practice after school, and he forgot his violin," Casey says. "I know this is annoying, but could you get it? I have a meeting with the superintendent."

"I don't think I can," Kirsten says. "Sheila's in a really bad mood today. Anyway, maybe Ian should deal with the consequences. You want him to develop grit, right?"

"You think he should just sit there while everyone else practices?"

"I can imagine more traumatizing childhood experiences." Kirsten is nevertheless about to relent when Casey says, "God damn it, Kirsten."

"I thought we didn't swear anymore," Kirsten says. There's a silence, and she asks, "Did you just hang up on me?"

"No," Casey says. "But I need to prepare for my meeting. I'll see you at home."

Which, if either of them, is delivering the violin? This is how Casey wins, Kirsten thinks—by *not* insisting on resolution, which compels Kirsten toward it. On a regular basis, Kirsten wonders if Casey is using middle-school pedagogical techniques on her.

She stews for the next ninety minutes, until she has to go home and get the violin or it will be too late, then she stands and grabs her purse. Like an apparition, Frank is back in her office.

He says, "If we leave now, we can go to Flanagan's and watch Lucy on *Mariana*. And I do mean *on*."

"I'm sure it'll be online later today."

"Don't you want to know if she mentions you?"

Kirsten hesitates, then says, "Fuck it. I'll come with you."

"For realsies? What were you about to do instead?"

Kirsten sighs. "Good question."

It is seven minutes to three when Kirsten and Frank enter Flanagan's Ale House. Four other patrons are there, two old men sitting side by side at the bar and two younger men sitting by themselves at tables.

Frank gestures toward the TV above the bar and says to the bartender, "Can you change the channel to *The Mariana Show*?"

"We'll buy drinks," Kirsten adds. But then the thought of returning to the office with beer on her breath makes her wonder if Sheila will fire her, and she orders seltzer water and French fries; Frank asks for a gin and tonic, and when their drinks are in front of them he clinks his glass against hers and says, "To lesbians."

Kirsten has only ever seen clips of *The Mariana Show,* and it turns out that there's a lot to get through before Lucy appears —Mariana's monologue, then a trivia contest among audience members, then a filmed segment in which Mariana takes a belly-dancing class. Plus endless commercials. As the minutes tick by, the afternoon is drained of the caperlike mood it had when she and Frank left the office. They speak intermittently. She says, "I don't think she *could* mention me, even if she wanted to. Like, from a legal perspective, since I'm a private citizen. And I'm sure she was involved with other girls."

Finally, after more commercials, Mariana introduces Lucy, and Lucy walks out to energetic cheering and applause. She sits on a purple armchair next to Mariana's purple armchair, and the cover of *Dishin' with the Prairie Wife* is projected onto an enormous screen behind them.

Lucy looks great—she's wearing a short-sleeved, belted blue dress with a pattern of roses—and she's also palpably nervous in a way that Kirsten finds surprisingly sympathetic. Lucy is smiling a lot, but she keeps widening her eyes in an oddly alert way, and she appears to be shaking.

Lucy and Mariana discuss a recipe in the memoir for raccoon stew; Lucy says that she personally isn't crazy about it but that it was given to her by her mother-in-law.

"You weren't raised on a farm," Mariana says.

"I wasn't," Lucy says. "I grew up in the suburbs of Phoenix. My dad was an engineer, and my mom was a teacher." Her matter-of-factness also elicits Kirsten's sympathy. Even if her fame is country-fried, even if she speaks in a nebulous drawl, Kirsten cannot remember ever seeing Lucy outright lie. "A few years after college, I enrolled in social-work school at the University of Missouri," Lucy continues. "It was while I was doing field work way out in the country that I met my husband. And that was it for both of us. I never expected to fall in love with a farmer, and he never expected to fall in love with a food blogger."

As the image on the screen behind them changes from the

book to a photograph of Lucy and a handsome man wearing a checked shirt and a cowboy hat, Mariana says, "Something in your book—and it's a fantastic read—but something that surprised me is before you got married to the Stud in Overalls, as we fondly refer to him, you describe how you dated women."

Lucy nods and says both matter-of-factly and shakily, "I did, in my late teens and early twenties. I consider myself bisexual."

"Oh yeah, you do, bitch," Frank says. "Booyah!"

"Can you not talk over her?" Kirsten says.

Mariana, who Kirsten hopes is feigning naïveté for her viewers, says, "But if you're married to a man you're not still bisexual, are you?"

"Well, my husband and I are monogamous, but I think even if your circumstances change your core identity remains. Like, heaven forbid, if my husband passed away I'd still be madly in love with him."

Really? Kirsten thinks. *Madly?*

Mariana asks, "Do you worry about how your fans will react to this news?"

"I love my fans," Lucy says, and turns and waves at the studio audience, who explode in applause. Though, surely, an audience in Southern California is not representative of Lucy's base.

Over the cheering, Mariana says, "This is just a hunch, but it seems like they love you, too." More thunderous cheering ensues.

"Really," Lucy says. "I gave this serious thought. I prayed on it, I talked to my preacher, I talked to my family. And obviously things are a lot better now for the LGBT community than they once were, but you still hear about teenagers taking their lives, or being made to feel like they're less than. So I decided to let them know, Hey, you're not alone."

Kirsten thinks of Lucy at the camp-counselor orientation in 1994, and then she thinks, What if Lucy *isn't* a greedy, phony hypocrite? What if she's still herself, as surprised by the turns her life has taken as Kirsten sometimes is by hers? In Flanagan's, it occurs to Kirsten that she might be witnessing a genuinely important cultural moment, which makes her wish that she were with someone other than Frank.

"I'm so verklempt," he says. "I need a hug." She assumes he's being sarcastic, but when she glances at him he's teared up for real.

He makes a sheepish expression and says in a thick, wet voice, "I can't believe your girlfriend is ruining my mascara."

What choice does she have? In her arms, he smells like gin and some leathery cologne, and she's still holding him when he lets loose with a huge, guttural sob.

"Oh, Frank," Kirsten says.

After she leaves work, Kirsten doesn't stop to buy Lucy's book. When she arrives home, the boys greet her at the front door.

"Mama, how many tickles do you need to make an octopus laugh?" Jack says.

"I don't know, how many?"

"I forgot my violin, but Mom brought it to me," Ian says.

"I hope you thanked her," Kirsten says.

"You need ten tickles," Jack says.

In the kitchen, Casey is dumping mayonnaise into a large clear bowl, onto chunks of canned tuna.

"Melts?" Kirsten says by way of greeting, and Casey nods. As Kirsten washes her hands, Casey says, "Will you pull out the salad ingredients? There's a yellow pepper."

"I appreciate your getting Ian's violin."

"We need to be better organized in the morning," Casey says. "I'm setting my alarm for fifteen minutes earlier tomorrow."

"O.K." After a pause, Kirsten says, "Did you hear that Lucy Headrick came out on *The Mariana Show*? Or whatever coming out is called if it's retroactive."

"Who's Lucy Headrick again?"

Oh, to be Casey! Calm and methodical, with a do-gooder job. To be a person who isn't frittering away her life having vengeful thoughts about people from her past! It happens that Casey is both a former farm girl, of the authentic kind—she grew up in Flandreau, South Dakota—and a gold-star lesbian. She and Kirsten met thirteen years ago, at the Christmas-caroling party of a mutual friend. Kirsten got very drunk and climbed onto Casey's lap during "Good King Wenceslas," and that night she stayed over at Casey's apartment.

"Lucy Headrick is the Prairie Wife," Kirsten says. "She just wrote a book."

"Got it," Casey says.

"She was actually very eloquent. And her fans are definitely the kind of people who are still bigots."

"Good for her."

"Are you pissed at me?"

"No," Casey says. "But I'm trying to get dinner on the table."

Kirsten puts the boys to bed, then lies down in the master bedroom and looks at her phone. It's difficult to estimate what portion of the tweets Lucy has received this afternoon are ugly—they're mixed in with "Yay for standing your truth Lucy!" and "I love you no matter what!!!" Maybe a third?

"why u like to eat pussy did u ever try a hard cock"

"You are A LESBIAN ADULTERER. You are DISGUSTING + BAD for AMERICA!!!!!"

"Romans 1:26 two women is 'against nature.'"

Quickly, before she can talk herself out of it, Kirsten types, "I thought you were very brave today." After hitting Tweet, she feels a surge of adrenaline and considers deleting the message, but for whose benefit? Her three bots'? In any case, Lucy hasn't tweeted since before noon, and Kirsten wonders if she's gone on a Twitter hiatus.

In the summer, Kirsten and Casey usually watch TV together after the boys are asleep, but during the school year Casey works in the den—responding to parents' emails, reading books about how educators can recognize multiple kinds of intelligence. Sometimes she keeps a baseball or a football game on mute, and the sports further deter Kirsten from joining her. Thus, almost every night, Kirsten stays upstairs, intending to fold laundry or call her mother while actually fucking around on her phone. At 9:45, she texts Casey "Going to bed," and Casey texts back "Gnight hon," followed by a sleeping-face emoji with "zzz" above the closed eyes. This is their nightly exchange, and, every night, for about four seconds, Kirsten ponders Casey's choice of the sleeping-face emoji versus something more affectionate, like the face blowing a kiss, or just a heart.

While brushing her teeth, Kirsten receives a text from Frank: "Bitch did u see this?" There's a link to what she's pretty sure is a Prairie Wife article, and she neither clicks on it nor replies.

She is still awake, in the dark, when Casey comes upstairs almost an hour later, uses the bathroom, and climbs into bed without turning on the light; Kirsten rarely speaks to Casey at this juncture and always assumes that Casey thinks she's asleep. But tonight, while curled on her side with her back to Casey, Kirsten says, "Did you sign Ian's permission slip for the field trip to the science museum?"

"Yeah, it was due last Friday."

"Oh," Kirsten says. "Imagine that."

They're both quiet as Casey settles under the blankets, then she says, "Did the prairie lady mention you on TV?"

"I probably would have told you if she had."

"Good point." Unexpectedly, Casey leans over and kisses Kirsten's cheek. She says, "Well, no matter what, I owe her a debt of gratitude for initiating you."

For some reason, Kirsten tears up. She swallows, so that she won't sound as if she's crying, and says, "Do you really feel that way, or are you joking?"

"Do you think you'd have dated women if she hadn't hit on you behind the arts-and-crafts shed?"

"And your life is better because you ended up with me?"

Casey laughs. "Who else would I have ended up with?"

"Lots of people. Someone less flaky and petty."

"I like your flakiness and pettiness."

Kirsten starts crying harder, though still not as hard as Frank was crying at the bar. But enough that Casey becomes aware of it and scoots toward Kirsten, spooning her from behind.

"Baby," Casey says. "Why are you sad?"

"This will sound self-centered," Kirsten says. "But Lucy was really into me. I'm sure it was partly because I wasn't that into her, and I wasn't even playing hard to get. I just—" She pauses.

"What?" Casey says.

"I know we have a good life," Kirsten says. "And the boys—they're amazing. They amaze me every day. Did I tell you, when we were at the mall last weekend Jack wanted to buy you this purse that was like a fake-diamond-encrusted jaguar head? Its eyes were emeralds."

"Oh, man," Casey says. "I can't wait for my birthday."

"It's not that I'm jealous of Lucy Headrick because she's a rich celebrity," Kirsten says. "It seems awful to be famous now." Her voice breaks as she adds, "I just wish that there was someone who was excited about me. Or that when someone *was* excited about me, I wish I hadn't taken it for granted. I didn't understand that would be the only time."

"*Kirsten.*" Casey uses her top hand to pet Kirsten's hip.

"I don't blame you for not finding me exciting," Kirsten says. "Why would you?"

"We have full-time jobs and young kids," Casey says. "This is what this stage is like."

"But do you ever feel like you'll spend every day slicing cucumbers for lunchboxes and going to work and driving to Little League on the weekend and then you'll look up and twenty years will have passed?"

"God willing," Casey says. She moves both her arms up so she's cupping Kirsten's breasts over her pajama top. "Do you want me to pretend to be Lucy at camp? Or Lucy now? Do you want me to make you a chocolate soufflé?"

"Soufflé is too French," Kirsten says. "Lucy would make apple pie."

They're both quiet, and, weirdly, this is where the conversation ends, or maybe, given that it's past eleven and Casey's alarm is set for six-fifteen or possibly for six, it isn't weird at all. They don't have sex. They don't reach any resolutions. But, for the first time in a while, Kirsten falls asleep with her wife's arms around her.

In the middle of the night, because she can't help herself, Kirsten checks to see if Lucy has responded to her tweet; so far, there's nothing.

Whose Heart I Long to Stop with the Click of a Revolver

FROM *Emrys Journal*

MY KID WALKS down Blue Street Diner's central aisle before slumping into a booth near the toilets. She's on meds that make her urinate nonstop and requires round-the-clock access to the facilities. Her words.

"The name of the drug is spironolactone, if you're wondering," she'd said on our pre-meeting phone call. "Also, I'm trans. The name you gave me is dead and incinerated and I spread its ashes over the Hudson. Say it to my face, and you'll meet the same fate. I'm Luciana now. Or Luz."

"You mean trans, like, you're transsexual?"

"Trans like gender is dead. When can we meet? Should I call you Mom or Jo?"

"Jo's fine," I'd said, though I find that name embarrassingly predictable in retrospect. It's a name I picked for myself after reading *Little Women,* obsessed, like so many little girls, with the bookish, tomboyish heroine. I should have gone for Beth, or better yet, Amy or Meg.

"Luciana. I really like that. She's only a minor figure in *Catch-22,* but something about her kind of sticks with you. Good choice," I said.

"Whatever. I was just trying to think of a girl version of Lucifer."

I meet her at Blue Street Diner because I've never been. Seemed appropriate to reunite with my stranger of a daughter on neutral ground.

An employee busses tables, pocketing pennies and dollar bills left under jars of Dijon mustard. The screams of a toddler fill the background. For my part there's some throat clearing, a few aborted questions. Every few seconds I venture a glance in Luciana's direction. This is the first time I've seen my daughter since shortly after she was born, and I am admittedly overwhelmed.

I keep one hand tucked into my handbag, palm secured around the handle of my revolver, ready to shoot if this girl, my child, has re-entered my life in order to harm me in some way, to exact vengeance because I chose to leave her in the care of the state.

Giving up on conversation, I hum the old bluegrass tune "Whiskey Before Breakfast" as I page through the menu. It's the first song I taught myself on the fiddle, slowly and painfully, when I decided I did not belong to my parents after all and wanted to travel to the South in a caravan.

Mr. Wheelock, Luciana's father, always wanted me to listen to blues and jazz. He said as a black girl I had no business not knowing Muddy Waters or Billie Holiday, but the fast-paced string melodies of country folk songs spoke to my youthful mania. I told him that as a white man, he had no business not knowing the Osborne Brothers or the Foggy Mountain Boys. Besides, black folks invented country and bluegrass, so I was just going back to the source.

That's when he told me that I was the *most mature young woman* he'd ever met. If he'd known then that he'd be dead at my own hands, would he have introduced himself to me that first time? Or would he have gone for another girl? Prone toward awkwardness, I like to think that maybe I was too pretty to resist, that were he able to do it again, he'd choose me knowing I'd murder him.

I suppose that's why I hated him most—that he found me pretty, and that made me want him. That he knew that and used it. The things an ugly black girl from Brooklyn will do to feel pretty. She'll dismantle her soul, if it's required.

"Can I get you guys started with some drinks?" a man says, holding a pen and pad of paper at me and Luz's table.

"Coffee," I say. "Says here you guys use a percolator, right? A stove top one?"

"Yeah, miss. And it's fresh, too."

"Cookies and cream milkshake, please," says Luciana. The

waiter scribbles down our order before leaving. "What's a percolator?" Luciana asks.

"You serious?" I say.

"I mean I'm assuming it's something that percolates, but I could do with a more precise definition."

When Luciana first walked up the diner, I wondered how much her personality would match up with her appearance. A good deal of it, it turns out. Her hair, coarse red threads that tangle and twist in on each other, contrasts sharply against her noncommittally brown skin, and the effect is overall very striking. She's got a wide jaw and a wide nose, big lips, like mine. Mascara and eyeliner. Rouge. She's cute in a kind of dykey way, and I wonder if she's gay like me. At least I passed down that gift.

The morning after meeting Luz at the diner, I notice frost for the first time on the grass. Autumn is here. The curious chortles of chirping birds are absent. They've gone south by now, abandoned upstate New York for Florida, like old rich white people tired of the cold. Flying to warmer climates when the weather turns foul, it's a pleasant notion. Back in the City, I suspect, New Yorkers are holding fiercely on to the season of sun, beach, and Italian ice. Flip-flops until Halloween, at least.

I remember Mr. Wheelock at about this time of the year buying me a ham and cheese sandwich on a soft white roll at the bodega, preparing us for a picnic on the beach. We'd watch West Indian men play dominoes and backgammon, ignoring the brisk breeze, holding fast on to what was left of September.

See, Coney Island is in decline, preparing for hibernation, and we enjoy a final day. He buys me hot dogs and funnel cakes and cotton candy. I tell him about my dreams, and he tells me I can do anything. He kisses me here, for the first time, a tentative thing that still manages to be sloppy, intrusive. I wonder if this is how it's supposed to feel. I wonder if I'm supposed to gag, to want to run to the bin and hurl. People stare, but no one says anything because people are people. I see their faces. I know their thoughts. "She can't be more than fourteen." I was twelve.

Mr. Wheelock tells me, "Don't you worry. I'll take care of you," after he finishes the kiss. He smiles smugly to anyone who tries to look down on him.

This is how I always remember him.

*

"It's cold," says Luz. She's moved in. That's why she got in touch. Eighteen years old, she's been coughed out the throat of social services onto the street.

"Knock much?" I ask.

"Sorry, I was bored. And I'm cold. Can you turn the heat up or something?"

"If you got turn-the-heat-up money," I say. "Here, wear that." There's a sweatshirt from my college hanging from one of the knobs on my dresser. Fleece-lined. Real thick.

She pulls it on over her chubby body, but it still hangs nice and loose. "Put on some socks or something," I say.

"I don't have any."

"What?"

"It was literally just summer, I don't know," she tells me, pouting. All her bravado from our pre-meeting is gone. She looks like a little girl with her arms crossed over her chest.

"We should go shopping," I say.

"Oh. So you got shopping money?" Luciana shoots back.

"Ok, a pack of socks is cheaper than heating this drafty-ass Victorian, smartass. Go clean yourself up so we can get out of here. We can even see a movie or whatever if you want."

Luciana shrugs and leaves, then I remove a gun from my bedside table. When I go to the city, I always take her with me. She's a brass and steel Smith and Wesson that clicks soothingly when cocked. A metal machine. A perfect contraption.

I've had this thing since I was fourteen. The wooden handle, simultaneously slick with polish and rough with overuse, contains my initials. Mr. Wheelock etched them with his carving knife, giving me the relic on my birthday. Intricate engravings, curls and loops like flowering vines, cover the barrel, cylinder, and frame.

Over two pounds she weighs. It felt like rocking an infant child when I first held the revolver in my hands. There's weight to it.

"Is that real?" Luciana asks. She's burst into my room without invitation again. If she's going to stay here, I need to get locks. This is one of Wheelock's old places, left to me in a trust, and it's nice but needs modernizing.

"Old as hell but works just the same. I practice with her every week at the range. She never fails me."

"Why do you have it out?" she asks. "Shouldn't that be behind lock and key? Or some glass display case? Are you an assassin?"

"I carry her with me whenever I go into the City. Just in case."

"Just in case what?" she says. She crosses her hands across her chest in a way that reminds me so much of my indignant, younger self, I almost cry on the spot.

"Just in case I need to kill someone," I say. "You should get a piece, too. I have eleven, most of them antiques, but a few modern enough for a kid like you. You can try one out. Revolvers are best because they don't jam, but a baby Glock will serve you well as long as you practice."

"I don't want to kill anyone," she says, and I tell her that she'll change her mind about that. "You don't know shit about me. You don't know what's been done to me. You don't think I ain't been through some shit? Doesn't change the fact that I don't want to kill."

"Even if it's you or them? You'd spare their life even if it was certain you'd lose your own?" I ask.

"Shut up!" she shouts, and walks out the room, slams the door. Gentle, tender, baby thing. My fledgling. Softer than me but just as bitter.

I want to tell her—know this:

The world plays out as games of power, who has it, who doesn't. An invisible puppeteer pulls the strings of each person's life, determining her fate based on race, gender, religion. Luz got a particularly unfortunate set of strings.

Imagine a large man gifted with athleticism and strength, favored in life because of his class and wealth and color. Now imagine a child, young and poor and thoroughly pathetic. See the two of them together, in a room, butting heads.

Now imagine the scene again, but this time the child has a gun, and the man does not. He steps back, suddenly fearful of her scrawny figure, her shaking frame, her tearing eyes. Everyone fears the bullet, no matter what gift the invisible puppeteer has bestowed upon him.

Something with that much weight in this world is to be saved and savored, so even though I was an anti-gun progressive when Mr. Wheelock handed me my gift, I could not say no to the revolver when I felt its heaviness in my hand.

He never knew the exact date on it, but said that it no doubt dated to the Civil War era and was likely used for an elite officer on the side of the Union. "Of course, you'll never shoot anyone with it," he said.

The wind sweeps through the valley quiet-like and unassuming, animating the leaves and branches of the trees. The maples and the birches dance with soul. Like the women in Baptist churches who holler and scream 'cause they think they are filled with the Holy Ghost.

I go here before every trip into New York, even in winter. It's my portal. My wardrobe.

I like to watch the trees shimmy as I sit on the edge of the river bank, feet in the water, butt in the wet clay, wishing for a water moccasin to come my way so I can shoot the creature dead. I'll watch it wiggle. Watch it convulse and carry on after I put bullets into its spiraling body.

I'll step back then, keep up my aim, and carefully unlock the barrel from my revolver before inserting fresh bullets. Laws of the universe don't fool me. I've always known that snakes live a long time after they die, battling on all warrior-like even once unhinged from this here mortal coil. Decapitated, the snake will still try to plunge its teeth into an unsuspecting person's flesh.

Snakes are even more dangerous when they're dead. Without any control over the chemical impulses in their bodies, they'll release all their venom into a piece of prey, not having the sense or ability to conserve for later attacks.

I stand up and remove my jeans, letting the evening chill trickle down my thighs to my ankles as I shuck off the denim. Next comes my sweater. Finally my shirt. Looking over each of my shoulders first, I rid myself of my underwear. My body shivers and shakes as I submerge myself into the river.

On the train with Luz, I almost remember what it's like to be a kid. The picture renders itself a little blurry, but I can just make out a creamy coffee drink in one hand and a book of Emily Dickinson's poetry in the other.

I take my thumb and smudge it along Luciana's cheeks. "You went a bit overboard with the blush."

"I always do," she says. "That's how I like it. I'm not tryna pretend like I'm some blushing virginal swan. I like the color, so I put it on heavy. If you have a problem with that, go sit somewhere else on the train."

She checks her makeup in a small mirror that she pulls from her handbag. "Besides, we're looking for clothes for me. Practical. Functional. It's not like I want anybody to fall in love with me tonight or ever," Luciana says, placing the mirror back into her bag. She crosses her legs and leans back into the cushioned seat of the Amtrak train.

"Sorry. I was just trying to be motherly, I guess," I say.

She shrugs, rolls her eyes, and puts her headphones back on. The teenage trifecta.

That night, after we return home with eight shopping bags, high off the spell of Manhattan, I dream about him. It's the day we met, and I've run away from home to see an exhibit on Dadaism at the MoMA. Saw an ad for it on the 2 train, and it's the summer between seventh and eighth grade. The art presents itself as an indistinct mist, and only the sharp angles of the walls and room edges are clear to me in the dream. The dress I'm wearing is short, too short, but I've grown a lot in the last year, and I was never one to be too concerned about the latest fashions.

"Big Francis Bacon fan?" he asks. He's wearing dark green khakis, a button-up shirt, and a skinny tie.

I've forgotten his voice by now, but in the dream I think it sounds just like him.

"I think it's so funny that there are two Francis Bacons," I say, a precocious little shit, looking at the painting before me. My voice doesn't quite make it out my throat, though, and it's like one of those nightmares when you need to scream for help, but no matter how much you want it your voice isn't going to come.

I can't speak, so I take the gun in my hand and point it to the world. "Here I am," I say. "And yes, I am a big Francis Bacon fan." The blast from the revolver says what I can't.

I awake to the sound of Luz loudly watching cartoons. Sunday mornings should be easier than this. They tend to wait patiently.

"Sorry if I woke you," she says, looking up from her cartoon. "How come you don't work?"

"What?"

"How come you don't work?" she asks again, crossing her legs together. She's got on the polka dot knee socks we bought yesterday.

"I live off of an inheritance," I say.

"Whoa," she says. "Bourgie. Shit. So I had rich grandparents? Were they like, those W.E.B. DuBois black assimilationist intellectuals? Did they pressure you to have someone else raise me?"

"No," I say. "Daddy was a bus driver. My mama was in medical billing. When was the last time you combed that head?" I ask. Her long strands are starting to mat together. "Looks like a bird's nest."

"I like my hair how it is," she says. "One of my foster mothers said she thought I had Irish in me. Do I?"

I walk to the kitchen, flummoxed by the question. I set my percolator on the stove.

"What does it even mean to have Irish in you?" I ask. "That's a child's question and not worthy of an answer. Do you think there's a piece of a country inside your bones? Or in your belly? Floating around? Making tea?"

"You know what I mean. Is my father Irish?" she asks. "Or part Irish?"

"I don't know. He had red hair, yes, if that's what you want to know."

"Is he how you got all the money?" she asks, standing up to join me in the question. It's not an accusation, but I take it that way, so defensive.

"I didn't ask for it," I say, remembering being contacted by police and lawyers.

"Was he a good man?" she asks. "Did he play music at all? I can play the violin, you know. I don't see any instruments around here. Maybe it comes from him?"

"Maybe it comes from you," I say, not wanting to think any part of her is from me, ruined, pathetic woman.

"I thought you'd have answers for me." Her breath comes out in a loud huff as she curls up next to the arm of the sofa. "I want to know everything, and you don't know anything."

I take a seat next to her, making sure a foot of distance remains between us. "Not even Sir Isaac Newton knew everything," I say.

"Who is that?"

Luciana decides to go for a walk, and she wears the brown leather jacket I got her over the sweatshirt from my alma mater.

She stops at the door, resting her shoulder against the frame. "Do you hate me?" she asks.

"No," I say. "Don't catch cold out there. The weather's getting bad."

I wave at her retreating form until she disappears around the block.

Before I had Luz, Wheelock asked me, "What are you going to do?"

"Adoption, I think," I said. "I'm not ready to be a mother and I don't know. I'm too far along to do the other thing. I can't provide a good home. I just can't."

He said, "I'll provide you a home. It's ours to raise." He was always like this, so sure that his way was the right away. "If you try to give my child away," he went on, "I'll have no choice but to claim my rights as father."

"They're not going to make me give my baby to a sick pervert," I said, meaning every word. I knew what he was. I knew that I was nothing to him but my youth.

"You really think they're going to believe the word of some slut black girl over me? Who would want you?"

And it's wrong and a lie, but I'm sixteen and don't know any better. His words sound like truth to me, like something to be afraid of, and all my life he has only ever given me what at the time felt like honesty.

I turned from him, stomping toward the door in a fit of adolescent theatrics. He snatched me by the wrist and twisted me backwards, pulling me close against his body. I'm trapped in his embrace, and a looker-on might think that the whole thing was affectionate, but there is vomit in my throat. Mr. Wheelock pushes me against the wall with enough force to snap my head back against the exposed brick. He steps back, then, taking in the sight of me, a desperate apology on his lips.

I shoot him in the chest three times, and it isn't even hard.

"The Tell-Tale Heart" is all lies.

I hear a crack of thunder and worry after Luciana. She's been gone for half an hour now, and the storm's picking up.

Like a high schooler, I recite one of my favorite poems. "Rain, midnight rain, nothing but the wild rain . . . / Remembering again that I shall die / And neither hear the rain nor give it thanks / For washing me cleaner than I have been / Since I was born into this solitude." Edward Thomas.

Mr. Wheelock introduced me to war poetry.

Sometimes I think he left me all this stuff to keep his hold on me. To strangle me. As I look out the window out into the gray, I think it's worked. Jobless, damaged, friendless, I do not feel like a full-grown adult. Luciana will tire of me when she realizes I have nothing to offer beyond shopping trips and random historical and literary trivia.

I walk barefoot to my room, feeling the texture change from hardwood to soft carpet. A draft is coming through, and thinking of Luz, I turn up the thermostat.

I write my girl—yes, my girl, mine—a note:

> A percolator: a type of coffee-pot in which boiling water rises through a cylindrical compartment, then falls again into the pot by way of diversion, all the while passing through a basket containing ground coffee beans.

> In this, I pass along to you one of the only things that your father did not teach me.

I cannot talk to the girl directly about so many things, not yet, but I leave her this small piece of myself on the coffee table so that she'll see it when she comes home.

Or perhaps she'll stay out, walk along the street until the paved road meets the dirt road and eventually the small wood by the river. Maybe she'll jump in, lose herself in the current, and find she doesn't need me at all. Part of me wishes for that to happen, so that I do not have to see her face again. There's too much feeling going on here lately.

Mr. Wheelock used to read me the letters of James Joyce while I lounged at his breakfast nook eating Lucky Charms. I would memorize the lines, recite passages to my English teachers in order to prove to them that I was worldly and experienced. One in particular I said aloud many an evening but never shared with another, holding it close to me like a twisted secret: "When that person . . . whose heart I long to stop with the click of a revolver, put his hand or hands under your skirts[,] did he only tickle you outside or did he put his finger or fingers up into you? . . . Did you feel it?"

I felt it, yes. I felt everything.

Sometimes, you hope for the viper to come, and it does, but you can't get off your shot fast enough. When that happens you squeeze your eyes shut and just endure the bite, let the venom rush through you, allow your blood to slow and clog, and wait for the toxin to invade every part of you.

What Terrible Thing It Was

FROM *Granta*

Becky Guo, Becky Guo, won't you play with me
I can't, said Becky, I'm hanging in a tree.
Becky Guo, Becky Guo, let me braid your hair.
I can't, said Becky, I've died way over there.
Becky Guo, Becky Guo, where are you today?
I'm here, said Becky, and I'll remain until you pay.

My toes are ice-cold when I enter Wellbrook Psychiatric Hospital. I know without looking that they've gone deathly pale beneath my socks and shoes, as though shuttling blood to my vital organs will sustain me in this place that is not old enough to be quaint: stained orange carpet, cement walls, cottage-cheese ceiling. I think briefly of fleeing, and how no one would stop me because no laser-printed hospital bracelet has yet been clipped to my wrist. But I've promised to come, and I am attempting to be brave. I approach the front desk while fingering the tin milagro that dangles from my neck.

The receptionist raises her head and asks, "Can I help you?"

"I'm Wendy Chung. I have an ECT consult at 2 p.m. with Dr. Richards."

"I see," she says, typing. "That you do. Well, follow me." She leads me to a group of hulking PCs, seating me at one of them. "You need to fill out these questionnaires before you see him. It's simple, but feel free to ask me if you have any questions." And then: "You know—I *love* your hair."

I put my hand to the top of my head, as if to emphasize the location of my hair.

"I love how long and black it is," she says. "Just beautiful. I always find it upsetting when Asian women dye their hair."

She goes back to her desk. I sit and look at the middle of the screen before me, which reads, in blocky green type:

PLEASE ANSWER THE FOLLOWING QUESTIONS ABOUT THE LAST TWO WEEKS (PRESS RETURN TO CONTINUE).

I press the return key. The next screen offers me four selections.

I DO NOT FEEL SAD.

I FEEL SAD.

I AM SAD ALL THE TIME AND I CAN'T SNAP OUT OF IT.

I AM SO SAD AND UNHAPPY THAT I CAN'T STAND IT.

I glance at the receptionist as though she can help me, but she's looking at her phone. She is perhaps checking the polls, which is what I would be doing if I weren't obligated to complete an intake survey. I examine her face. Has she voted? If so, who did she vote for?

PLEASE ANSWER THE FOLLOWING QUESTIONS ABOUT THE LAST TWO WEEKS (PRESS RETURN TO CONTINUE).

The first question stymies me because I'm not here for depression, which is what THE FOLLOWING QUESTIONS are clearly meant to evaluate. Even a person without depression could answer I FEEL SAD for a galaxy of reasons. If this survey were about the election I might choose I AM SAD ALL THE TIME AND I CAN'T SNAP OUT OF IT, or even I AM SO SAD AND UNHAPPY THAT I CAN'T STAND IT, which are both interesting ways of describing inner turmoil. Who knows what we can and can't stand. In my opinion, I've been able to stand it if I'm still alive, and maybe my psychiatrist was wrong and I don't need this consultation for electroconvulsive therapy; on the other hand, perhaps I said yes to the consultation because I can no longer stand the voices and the visions.

In terms of depression, however, sadness is not so much my problem, in which case it might make the most sense to choose I

DO NOT FEEL SAD. Yet it is my belief that this could never be the right answer as long as I am alive.

"Wendy?" a voice says, and I flinch so dramatically that I almost fall out of my chair. It's the doctor. He is white, like the receptionist; his glasses are John Lennon spectacles; his smile is bland. He is handsome in an unexciting way, like a bachelor on a reality television show. Out of the corner of my eye I see glossy black shoes hanging, and involuntarily I turn to look at the nothing that is there.

"I'm sorry," I say, composing myself.

His name is Dr. Richards. We shake hands with a grip. He says, "Come with me."

Dr. Richards brings me to a messy office with pockmarked walls. The easy chair I sit in smells of bodies and terror—I imagine the others who have sat here before me. I wonder how many of them have ended up getting electricity shocked through their skulls.

"Tell me what's brought you here," Dr. Richards says.

Becky Guo, Becky Guo, won't you play with me

I've prepared for this. On the bus to the hospital I stared straight ahead and told myself that it was imperative for me to be honest about my situation, no matter how terrified I was or how many stories I'd read online about people who had permanently damaged their ability to form new memories: goldfish people, I said to Dennis, my husband, who couldn't be here because of work and is very sorry that he cannot be here to hold my hand. I'm prepared to tell Dr. Richards my medical history and about the first voice I heard when I was twenty and how the election has made my stress so much worse, which has in turn escalated psychotic symptoms that have proven to be medication-resistant. And yet Dr. Richards's face, which warps and flattens and suddenly seems made of plaster, sucks out all the words I had carefully constructed and lined up delicately in impeccable rows, until I am vacant; the erasure of my likes and dislikes and the hopes I harbor, leaving nothing but agitation behind, is something that terrifies me about psychosis—I cannot survive another bout of catatonia.

"I hallucinate."

"What do you hallucinate?"

It doesn't matter, I try to say, but the words won't come out.

I'm afraid, is what I want to say.
Have you voted?
We're all going to die.
Respond; that is how to clear the river.
"I see," he says.

When I was seventeen, Rebecca Mei-Hua Guo was found hanging
from a eucalyptus tree near the outskirts of Polk Valley, where I
live. To be hanged from this tree was a feat, given its size; her
gleaming shoes dangled far above the heads of the two huntsmen
who found her, too high for them to reach, and certainly too high
for them to undo the knots that made her noose, or the rope that
bound her to the branch. By the time they summoned the police and the fire brigade, she had been hanging for over fourteen
hours—so said the medical examiner who evaluated her body.

I am well aware that any narrative involving a dead girl ultimately fails to animate the dead girl, who remains a corpse—or
in this case, a ghost—for the duration. I do believe in ghosts. I
believe that the living carry patterns of energy created by atoms
and molecules and cells and organs, and that these patterns remain vibrating in the air after we die. Sometimes they disassemble
and form other patterns, such as in the Buddhist belief of rein-
carnation, and sometimes they remain what they were before the
death occurred.

As an amateur Tarot reader, I pulled a card for Becky the day
her body was found, and I did not pull the World or the Wheel
of Fortune. I pulled the Nine of Swords: despair, nightmares. For
years I had dreams in which I was the one hanging, and that the
children were singing of me while I gasped for breath, wriggling
like an exotic dark-haired worm on a hook, watching the towns-
people laughing from below. It could have been any of them who
killed Becky. It would have been any of them. As long as the mur-
derer was free I would not know who had sedated and then hung
Becky from that high-up branch. I would not know why or how
the killer had done it, and because there seemed to be no reason
for the act I would have to keep my head bowed. If she had not
been killed in part because of her race I could, as the saying goes,
breathe easier, but I could not assure myself of that any more than
I could wipe off my own face.

We, the Guo family, insist that the eucalyptus tree where our daughter
Rebecca died be cut down. It is too much to bear for us to see the reminder of her terrible death, or to even know that it is there.

Mr. and Mrs. Guo came to me to write the letter because they
wanted it to be written in perfect English, which they could not do
themselves. It was the kind of thing, I knew, that they would have
had Becky do, had she lived. Because I wrote this letter for them
I know that they did not ask for a plaque to be installed at the site
of her death; they believed without question that the town would
deny them such a thing, and I too knew this and agreed with them
without a word spoken.

They came to our apartment in the afternoon, when neither
of my parents were home, and asked me to write this letter to the
mayor of Polk Valley. I had never before seen Mr. Guo so rumpled,
or Mrs. Guo so casual—my life had carried enough weight by then,
but I'd never seen two people so heavy with sadness.

When they asked if I would please do this favor for them I was
immediately embarrassed because I knew they would want me to
write the letter on a computer, which my family did not have, but
the couple before me was bent with such sorrow that I said yes
and let them inside, mentally scanning the disarray in our tepid
home. I could tell that they were trying not to see Becky in me,
but that they couldn't help doing so. I look nothing like Becky
—she was round-faced, had enviable double eyelids—and yet the
comparison was inevitable and caused their eyes to snag on me before ripping away. I gestured to the kitchen table and asked if they
wanted tea, but they were staring into emptiness. I asked again in
Mandarin, and Mrs. Guo's head lifted slightly.

"You can speak Mandarin?" she asked, in Mandarin.

"*Hai hao,*" I said, which was to say, "My Mandarin is serviceable,
but I'm by no means fluent."

"We tried to teach Becky, but she only ever spoke English," Mrs.
Guo said in English.

I went to the kitchen and searched for tea, vaguely aware that
we had run out the day before and that I hadn't asked my parents
for the money to buy some. I told the Guos with apology that we
had run out of tea, but did they want some water? With enough
mundane dillydallying my heart would stop drumming, I thought.

Nor did I know why I was so afraid, though in hindsight I think it was because they emanated grief like a contagion.

Mr. Guo tried to pay me after I gave him the letter, and even though I had no money and my parents were always talking about how hard they worked and how poor we were, I refused the twenty-dollar bill. But for hours after they left, the apartment smelled like death: pale and blank, dry like dead leaves. I opened all the windows and turned on all the fans for fifteen minutes, and then I went through the apartment and turned them all off, but I left the windows open. It was summer and I could hear people talking and laughing and carrying on while I went into my bedroom and did my calculus homework, and the Guos went home and, I am sure, painstakingly rewrote my letter on their computer before sending it to our mayor. I wondered whether I should have taken the money. I decided that I was right not to.

After the crime-scene tape was removed, I would go to the eucalyptus tree and press my hands against the bark, feeling its warmth beneath my palms and knowing that it was breathing, a living thing; each time I returned I half-expected it to be nothing but a stump, but there it remained, its leaves rustling, its branches looming to remind me of all the corpses that could still hang there.

At the time there were always two or three bouquets at the base of the tree—red roses, calla lilies. I would bring flowers sometimes, when I remembered. I imagine there are no flowers left there now. I no longer go to the tree, and I avoid the Guos when I can. It seems heartless, but if I must stay and care for my mother it is important that I distance myself from Becky, because we still don't know who killed her, and if I remain too close to the situation I will corrode from fear.

"Electroconvulsive therapy," Dr. Richards says, "is extremely effective for those with intractable depression. It has rarely been shown to work well for those with schizophrenia. I usually recommend ECT for the former, and not so much for the latter, because of the potential for undesirable side effects. Memory loss is the greatest side effect, as you've probably heard. I'm sure you've looked it up. There are those who advocate against ECT because of what they've gone through. I don't blame them for it; they are entitled to their experiences. But there are some cases of schizophrenia in which I do think ECT should be considered, and yours is one of them. ECT is most effective for people who have been diagnosed with schizophrenia and experience hallucinations—in your case, auditory and visual hallucinations—yet don't respond to the atypical antipsychotics, Clozaril, or even the older antipsychotics. For people like you, Wendy, ECT might shake up your brain enough to get things working right again."

I am trying not to look at his face, focusing only on the words coming out of it. I am a good candidate for ECT. My health insurance would cover the treatment. I would be an inpatient at the hospital for approximately one week and receive electroconvulsive therapy each morning. They can best monitor me this way. I might be able to go back to work.

"The Wheel of Fortune is a reminder of the impermanence of life," says a neutral voice.

"I need to talk about this with my husband before I agree to anything," I say.

"The roots of the word 'innocent' mean to be free of injury or hurt."

"That's fine," says Dr. Richards, looking back at his computer.

The bus ride back to Polk Valley takes an hour, and the line at the polling place is long, yawning down the perimeter of the high school and around the sidewalk to the corner, across the street from a convenience store that sells cigarettes to minors and Slim Jims at the counter. I wait between a twenty-something white guy scrolling through his phone and an older white woman scuffing the toes of her red cowboy boots. I don't talk to them about who they're going to vote for; I remind myself that California always goes blue.

I can't, said Becky, I've died way over there.

I text Dennis: "Consult went okay. Dr. says I should do it. Insurance will probably cover."

In two minutes he texts back: "Let's talk when I get home."

I look briefly at Twitter and see that the man I am afraid will become president has insinuated that it would be best if his supporters harassed people at the polls, particularly people of color; of course, he never says "people of color," but we know what he means. I click on the tweet and scroll down; the woman who shared this article received fifteen misspelled and angry replies from people with names like WhiteIsRight19887 and ((Aryan

Queen)). "Muslim Obama HATES America, LOVES terrrerists!" ((Aryan Queen)) is using a photo of Taylor Swift as her avatar. My coworker at the deli used to blast *Red* while we cleaned the kitchen, singing, "Don't you see the starlight, starlight? Don't you dream impossible things?"

When I go to sign in at the polls I see that Mrs. Guo is one of the women at the table, which surprises me; I have never thought of her as someone to volunteer for anything, but perhaps I am mostly thinking of my own mother, who felt that to volunteer in Polk Valley was to extend herself too far into America. I haven't spoken to Mrs. Guo in years, but she beckons me forth, a lipsticked smile blooming. Her hair is short and permed, puffy like a cloud. She says, "Wendy-ah."

"Hi."

"Can I see your ID?"

"Yes." I remove it from my wallet. She takes it and scans the names in front of her. "Voting today. Good girl," she says. "You are still so beautiful."

"Thank you."

"Are you married yet?"

"Um," I say, "yes. I am." I think of Dennis, his image slotting neatly into my mind. "I got married last year."

"That's good," Mrs. Guo says. She makes a mark with her pen. "Mr. Guo and I are moving to San Francisco. We're leaving in a month."

I don't know what to say to that.

"We never forgot . . . Mr. Guo and I are always grateful that you wrote that letter for us."

"It was nothing, really."

"No," she says, "it was a kindness. A true kindness."

"I'm sorry it didn't work out," I said.

"*Mei you guanxi.*" She gestures to an empty voting booth, and says, "You take care, Wendy," as I walk away.

After her body was found, and even after it was clear that suicide was an impossible explanation, there remained a contingent that insisted Becky must have killed herself. Such a strange girl, with such dark thoughts—no surprise that she had ended up dangling from a tree. And yet Becky was strange in the most conventional of ways: a Sex Pistols pin on her JanSport, a streak of hair the color of holly berries. Witchcraft or Satanic practices could explain the otherwise physical impossibility of *how*, but I bristled at such associations, which only accelerated Becky's inevitable mythology. Becky could be anything, once she died, and the rest of us would have to live.

I used to avoid being in the same room as Becky. It was too much to have two Chinese girls in one place, I thought, and Becky must have felt the same way because she often entered a room, spotted me, and then backed out to find her own domain. Usually this happened at parties. Sometimes it happened at restaurants. Once at a museum: a gallery of watercolors that looked like wounds.

After she died, of course, this was no longer the case. Now I find myself wanting to talk to her. I want to ask, Are you scared, too? Even knowing that I am not alone would be its own strange balm.

Dennis and I own a television, but we use it primarily for movies and his video games, and only recently activated the free cable that comes with our internet connection. I have, till now, resisted watching the breakneck election coverage, but it is already on when I get home. I find Dennis sitting in the corduroy easy chair, checking his phone with the television glowing and muttering across the room; I kiss him and put down my bag and stretch out on the sofa, staring at the ceiling. Right now, the news anchor says, the electoral votes are 129 to 97, which seems impossible—it was not so long ago that the candidate was thought too volatile to even win a primary.

"How was the consult?" he asks.

I had almost forgotten the consult. "It was okay."

We are silent. Polls are now closed in forty states.

"Do you think you'll do it?"

"I'm not sure."

He asks, "Are you scared?" I wish I could see his face, but I imagine it: Dennis with his bespectacled eyes on his phone, performing the act of emotional multitasking. While I've been psychotic, he's been phone banking. He even went canvassing door-to-door, which sounds nightmarish to me—but Dennis is white and male and good-looking without being threatening—I never use the word *disarming*, but he is that, too.

"I read a book about ECT earlier this week. In the worst-case scenario, I won't remember major events in my life. I might even have trouble forming new memories. They don't even know *how* ECT works—a guy named Ugo Cerletti decided to use electricity on the brain because they thought epilepsy and schizophrenia were somehow antagonistic. Before ECT, they'd use camphor to induce convulsions, but camphor never became as popular as shock therapy."

"What are the odds you'll have memory loss?"

"I don't have hard numbers. I don't know if there *are* any. It's something that might happen. I would have to make peace with that."

"When do you have to decide?"

"Soon, I guess." I realize I'm drawing a red X on my thigh with the nail of my right index finger. "I know Dr. Hoch wants to get me on the wait list as soon as possible, if I'm going to do it."

Dennis says that it's my decision and that he'll support me no matter what, which is kind and supportive and the right thing to say.

I look at Twitter again. Everyone is talking about the election, about moving to Canada, about the apocalypse. A Canadian writer says, "The grass is always greener!" The Southern Poverty Law Center is still reporting election-related hate crimes. One friend is live-tweeting her experience of watching *Casablanca* for the first time. "Does anyone else think Humphrey Bogart looks like J. D. Salinger?" she asks. I read an article about people chanting "Lock her up!" at a rally. I read about a Muslim schoolteacher in New York City who had her hijab torn off by a stranger in broad daylight. ("MCM LIES," is one reply.) I read about gaslighting. I read an essay about having a younger brother with brain cancer, and I start to cry even though I don't have any siblings and no one I know is dying.

"Oh my God, Florida," Dennis says. "He just took Florida."

I look at the TV through wet eyes, where his fleshy, grinning face appears with the words FLORIDA and 29 ELECTORAL VOTES. He has won. No one has conceded yet, but still, he has won.

I'm here, said Becky.

"It's over," I say.

Dennis says, "I think so."

I tell him that I'm going to bed. He says something back.

In the bathroom, where I avoid looking in the mirror—an aversion to my own face is one of my latest symptoms—I turn on the tap and let the water run cool over my fingers. I stand at the sink for a long time, until I cannot remember what I am doing; I lose the next move. Suddenly, and too loudly, a girl calls my name.

Contributors' Notes

Other Distinguished Stories of 2017

American and Canadian Magazines Publishing Short Stories

Contributors' Notes

MARIA ANDERSON'S fiction is forthcoming or has appeared in the *Mississippi Review*, the *Missouri Review*, the *Iowa Review*, and the *Atlas Review*. She's an editor at Essay Press, and she has been awarded residencies from Joshua Tree National Park, the AMK Ranch Research Center in Grand Teton National Park, and the Crosshatch Center for Art & Ecology. She lives in Bozeman, Montana.

• I lived in Missoula, Montana, for a short time and had always been fascinated by Bonner, the tiny town a couple miles east on the interstate where a few of our friends lived. I wanted to set a story there. I grew up on a cattle ranch outside of town, and spent a lot of time alone as a child, wandering through the woods with our German shepherd. I wanted to work through some of the feelings that go with this kind of deep-seated physical and emotional isolation.

I wrote the first draft of this story at Coal Creek Tap while doing my MFA in Laramie, at the University of Wyoming. It felt easier to focus with people drinking beer and playing cribbage around me. My early readers will remember several especially awful middles and endings to this story —a scene in a strip club with a dancer named Anaconda, a moment in a hotel where men attempt to steal dog semen from a fridge. But what I kept returning to was the main character, and how it feels to have a loved one vanish, whether emotionally or physically, and to know that this is one of the old mysteries you hear about. Someone is there one moment and irreversibly gone the next. Even if that person is right in front of you, you can feel the horror of having lost them already. The horror isn't that they're gone, but that this vanishing is unfair and unexplainable.

JAMEL BRINKLEY is the author of *A Lucky Man: Stories*. His fiction has appeared in *A Public Space, Ploughshares, Gulf Coast, Glimmer Train, Ameri-*

can *Short Fiction, Threepenny Review, Epiphany,* and *LitMag.* He has received scholarships and fellowships from Kimbilio Fiction, the *Callaloo* Creative Writing Workshop, the Napa Valley Writers' Conference, *Tin House,* Ragdale, and the Bread Loaf Writers' Conference. A graduate of the Iowa Writers' Workshop, he was also the 2016–17 Carol Houck Smith Fiction Fellow at the Wisconsin Institute for Creative Writing. He is currently a 2018–20 Wallace Stegner Fellow in Fiction at Stanford University.

• As I worked on the initial draft of "A Family," I had a few stories swimming around in my mind: "Old Boys, Old Girls" by Edward P. Jones, "Three People" by William Trevor, and the brilliant reply to that Trevor tale, "Gold Boy, Emerald Girl" by Yiyun Li. In addition to those stories, I was, as I came to discover along the way, also thinking about black men and mass incarceration, a changing New York City, the urgency and variety of human companionship, the way a friend can be the love of one's life, the multiple forms that families can take, and both the speed and stickiness of time. My first working title was "Lena's Men," which I'm still fond of in many ways. She's my favorite person in the piece, the story's true living link, connecting each of the other principal characters. I decided against that title, ultimately, because I wanted to emphasize all the characters together as one unit, even on the level of grammar. The next working title was "A Kind of Family," but I decided against that one because I wanted to avoid any unconscious or deliberate misinterpretation on the part of some readers (in, say, the tradition of the Moynihan Report) that I was writing about *kind of* a family or *sort of* a family, *not quite* a family, a family only in degraded form. The title I settled on asserts, simply and directly, what I believe to be true about these characters in the end, who and what they are with one another.

YOON CHOI lives in Anaheim Hills, California, with her husband and four children. Her work has been published in *Michigan Quarterly Review* and *New England Review.* A current Wallace Stegner Fellow at Stanford University, she is working on a collection of short stories.

• This story began as a promise to myself, after the last of our children was born, to find an hour a day to write. What I came up with in those hours was perfunctory at best. An old man with Alzheimer's wanders from home and drowns in a municipal pond. Six thousand words, tops. But one night, as I was typing toward the inevitable, it occurred to me that the old man would probably have a wife. The wife gave me the structure of the story—and then the story itself. Structurally, the use of his/her sections solved the problem of narrating from a single unreliable perspective. But the double narration also raised questions. There was a wife. This probably meant there were children. Maybe even grandchildren. A grandchild in particular. I thought: What if the old man was left alone with his grandson?

What if he brought that child to the edge of the water? What if the old woman had left the two of them together, against her better judgment, because of . . . what? A secret. Suddenly, I was not so sure that the old man would be the one to die. I was not sure about anything at all. That's when the story found in these pages slowly began to get written.

EMMA CLINE is the author of *The Girls,* nominated for a National Book Critics Circle Award, the First Novel Prize from the Center for Fiction, and an LA Times Book Prize. Her stories have appeared in *The New Yorker, Granta, Tin House,* and the *Paris Review.* In 2014 Cline won the Plimpton Prize from the *Paris Review,* and in 2017 she was named by *Granta* as one of the Best Young American Novelists of her generation.

  • I wanted to think about "cost" in this story, both in terms of the actual exchange of goods for a set price, and in terms of the cost of our experiences, what they exact from us. Alice thinks she understands how the world works, but she consistently mistakes surface information — how things look, their external value — for reality. Her life is a kind of recurring anecdote, her painful experiences just fodder for stories. As long as she squints a certain way, keeps certain information from herself, nothing can really hurt or affect her. I didn't want to moralize about her choices — the danger doesn't come from what Alice is actually doing, but from her inability to fully inhabit her own life. I wanted the reader to think about what living this way might cost, what the price might eventually be, even if Alice can't.

ALICIA ELLIOTT is a Tuscarora writer living in Brantford, Ontario, with her husband and child. Her writing has been published by *The Malahat Review, New Quarterly, The Walrus, Globe and Mail, VICE,* and many others. Her essay "A Mind Spread Out on the Ground" won Gold at the National Magazine Awards and was published in *Best Canadian Essays 2017.* Most recently, she was the 2017–18 Geoffrey and Margaret Andrew Fellow at UBC. Elliott is currently Creative Nonfiction Editor at *The Fiddlehead,* Associate Creative Nonfiction Editor at *Little Fiction | Big Truths,* and a consulting editor at *New Quarterly.* Her first book of essays is forthcoming from Doubleday Canada in spring 2019.

  • The first line came to me while I was sitting in a coffee shop in a city I didn't know. "They found him while laying the groundwork for a fast food restaurant." I wasn't sure what I was writing about at first, but the idea of consumption loomed large in my mind. I initially tried to write the story about a white family, but nothing was gelling. It always felt wrong, unfinished.

After visiting the Mohawk Institute, otherwise known as the Mush Hole, the residential school closest to my rez, I realized where Henry had gone, and why he hadn't come back. I realized why I was continually circling back around to the idea of consumption, and why it was so painful that a fast food restaurant was being built on those lands. Canada has fed so many of my people to the monster of colonialism. They've stripped away our lands, eroded our rights, stolen our children, then criminalized them, then imprisoned them—all for the purpose of pushing forward white, Western capitalism. A fast food restaurant is the perfect symbol for this sort of capitalistic, colonial consumption.

As soon as I realized Beth and her family were Mohawk, it was like the story opened up. Everything came fast. Everything made sense. What didn't make sense—what was painful to ask myself—was why I was writing all my characters as white before this. It's important to recognize the ways that whiteness works its way into our imaginations as Indigenous writers, the way it forces us to diminish our own people, our own stories, and elevate either whiteness itself, or a version of Indigeneity that pleases white audiences. This story helped me realize that my writing didn't have to do either of those things. My writing could center Indigenous people, voices, and experiences instead.

I'm beyond grateful that this messy, complicated, and (I think) ultimately hopeful story was chosen to be included in this collection. It gives me faith that the old standards of what's been traditionally considered literary and acceptable are changing. It tells me that Indigenous stories, which we as Indigenous people have always cherished and revered, are finally being cherished and revered by non-Indigenous readers, as well. What a gift.

DANIELLE EVANS is the author of the story collection *Before You Suffocate Your Own Fool Self,* winner of the PEN American Robert W. Bingham Prize, the Hurston-Wright Award, the Paterson Prize, and a National Book Foundation 5 under 35 selection. Her stories have appeared in magazines and anthologies including the *Paris Review, A Public Space, American Short Fiction, Callaloo, New Stories from the South,* and *The Best American Short Stories 2008, 2010,* and *2017.* She teaches creative writing at Johns Hopkins University.

• I had sketched out what I thought would be a campus novel someday, where one inciting event triggered a progression of responses, and multiple narrators would tell the story. A few years later, I realized I was most interested in only one of the narrators. Having written a lot about the experience of racism, I wanted to find a different way to inhabit that narrative. I think a lot about the James Baldwin line "It is the innocence which constitutes the crime." I wanted to write a story that invited not just empathy but implication, and explored the relationship between the two. I wanted to write about what it is to live always in the present and avoid a sense of history and consequence, which was about race and politics, but also, I realized once I started writing, about the messy spiraling of grief and denial. I was drafting the story during a time when I was spending a lot of time in hospitals, sharing a kind of forced intimacy and vulnerability with some people I realized wouldn't like me or be likable in other contexts. That grief and intimacy let me get closer to Claire, let me care about her, without forgetting that as much as the story is about her real human grief, it's also about what the desire to generously and forever forgive some people costs others. A few times during the years I was writing and revising this story, I put it away for a while because I thought the national conversation around Confederate imagery might have changed enough that I'd have to factor it into the story. The story got finished faster than the changing did.

CAROLYN FERRELL's story collection *Don't Erase Me* (1997) was awarded the Art Seidenbaum Award of the *Los Angeles Times,* the John C. Zachiris Award given by *Ploughshares,* and the Quality Paperback Book Prize for First Fiction. Her stories and essays have appeared in the *New York Times, Literary Review, Ploughshares,* and other places; her story "Proper Library" was included in *The Best American Short Stories of the Century,* edited by John Updike. A recipient of a fellowship from the National Endowment for the Arts, Ferrell teaches at Sarah Lawrence College and lives in New York with her husband and children.

• I'd long tried to figure out how to approach the individual pieces of "A History of China" while also thinking about the larger story. Ultimately, I was guided by a few short stories that have helped me consider form and content in new ways: Steven Millhauser's brilliant "Phantoms" was one such guide, as was Edward P. Jones's incredible "All Aunt Hagar's Children," and Alice Munro's harshly poignant "Wild Swans." Robin Hemley's "Sympathy for the Devil: How to Deal with Difficult Characters," an essay I've taught for years, was another beacon.

"A History of China" has its earliest roots in an experience I had with a now-defunct German porcelain company, my first job out of college. I was fascinated by the role a five-piece place setting could play in a world that cherished patterns and platters, soup tureens and replacement soup tureens—a world about which I knew nothing. In fact, I was fired a few months in, my supervisor explaining that I didn't have what it took to make it in that world. Years later I went and used those dishes to my advantage.

ANN GLAVIANO is a writer, dancer, DJ, and born-and-raised New Orleanian. Her work has appeared in *Tin House, Ninth Letter, Prairie Schooner, Fairy Tale Review,* the *Atlas Review, Slate,* and the anthology *Please Forward: How Blogging Reconnected New Orleans After Katrina* (University of New Orleans Press), among other publications. Her novella, *Dickbeer,* was published by Amazon's *Day One.* Glaviano is an alumna of Louisiana State University and the MFA program at Ohio State.

• I attended sleepaway summer camp of the traditional outdoors variety from the ages of eight to ten, followed by nerd camp (shoutout to the ADVANCE Program for Young Scholars!) every summer till I was sixteen. Camp changed my life utterly and for the better—in fact, nerd camp was where I took my first creative writing course—so I have a real soft spot for camp stories, plus a wealth of material to draw from.

I came across a writing prompt years ago, and I wish I could credit the source but I can no longer find it, that suggested writing a story about a camp organized around a theme we don't usually have camps for—such as wife camp. When it was time to start a new story, I pulled out this camp prompt, and I considered other weird camp concepts, and finally I realized that my favorite thing about the prompt was the idea of wife camp. What would one do at a wife camp?

It turns out wife camps exist, usually in a religious context, and this took me down a deep rabbit hole of research on the ways we teach girls, across different cultures, what will be expected of them as women. I looked at initiation rituals, both formal and informal, and superstitions regarding menstruation. I also thought about how baffled kids often are when they first encounter adult behaviors that are upheld as norms but are, from an outsider perspective, bizarre and absurd; I wrote from that place of absurdity. I had a great deal of fun.

I have hated epistolary stories my whole life, starting with *Dear Mr. Henshaw* (no shade toward Beverly Cleary), but Donald Barthelme changed my mind; the structure of this story was inspired by "Me and Miss Mandible."

JACOB GUAJARDO is a graduate of MFA@FLA at the University of Florida. His fiction has appeared in *Passages North, Hobart, Necessary Fiction, The Mondegreen,* and elsewhere. He lives in Gainesville, Florida, but was born and raised in St. Louis, Michigan.

• This story took two years and eleven drafts to write. It took about the same amount of time to get it published. I grew up in St. Louis, Michigan, the geographic center of the state. My family lived two hours from all of the beaches on the Great Lakes. When we did get to go to the beach (my parents both worked full-time jobs) it was a treat. When we were at the beach, it was like we were a different family. My favorite beaches are in Grand Haven, on the west side of the state, where this story takes place. I loved imagining what it would be like to grow up there. Would a boy like me, a queer, light-skinned halfie, survive? What if he fell in love? What if he fell in love with someone he shouldn't? Young, queer people of color become adept at hiding, but it's hard to hide that you are in love.

My dad grew up in a single-parent household with two sisters and two brothers. He's a first-generation kid. His mom worked hard to give him and his siblings what they had, but not without the help of her friends. I have always known that it takes more than a set of parents to raise kids. I knew I wanted to write about the people who raised me. I knew I wanted to write about beach boys, and I knew I wanted to write about first love.

CRISTINA HENRÍQUEZ is the author of three books, including, most recently, the novel *The Book of Unknown Americans,* which was longlisted for the Andrew Carnegie Medal for Excellence in Fiction and was a finalist for the Dayton Literary Peace Prize. Her work has appeared in *The New Yorker, The Atlantic,* the *Wall Street Journal, Oxford American,* the *New York Times Magazine,* and elsewhere. She is also the recipient of an Alfredo Cisneros Del Moral Foundation Award. She lives in Illinois.

• A few years ago, I went to a hotel by myself for one weekend to do nothing but write. Armed with Japanese whiskey and Goldfish crackers, I holed up in the room, intending to make progress on a novel I'd been struggling with. Instead, I sat down and wrote this story.

It's rare that I start a story with what could properly be called an idea. For me, the seed is always language, and when the words come, they open a path before me. So I wrote the first line — *On the first day, there's a sense of relief*—and continued from there, letting the story reveal itself. It's a scary way to write, and it requires a certain amount of faith, but by the end of that weekend, I had the first draft. From there, it was a matter of understanding what the story was really about, and one of the things I wanted to show was that in trying to find safety, the main character, this woman, only managed to trade one sort of horror for another.

Although most of the story came quickly, I did labor over the ending. The woman is unraveling, and I wanted the language to do that, too, for that final image to be one not of stasis but of movement, reflecting the change within the character, but also to evoke a kind of lyricism at odds with the bleakness of that change.

KRISTEN ISKANDRIAN'S debut novel *Motherest* was published by Twelve/ Hachette in 2017 and was chosen as a monthly pick by *Shondaland, Vanity Fair, The Millions,* and the *Wall Street Journal,* as well as being named a Best Book of the Year by *Publishers Weekly* and *Lenny Letter.* Her short fiction has appeared in *The O. Henry Prize Stories 2014, Tin House, McSweeney's, Ploughshares, Crazyhorse, Joyland,* and *Epoch,* among others. She lives in Birmingham, Alabama. For more information visit kristeniskandrian.com.

• My class in elementary school did an overnight at a museum of natural history, although I don't remember much about it beyond possibly sleeping beneath a terrarium of spiders, and even that detail may be an invention of memory. And, like my narrator, I adore E. L. Konigsburg's *From the Mixed-up Files of Mrs. Basil E. Frankweiler.* But mostly I wanted to explore longing from the point of view of a preteen, a child, because I think we forget that children experience desire in all kinds of powerful and devastating and transgressive ways. Jill knows who she is and what her strengths are; she doesn't need anyone to tell her how to be. From that self-assurance springs both her sense of humor and her capacity for deep hurt. I'm unendingly fascinated by where and how our two most human conditions —pain and pleasure—meet, blur, and swallow one another whole.

JOCELYN NICOLE JOHNSON'S essays and short stories have appeared in *Guernica, Prime Number, Literary Mama,* and elsewhere. Her work has twice been nominated for the Pushcart Prize. Johnson lives, writes, and loves on her people—her son, husband, friends, and art students—in Charlottesville, Virginia.

• In 2014, years before Charlottesville became known for a deadly white supremacists' rally, a black University of Virginia student was detained by local law enforcement after he was turned away from a bar near campus. Moments later, a video showed Martese Johnson pinned to the ground, blood pouring down his face. "I go to UVA!" he shouted, as if he'd once believed those words would shield him. The next week, I recognized his image in the local paper: a boy in a suit, flanked by lawyers, his forehead marked by ten fresh sutures. Looking on, I received some share of this young man's bewilderment and heartache; it collected in me. A year later, "Control Negro" spilled out.

This short story contains fragments of my mother, my father, my brother; I borrowed details, real and imagined, from their lives growing up in the '50s and '60s in the sand hills of South Carolina, a community perverted by Jim Crow racism. It contains a speck of bitterness that settled in me, years ago, after a conversation with a close college friend, who was white. She told me, excitedly, that she'd learned in class about a professor who'd "definitely" disproved the effects of racism. His method, she explained, was to compare the barriers faced by black communities—bondage, violence, discrimination—to comparable difficulties other ethnic groups had contended with—though not in aggregate, she conceded. The professor found that other groups had overcome the same hurdles that crippled black communities. And so, the logic seemed to go, the problem must be with blackness itself, and not the brutality it inspired. What I remember most was my friend's gleeful conclusion: "He was black!" she said. "The professor, who did the study, was a black man!"

It was only after "Control Negro" found a home at *Guernica* that I recognized myself in the story. Hadn't I felt curated during moments of my middle-class upbringing, choreographed even? And now I was watching my own biracial boy come of age in a newly vitriolic and outraged America.

MATTHEW LYONS is the author of dozens of short stories, appearing in *Black Dandy, Kzine,* and *Daily Science Fiction* among others. His work has been nominated for *Best Small Fictions, Best of the Net,* and more. Born in Colorado, he lives in New York City with his wife.

• I've always been fascinated with the phenomenon of American male rage, and how it's communicated down from generation to generation, from fathers to sons, more often than not mutating into something far worse than what it was before. In so many ways, that rage is a central driver in our society, and even if our bad decisions sometimes seem sensible, it's not difficult to track the destruction that they can cause as we flirt with total annihilation. Gods, humans, or something in-between, we all inherit the damage that was done before us. Even though we like to think of ourselves as better, sometimes all we can hope to do is redirect it. Sometimes we can only make things worse.

DINA NAYERI was born in Tehran and arrived in America at ten years old, after two years as a refugee. She is the author of the acclaimed *Guardian* Long Read "The Ungrateful Refugee" (soon to be a book by the same name), and the winner of an O. Henry Prize, a National Endowment for the Arts literature grant, and fellowships from the Macdowell Colony, Bogliasco Foundation, and others. Her work has been translated into fourteen languages and recently published in the *New York Times,* the *Guardian, Los Angeles Times, New Republic,* and others. Her second novel, *Refuge,* was published by Riverhead Books in 2017.

• "A Big True" began as an experiment. For months my mother and I had fought about my fiction, which she thinks of as an excuse to twist the truth. "You write these loser parents all the time and you use my details. You lie about me." "But they're not you!" I'd say again and again. She said, "And yet somehow you can't write a parent who's not a loser, or a child who isn't perfect." She was so wrong, but still I set out to prove her even *more* wrong (yes, I know). I said, "What if I write a story about a parent who's wildly different from you, a man maybe, whose daughter refuses to understand him? What if I make him an artist and she's the bland one? What if I show the color in a simple life and the dreariness in a seemingly successful one?" She loved the idea. So I wrote the story. I sent the first draft to her, and I was so nervous about how she'd react. She called me and after a silent beat, she said, "You did it again! Another loser immigrant parent and their amazing kid who knows everything!" A loser? I was in shock. Didn't she see what I saw, all the love in my story? Didn't she see that I adored Rahad? That I had adored every displaced mother and father I had ever created from the parts of her and of my father and my grandparents and myself? We fought, of course. I edited. We fought again. Finally, she threw me a bone. "Wyatt is funny," she said. "I understand the trick he plays at the end. It's very moving. Very true."

TÉA OBREHT'S debut novel, *The Tiger's Wife,* won the 2011 Orange Prize for Fiction, and was a 2011 National Book Award Finalist and a *New York Times* best seller. Her work has appeared in *The New Yorker, Zoetrope: All-Story, The Atlantic, Harper's, Vogue,* and *Esquire,* among others. She was a National Book Foundation 5 Under 35 honoree, and was named by *The New Yorker* as one of the twenty best American fiction writers under forty. She lives in New York and teaches at Hunter College. Her second novel is forthcoming in 2019.

• A few years ago, during the penultimate week of a fellowship at the New York Public Library, I had the fortune of taking a tour through the labyrinthine stacks of the Stephen A. Schwarzman building on Fifth Avenue. A controversial renovation had been announced, and for months New Yorkers had debated the logistics and consequences of moving the lion's share of the collection offsite in order to address concerns that the library's stacks might be too fragile to continue the twin tasks of housing its books and supporting its weight.

It was eerie to go all the way down into the warm, green-gray catacombs of the old girl and see her skeleton laid bare. Infinities of struts and empty rectangles receded in every direction. Halogen tubes flickered overhead. A right here, a left there, a deserted corridor, a stairwell leading to basement storage. On an otherwise empty shelf at the foot of a metal ladder I barely survived sat a box labeled:

ITEMS AWAITING PROTECTIVE ENCLOSURE

I'm not a note-taking kind of writer (managing to lose every single Moleskine I've ever carried has cured me of trying to catch those daily jolts of inspiration) but when I saw these words, I scrambled to grab them, get them down on paper, preserve their correct order. Right away I knew: this was something, a thread, a line if I'd ever seen one. A gift. Just sitting there in the library basement. A title — maybe. I told myself that I would wait as long as necessary for the right story to come along and claim it. Of course, this would turn out to be the one I had already been writing for the better part of a year — though two more years would pass before its hazy, disparate threads (shed hunting, unrequited first love, a father obsessed with littering transgressions) finally came together.

RON RASH is the author of the 2009 PEN/Faulkner finalist and *New York Times* best seller *Serena,* in addition to many prizewinning novels, including *The Risen, Above the Waterfall, The Cove, One Foot in Eden, Saints at the River,* and *The World Made Straight;* four collections of poems; and six collections of stories, among them *Burning Bright,* which won the 2010 Frank O'Connor International Short Story Award, and *Chemistry and Other Stories,* which was a finalist for the 2007 PEN/Faulkner Award. Twice the recipient of both *The Best American Short Stories* and the O. Henry Prize, he teaches at Western Carolina University.

• As with almost all of my fiction, this story began with an image: a baptism scene on a frozen river. I sensed the time period was the late nineteenth century and that the minister was deeply conflicted about performing the rite. Where the initial image came from I cannot say. It was not derived from anything I'd ever heard of happening. After finishing the first draft, I realized that my naming the child Pearl established a connection to the Pearl in *The Scarlet Letter,* but that too was, at least initially, subconscious. My perspective on stories is Jungian. They already exist; thus writers are more transmitters than creators. But how *well* the story will be told is conscious, a matter of craft.

AMY SILVERBERG is a writer and stand-up comedian based in Los Angeles. She's currently a Doctoral Fellow in Fiction at the University of Southern California. Her writing has appeared in *TriQuarterly, Los Angeles Review of Books, The Collagist,* and elsewhere. She will be performing stand-up on season 6 of Hulu's comedy showcase *Coming to the Stage.* She's now at work on a collection of short stories and a novel.

• The way I enter stories is almost always through voice; I rarely have a character or premise in mind. I just had that first line in my head for a while — the line of a character saying she made a bet with her father — so I wrote one paragraph and set it aside for months and months. I'm not sure why I decided to pick up the story again, but I know that line ran through my head enough times, stayed with me long enough, that I felt I wanted to revisit it and go from there. Maybe I just had a deadline! At the time, I was teaching an Intro to Composition class that was mostly freshmen, and I met with them three times a week, so I got to know them pretty well. We'd talk often about their relationships with their parents — who had a helicopter mom, whose dad wanted them to really embrace being on their own. I was definitely thinking about that at the time, the myriad of ways in which parents and children learn to let go. Eighteen has always struck me as a very strange, particular age — especially for the kids I was teaching — so many of them were living away from home, but still talking to their parents every day. I'd just read the short story "The Paperhanger" by William Gay and admired the mystery of it, how it seemed to go confidently into an unknown world, a world that felt a little surreal and a little absurd. At least that's how I remember feeling about the story at the time. I was also in a workshop taught by Aimee Bender, and while I hadn't set out to write anything with a magical realism element, I'm sure her stories (which I've read many, many times) rubbed off on me — or if not the stories, then at least the courage or freedom to go confidently into that so-called unknown world. Finally, I love writing about Los Angeles. I've lived here most of my adult life, and I perform comedy here. It still feels exciting that a friend of mine, who works as a waitress, might quit her job at any moment for an acting role. For as long as I've lived here, it's always felt like a city of transition and transformation—that you might be one thing and then become another over the course of a single day will always be compelling to me.

CURTIS SITTENFELD is the best-selling author of five novels—*Prep, The Man of My Dreams, American Wife, Sisterland,* and *Eligible*—and one story collection, *You Think It, I'll Say It.* Her books have been selected by the *New York Times, Time, Entertainment Weekly,* and *People* for their "Ten Best Books of the Year" lists, optioned for television and film, and translated into thirty languages. Her short stories have appeared in *The New Yorker,* the *Washington Post,* and *Esquire,* and her nonfiction has appeared in the *New York Times, Time, Vanity Fair, The Atlantic, Slate,* and on *This American Life.*
   • I joined Twitter in 2013 and, as someone who had been a social media skeptic, was both surprised and a bit alarmed by how quickly I took to it. (As the saying goes, the twenty minutes I spend on Twitter are the best four hours of my day.) I also thought about the strangeness of the fact that many tweets are exchanged between people whose identities are unclear. If a person from my own past about whom I had ambivalent feelings emailed me, the truth is that I might ignore the email. But if the same person reached out on Twitter, with a jokey username, I might, in the spirit of being a pleasant author, engage in a back-and-forth while having no idea who the person really was. Although I certainly am not famous like Lucy Headrick, it was this strangeness that inspired me to write "The Prairie Wife." Of course, the story ended up being about a few other things —celebrity culture, forty-something sadness—but its origins are in how weird I find Twitter.

RIVERS SOLOMON writes about life in the margins, where they are much at home. They graduated from Stanford University with a degree in comparative studies in race and ethnicity and hold an MFA in fiction writing from the Michener Center for Writers. Though originally from the United States, they currently reside in the United Kingdom. Their debut novel, *An Unkindness of Ghosts,* is out now.
   • When I wrote "Whose Heart I Long to Stop with the Click of a Revolver," some years ago now, I'd been thinking a lot about guns—specifically how much I liked them compared to others who hold socially progressive values. I'd never held one myself, but it seemed to me that the world's bank account, its balance of power, if you will, was mighty in arrears and needed to be set to rights. I couldn't envision a way of doing that that didn't involve a gun.

You can't rape a .38. I first saw that on a vintage photo of a protest march, but I've since seen it a number of places, including on advertisements for personal weapons. How strange it was, I thought, the way violence unfolds on both mass and individual scale, how the small violence of a single victim and perpetrator can reflect larger patterns and social values. How rape is a tool in an ongoing war against women. I wanted to write a story about a woman enmeshed in violence, who could not, no matter what, disentangle herself from it, because none of us can.

ESMÉ WEIJUN WANG is the author of the novel *The Border of Paradise,* which was called a Best Book of 2016 by NPR and one of the 25 Best Novels of 2016 by *Electric Literature.* She received a 2018 Whiting Award, was named by *Granta* as one of the "Best of Young American Novelists" in 2017, and is the recipient of the Graywolf Nonfiction Prize for her forthcoming essay collection, *The Collected Schizophrenias.* Born in the Midwest to Taiwanese parents, she lives in San Francisco, and can be found at esmewang.com and on Twitter @esmewang.

• The first thing that came to me, with this story, was the singsong rhyme from the very beginning, which led to a few questions: Who is Becky Guo, where is this taking place, and who is telling the story? I wrote most of "What Terrible Thing It Was" in New Orleans in December 2016, right after Trump's election — it was the beginning of a particular kind of anxiety for myself and most of my loved ones about the country and what was going to be coming next. Part of that felt like paranoia, but a paranoia with far too much truth behind it, which is what led to the inclusion of the narrator's psychosis and the convergence of her electroconvulsive therapy (ECT) consultation with Election Night. I wanted Wendy to have concerns outside of the election, and she does, but the election in the story and the social concerns surrounding it leave their fingerprints all over that day and her memories of Becky's murder. I consider it as much a story about trauma as anything else, and a narrative of how new traumas tend to revive old ones.

Other Distinguished Stories of 2017

American and Canadian Magazines Publishing Short Stories

Able Muse Review
African American Review
AGNI
Alaska Quarterly Review
Alligator Juniper
The American Scholar
American Short Fiction
Antioch Review
Appalachian Heritage
Arcadia
Arkansas Review
Arts & Letters
Ascent
Asterix Journal
The Atlantic
Baltimore Review
The Believer
Bellevue Literary Review
Bennington Review
Blackbird
Black Warrior Review
Bomb
Booth
Bosque
Boston Review
Boulevard
Brain, Child: The Magazine for Thinking Mothers
Briar Cliff Review
Bright Eight
BuzzFeed

Callaloo
Carolina Quarterly
Carve Magazine
Catamaran Literary Reader
Catapult
Chattahoochee Review
Chautauqua
Cherry Tree
Chicago Quarterly Review
Chicago Tribune, Printers Row
Cimarron Review
Cincinnati Review
Colere
Colorado Review
Commentary
The Common
Confrontation
Conjunctions
Consequence
Copper Nickel
Cossack Review
Crab Orchard Review
Crazyhorse
Cream City Review
CutBank
The Dalhousie Review
December
Delmarva Review
Denver Quarterly
Descant
Dogwood

Ecotone
805 Lit + Art
Electric Literature
Eleven Eleven
Emrys Journal
Epiphany
Epoch
Event
Fairy Tale Review
Fantasy and Science Fiction
Faultline
Fence
Fiction
Fiction International
The Fiddlehead
Fifth Wednesday
Five Points
The Flexible Persona
Florida Review
Flying South
Foglifter
The Forge
Four Way Review
Fourteen Hills
Freeman's
Gamut Magazine
Gemini
Georgia Review
Gettysburg Review
Glimmer Train
Gold Man Review
Grain
Granta
Green Mountains Review
Greensboro Review
Grist
Guernica
Gulf Coast
Hanging Loose
Harper's Magazine
Harvard Review
Hayden's Ferry Review
High Desert Journal
Hopkins Review
Hotel Amerika
Hudson Review
Huizache
Hunger Mountain

Idaho Review
Image
Indiana Review
Iowa Review
Iron Horse Literary Review
Isthmus
Jabberwock Review
Joyland
Juked
Kenyon Review
Kweli Journal
Lady Churchill's Rosebud Wristlet
Lake Effect
Lalitamba
The Lenny Letter
Lilith
Literary Review
Lit Mag
Little Patuxent Review
Louisiana Literature
Louisville Review
Lunch Ticket
Madison Review
Make
Manoa
Mary
Massachusetts Review
Masters Review
McSweeney's Quarterly
Memorious
Meridian
Michigan Quarterly Review
Mid-American Review
Midwestern Gothic
Minnesota Review
Mississippi Review
Missouri Review
Montana Quarterly
Moon City Review
Mount Hope
n + 1
Narrative Magazine
Natural Bridge
New England Review
New Guard
New Haven Review
New Letters
New Madrid

New Ohio Review
New Quarterly
New South
The New Yorker
Nimrod International Journal
Ninth Letter
Noon
The Normal School
North American Review
North Carolina Literary Review
North Dakota Quarterly
Notre Dame Review
Ocean State Review
The Offing
One Story
Opossum
Orion
Oxford American
Oyster River Pages
Pakn Treger
PANK
Paper Darts
Paris Review
Passages North
Pembroke Magazine
Pigeon Pages
The Pinch
Pleiades
Ploughshares
PoemMemoirStory
Portland Review
Post Road
Potomac Review
Prairie Fire
Prairie Schooner
Prism International
Profane
Provincetown Arts
Provo Canyon Review
A Public Space
Puerto del Sol
Pulp Literature
Raritan
Redivider
Reservoir
River Styx
Roanoke Review
Room Magazine

Ruminate
Salamander
Salmagundi
Santa Monica Review
Saturday Evening Post
Sewanee Review
Sierra Nevada Review
Sixfold
Slice
Solstice
Southampton Review
South Carolina Review
South Dakota Review
Southeast Review
Southern Humanities Review
Southern Indiana Review
Southern Review
Southwest Review
Sou'wester
StoryQuarterly
StringTown
Subtropics
Summerset Review
The Sun
Sycamore Review
Tablet
Tahoma Literary Review
Tampa Review
Terraform
Territory
Third Coast
This Land
Threepenny Review
Timber Creek Review
Tin House
The Tishman Review
Transition
TriQuarterly
The Turnip Truck(s)
upstreet
Vermont Literary Review
Vice
Virginia Quarterly Review
War, Literature, and the Arts
Washington Square Review
Water~Stone Review
Waxwing Magazine
Weber Studies

West Branch
Western Humanities Review
Whitefish Review
Wildness
Willow Springs
Wired
Witness

World Literature Today
Yale Review
Yellow Medicine Review
Your Impossible Voice
Zoetrope: All-Story
ZYZZYVA

THE BEST AMERICAN SERIES®

FIRST, BEST, AND BEST-SELLING

The Best American Comics

The Best American Essays

The Best American Food Writing

The Best American Mystery Stories

The Best American Nonrequired Reading

The Best American Science and Nature Writing

The Best American Science Fiction and Fantasy

The Best American Short Stories

The Best American Sports Writing

The Best American Travel Writing

Available in print and e-book wherever books are sold.

hmhco.com/bestamerican